The Erotic
ANNE
of
GREEN
GABLES
(Illustrated)

THE EROTIC
ANNE
OF
GREEN
GABLES
(ILLUSTRATED)

Anne Shirley
As Told to Frank Holtzer
Based on the Works of L.M. Montgomery

Secret Kiss Erotic Literature

TABLE of CONTENTS

The Erotic
ANNE
OF
GREEN
GABLES
(ILLUSTRATED)

I am the real Anne Shirley.

PREFACE

An Orphan Girl Grows Up

You may think you know my story, but you don't. I'm nothing like that innocent little girl you read about in those books by Lucy Maud Montgomery.

First of all, when I first came to live with Matthew and Marilla Cuthbert at Green Gables on Prince Edward Island I wasn't eleven years old; I was fifteen. And their name wasn't Cuthbert; it was Collins. Maud wisely changed that just like she changed the details of the story.

It's true I was pure in the beginning – well, kind of – but that didn't last long.

Although brother and sister, Martin and Matilda Collins secretly lived as if man and wife. And they were quite happy to add me to the family in a cozy *ménage a trois*. I lost my virginity to Martin within hours of my arrival at Green Gables.

Truth is, I didn't really mind. As it turned out, I liked to fuck. I did him, I did his sister, I did the neighborhood boys, I did the minister's wife, I even did a 60-year-old circus midget with one glass eye. But that's another story.

No, I wasn't the girl you read about. I wasn't even a redhead.

So continue on, gentle soul. I've left Maud's words in place, but corrected them to tell you the erotic adventures of yours truly, Anne Shirley.

- Anne

Matilda and Martin Collins (at Green Gables).

CHAPTER I

Mrs. Langston Is Surprised

That old busybody Mrs. Langston lived just where the Avonlea main road dipped down into a little hollow, fringed with alders and ladies' eardrops and traversed by a brook that had its source away back in the woods of the old Collins place; it was reputed to be an intricate, headlong brook in its earlier course through those woods, with dark secrets of pool and cascade; but by the time it reached Langston's Hollow it was a quiet, well-conducted little stream, for not even a brook could run past Mrs. Langston's door without due regard for decency and decorum; it probably was conscious that Mrs. Langston was sitting at her window, keeping a sharp eye on everything that passed, from brooks and children up, and that if she noticed anything odd or out of place she would never rest until she had ferreted out the whys and wherefores thereof. She was a voyeur who kept tabs on her neighbors with a spyglass, peering into bedroom windows, invading their privacy, following the secret sex life of certain inhabitants of Prince Edward Island.

Like that of Matilda and Martin Collins, the bachelor brother and spinster sister who lived at Green Gables. You could see everything that went on there if you focused a spyglass across the field that separated the Langston place from the big white farmhouse with green trim.

There are plenty of people in Avonlea, and out of it,

who can attend closely to their neighbor's business by dint of neglecting their own; but Mrs. Langston was one of those capable creatures who can manage their own concerns and those of other folks into the bargain. She was a notable housewife; her work was always done and well done; she ran the Sewing Circle, oversaw the Sunday School, and was the strongest supporter of the Church Aid Society and Foreign Missions Auxiliary. Yet with all this, Mrs. Langston found abundant time to sit for hours at her kitchen window, knitting "cotton warp" quilts – she had knitted sixteen of them, as Avonlea housekeepers were wont to tell in awed voices – while keeping a sharp eye on her neighbors' houses. There was a clutter of farmhouses within eyesight. What's more, with Avonlea occupying a little triangular peninsula jutting out into the Gulf of St. Lawrence with water on two sides of it, anybody who went out of it or into it had to pass over that hill road and so run the gauntlet of Mrs. Langston's all-seeing eye.

She was sitting there one afternoon in early June. The sun was coming in at the window warm and bright; the orchard on the slope below the house was in a bridal flush of pinky-white bloom, hummed over by a myriad of bees. Thomas Langston – Rita's husband, a meek little man whom Avonlea people called her "pet poodle" – was busily sowing his late turnip seed on the hill field beyond the barn; and their neighbor Martin Collins ought to have been sowing his on the big red brook field away over by Green Gables. Mrs. Langston knew that Martin ought because she had heard him tell Peter Maxwell the evening before in William J. Blair's store over at Carmody that he meant to sow his turnip seed the next afternoon. Peter had asked him about it, of course, for Martin Collins had never been known to volunteer information about anything in his whole life.

And yet Rita Langston spotted none other than Martin at half-past three on the afternoon of a busy day, placidly driving over the hollow and up the hill in a buggy pulled by his sorrel mare; moreover, he was wearing a white collar and his best suit, plain proof that he was going someplace outside of Avonlea. Now, the curious woman asked herself, where was Martin Collins going and why was he going there?

Had it been any other man in Avonlea, Mrs. Langston, might have had a pretty good guess as to both questions. But Martin so rarely left home that it must be something pressing that occasioned this journey; he was the shyest man alive and hated to go among strangers or to visit any place where he might have to talk. His neighbor, ponder as she might, could make nothing of it and thus her afternoon's enjoyment was decidedly spoiled. She liked to be "in the know."

"I'll just step over to Green Gables after tea and find out from his sister Matilda where he's gone and why," Mrs. Langston concluded. "He doesn't generally go to town this time of year and he NEVER visits; if he'd run out of turnip seed he wouldn't dress up and take the buggy to go for more; nor was he driving fast enough to be going for a doctor." Yet something must have happened since last night to start him off. "I'm clean puzzled, that's what," she muttered, "and I won't know a minute's peace of mind until I find out what has taken Martin Collins out of Avonlea today."

Accordingly after tea Mrs. Langston set out, but

she had not far to go; the big, rambling, orchard-embowered house where the Collins lived – a place known as Green Gables for its painted eaves – was located a scant quarter of a mile up the road from Langston's Hollow. While Green Gables was barely visible from the main road along which all the other Avonlea houses were so sociably situated, there happened to be a clear view across the open field from the Langston house to the Collins place.

"It's no wonder Martin and Matilda are both a little odd, living away back here by themselves," she said as she stepped along the deep-rutted, grassy lane bordered with wild rose bushes. "To be sure, they seem contented enough; hidden away where nobody can see their carryings-on. Brother and sister indeed!"

Night after night she'd witnessed their bedroom antics through her spyglass. Scandalous! Nonetheless, she had kept their secret, else risk disturbing the lascivious performances which provided her with a second-hand sex life. Goodness knows, her Thomas was all but useless in that department.

With this thought, Mrs. Langston stepped into the backyard of Green Gables. Very green and neat and precise was that yard, set about on one side with great patriarchal willows and the other with prim Lombardies. Not a stray stick nor stone was to be seen, for Mrs. Langston would have noticed it if there had been. Privately she was of the opinion that Matilda Collins swept that yard as often as she swept her house. One could have eaten a meal off the ground without overbrimming the proverbial peck of dirt.

Mrs. Langston rapped smartly at the kitchen door

and promptly stepped inside when Matilda's voice invited her to enter. The kitchen at Green Gables was a cheerful room – or would have been if it had not been so painfully clean as to give it the appearance of an unused parlor. Its windows looked east and west; through the west one, looking out on the backyard, came a flood of mellow June sunlight; but from the east one, you got a glimpse of the bloom-white cherry trees in the orchard and the slender birches down in the hollow by the brook.

Here sat Matilda Collins, when she sat at all, always slightly distrustful of sunshine, which seemed to her much too dancing and irresponsible a thing for a world which was meant to be taken seriously. And here she sat knitting, with the table behind her already laid for supper. She was obviously expected her brother to return by dark.

Mrs. Langston, before she had fairly closed the door, had taken a mental note of everything that was on that table. There were three plates laid, so that Matilda must be expecting someone to come home with Martin. Interesting.

"Good evening, Rita," Matilda said briskly. "This is a real fine evening, isn't it? Won't you sit down? How are all your folks?"

Something that might be called friendship existed between Matilda Collins and Mrs. Langston, in spite of – or perhaps because of – their dissimilarity.

Matilda was a pretty woman, with enticing curves, her blonde hair framing a heart-shaped face. She was a woman of more sophistication than you'd expect to find on Prince Edward Island; there was something about her mouth that hinted of ... sensuality.

"We're all pretty well," replied Mrs. Langston. "I was kind of afraid YOU weren't, though, when I saw Martin starting off today. I thought maybe he was going for a doctor."

Matilda's lips twitched understandingly. She had known that the sight of Martin's departure would be too much for her neighbor's curiosity. "Oh, no, I'm quite well, thank you for asking," she said politely. "Martin went to Bright River. We're getting a little boy from an orphanage in Nova Scotia and he's coming on the train tonight."

If Matilda had said that Martin had gone to Bright River to meet a kangaroo from Australia, Mrs. Langston could not have been more astonished. She was actually stricken dumb for about five seconds.

"Are you in earnest, Matilda?" she finally managed to utter.

"Yes, of course," said the blonde woman, as if getting boys from orphanages in Nova Scotia were part of the usual spring work on any well-regulated Avonlea farm.

This news had given Mrs. Langston a severe mental jolt. A boy! Matilda and Martin Collins of all people adopting a boy! From an orphanage! Well, the world was certainly turning upside down! She would be surprised at nothing after this! Nothing!

"What on earth put such a notion into your head?" she inquired, determined to get at the heart of this strange turn of events.

"Well, we've been thinking about it for some time – all winter in fact," replied Matilda. "Mrs. Alexander

Spencer was up here one day before Christmas and she said she was going to get a little girl from the orphanage over in Hopeton in the spring. So Martin and I talked it over and thought we'd get an orphan child too – a boy. Martin could use some help around the farm. And you know how hard it is to get decent workers. There's never anybody available but those stupid little French boys; and as soon as you get one trained he leaves to work in the lobster canneries or in the States. So we decided to ask Mrs. Spencer to pick one out for us when she went over to get her little girl. We heard last week she was going, so we sent word for her to bring us a smart boy of about sixteen. We decided that would be the best age – old enough to be of some use in doing chores right off and young enough to be trained up proper. We mean to give him a good home and schooling. We had a telegram from Mrs. Alexander Spencer today – the mailman brought it from the station – saying they were coming on the five-thirty train tonight. So Martin drove over to Bright River to meet the boy. Mrs. Spencer will drop him off there."

Mrs. Langston adjusted her mental attitude to this amazing piece of news. "Well, Matilda, I'll just tell you plain that I think you're doing a mighty foolish thing – a risky thing, that's what. I know a thing or two about your home life, and I think this energetic young boy is more for your pleasures than for farming. Why, you and your brother could get arrested for the corruption of a minor."

Seeming neither offended nor alarmed, Matilda Collins continued with her knitting, not missing a stroke.

"I don't deny there's something in what you say, Rita. I know you watch our house with your telescope. But you'll keep our secrets lest we reveal yours. We know you like to tie Thomas to a post in the barn and whip him. Bondage and discipline, I believe it's called. A deviant fetish."

"Why I never –!"

"Of course you do. We have eyes and ears too. As for our getting a boy, there are risks to be sure. But after all these years I'm growing tired of a steady diet of Martin. We've been going at it since we were children. There are not many eligible suitors her on Prince Edward Island, so we made do with what we had. But an orphan boy – that's a new wrinkle."

"Well, I hope it will turn out all right," said Mrs. Langston in a tone that plainly indicated her doubts. "Only don't say I didn't warn you if he burns Green Gables to the ground or puts strychnine in the well water – I heard of a case over in New Brunswick where an orphanage child did just that, and the whole family died in fearful agonies. Only, it was a girl in that instance. It was her revenge for the sexual abuse she was suffering in their hands."

"Well, we're not getting a girl," said Matilda, as if poisoning wells were a purely feminine accomplishment and not to be dreaded in the case of a boy. "I'd never dream of taking a girl into our bed. It might be too much temptation for Martin to dump me for a younger partner. I am getting up there – nearly thirty. The ripe old age of an unclaimed spinster."

"That's the curse of Prince Edward Island," nodded Mrs. Langston. "Not many eligible men hereabouts."

"A few traveling medicine men have proposed and asked me to come away with them, but I'd never leave Green Gables. It's my home. Always has been; always will be."

Mrs. Langston sighed in agreement. She would have liked to stay until Martin came home with his imported orphan. But reflecting that it would be a good two hours at least before his arrival she took herself away, somewhat to Matilda's relief. She was uncomfortable that Mrs. Langston had ferreted out their plan.

"Well, of all things that ever were or will be!" Mrs. Langston said to herself when she was safely out in the lane. "It seems as if I must be dreaming. Well, I'm sorry for that poor boy, a sexual slave to that depraved couple. Martin and Matilda will expect him to satisfy their basest desire. My, but I pity him, that's what."

But if Mrs. Langston could have seen the child who was waiting patiently at the Bright River station at that very moment her pity would have been even more profound indeed.

I arrive on Prince Edward Island, bag in hand.

CHAPTER II

Martin Collins is surprised

Martin Collins and the sorrel mare jogged comfortably over the eight miles to Bright River. It was a pretty road, running along between snug farmsteads. The air was sweet with the breath of many apple orchards and the meadows sloped away in the distance to horizon mists of pearl and purple; while ...

"The little birds sang as if it were
The one day of summer in all the year."

Martin enjoyed the drive after his own fashion, except during the moments when he met women and had to nod to them – for in Prince Edward Island it is customary to nod to all and sundry you meet on the road whether you know them or not.

Martin dreaded all women except his sister Matilda; the two of them had been close since childhood, eventually sharing the family home after their parents passed away. With few suitable candidates for marriage on the island, the siblings had drifted into a connubial kind of relationship. Everyone had a sexual itch to be scratched.

They made a handsome couple, this broad-shouldered young man and his pretty blonde sister. People commented on their family resemblance, their even features and well-proportioned bodies. "They look just like their mother," it was said. "She was such a beauty."

Their parents had died in a ferry accident when

they were teenagers, leaving them to manage Green Gables and the surrounding farm on their own. People hereabouts considered them "brave" and "stalwart," two youngsters surviving on their own.

When Martin reached Bright River there was no sign of any train; he thought he was too early, so he tied his horse in the yard of the small Bright River hotel and went over to the station house. The long platform was almost deserted; the only living creature in sight being a pretty teenage girl who was sitting on a pile of shingles at the far end. Martin noted her shapely legs and the swell of her bosom. Quite a looker for one so young. He found pubescent girls attractive, having begun his sexual relationship with his sister even before she had hair between her legs. Studying the girl on the platform, he told himself he wouldn't mind sampling that young snatch. Maybe he should find out whom she was visiting on the island, then call on her some evening. He and his sister had an open relationship, no jealousy over the occasional dalliance, her sometimes coupling with traveling salesmen, him with willing barmaids.

Had he looked beyond the girl's budding titties, he would have noticed the tense rigidity of her expression. She was sitting there waiting for something or somebody and since sitting and waiting was the only thing to do just then, she sat and waited with all her might and main.

Martin came upon the stationmaster locking up the ticket office preparatory to going home for supper, and asked him if the five-thirty train would soon be along.

"Wind your watch. The five-thirty train has come and gone a half hour ago," answered the brusque official. "But there was a passenger dropped off for you – a girl. She's sitting out there on the shingles. I asked her to go into the ladies' waiting room, but she informed me gravely that she preferred to stay outside. 'There was more scope for imagination on the platform,' she said. She's a case, I should say. I think she didn't trust being alone in the station with me."

"Wait – I'm not expecting a girl," Martin said blankly. "It's a boy I've come for. Mrs. Alexander Spencer was to bring him over from Nova Scotia for us. We've agreed to provide a foster home for a needy youngster willing to help out on the farm."

The stationmaster whistled. "Guess there's been some mistake," he said. "Mrs. Spencer came off the train with that girl and delivered her into my charge. Said you and your sister were adopting her from an orphanage and that you would be along for her presently. That's all I know about it – and I haven't got any more orphans concealed hereabouts. You'll have to take her instead of a boy."

"I don't understand," said Martin helplessly, wishing that his sister were here to cope with the awkward situation. Matilda was the smarter sibling, always several steps ahead of him. She ran the farm, kept the records, planned the meals, and managed the money. He was just a handy stud muffin, a bit worse for the wear, being nudged aside by her plans to bring a boy into their bed.

"Well, you'd better question the girl," said the stationmaster. "I dare say she'll be able to explain –

she's got a tongue of her own, that's certain. Maybe they were out of boys for adoption."

"Out of boys –?"

"It happens. There's a greater demand for them. Just like you, people wanting them to help on farms."

As the stationmaster walked jauntily away, the unfortunate Martin was left to walk up to this stranger – an orphan girl – and demand of her why she wasn't a boy. Martin groaned resignedly as shuffled down the platform in her direction.

She had been watching him ever since he arrived, her eyes following his every move as he approached where she sat. Martin returned her gaze, studying her: A pretty young woman of about fifteen or sixteen, garbed in a very long skirt and a blouse of yellowish-gray wincey. She wore a dark brown top hat and beneath the hat, extending down her back was a shock of brunette hair. Her face was small, white and thin; her mouth was large and so were her eyes, which looked green in some lights and gray in others.

So far, the ordinary observer might have seen that those big eyes were full of spirit and vivacity; that the mouth was sweet-lipped and expressive, with just a touch of lipstick; that the forehead was broad and full; in short, a discerning observer might have concluded that no commonplace soul inhabited the body of this stray woman-child of whom shy Martin Collins was so ludicrously afraid.

Martin, however, was spared the ordeal of speaking first, for as soon as she concluded that he was coming her way she stood up, grasping the handle of an old-fashioned carpetbag, and held out her free hand to him.

"I suppose you are Mr. Martin Collins of Green Gables?" she said in a peculiarly clear, sweet voice. "I'm very glad to see you. I was beginning to be afraid you weren't coming for me and I was imagining all the things that might have happened to prevent you. I had made up my mind that if you didn't come for me tonight I'd go down the track to that big wild cherry tree at the bend, and climb up into it to stay all night. I wouldn't be a bit afraid, and it would be lovely to sleep in a wild cherry tree all white with bloom in the moonshine, don't you think? You could imagine you were dwelling in marble halls, couldn't you? And I was quite sure you would come for me in the morning, if you didn't tonight."

Martin had taken the hand awkwardly in his; then and there deciding that he could not tell this woman-child with the twinkling eyes that there had been a mistake. No, he would take her home and let Matilda do that. She couldn't be left here at the Bright River station in any case, no matter what mistake had been made, so all questions and explanations might as well be deferred until they were safely back at Green Gables.

"I'm sorry I was late," he said. "Come along. The horse is over in the yard. Give me your bag."

"Oh, I can carry it," she responded cheerfully. "It isn't heavy. I've got all my worldly goods in it, but it isn't heavy. And if it isn't carried in just a certain way the handle pulls out – so I'd better keep it because I know the exact knack of it. It's an extremely old carpetbag. Oh, I'm very glad you've come, even if it would have been nice to sleep in a wild cherry tree.

We've got to drive a long piece, haven't we? Mrs. Spencer said it was eight miles. I'm glad because I love riding in a buggy. Oh, it seems so wonderful that I'm going to live with you and belong to you. I've never belonged to anybody – not really. But the orphanage was the worst. I've only been in it four months, but that was enough. I don't suppose you ever were an orphan in an orphanage, so you can't possibly understand what it is like. It's worse than anything you could imagine. Mrs. Spencer said it's wicked of me to talk like that, but I don't mean to be wicked. It's so easy to be wicked without knowing it, isn't it? They were good, you know – the orphanage people. But there is so little scope for the imagination in an orphanage. However, it was pretty interesting to imagine things about the other orphans – to imagine that perhaps the girl who sat next to you was really the daughter of a belted earl, who had been stolen away from her parents in her infancy by a cruel nurse who died before she could confess. Or that the headmistress was a Russian aristocrat who had fallen on bad times, lost her title and been forced to work for a living. Or that the handyman was a secret agent, posing as a maintenance worker while gathering state secrets for the Germans. I used to lie awake at nights and imagine things like that, because I didn't have time during the day. I guess that's why I'm so thin – I am dreadful thin, aren't I? Other than my boobies. I do love to imagine I'm nice and plump, with dimples in my cheeks. But I'll have to settle for having nice boobies. They're quite a handful, the boys at the orphanage used to tell me."

With this, Martin's companion stopped talking,

16

partly because she was out of breath and partly because they had reached the buggy. Not another word did she say until they had left the village and were driving down a steep little hill, the road part of which had been cut so deeply into the soft soil, that the banks, fringed with blooming wild cherry trees and slim white birches, were several feet above their heads.

Martin's mind was occupied by thoughts of the girl's boobies. They did look like a handful, jiggling there under her thin blouse. When he glanced her way, he could make out the imprints of her nipples against the flimsy fabric.

The girl put out her hand and broke off a branch of wild plum that brushed against the side of the buggy. "Isn't that beautiful? What did that tree, leaning out from the bank, all white and lacy, make you think of?" she asked.

"Well now, I dunno," said Martin. Unable to cease thinking about what her rosy nips might taste like. He could imagine holding one gently between his teeth, sucking on it like a strawberry. "What do they make YOU think of?"

"Why, a bride, of course – a bride all in white with a lovely misty veil. I've never seen one, but I can imagine what she would look like. I don't ever expect to be a bride myself. But I sometimes try to imagine what a wedding night must be like, becoming a woman for the first time. I'm a virgin, you know. You are not getting spoiled goods. I only let the boys at the orphanage put their fingers in, not their John Thomases. I do hope that some day I shall have a white dress. That is my highest ideal of earthly bliss. I just love pretty clothes. And I've never had a pretty dress in my life that I can remember – but of course it's all the more to look forward to, isn't it? That and my wedding night, should I ever have one. This morning when I left the orphanage I felt so ashamed because I had to wear this horrid old wincey blouse. All the orphans had to wear them, you know. A merchant in Hopeton donated three hundred yards of wincey to the orphanage last winter. Some people said it was because he couldn't sell it, but I'd rather believe that it was out of the kindness of his heart, wouldn't you? When we got on the train I felt as if everybody must be looking at me and pitying me. It's so thin you can practically see my boobies through the fabric. People were looking at them, but I just imagined to myself that I had on the most beautiful pale blue silk dress – because when you ARE imagining you might as well imagine something worthwhile – and a big hat all flowers and nodding plumes, and a gold watch, and kid gloves and boots. I felt cheered up right away and I enjoyed my trip to the Island with all my might. I wasn't a bit seasick coming over in the boat. Neither was Mrs. Spencer although she generally is. She said she hadn't time to get sick, watching to see that I didn't fall overboard. She said she never saw the beat of me for prowling about. But I wanted to see everything that was to be seen on that boat, because I didn't know whether I'd ever have another opportunity. Oh, look! There are a lot more cherry trees all in bloom! This Island is the bloomiest place. I just love it already, and I'm so glad I'm going to live here. I've always heard that Prince Edward Island was the prettiest place in the world, and I used to imagine I was living here, but I never really expected I would. It's delightful when your imaginations come true, isn't it? What imagination would you like to come true?"

He didn't dare say what he'd been thinking as he watched those pert nipples moving about beneath the wincey with each jolt of the buggy on the uneven red-dirt road.

She turned toward him, as if deliberately displaying her bosom, the rosy areolae of her nipples visible beneath the thin fabric. "When we got into the train at Charlottetown and the red roads began to flash past I asked Mrs. Spencer what made them red and she said she didn't know and for pity's sake not to ask her any more questions. She said I must have asked her a thousand already. I suppose I had, too, but how are you going to find out about things if you don't ask questions? And what DOES make the roads red?"

"Well now, I dunno," said Martin. Barely able to keep his mind on driving the buggy. Those pointy nipples were driving him crazy with desire.

"Well, that is one of the things to find out sometime. Isn't it splendid to think of all the things there are to find out about? It just makes me feel glad to be alive – it's such an interesting world. It wouldn't be half so interesting if we know all the answers about everything, would it? There'd be no scope for imagination then, would there? But am I talking too much? People are always telling me I do. Would you rather I didn't talk? If you say so I'll stop. I can STOP when I make up my mind to it, although it's difficult."

"Oh, you can talk as much as you like. I don't mind," said Martin, much to his own surprise.

Although he found it rather difficult for his slower intelligence to keep up with her brisk mental processes, he decided that he kind of liked her chatter. It distracted her from the fact that he was looking at her bobbling breasts.

"Oh, I'm so glad. I know you and I are going to get along together fine." She put a hand on his knee. It felt to him like a branding iron. "It's so nice to talk when one wants to and not be told that children should be seen and not heard. I've had that said to me a million times if not more. And people laugh at me because I use big words. But if you have big ideas you have to use big words to express them, don't you?"

"Well now, that seems reasonable," said Martin.

"It's so hot out here. Is it always this hot in Avonlea? I wish I could unbutton my blouse to take in some air."

"Yes, it is rather hot," he acknowledged. "Go ahead, unbutton your blouse and make yourself more comfortable. There are no other travelers on the road today, so no one will see you."

"But you will see me, Mr. Collins. I might be embarrassed to expose myself to you. Although I'm sure after I get used to living with you and your sister, my modesty will fade. I expect I will be bathing in the kitchen in front of you before you know it."

Martin Collins nearly fell off the buggy seat. "Uh, yes, familiarity comes from sharing a home," he allowed. "Go ahead, unbutton your blouse and take in some cooler air. You may as well get used to being unembarrassed around me."

"That's true. There's no time to start getting used

to each other like the present. I think I will do just that. But I must warn you, I'm not wearing a camisole under this blouse."

He could readily tell that, studying the movement of her pink nipples against the wincey.

"Here," she said, unbuttoning her top and peeling it back off her shoulders. Martin practically fainted at the sight of her bared breasts. The nipples stood out like little pegs, stiffened by the breeze.

"Ohmygod," he muttered.

"What?" she asked. "Should I put my blouse back on?"

"No, no, you're fine. Enjoy the fresh air."

"Yes, it feels good on my skin. That blouse was so hot. I'm glad I can be free around you. I often romp around with no clothing on. I'm a naturalist at heart."

"A naturalist? You mean you like being naked?"

"Yes, indeed I do. Oh, I hope I'm not being too candid. Mrs. Spencer said that my tongue must be hung in the middle. But it isn't – it's firmly fastened at one end. Mrs. Spencer said your place was named Green Gables. I asked her all about it. And she said there were trees all around it. I was gladder than ever. I just love trees. And there weren't any at all about the orphanage, only a few poor weeny-teeny things out in front with little whitewashed cagey things about them. They just looked like orphans themselves, those trees did. It used to make me want to cry to look at them. I used to say to them, 'Oh, you POOR little things! If you were out in a great big woods with other trees all around you and little mosses and Junebells growing over your roots and a brook not far away and birds singing in your branches, you could grow, couldn't you? But you can't where you are. I know just exactly how you feel, little trees.' I felt sorry to leave them behind this morning. You do get so attached to things like that, don't you? Is there a brook anywhere near Green Gables? I forgot to ask Mrs. Spencer that."

"Well now, yes, there's one right below the house."

"Fancy. It's always been one of my dreams to live near a brook. I never expected I would, though. Dreams don't often come true, do they? Wouldn't it be nice if they did? But just now I feel pretty nearly perfectly happy. I can't feel exactly perfectly happy because – well, what color would you call this?"

She twitched one of her long glossy braids over her thin shoulder and held it up before Martin's eyes. Martin was not used to deciding on the tints of ladies' tresses, but in this case there couldn't be much doubt.

"It's brunette, ain't it?" he said.

The girl let the braid drop back with a sigh that seemed to come from her very toes and to exhale forth all the sorrows of the ages. "Alas, it's what the headmistress called 'piss-burnt brown'," she said resignedly. "Now you see why I can't be perfectly happy. Nobody could who has piss-colored hair. I don't mind the other things so much – the freckles and the green eyes and my skinniness. I can imagine them away. I can imagine that I have a beautiful roseleaf complexion and lovely starry violet eyes. But I CANNOT imagine this piss-burnt brown hair away. I do my best. I think to myself, 'Now my hair is a glorious blonde, as blonde as corn silk.' But all the time I KNOW it is just plain brown and it breaks my heart. It will be my lifelong sorrow. I read of a girl once in a novel who had a lifelong sorrow but it wasn't brown hair. Her hair was pure gold rippling back from her alabaster brow. What is an alabaster brow? I never could find out. Can you tell me?"

"Well now, I'm afraid I can't," said Martin, who was getting a little dizzy. He felt as faint as he had once felt in his rash youth when a girl had enticed him on the merry-go-round at a picnic. In vertiginous circles, it went.

Anne continued, "Well, whatever it was it must have been something nice because she was divinely beautiful. Have you ever imagined what it must feel like to be divinely beautiful?"

"Well now, no, I haven't," confessed Martin ingenuously.

"I have, often. Which would you rather be if you had the choice – divinely beautiful or dazzlingly clever or angelically good?"

"Well now, I – I don't know exactly."

"Neither do I. I can never decide. But it doesn't make much real difference for it isn't likely I'll ever be any of those things. It's certain I'll never be angelically good. After all, I liked it when the boys at the orphanage put their fingers inside me. It made me feel all warm and tingly down there. Mrs. Spencer says – oh, Mr. Collins! Oh, Mr. Collins!! Oh, Mr. Collins!!!"

That was not what Mrs. Spencer had said; neither had the child tumbled out of the buggy; nor had Martin done anything astonishing. They had simply rounded a curve in the road and found themselves in the "Avenue."

The "Avenue," so called by the Newbridge people, was a stretch of road four or five hundred yards long, completely arched over with huge, wide-spreading apple trees, planted years ago by an eccentric old farmer named Granger. Overhead was one long canopy of snowy fragrant bloom. Below the boughs the air was full of a purple twilight and far ahead a glimpse of painted sunset sky shone like a great rose window at the end of a cathedral aisle.

Its beauty seemed to strike the child dumb. She leaned back in the buggy, her thin hands clasped before her, her face lifted rapturously to the white splendor above. Even after they had passed from under the arbor of apple trees and were driving down the long slope toward Newbridge she did not move or speak. Still with rapt face she gazed afar into the sunset with green eyes that saw visions trooping splendidly across that glowing background. Through Newbridge, a bustling little village where dogs barked at them and small boys hooted and curious faces peered from the windows, they drove, still in silence. She'd discretely closed her blouse as they passed. When three more miles had dropped away behind them the child had not yet spoken. She could keep silence, it was evident, as energetically as she could talk.

"I guess you're feeling pretty tired and hungry," Martin ventured to say at last, accounting for her long visitation of dumbness with the only reason he could think of. "But we haven't very far to go now – only another mile."

She came out of her reverie with a deep sigh and looked at him with the dreamy gaze of a soul that had been wondering afar, star-led. Her blouse had draped open again, exposing her pink-tipped breasts.

"Oh, Mr. Collins," she whispered, "that place we came through – that white place – what was it?"

"Well now, you must mean the Avenue," said Martin after a few moments' profound reflection on her pointy nipples. "It is a kind of pretty place."

"Pretty? Oh, PRETTY doesn't seem the right word to use. Nor beautiful either. Those descriptions don't go far enough. Oh, it was wonderful – wonderful. It's the first thing I ever saw that couldn't be improved upon by imagination. It just satisfies me here" – she put one hand on her breast – "it made a queer funny ache and yet it was a pleasant ache. Did you ever have an ache like that, Mr. Collins?"

"Well now, I just can't recollect that I ever had."

"I have it lots of time – whenever I see anything royally beautiful. Here, feel the ache in my heart," she said, replacing her hand with his.

Martin drew a sharp breath. He could barely believe that her firm young breast was cupped there in the palm of his hand. "The boys at the orphanage were right," he muttered, discombobulated as she pressed his hand against her bosom.

"Oh, how so?"

"You are quite a handful."

"The headmistress says so too, but she doesn't mean it like that."

He could feel her nipple poking against his palm, as hard as a pebble. "Weren't you going to finish removing your blouse to take in the air?" he reminded her.

"Yes, I was," she said, brushing his hand aside to fumble with her remaining buttons. In short order, her wincey garment lay beside her on the buggy seat. "There," she said. "That feels better."

Martin studied her magnificent titties. Round and firm, defying gravity with their youth, the tips as pink as rose petals. "Ohmygod," he muttered at the delightful sight. This introduction to the new girl was going much better than he might have ever imagined in his wildest fantasies.

"What is it?" she started, looking around. "Did someone along the road see my bobbies?"

"No, the road is deserted. It was just my surprise at your unadorned beauty."

"Oh? You like my boobies?"

"They look perfect."

"I do hope you like them. Now that I belong to you and your sister, they are yours. You can touch them anytime you like, I don't mind. You can even put them in your mouth and suck on them, the way the boys did at the orphanage. I would enjoy that. It feels so good to have someone nibble them."

"Really?"

"Oh yes, it's true. They are yours to do as you will. Do you want to taste one now?" Without waiting for a response, she rose from the buggy seat to lean toward him, thrusting her right breast against his lips. He had little choice but take the nipple into his mouth and explore its contours with his tongue.

"Mmmph," he responded.

"Pull the buggy to the side of the road," she commanded, "else you may wreck us. And while we're stopped. You can put your finger inside me. I don't mind. Just slip it under the edge of my panties. You'll find I'm already moist from anticipation."

"Anticipation?"

"Yes, you're going to fuck me, aren't you?"

"Well, I just might at that."

The sorrel mare waited patiently, munching on a clump of grass as the passengers dallied. Martin had the hem of the girl's skirt over her knees, exposing shapely legs, his finger frigging her with ferocity.

She talked as his applied his ministrations: "They shouldn't call that lovely place the Avenue," she referred to the apple-tree arbor. "There is no meaning in a name like that. They should call it – let me see – the White Way of Delight. Isn't that a nice imaginative name?"

"Yes it is," he said, removing her panties and inserting his erect member between those moist lower lips. They engulfed him like a vacuum tube.

"When I don't like the name of a place or a person I always imagine a new one," she prattled on. "There was a girl at the orphanage whose name was Hepzibah Jenkins, but I always imagined her as Rosalia DeVere. Other people may call that place the Avenue, but I shall always call it the White Way of Delight."

Way of Delight indeed, thought Martin. It wasn't long before he'd cummed inside the girl. He hastened to straighten her clothing, lest any passerby might spot them in a state of dishabille. "We best be going," he suggested awkwardly. "My sister will have supper waiting."

"Yes indeed," she responded eagerly, unmindful of

the sexual encounter they had just shared. "I can't wait to meet your sister. I hope she takes to me as well as you have."

"Best to button your blouse. We've not got far to go." He was concerned about Mrs. Langston's prying eyes. No need to give the old biddy more to gossip about that he and Matilda already had!

Anne tidied herself up, looking none the worse for the wear. "Have we really only another mile to go before we get home? I'm glad and I'm sorry. I'm sorry because this drive has been so pleasant and I'm always sorry when pleasant things end. Something still pleasanter may come after, but you can never be sure. And it's so often the case that it isn't pleasanter. That has been my experience anyhow. But I'm glad to think of getting home. You see, I've never had a real home since I can remember. It gives me that pleasant ache again just to think of coming to a really truly home."

By then they had driven over the crest of a hill. "Oh, isn't that pretty!" she suddenly exclaimed.

Below them was a pond, looking almost like a river so long and winding was it. A bridge spanned it midway. The water was a glory of many shifting hues – the most spiritual shadings of crocus and rose and ethereal green, with other elusive tintings for which no name has ever been found.

Above the bridge the pond ran up into fringing groves of fir and maple and lay all darkly translucent in their wavering shadows. Here and there a wild plum leaned out from the bank like a white-clad girl tiptoeing to her own reflection. From the marsh at the head of the pond came the clear, mournfully sweet chorus of the frogs.

"That's Barry's Pond," said Martin.

"Oh, I don't like that name, either. I shall call it – let me see – the Lake of Shining Waters. Yes, that is the right name for it. I know because of the thrill. When I hit on a name that suits exactly it gives me a thrill. Do things ever give you a thrill?"

"What we did back there on the side of the road gave me a thrill," he admitted shyly.

"Yes, it was thrilling, wasn't it? We must do it again and often. I shall be such a good daughter to you."

Daughter? He had more in mind than that. A live-in concubine, a young mistress perhaps. That is, if his sister would allow it. But instead he replied, "Welcome to Avonlea."

Her thoughts already had raced on. "Why do other people call it Barry's Pond?" she asked as she surveyed the shining water.

"I reckon because Mr. and Mrs. John Barry lives up there in that house." He pointed toward a little gray house peering around a white apple orchard on a slope beyond and, although it was not yet dark, a light was shining from one of its windows. "Orchard Slope's name of his place."

"Oh?"

"Named after that orchard you see over there. If it wasn't for that line of trees you could see Green Gables from here. But we have to go over the bridge and round by the road, so it's near half a mile further."

"Have the Barrys got any little girls? Well, not so very little either – about my size."

"They've got one about fifteen. Her name is Diana."

"What a perfectly lovely name!"

"Well now, I dunno. There's something dreadful heathenish about it, seems to me. I'd rather Jane or Mary or some sensible name like that. But when Diana was born there was a schoolmaster boarding there and they gave him the naming of her and he called her Diana. After a Greek goddess or some such."

"I wish there had been a schoolmaster like that around when I was born. I could have been named Athena. Oh, my goodness, here we are at the bridge. I'm going to shut my eyes tight. I'm always afraid going over bridges. I can't help imagining that just as we get to the middle, it'll crumple up like a jackknife and nip us. So I shut my eyes. But I always have to open them when I think we're getting near the middle. Because, you see, if the bridge DID crumple up I'd want to SEE it crumple. What a jolly rumble it makes under the buggy's wheels! I always like the rumble part of it. Isn't it splendid there are so many things to like in this world? There we're over. Now I'll look back. Goodnight, dear Lake of Shining Waters. I always say goodnight to the things I love, just as I would to people. I think they like it. That water looks as if it's smiling at me."

He wondered if the girl might be a bit daft. But no matter. With that firm little body and ample bosom and tight pussy she'd do just fine. He wasn't much of a talker anyway.

When they had driven up the hill and around a corner Martin said: "We're pretty near home now. That's Green Gables over – "

"Oh, don't tell me," she interrupted breathlessly,

catching at his partially raised arm and shutting her eyes that she might not see his gesture. "Let me guess. I'm sure I'll guess right."

She opened her eyes and looked about her. They were on the crest of a hill. The sun had set some time since, but the landscape was still clear in the mellow afterlight. To the west a dark church spire rose up against a marigold sky. Below was a little valley and beyond a long, gently rising slope with snug farmsteads scattered along it. From one to another the girl's eyes darted, eager and wistful. At last they lingered on one house away to the left, far back from the road, dimly white in the twilight of the surrounding woods. Over it, in the stainless southwest sky, a great crystal-white star was shining like a lamp of guidance and promise.

"That's it, isn't it?" she said, pointing.

Martin slapped the reins on the sorrel's back delightedly. "Well now, you've guessed it! But I reckon Mrs. Spencer described it so's you could tell."

"No, she didn't – really she didn't. I hadn't any real idea what it looked like. But just as soon as I saw it I felt it was home. Oh, it seems as if I must be in a dream. Do you know, my arm must be black and blue from the elbow up, for I've pinched myself so many times today. Every little while a horrible sickening feeling would come over me and I'd be so afraid it was all a dream. Then I'd pinch myself to see if it was real – until suddenly I remembered that even supposing it was only a dream I'd better go on dreaming as long as I could; so I stopped pinching. But it IS real and we're nearly home, aren't we?"

With a sigh of rapture she relapsed into silence.

Martin stirred uneasily. He felt glad that it would be Matilda and not he who would have to tell this waif that the home she longed for was not to be hers after all. As much as he would like to add a mistress to his household, he knew his sister would never agree to share their bed with another woman. It wasn't fair, he told himself. After her repeated haranguing, he'd agreed to add a boy to their sexual menagerie. It wasn't his fault Mrs. Spencer had delivered a girl instead.

They drove over Langston's Hollow, where it was already quite dark, but not so dark that Mrs. Langston could not see them from the vantage of her kitchen window as they approached. He was tempted to offer a wave, certain that the woman would be following their progress with the aid of her spyglass.

By the time they arrived at Green Gables he was dreading the approaching revelation with a reluctance he did not understand. He was not worried about the trouble this mistake might cause him and his sister, but more his concern was for the child's disappointment. When he thought of that rapt light in her eyes being quenched he had an uncomfortable feeling that he was going to assist at murdering something – much the same feeling that came over him when he had to kill a lamb or calf or any other innocent little creature.

The yard was quite dark as they turned into it and the poplar leaves were rustling silkily all round it. "Listen to the trees talking in their sleep," the girl whispered as he lifted her to the ground. "What nice dreams they must have!"

Then, holding tightly to the carpetbag which contained "all her worldly goods," she followed him silently into the house.

Listening to Martin and Matilda having sex.

CHAPTER III

Matilda Collins is Surprised

Matilda came briskly forward as Martin opened the door. But when her eyes fell of the attractive figure with luxurious brunette hair and luminous gray-green eyes she stopped short in amazement.

"Martin Collins, who's that?" she exclaimed. "Where is the boy?"

"There wasn't any boy," said Martin wearily. "There was only this girl." He nodded toward the teenager, remembering that he had never even asked her name beyond the given Anne.

"No boy! But there MUST have been a boy," insisted Matilda. "We sent word to Mrs. Spencer to bring a boy."

"Well, she didn't. She brought HER. I asked the stationmaster. And I had to bring her home. She couldn't be left there, no matter where the mistake had come in."

"Well, this is a pretty piece of business!" sighed Matilda. "Do you expect me to have sex with a girl?"

"Why not? You might like it."

"It would be a new experience," she admitted, appraising the young woman from a new perspective.

"This works out fine for me," her brother allowed. "I wouldn't mind having an extra female around the house."

"No doubt," said his sister with an air of disapproval.

During this dialogue the girl had remained silent, her eyes roving from one to the other, all the animation fading out of her face. Suddenly she seemed to grasp the full meaning of what had been said. Dropping her precious carpetbag she sprang forward a step and clasped her hands. "You don't want a daughter?" she cried. "I might have expected it. You simply took advantage of me on the way here, fondling my boobies and putting your John Thomas in my pussy. And I let you, thinking I was coming to a new home. I've heard of debauched couples who prey on innocent young girls. I might have known you were simply taking advantage of my generosity with no intention of keeping me. Oh, what shall I do? I'm going to burst into tears!"

Burst into tears she did. Sitting down on a chair by the table, flinging her arms out upon it, and burying her face in them, she proceeded to cry stormily. Matilda and Martin looked at each other deprecatingly across the stove. Neither of them knew what to say or do.

The girl looked up, tears streaming down her cheeks. "I cannot believe you'd turn me away," she said to Martin, "after I let you take my most precious gift -- my virginity."

Matilda eyed her brother, "Now look what you've done. You couldn't wait could you, abusing that poor girl before you even got her home?"

"She threw herself at me."

"Did not," sobbed the girl. "You took advantage of me."

"Well, well, there's no need to cry so about it," sighed Matilda, giving her brother the evil eye.

"Yes, there IS need!" The girl raised her head quickly, revealing a tear-stained face and trembling lips. "YOU would cry, too, if you were an orphan and had come to a place you thought was going to be home and then found that they didn't want you because you weren't a boy. And one of them —" she glanced accusingly at Martin "— sampled your body with no intention of keeping you. It's not fair. Sharing your favors with your new family is one thing, but being used and then cast aside is another. Oh, this is the most TRAGICAL thing that ever happened to me!"

Something like a reluctant smile, rather rusty from long disuse, mellowed Matilda's grim expression. "Well, don't cry. We're not going to turn you out-of-doors tonight. You'll have to stay here until we investigate this affair. What's your name?"

The girl hesitated for a moment. "Will you please call me Cordelia?" she said eagerly.

"CALL you Cordelia? Is that your name?"

"No-o-o, it's not exactly my name, but I would love to be called Cordelia. It's such a perfectly elegant name."

"I don't know what on earth you mean. If Cordelia isn't your name, what is?"

"Anne Shirley," reluctantly admitted the owner of that name, "but, oh, please do call me Cordelia. It can't matter much to you what you call me if I'm only going to be here a little while, can it? And Anne is such an unromantic name."

"Unromantic fiddlesticks!" said the unsympathetic

Matilda. "Anne is a real good plain sensible name. You've no need to be ashamed of it."

"Oh, I'm not ashamed of it," explained Anne. "Only I like Cordelia better. I've always imagined that my name was Cordelia – at least, I always have of late years. When I was young I used to imagine it was Geraldine, but I like Cordelia better now. But if you call me Anne please call me Anne spelled with an E."

"What difference does it make how it's spelled?" asked Matilda. "It sounds the same either way."

"Oh, it makes SUCH a difference. It LOOKS so much nicer. When you hear a name pronounced can't you always see it in your mind, just as if it was printed out on a page? I can; and A-n-n looks dreadful, but A-n-n-e looks so much more distinguished. If you'll only call me Anne spelled with an E I shall try to reconcile myself to not being called Cordelia."

"Very well, then, Anne spelled with an E, can you tell us how this mistake came to be made? We sent word to Mrs. Spencer to bring us a boy. Were there no boys at the orphanage?"

"Oh, yes, there was an abundance of them. But Mrs. Spencer said DISTINCTLY that you wanted a girl about fifteen or sixteen years old. And the matron said she thought I would do. You don't know how delighted I was. I couldn't sleep all last night for joy."

"Mrs. Spencer was in error," said the blonde woman with a roll of her eyes.

The girl turned reproachfully to Martin, "Oh, why didn't you tell me at the station that you didn't want me and leave me there? If I hadn't seen the White Way of Delight and the Lake of Shining Waters it wouldn't be so hard."

"She – she's just referring to some conversation we had on the road," said Martin hastily.

"Before or after you fucked her?"

"She was more than willing."

"That's when I thought I was going to stay and be a part of your family," pouted Anne Shirley. "I wouldn't mind being fucked if I were staying. I'd gladly do the both of you."

"You'll have to talk to my sister about that. Go or stay – it's her decision."

"Oh my," said Matilda, mulling over this new idea. A girl in her bed instead of a boy. That was an interesting thought.

Martin headed for the door. "I'm going out to put the mare in, Matilda. We may as well have supper when I finish with that."

"Yes, dear."

He stomped out without bothering to look back.

Matilda turned to the girl. "Did Mrs. Spencer bring anybody over besides you?"

"Just one other. She brought Lily Jones for herself. Lily is only five years old and she is very beautiful and had blonde hair. If I was very beautiful and had blonde hair would you keep me?"

"No. We want a boy to help Martin on the farm. A girl would be of no use to us. Take off your hat. I'll lay it and your bag on the hall table."

Anne took off her hat meekly. "Shall I take my dress off too?"

"No, why would you do that?"

"I thought you might change your mind if you saw

me in my natural glory. My boobies are quite nice. Even Martin said so."

"He did, did he?"

"He said they were quite a handful. Would you like to see for yourself. I wouldn't mind if you touched them. In fact, I'd like that. We girls at the orphanage used to touch each other all the time. It felt good, I must say."

"Keep your clothes on for now. We'll sort this matter out after supper. Martin likes to eat on time. I imagine he's real hungry after the workout you gave him."

"I did my best. But I'm sure I could do much better with practice. I do so want a family of my own to make happy."

"It would make me happy if you'd help set the table."

"Yes, ma'am."

Martin came back presently and they sat down to the food. But Anne could not eat. In vain she nibbled at the bread and butter and pecked at the crab apple preserves in the little scalloped glass dish by her plate. She did not make much headway at all.

"You're not eating anything," said Matilda sharply, eying her as if it were a serious shortcoming.

Anne sighed. "I can't. I'm in the depths of despair. Can you eat when you are in the depths of despair?"

"I've never been in the depths of despair, so I can't say," responded Matilda.

"Well, did you ever IMAGINE you were in the depths of despair?"

"No, I haven't."

"Then I don't think you can understand what it's like. It's a very uncomfortable feeling indeed. When you try to eat, a lump comes up in your throat and you can't swallow anything, not even if it was a chocolate caramel. I had a chocolate caramel once two years ago and it was simply delicious. I've often dreamed since then that I had a lot of chocolate caramels, but I always wake up just when I'm going to eat them. I do hope you won't be offended because I can't eat. Everything is extremely nice, but still I cannot eat."

"I guess she's tired," said Martin, who hadn't spoken since his return from the barn. "Best put her to bed."

Matilda had been wondering where Anne should be put to bed. She had prepared a couch in the kitchen chamber for the desired and expected boy. Although it was neat and clean, it did not seem quite right to put a girl there in the kitchen. There remained only the east gable room. Matilda lighted a candle and told Anne to follow her. Taking her hat and carpetbag from the hall table as she passed, the girl spiritlessly trudged up to the small gable chamber.

Matilda set the candle on a three-cornered table and turned down the bedclothes. "I suppose you have a nightgown?" she questioned.

Anne nodded. "Yes, the matron of the orphanage made one for me. It's fearfully skimpy. There is never enough to go around in an orphanage, so things are always skimpy – at least in a poor orphanage like ours. I hate skimpy nightdresses. But one can dream just as well in them as in lovely trailing ones, with frills around the neck. So I guess it doesn't really matter what I wear to bed."

"Well, undress as quick as you can and climb into bed. I'll come back in a few minutes for the candle. I daren't trust you to put it out yourself. You'd likely set the place on fire," she said, remembering Mrs. Langston's warnings.

When Matilda had gone, Anne looked around her wistfully. The whitewashed walls were so painfully bare and staring that she thought they must ache over their own bareness. The floor was bare, too, except for a round braided mat in the middle such as Anne had never seen before. In one corner was the bed, a high, old-fashioned one, with four dark, low-turned posts. In the other corner was the aforesaid three-corner table adorned with a fat, red velvet pincushion hard enough to turn the point of the most adventurous pin. Above it hung a little six-by-eight mirror. Midway between table and bed was the window, covered with an icy white muslin frill, and opposite it was the washstand. The whole apartment was of a rigidity that sent a shiver to the very marrow of Anne's bones.

With a sob she hastily discarded her garments, put on the skimpy nightgown and sprang into bed where she burrowed face downward into the pillow. When Matilda came up for the light she found various articles of raiment scattered untidily over the floor.

"Pick those up and hang them in the closet," she instructed. Neatness was a mantra with Matilda Collins.

Timidly, Anne crawled out of bed and began gathering the clothing off the floor. "Sorry," she said as she put them in the narrow closet. "I was just so very upset –"

Matilda examined the girl, standing there in her nightgown. It WAS very skimpy, barely covering her crotch. And with the candle behind her on the nightstand, the silhouette of her lithesome body was as plain as day. Her breasts were pert. And she was obviously not wearing panties for you could see a trace of youthful pubic hair through the thin fabric. Nice, Matilda had to admit.

"Goodnight," the woman said, a little awkwardly, but not unkindly. Growing up with her brother, she'd never had the opportunity to see many naked girls. She was surprised to find herself attracted to Anne's slender body.

Anne's white face seemed near tears. "How can you call it a GOOD night when you know it must be the very worst night I've ever had?" she said reproachfully. Then she dived down into the bedcovers, pulling a quilt over her head in an effort to achieve invisibility.

Matilda went slowly down to the kitchen and proceeded to wash the supper dishes. Martin was smoking – a sure sign of perturbation of mind. He seldom smoked, for Matilda considered it a filthy habit; but at certain times and seasons he felt driven to it and then Matilda winked at the practice, realizing a man must have some vent for his pent-up emotions.

"Well, this is a pretty kettle of fish," she said wrathfully. "This is what comes of sending word instead of going ourselves. Richard Spencer's folks have twisted that message somehow. One of us will have to drive over and see Mrs. Spencer tomorrow, that's certain. This girl will have to be sent back to the orphanage."

"Yes, I suppose so," said Martin.

"You SUPPOSE so! Don't you know it?"

"Well now, she's a real nice little thing, Matilda. It's kind of a pity to send her back when she's so set on staying here. And she's quite willing to fuck us both."

His sister's astonishment could not have been greater if Martin had expressed a predilection for standing on his head. "Martin Collins, you don't mean to say you think we ought to keep her!"

"Well, now, no, I suppose not – not exactly," stammered Martin, uncomfortably driven into a corner for his precise meaning. "I suppose – we could hardly be expected to keep her."

"I should say not. What good would she be to us?"

"We might have some fun in bed with her."

"Martin Collins, I believe that child has bewitched you! I can see as plain as plain that you want to keep her."

"Well now, she's a real interesting little thing," persisted Martin. "You should have heard her talk a mile a minute as we were coming from the station."

"Oh, she can talk fast enough. I saw that at once. It's nothing in her favor, either. I don't like young people who have so much to say. I don't want an orphan girl and if I did she isn't the style I'd pick – her with those big eyes and pouty lips."

"Don't forget those nice titties and long legs."

"Those too. She is quite enticing, if I do say so. But I've never been with a woman and I don't plan to start now. No, she's got to be dispatched straightway back to where she came from."

"Don't be so hasty. I can tell you fancy her too. It's just the idea of being with a woman that's strange to you. I hear that happens in Paris all the time."

"This is not Paris, France. This is a faraway island at the northeastern edge of Canada. Deviant sexual shenanigans – people don't do that sort of thing here."

"You and I do that sort of thing. Incest is not on most Christian menus."

"We're different."

"My point exactly."

"Well –"

"I could hire a French boy to help me with the farm work," said Martin, "and Anne would be company for you."

"I'm not suffering for company," said Matilda shortly.

"But you might enjoy an extra bed partner," he persisted.

"No, I'm not going to keep her," his sister replied. But he heard a hesitation in her voice. That was good enough for now.

"Well, it's just as you say, of course, Matilda," smiled Martin, rising from his easy chair and putting away his pipe. "I'm going to bed. Are you coming?"

"Not yet. But I expect to be cumming in about fifteen minutes."

"Then move that pretty ass."

"First I need to clean up the dishes."

"Save them till morning. I'm horny." He didn't add that screwing the new girl on the way back to Green Gables had whetted his appetite for more.

So to bed went Martin. And to bed went Matilda,

eager to feel her brother's hard member between her loins. Sex with a girl indeed! she scolded herself as he entered her. She preferred dicks, right?

And upstairs in the east gable, Anne Shirley was crying herself to sleep. She had been certain that episode in the buggy would secure herself a place in Martin Collins's bed. But apparently not. She could hear him in there fucking his sister while she lay here in bed masturbating alone.

A glorious first morning in Avonlea.

CHAPTER IV

Morning at Green Gables

It was broad daylight when Anne awoke and sat up in bed, staring confusedly at the window through which a flood of cheery sunshine was pouring. For a moment she could not remember where she was. First came a delightful thrill, as something very pleasant; then a horrible remembrance. This was Green Gables and they didn't want her because she wasn't a boy!

Yes, it was morning and there was a cherry tree in full bloom outside her window. With a bound she was out of bed and across the floor. She pushed up the sash – it went up stiffly and creakily, as if it hadn't been opened for a long time, which was the case; and it stuck so tight that nothing was needed to hold it up.

Anne dropped on her knees and gazed out into the June morning, her eyes glistening with delight. Oh, wasn't it beautiful? Wasn't it a lovely place? Even if she wasn't really going to stay here, she would imagine she was. There was scope for imagination here.

The cherry tree grew so close that its boughs tapped against the house, and it was so thickset with blossoms that hardly a leaf was to be seen. On both sides of the house were big orchards, one of apple trees and one of cherry trees. In the garden below were lilac trees purple with flowers, and their dizzily sweet fragrance drifted up to the window on the morning wind.

Below the garden a green field lush with clover

sloped down to the hollow where the brook ran and where scores of white birches grew, upspringing airily out of an undergrowth suggestive of delightful possibilities in ferns and mosses and woodsy things generally. Beyond it was a hill, green and feathery with spruce and fir; there was a gap in it where the gray gable end of the little house she had seen from the other side of the Lake of Shining Waters was visible.

Off to the left were the big barns and beyond them, away down over green, low-sloping fields, was a sparkling blue glimpse of the sea.

Anne's beauty-loving eyes lingered on it all, taking everything greedily in. She had looked on so many unlovely places in her life, poor child; but this was as lovely as anything she had ever dreamed.

She knelt there, lost to everything but the loveliness around her, until she was startled by a hand on her shoulder. Matilda had come into the room, unheard by the small dreamer.

"It's time you were dressed," she said curtly.

Matilda really did not know how to talk to the child, and her uncomfortable ignorance made her crisp and curt when she did not mean to be.

Anne stood up and drew a long breath. "Oh, isn't it wonderful?" she said, waving her hand comprehensively at the world outside.

"It's a big tree," said Matilda, "and it blooms great, but the fruit don't amount to much never – small and wormy."

"Oh, I don't mean just the tree; of course it's lovely – yes, it's RADIANTLY lovely – it blooms as if it meant it – but I'm referring to everything, the garden and the orchard and the brook and the woods, the whole big dear world. Don't you feel as if you just love the world on a morning like this? And I can hear the brook laughing all the way up here. Have you ever noticed what cheerful things brooks are? They're always laughing. Even in wintertime I've heard them under the ice. I'm so glad there's a brook near Green Gables. Perhaps you think it doesn't make any difference to me when you're not going to keep me, but it does. I shall always like to remember that there is a brook at Green Gables even if I never see it again. If there wasn't a brook I'd be HAUNTED by the uncomfortable feeling that there ought to be one. I'm not in the depths of despair this morning. I never can be in the morning. Isn't it a splendid thing that there are mornings? But I feel very sad. I've just been imagining that it was really me you wanted after all and that I was to stay here forever and ever. It was a great comfort while it lasted. But the worst of imagining things is that the time comes when you have to stop and that hurts."

Matilda barely heard the burble of words as she stared at the girl's body, visible through the skimpy nightgown. Those rosy nipples seemed to be pointing at her. They poked against the fabric of the nightgown as if wanting to escape. She wanted to reach out and touch those breasts but thought better of it. "You'd better get dressed and come downstairs and never mind your imaginings," she said as soon as she could get a word in edgewise. "Breakfast is waiting. Wash your face and comb your hair. Get dressed, for god's sake. Leave the window up and turn your bedclothes back over the foot of the bed. Be as smart as you can."

51

Anne could evidently be smart to some purpose for she was downstairs in ten minutes time, with her clothes neatly on, her hair brushed and braided, her face washed, and a comfortable consciousness pervading her soul that she had fulfilled all Matilda's requirements. As a matter of fact, however, she had forgotten to turn back the bedclothes.

"I'm pretty hungry this morning," she announced as she slipped into the chair Matilda had placed for her. "The world doesn't seem such a howling wilderness as it did last night. I'm so glad it's a sunshiny morning. But I like rainy mornings real well, too. All sorts of mornings are interesting, don't you think? You don't know what's going to happen through the day, and there's so much scope for imagination. But I'm glad it's not rainy today because it's easier to be cheerful and bear up under affliction on a sunshiny day. I feel that I have a good deal to bear up under. It's all very well to read about sorrows and imagine yourself living through them heroically, but it's not so nice when you really come to have them, is it?"

"For pity's sake, hold your tongue," instructed Matilda. "You talk entirely too much for a little girl."

Thereupon Anne held her tongue so obediently and thoroughly that her continued silence made Matilda rather nervous, as if in the presence of something not exactly natural. Martin also held his tongue, – but this was natural – so that the meal was a very silent one.

As it progressed Anne became more and more abstracted, eating mechanically, with her big eyes fixed unswervingly and unseeingly on the sky outside the window. This made Matilda more nervous than ever;

she had an uncomfortable feeling that while this odd girl's body might be sitting there at the table, her spirit was far away in some remote airy cloudland, borne aloft on the wings of imagination. Who would want such a distracted dreamer about the place?

Yet Martin wished to keep her, of all unaccountable things! Matilda felt that he wanted it just as much this morning as he had the night before, and that he would go on wanting it. That was Martin's way – take a whim into his head and cling to it with the most amazing silent persistency – a persistency ten times more potent and effectual in its very silence than if he had talked it out. Why did they need an extra person in bed, she thought to herself. Why can't he be satisfied with just me?

Then she remembered that it was her who had been lobbying for an extra bed partner – a boy! Was she being disingenuous, rejecting Martin's sexual inclinations when he'd been supportive of her own. Would she really object to a little hanky-panky with this attractive girl sitting across the table?

When the meal was ended Anne came out of her reverie and offered to wash the dishes. She delivered a bright smile to show her willingness to help out.

"Can you wash dishes right?" asked Matilda distrustfully.

"Pretty well. I'm better at looking after children, though. I've had so much experience at that. It's such a pity you haven't any here for me to look after."

"I don't want any more children to look after than I've got at present. YOU'RE problem enough in all conscience. What's to be done with you I don't know.

Martin is a most ridiculous man."

"I think he's lovely," said Anne reproachfully. "He is so very sympathetic. He doesn't mind how much I talk – he seems to like it. I felt that he was a kindred spirit as soon as ever I saw him."

"You're both queer enough, if that's what you mean by kindred spirits," said Matilda with a sniff. She wondered if her brother had already been in the girl's knickers this morning before she'd gotten up. She wouldn't put it past that horny rascal. "Yes, you may wash the dishes. Take plenty of hot water, and be sure you dry them well. I've got enough to attend to this morning for I'll have to drive over to White Sands in the afternoon and see Mrs. Spencer. You'll come with me and we'll settle what's to be done with you. After you've finished the dishes, go upstairs and make your bed."

Anne washed the dishes deftly enough, while Matilda kept a sharp eye on the process. Later on the girl made her bed less successfully, for she had never learned the art of wrestling with a feather tick. But it was done somehow and smoothed down; and then Matilda, to get rid of her, told her she might go out-of-doors and amuse herself until lunch.

Anne flew to the door, face alight, eyes glowing. "Oh, I must go down to look at the sea. The sun is barely up and the water's still shimmering with a golden hue." With that, she shucked her dress, tossing it on the stone bench outside the door, and raced off down the hill as naked as a wood sprite.

"Holy Mother of God," murmured Matilda at the sight of the bare-bottomed girl. "I hope Mrs. Langston doesn't see her. Or those Barston boys who are always traipsing through our pasture uninvited."

Martin came out of the barn. "Did I just see Anne go running by as naked as the day she was born?" he stared into the distance. She was nearly to the seacoast by now.

"I'm afraid so. I could hardly believe my eyes."

"She told me she was a naturalist."

Matilda frowned. "You mean like those sun worshippers I read about in the *Police Gazette*. They gather in nudist camps where they walk around without a stitch of clothing."

"Sure looks like it," Martin said, continuing to stare into the distance.

≈≈≈

Eventually Anne came back to the house and sat dejectedly at the table, light and glow as effectually blotted out as if some one had clapped an extinguisher on her. Her face was screwed up in a frown, almost on the verge of tears.

"What's the matter now?" demanded Matilda, handing the girl her dress.

"I don't dare enjoy myself," said Anne in the tone of a martyr relinquishing all earthly joys. "If I can't stay here there is no use in my loving Green Gables. And if I go out there and get acquainted with all those trees and flowers and the orchard and the brook, I'll not be able to help loving it. It's hard enough now, so I won't make it any harder. I want to go out so much – everything seems to be calling to me, 'Anne, Anne, come out to us. Anne, Anne, we want a playmate' – but I'd better not. There is no use in loving things if you have to be torn from them, is there? And it's so hard to keep from loving things, isn't it? That was why I was so glad when I thought I was going to live here. I thought I'd have so many things to love and nothing to hinder me. But that brief dream is over. I am resigned to my fate now, so I don't think I'll go out for fear I'll get unresigned again."

"Good."

"What is the name of that geranium on the windowsill, please?"

"That's an apple-scented geranium."

"Oh, I don't mean that sort of a name. I mean just a name you gave it yourself. Didn't you give it a name?"

"No, of course not."

"May I give it one then? May I call it – let me see – Bonny would do. May I call it Bonny while I'm here? Oh, do let me!"

"Goodness, I don't care. But where on earth is the sense of naming a geranium?"

"Oh, I like things to have names even if they are only geraniums. It makes them seem more like people. How do you know but that it hurts a geranium's feelings just to be called a geranium and nothing else? You wouldn't like to be called nothing but a woman all the time. Yes, I shall call it Bonny. I named that cherry tree outside my bedroom window this morning. I called it Snow Queen because it was so white. Of course, it won't always be in blossom, but one can imagine that it is, can't one?"

"I never in all my life saw or heard anything to equal her," muttered Matilda, beating a retreat down to the cellar after potatoes. "She is kind of interesting as Martin says. I can feel already that I'm wondering what on earth she'll say next. Better watch out or she'll be casting a spell over me, too. She's already cast it over Martin. That look he gave me when he went out said everything he said or hinted last night over again. I wish he was like other men and would talk things out. A body could answer back then and argue him into reason. But what's to be done with a man who just LOOKS? And he's certainly looking at Anne ... like a dog sniffing after a bitch in heat."

When Matilda returned from her cellar pilgrimage, Anne Shirley had relapsed into reverie, her chin in her hands and her eyes on the sky. There Matilda left her until the lunch was on the table.

"Can I have the mare and buggy this afternoon, Martin?" asked Matilda.

Martin nodded and looked wistfully at Anne. Matilda intercepted the look and said grimly: "I'm going to drive over to White Sands and settle this thing. I'll take Anne with me and Mrs. Spencer will probably make arrangements to send her back to Nova Scotia at once. I'll set your tea out for you and I'll be home in time to milk the cows."

Still Martin said nothing and Matilda had a sense of having wasted words and breath. There is nothing more aggravating than a man who won't talk back – unless it is a woman who won't. She glanced at Anne, sitting silently at the table, toying with her food.

~ ~ ~

Martin hitched the sorrel to the buggy and Matilda and Anne set off. Martin opened the yard gate for them and as they drove slowly through, he said to nobody in particular: "Harley Buote from the Creek was here this morning, and I told him I guessed I'd hire him for the summer."

Matilda made no reply, but she hit the unlucky sorrel such a vicious clip with the whip that the fat mare, unused to such treatment, whizzed indignantly down the lane at an alarming pace. For some reason Matilda was irked. Maybe it was because Harley Buote was a big handsome man with steely eyes and a physique befitting a blacksmith. She found him attractive, but knew nothing could ever come of her daydreams. Sleeping with the occasional door-to-door peddler was one thing, but Harley was a local man, too close to home to risk a dalliance.

Matilda looked back once as the buggy bounced along and saw Martin leaning over the gate, looking curiously after them. Had she been too obvious in her reaction?

Matilda and I get acquainted.

CHAPTER V

Anne's History

"**D**o you know," said Anne confidentially, "I've made up my mind to enjoy this drive. It's been my experience that you can nearly always enjoy things if you make up your mind firmly that you will. Of course, you must make it up FIRMLY. I am not going to think about going back to the orphanage while we're having our drive. I'm just going to think about the drive. Oh, look, there's one little early wild rose out! Isn't it lovely? Don't you think it must be glad to be a rose? Wouldn't it be nice if roses could talk? I'm sure they could tell us such lovely things. And isn't pink the most bewitching color in the world? I love it, but I can't wear it."

"Don't be silly. Pink would look good on you."

"The nipples on my boobies are pink. I suppose that looks good on me."

"Yes, it does –" Matilda began, then stopped herself.

"And if I spread apart the lips of my pussy, it is pink there too."

"That's true of all women," Matilda replied cautiously.

"You too?"

"Me too."

"May I see? I am curious."

Matilda cleared her throat nervously. "That might not be appropriate."

"You saw me in my nightie. That didn't hide much of me. Turn about is fair play."

Matilda started to say, "This is not a game –" but then halted her words before they came out. "Alright," she told the girl, "but this must remain our secret."

"Of course. You can see my pink too, if you like."

"Well, alright."

Matilda guided the sorrel into a side road that led down to the Langston's hayfield. A dead end, nobody would be there this time of year. The cedars that bordered it would provide ample privacy.

"You sure about this?" asked the blonde woman.

"Oh yes."

"Then we should both get undressed," said Matilda, pulling her housedress over her head. That left her in knickers and a camisole.

Anne reciprocated, slipping out of her skirt and blouse. That left her completely nude. "Now the rest," she nodded at the older blonde.

Matilda up-ended the camisole, shaking her hair free. That made her pendulous breasts sway like a metronome.

"Ooo, I like the way you look," said Anne.

"Thank you." Matilda stepped out of the cotton panties and kicked them aside. "Let's sit on these logs facing each other," she suggested. "Then we can spread our legs and show all."

"Alright then," Anne took her place.

"On the count of three."

"One-two-three," said Anne as if it were one word. She opened the V of her thighs, revealing a sprig of dark hair that barely covered her pubis.

Matilda moved her knees apart, exposing her more luxurious bird's nest of hair. "There," she said. Her vulva was parted enough to offer a hint of pink.

Anne's fingers moved her lower lips apart to display the moist interior. "Want me to lick your pussy? A girl at the orphanage did that to me once and I liked it."

"Here, lay down beside me on the grass," directed Matilda. "Feet toward my head. That way we can lick each other at the same time."

Oddly enough, the fifteen-year-old girl seemed more adept at it than the older woman. Burying her face in Matilda's crotch, he tongue was like that of a serpent. In short order, she had the blonde whimpering and moaning, lost in the throes of ecstasy. "Ohmygod ... ohmygod ... ohmygod," Matilda repeated. That was followed by an orgasmic shriek.

≈≈≈

Later, the two of them dressed and tidied themselves up. "You must not tell my brother of this," said Matilda Collins as she brushed her hair back with the comb of her fingers.

"How can I? You are sending me back to the orphanage and I'll not likely see him again."

"I see your point. I hope you do not think I've taken advantage of you as my brother did."

"No, not at all. Did you enjoy it?"

"Very much, my dear. It was my first time with a member of the same sex."

"How nice. I'm glad you chose me."

Matilda wagged a finger at the girl. "This does not change matters. You cannot stay. I'm taking you back to Mrs. Spencer for return to the orphanage."

"If you let me stay, we could do that every night."

"No, we cannot," said Matilda mercilessly. "That was a one-time experiment."

"I thought you said you liked it," interjected Anne.

"I did. But it shan't happen again."

Anne sighed. "Well, that is another hope gone. 'My life is a perfect graveyard of buried hopes.' That's a sentence I read in a book once, and I say it over to comfort myself whenever I'm disappointed in anything."

"I don't see where the comfort comes in," said Matilda.

"Why, because it sounds so nice and romantic, just as if I were a heroine in a book, you know. I am so fond of romantic things, and a graveyard full of buried hopes is about as romantic a thing as one can imagine, isn't it? I'm rather glad I have one. Will we be going across the Lake of Shining Waters today?"

"We're not going over Barry's Pond, if that's what you mean by your Lake of Shining Waters. We're going by the shore road."

"Shore road sounds nice," said Anne dreamily. "Is it as nice as it sounds? Just when you said 'shore road' I saw it in a picture in my mind, as quick as that! And White Sands is a pretty name, too; but I don't like it as well as Avonlea. Avonlea is a lovely name. It just sounds like music. How far is it to White Sands?"

"It's five miles; and as you're evidently bent on talking you might as well talk to some purpose by telling me what you know about yourself."

"Oh, what I KNOW about myself isn't really worth

telling," replied Anne. "If you'll only let me tell you what I IMAGINE about myself you'll find it ever so much more interesting."

"No, I don't want any of your imaginings. Just you stick to bald facts. Begin at the beginning. Where were you born and how old are you?"

"I turned fifteen last March," said Anne, resigning herself to telling the bald facts. "And I was born in Bolingbroke, Nova Scotia. My father's name was Walter Shirley, and he was a teacher in the Bolingbroke High School. My mother's name was Bertha Shirley. Aren't Walter and Bertha lovely names? I'm so glad my parents had nice names. It would be a real disgrace to have a father named – well, say Jebediah, wouldn't it?"

"I guess it doesn't matter what a person's name is as long as he behaves himself," said Matilda, feeling herself called upon to inculcate a good and useful message. After their earlier encounter, she felt it necessary to make amends for her moral turpitude.

"Well, I don't know." Anne looked thoughtful. "I read in a book once that a rose by any other name would smell as sweet, but I've never been able to believe it. I don't believe a rose WOULD be as nice if it was called a thistle or a skunk cabbage. I suppose my father could have been a good man even if he had been called Jebediah; but I'm sure it would have been a cross to bear. Well, my mother was a teacher in the high school, too, but when she married father she gave up teaching, of course. A husband was enough responsibility. Mrs. Thomas said that they were as poor as church mice. They went to live in a weeny-teeny little yellow house in Bolingbroke. I've never seen that house, but I've imagined it thousands of times. I think it must have had honeysuckle over the parlor window and lilacs in the front yard and lilies of the valley just inside the gate. Yes, and muslin curtains in all the windows. Muslin curtains give a house such an air. I was born in that house. Mrs. Thomas said I was the homeliest baby she ever saw, I was so scrawny and tiny and nothing but eyes, but that mother thought I was perfectly beautiful. I should think a mother would be a better judge than a poor woman who came in to scrub, wouldn't you? I'm glad she was satisfied with me. I would feel so sad if I thought I was a disappointment to her – because she didn't live very long after that, you see. She died of fever when I was just three months old. I do wish she'd lived long enough for me to remember calling her mother. I think it would be so sweet to say 'mother,' don't you? And father died four days afterwards from fever too. That left me an orphan and folks were puzzled as what to do with me. You see, nobody wanted me even then. It seems to be my fate. Father and mother had both come from places far away and it was well known they hadn't any relatives living. Finally Mrs. Thomas said she'd take me, though she was poor and had a drunken husband. She brought me up by hand.

"I lived with them until I was eight years old. I helped look after the Thomas children – there were four of them younger than me – and I can tell you they took a lot of looking after. Then Mr. Thomas was killed falling under a train and his mother offered to take Mrs. Thomas and the children, but she didn't want me. Mrs. Thomas was at her wit's end as what to do with me. Then Mrs. Hammond from up the river said she'd take me, seeing I was handy with children, and I went up the river to live with her. It was a very lonesome place. I'm sure I could never have lived there if I hadn't had an imagination. Mr. Hammond worked a little sawmill up there, and Mrs. Hammond had eight children. She had twins three times. I like babies in moderation, but twins three times in succession is TOO MUCH. I told Mrs. Hammond so when the last pair came. I used to get so dreadfully tired carrying them about.

"I lived up river with the Hammonds for about two years, and then Mr. Hammond died and Mrs. Hammond divided her children among her relatives and moved to the States. I had to go to the orphanage at Hopeton, because nobody would take me. They didn't want me at the orphanage, either; they said they were overcrowded as it was. But they had to take me and I was there four months until Mrs. Spencer came."

Anne finished up with another sigh, of relief this time. Evidently she did not like talking about her experiences in a world that had not wanted her.

"Did you ever go to school?" demanded Matilda, turning the sorrel mare down the shore road.

"Not a great deal. I went a little the last year I stayed with Mrs. Thomas. When I went up river we were so far from a school that I couldn't walk it in winter and there was a vacation in summer, so I could only go in the spring and fall. But of course I went while I was at the orphanage. I can read pretty well and I know ever so many pieces of poetry by heart – 'The Battle of Hohenlinden' and 'Edinburgh after Flodden,' and 'Bingen of the Rhine,' and most of the 'Lady of the Lake' and most of 'The Seasons' by James Thompson. Don't you just love poetry that gives you a crinkly feeling up and down your back? There is a piece in the Fifth Reader – 'The Downfall of Poland' – that is just full of thrills. Of course, I wasn't in the Fifth Reader – I was only in the Fourth – but the big girls used to lend me theirs to read."

"Were those women – Mrs. Thomas and Mrs. Hammond – good to you?" asked Matilda, looking at Anne out of the corner of her eye.

"O-o-o-h," faltered Anne. Her sensitive little face suddenly flushed scarlet with embarrassment. "They MEANT to be – I know they meant to be just as good and kind as possible. And when people mean to be good to you, you don't mind very much when they're not always good. They had much to worry them, you know. It's very trying to have a drunken husband, you see; and it must be very trying to have twins three times in succession, don't you think? But I feel sure they really meant to be good to me."

Matilda asked no more questions. Anne gave herself up to a silent rapture over the shore road and Matilda guided the sorrel abstractedly while she pondered deeply. Pity was suddenly stirring in her heart for the child. What a starved, unloved life she had had – a life of drudgery and poverty and neglect, for Matilda was shrewd enough to read between the lines of Anne's history and divine the truth. No wonder she had been so delighted at the prospect of a real home, willing to do anything to secure herself a place. Matilda felt ashamed that she had taken sexual advantage of the child.

Anne seemed a nice, teachable little thing. It was a pity she had to be sent back. What if they should indulge Martin's whim and let the girl stay? She *would* make a nice plaything for the two of them.

Matilda thought about that possibility as the mare made her way along the narrow road. On the left were steep red sandstone cliffs, so near the track that a mare of less steadiness might have tried the nerves of people riding in the buggy. Down at the base of the cliffs were little sandy coves surrounded by heaps of surf-worn rocks. Beyond lay the sea, shimmering and blue, and over it soared gulls, their pinions flashing silvery in the sunlight.

"Isn't the sea wonderful?" said Anne, rousing from a long silence. "Once, when I lived in Marysville, Mr. Thomas took us all to spend the day at the shore. I enjoyed every moment of that day, even if I had to look after the children all the time. I lived it over in happy dreams for years. But this shore is even nicer than the Marysville shore. Aren't those gulls splendid? Would you like to be a gull? I think I would – that is, if I couldn't be a human girl. Don't you think it would be nice to wake up at sunrise and swoop down over the water and away out over that lovely blue all day, and then at night to fly back to one's nest? Oh, I can just imagine myself doing it. What big house is that just ahead, please?"

"That's the White Sands Hotel. Mr. Kirke runs it, but the season hasn't begun yet. Heaps of Americans come there in the summer. They think this shore is just about right for a vacation."

"I was afraid it might be Mrs. Spencer's place," said Anne mournfully. "I don't want to get there. Somehow, it will seem like the end of everything."

My fate in the balance.

CHAPTER VI

Matilda Makes Up Her Mind

Get there they did, however. Mrs. Spencer lived in a big yellow house at White Sands Cove, and she came to the door with surprise on her face.

"Dear me," she exclaimed, "you're the last folks I was expecting to see today, but I'm real glad to see you. You'll put your horse in? And how are you, Anne?"

"I'm as well as can be expected, thank you," said Anne solemnly. A blight seemed to have descended on her.

"I suppose we'll stay a little while to rest the mare," said Matilda, "but I promised Martin I'd be home early. The fact is, Mrs. Spencer, there's been a big mistake. We sent word, Martin and I, for you to bring us a boy from the orphanage. We told your brother Robert to tell you we wanted a boy ten or eleven years old."

"Matilda Collins, you don't say so!" said Mrs. Spencer in distress. "Why, Robert sent word down by his daughter Nancy and she said you wanted a girl — didn't she, Flora?" appealing to her daughter who had come out to the steps.

"She certainly did, Miss Collins," corroborated Flora earnestly.

"I'm dreadful sorry," said Mrs. Spencer. "I thought I was following your instructions. Nancy is a terrible flighty thing. I've often had to scold her for her heedlessness."

"It was our own fault," said Matilda resignedly.

73

"We should have come to you ourselves and not left an important message to be passed along by word of mouth in that fashion. Anyhow, the mistake has been made and the only thing to do is to set it right. Can we send the child back to the orphanage? I suppose they'll take her back, won't they?"

"I suppose so," said Mrs. Spencer thoughtfully, "but I don't think it will be necessary to send her back. Mrs. Peter Blewett was up here yesterday, and she was saying to me how much she wished she'd sent by me for a little girl to help her. Mrs. Blewett has a large family, you know, and she finds it hard to get help. Anne will be the very girl for her."

Matilda did not look happy. Here was an unexpectedly good chance to get this unwelcome orphan off her hands, but she did not feel good about it. She had heard of Mrs. Blewett. Discharged servant girls told fearsome tales of her temper and stinginess. Matilda felt a qualm of conscience at the thought of handing Anne over to the woman's tender mercies.

"Look," exclaimed Mrs. Spencer, "that's Mrs. Peter Blewett coming up the lane at this blessed minute. That is real lucky, for we can settle the matter right away. Take the armchair, Miss Collins. Anne, you sit here on the ottoman and don't wiggle. Flora, go put the kettle on."

The new visitor waddled into the parlor.

"Good afternoon, Mrs. Blewett," greeted their hostess. "We were just saying how fortunate it was you happened along. Let me introduce you two ladies. Mrs. Blewett, Miss Collins."

The women nodded at each other.

"Please excuse me for just a moment," apologized Mrs. Spencer. "I forgot to tell Flora to take the buns out of the oven."

Anne sat mutely on the ottoman, with her hands clasped tightly in her lap, staring at Mrs. Blewett. Was she to be given into the keeping of this sharp-faced, sharp-eyed woman? She felt a lump coming up in her throat and her eyes smarted painfully. She was afraid she couldn't keep the tears back.

Mrs. Spencer returned, flushed and beaming. "It seems there's been a mistake about this little girl, Mrs. Blewett," she interjected. "I was under the impression that Mr. and Miss Collins wanted a little girl to adopt. But it seems they wanted a boy instead. So if you're still interested, I think she'll be just the thing for you."

Mrs. Blewett darted her eyes over Anne from head to foot. "How old are you and what's your name?" she demanded.

"Anne Shirley," faltered the girl, not daring to make any stipulations regarding the spelling thereof, "and I'm fifteen years old."

"Humph! You don't look as if there's much to you. But you're wiry. Well, if I take you you'll have to be a good girl, you know – good and smart and respectful."

"Yes, ma'am," Anne nodded.

Mrs. Blewett cleared her throat. "I suppose I can take her off your hands, Miss Collins. The baby's awful fractious, and I'm clean worn out attending to him. If you like I can take her home right now."

Matilda looked at Anne and softened at sight of the girl's pale face with its look of mute misery – the misery of a helpless little creature who finds itself once more caught in the trap from which it had escaped. Matilda felt an uncomfortable conviction that, if she denied the appeal of that look, it would haunt her to her dying day.

"Well, I don't know," she said slowly. "I didn't say that Martin and I had absolutely decided that we wouldn't keep her. In fact, I may say that Martin is quite disposed to hold onto her. I just came over to find out how the mistake had been made. I think I'd better talk it over with Martin. If we make up our mind not to keep her we'll bring her over to you tomorrow night. If we don't, you may know that she is going to stay with us. Will that suit you, Mrs. Blewett?"

"I suppose it'll have to," said Mrs. Blewett ungraciously.

During Matilda's speech a sunrise had been dawning on Anne's face. First the look of despair faded out; then came a faint flush of hope; her eyes grew deep and bright as morning stars. The child was quite transfigured; and, a moment later, when Mrs. Spencer and Mrs. Blewett went out in quest of a recipe the latter had come to borrow she sprang up and flew across the room to Matilda.

"Oh, Miss Collins, did you really say you'd let me stay at Green Gables?" she said in a breathless whisper, as if speaking aloud might shatter the glorious possibility. "Did you really say that? Or did I only imagine it?"

"You'd better learn to control that imagination of yours, Anne," said Matilda crossly. "It hasn't been decided yet. Mrs. Blewett certainly needs you more than I do."

"I'd rather go back to the orphanage than live with

her," said Anne passionately. "She looks like a big fat pig."

Matilda smothered a smile under the conviction that Anne must be reproved for such a speech. "You should be ashamed of talking so about a lady like Mrs. Blewett," she spoke to her severely. "Go back and sit down quietly and hold your tongue and behave as a good girl should."

"I'll try to do that and anything else you want, if you'll only keep me," said Anne, returning meekly to her ottoman. "That includes getting naked with you on the rug."

"We'll see about that," Matilda Collins replied noncommittally.

~ ~ ~

When they arrived back at Green Gables that evening Martin was waiting for them. Matilda noted the relief in his face when he saw that she had brought Anne back with her. She waited until they were milking the cows before she told him about the interview with Mrs. Spencer.

"I'm glad you brought Anne back," he said. "I wouldn't give a dog I liked to that Blewett woman."

"I don't fancy the old biddy's style myself," nodded Matilda. "But it's that or keeping the girl ourselves. And since you seem to want her, Martin, I suppose I'm willing. I've been thinking it over until I've kind of got used to the idea."

Martin's face glowed of delight. "Well now, I hoped you'd come to see it in that light, Matilda," he said. "She's such an interesting little thing."

"It would be more to the point if you said she's a *sexy*

little thing," responded Matilda.

"You've sampled her, haven't you?" He gave her a big grin, as if a light had come on inside his brain.

"So what if I have? You fucked her before you got her home from the train station, did you not?"

"Indeed I did."

"Even-steven then. Forget Mrs. Blewett. We'll keep the girl and you can fuck her all you want. Me too."

"Hmm, I like the idea of having our own sex slave."

"I'll make it my business to see she's trained to be a good little whore. And mind, Martin, you're not to go interfering with my methods. Perhaps I've not had a lot of sexual experience, but I've satisfied you adequately for the past ten years."

"That's true," he grinned.

"Just leave me to manage her. I'll have her fucking us on cue before you know it."

"There, there, Matilda, you can have your own way," Martin reassured his sister. "I kind of think she's the sort you can do anything with if you get her to love you."

"Love?" Matilda sniffed, to express her contempt for Martin's opinion. "We're talking about sex. That doesn't require any emotions. She just needs conditioning, like Pavlov's dog. Ring a bell and she spreads those lovely long legs."

"I suspect it's a little more complicated than that," said her brother as he walked off to the dairy carrying the milk pails.

I get to stay.

CHAPTER VII

Anne Says Her Prayers

When Matilda took Anne up to bed that night she said stiffly: "Now, Anne, I noticed last night that you threw your clothes all about the floor when you took them off. That is a very untidy habit, and I can't allow it. As soon as you take off any article of clothing fold it neatly and place it on the chair. I haven't any use for girls who aren't neat."

"I was so harrowed up in my mind last night that I didn't think about my clothes at all," said Anne. "I'll fold them nicely tonight. They always made us do that at the orphanage. Half the time, though, I'd forget, I'd be in such a hurry to get into bed where I could imagine things."

"You'll have to remember a little better if you want to stay here," admonished Matilda."

"Here, watch me. I'll fold them in front of you right now." With that, Anne slipped her blouse off her shoulders and dropped her skirt. Then stepping out of her panties, she stood entirely naked before her new mistress. "See?" she said, neatly folding her garments and putting them on the dresser.

"Well, that's the spirit," nodded Matilda, her eyes drifting over the young girl's body. Her breasts were well developed for a fifteen-year-old. Matilda remembered the taste of them in her mouth that very afternoon. Like lilac. "Now say your prayers and get into bed before I'm tempted to crawl in with you."

"I never say any prayers," announced Anne. "But tonight I'll make an exception and pray that you'll let me stay at Green Gables. Then you – and your brother – could crawl into my bed anytime you like. Wouldn't that be nice?"

Matilda looked horrified. "Why, Anne, what do you mean? Were you never taught to say your prayers? God always wants little girls to say their prayers. Don't you know who God is, Anne?"

"'God is a spirit, infinite, eternal and unchangeable, in His being, wisdom, power, holiness, justice, goodness, and truth,'" responded Anne promptly and glibly.

Matilda looked rather relieved. "So you do know something then, thank goodness! You're not quite a heathen. Where did you learn that?"

"Oh, at the orphanage's Sunday School. They made us learn the whole catechism. I liked it pretty well. There's something splendid about some of the words. 'Infinite, eternal and unchangeable.' Isn't that grand? It has such a roll to it – just like a big organ playing. You couldn't quite call it poetry, I suppose, but it sounds a lot like it, doesn't it?"

"We're not talking about poetry, Anne – we are talking about saying your prayers. Don't you know it's a terrible wicked thing not to say your prayers every night? I'm afraid you are a very bad little girl."

"It's easier to be bad than good if you're a homeless orphan," said Anne. "God made me an orphan and I've never cared about Him since."

Matilda decided that Anne's religious training must be begun at once. Plainly there was no time to be lost. "You must say your prayers while you are under my roof, Anne."

"Why, of course," assented Anne. "I'd do anything to oblige you. I'll lick your pussy till you cum. And I've already let your brother Martin take my virginity. I'd always wondered what'd it be like to have a man put his John Thomas inside me. It felt very good, so big and long. But you know that. After all, you and your brother are VERY close."

"What makes you say that?"

"I heard the two of you doing it last night."

"Yesterday – with my brother – that was your first time?"

"Yes, ma'am. I wouldn't let the boys at the orphanage do that – fingers only. I knew I should save myself as something special for my new family, if I ever got one."

"Oh my," said Matilda in embarrassment. "You must kneel down and pray."

Anne knelt at Matilda's knee and looked up gravely. "Why must people kneel down to pray? If I really wanted to pray I'll tell you what I'd do. I'd go out into a great big field all alone or into the deep, deep, woods, and I'd look up into the sky – up – up – up – into that lovely blue sky that looks as if there was no end to its blueness. And then I'd just FEEL a prayer. Well, I'm ready. What am I to say?"

Matilda felt more embarrassed than ever. She had intended to teach Anne the childish classic, "Now I lay me down to sleep." But she had, as I have told you, the glimmerings of a sense of humor – which is simply another name for a sense of fitness of things; and it suddenly occurred to her that that simple little prayer, sacred to white-robed childhood lisping at motherly knees, was entirely unsuited to this sexy little witch of a girl who knew and cared nothing about God's love.

"You're old enough to pray for yourself, Anne," she said finally. "Just thank God for your blessings and ask Him humbly for the things you want."

"Well, I'll do my best," promised Anne, burying her face in Matilda's lap. "*Gracious heavenly Father –* that's the way the ministers say it in church, so I suppose it's all right in private prayer, isn't it?" she interjected, lifting her head for a moment.

"Yes, go ahead."

"*Gracious heavenly Father, I thank Thee for the White Way of Delight and the Lake of Shining Waters and Bonny and the Snow Queen. I'm really extremely grateful for them. And that's all the blessings I can think of just now to thank Thee for. As for the things I want, they're so numerous that it would take a great deal of time to name them all so I will only mention the two most important. Please let me stay at Green Gables; and please let me be good-looking when I grow up. I remain, yours respectfully, Anne Shirley.*"

"Amen," Matilda corrected her ending.

"I could have made it much more flowery if I'd had a little more time to think it over," said Anne. "Now do you want me to do you?"

Poor Matilda was only preserved from complete collapse by remembering that it was not irreverence, but simply spiritual ignorance on the part of Anne that was responsible for this extraordinary petition. "No, not while God is looking down on us."

"Doesn't God look down us all the time?" inquired Anne as she slid the blonde woman's skirt over her knees. "Oh look, you're wearing silk panties. They're so very pretty. I hope I will have silk panties to wear some day."

As the girl spoke, she tugged the undergarment forward and over the knees, uncovering the nest of blonde curls. "Oh how very pretty your pussy is," she gushed, "all nestled away inside that corn-silk hair. I wish I were blonde like you. Anything but this non-descript brown hair."

"Wait," said Matilda. But the girl had already burrowed her face in the woman's lap and was exploring the folds of her sex with a snake-like tongue.

"Mmmph," said Anne, busily teasing the nether regions of her new mistress.

"Oooo," responded Matilda, giving in to the pleasurable sensations.

≈≈≈

Later Matilda tucked the girl in bed, mentally vowing that she should be taught a prayer the very next day, and was leaving the room with the light when Anne called her back.

"I've just thought of it now. I should have offered to do Martin too. Do you suppose it will make any difference in his decision about letting me stay that he didn't get to fuck me tonight?"

"I – I don't suppose it will," said Matilda. "He has plenty of time to do that tomorrow. Now go to sleep like a good girl. Goodnight."

"Goodnight, Matilda," the girl said, cuddling luxuriously down among her pillows. "By the way, I like how you taste."

"Why thank you, Anne."

Matilda retreated to the kitchen, set the candle firmly on the table, and glared at her brother. "Martin Collins, it's about time somebody adopted that child and taught her something. She's practically a heathen. Will you believe that she never said a prayer in her life till tonight? I'll be sending her to Sunday School just as soon as I can get some suitable clothes made for her."

"Well, well, she got you off," observed Martin. "I can tell by the flush of your cheeks. When do I get my turn with that little vixen?"

"Let her sleep tonight. Then tomorrow you can continue with her initiation into womanhood, just like you did me some twenty years ago."

"Yes, I remember that well. You were a willing pupil. I hope Anne will be so, too."

"Oh, she's more than willing, that horny little tart. You and I are going to have our hands full with her. We've had a pretty easy sex life of it so far, just the two of us. But the time to share our bed has come at last and we'll just have to make the best of it."

A willing pupil.

CHAPTER VIII

Anne's Bringing-up Is Begun

For reasons best known to herself, Matilda did not tell Anne that she was to stay at Green Gables until the next afternoon. During the forenoon she kept the girl busy with various tasks and watched over her with a keen eye while she did them. By noon she'd concluded that Anne was smart and obedient, willing to work and quick to learn; her most serious shortcoming seemed to be a tendency to fall into daydreams in the middle of a task and forget all about it until such time as she was sharply recalled to earth by a sharp reprimand.

When Anne had finished washing the dinner dishes she suddenly confronted Matilda with the air of one desperately determined to learn the worst. Her thin little body trembled from head to foot; her face flushed and her eyes dilated until they were almost black; she clasped her hands tightly and said in an imploring voice: "Oh, please, Miss Collins, won't you tell me if you are going to send me away or not? I've tried to be patient all the morning, but I really feel that I cannot bear not knowing any longer. It's a dreadful feeling. Please tell me."

"You haven't scalded the dishcloth in clean hot water as I told you to do," said Matilda immovably. "Just go and do it before you ask any more questions, Anne."

Anne went and attended to the dishcloth. Then she returned to Matilda and fastened imploring eyes of the latter's face. "Please, ma'am, tell me if you're going to send me back. I tried so hard to please you last night. And I'm more than willing to please Mr. Collins too."

"Well," said Matilda, unable to find any excuse for deferring the answer any longer, "I suppose I might as well tell you. Martin and I have decided to keep you – that is, if you will try to be a good little girl and show yourself grateful in a sexual way. Why, Anne, whatever is the matter?"

"I'm crying," said Anne in a tone of bewilderment. "I can't think why. I'm glad as glad can be. Oh, GLAD doesn't seem the right word at all. I was glad about the White Way and the cherry blossoms – but this! Oh, it's something more than glad. I'm so happy. I'll try to satisfy the both of you. It will be a challenge, I expect, for Mrs. Thomas often told me I was desperately wicked."

"That's what we want, a girl who is pious in Sunday School but wicked in our bed."

"Oh, I'll do my very best. But can you tell me why I'm crying?"

"I suppose it's because you're all excited and worked up," shrugged Matilda. "Sit down on that chair and try to calm yourself. I'm afraid you both cry and laugh far too easily. Yes, you can stay here and we will try to do right by you. You must go to school; but it's only a fortnight till vacation so it isn't worthwhile for you to start before it opens again in September."

"What am I to call you?" asked Anne. "Shall I always say Miss Collins? Can I call you Aunt Matilda?"

"No; you'll call me just plain Matilda. I'm not used to being called Miss Collins and it would make me nervous."

"It sounds awfully disrespectful to just say Matilda," protested Anne.

"I guess there'll be nothing disrespectful in it if you're careful to speak respectfully. Everybody, young and old, in Avonlea calls me Matilda except the minister. He says Miss Collins – when he thinks of it."

"I'd love to call you Aunt Matilda," said Anne wistfully. "I've never had an aunt or any relation at all – not even a grandmother. It would make me feel as if I really belonged to you. Can't I call you Aunt Matilda?"

"No. I'm not your aunt and I don't believe in calling people names that don't belong to them."

"But we could imagine you were my aunt."

"I couldn't," said Matilda grimly.

"Do you never imagine things different from what they really are?" asked Anne wide-eyed.

"No."

"Oh!" Anne drew a long breath. "Oh, Miss – Matilda, how much you miss!"

"I don't believe in imagining things different from what they really are," retorted Matilda. "When the Lord puts us in certain circumstances He doesn't mean for us to imagine them away. And that reminds me. Go into the sitting room, Anne – be sure your feet are clean and don't let any flies in – and bring me out the illustrated card that's on the mantelpiece. The Lord's Prayer is on it and you'll devote your spare time this afternoon to learning it off by heart. There's to be no more of such praying as I heard last night."

"But afterwards ... what we did ... I suppose I was very awkward," said Anne apologetically, "but, you see,

I'd never had any practice in pleasuring another woman. Or a man. I do so hope your brother will not be disappointed in sex with me. You couldn't really expect a person to fuck very well the first time she tried, could you? But I promise to learn. I'm sure I will become a very good sex partner with practice. People get better at things with practice. Have you ever noticed that?"

"Here is something for you to notice, Anne. When I tell you to do a thing I want you to obey me at once and not stand stock-still and discourse about it. Just you go and do as I bid you."

Anne promptly departed for the sitting room across the hall; she failed to return; after waiting ten minutes Matilda laid down her knitting and marched after her with a grim expression. She found Anne thumbing through an issue of *Harper's Weekly*, her eyes astar with dreams. The white and green light strained through apple trees and clustering vines outside fell over the rapt little figure with a half-unearthly radiance.

"Anne, whatever are you thinking of?" demanded Matilda sharply.

Anne came back to earth with a start. "That," she said, pointing to a page in the magazine – a rather vivid chromo of a nude woman.

"My lord, where did that smutty picture come from?"

"It's fine art, a painting by a Frenchman named Édouard Manet. Says here that it's part of an exhibition at the Metropolitan Museum of Art in New York City."

Matilda bent over her to study the image. Titled "Olympia," it depicted a young woman lounging in the nude, with a black maid hovering in the background. "Art, you say?"

"Well, that's what this magazine calls it. Magazines seem to know everything, don't you think? I found it here on the side table with today's mail. Do you subscribe to it? It looks like a fine publication, filled with articles on art and politics and news of the world."

"Perhaps Martin subscribed to it. It looks rather scandalous to me. You shouldn't be looking at such pictures, fine art or not!"

"I was just imagining I was the girl in the picture – that I had a maid standing off by herself in the corner while I primped for an assignation with a man – Martin, perhaps – coming to ravish my naked body. The girl in the painting, she looks lonely and sad, don't you think? I guess because she has never had a lover. But now all that's going to change. I'm sure I know just how she feels. Her heart must be beating like a snare drum and her hands as cold as ice, like mine got when I asked you if I could stay. She's afraid her new lover mightn't come to ravish her. But it's likely he will, don't you think? I've been trying to imagine it all out – her getting moist between her legs as she anticipates what is about to occur; and then he walks into the room, waves the maid away, and proceeds to fuck the girl until she well-nigh passes out from the ecstasy of it all. Such a thrill of joy would run over her! But I wish the artist hadn't painted the girl so sorrowful looking. She should be as happy as I am about the prospect of being fucked."

"Anne," scolded Matilda, "you shouldn't talk that way. It's irreverent – positively irreverent."

Anne's eyes marveled. "Why, I felt just as reverent as could be. I'm sure I didn't mean to be irreverent."

"Well I don't suppose you did – but it doesn't sound right to talk so familiarly about such things. 'Fuck' is not a word to be used by a girl as young as you."

"But why not? Isn't that what you and Martin are going to do with me? If I am old enough to be fucked, I should think I'm old enough to say the word."

"Oh, alright. Say 'fuck' any time you like, but not in front of people outside this family. The arrangement between you and me and Martin is a private one, a secret not to be shared with others."

"By 'not to be shared with others,' do you mean not talk about it ... or not fuck them too."

"Not talk about it of course. I care not whom you fuck. You can fuck minister Cleary on the baptismal font of the First Presbyterian Church for all I care."

"Yes, ma'am. I'll keep that in mind. In case I have occasion to go to church."

"And another thing, Anne, when I send you after something you're to bring it at once and not fall into mooning over pictures. Remember that. Take that prayer card and come right to the kitchen. Now, sit down in the corner and learn 'The Lord's Prayer' by heart."

Anne set the card up against the jugful of apple blossoms she had brought in to decorate the dinner table – Matilda had eyed that decoration askance, but had said nothing – propped her chin on her hands, and fell to studying it intently for several silent minutes.

"I like this," she announced at length. "It's

beautiful. I've heard it before – I heard the superintendent of the orphanage's Sunday School recite it once. But I didn't like it then. He had such a cracked voice and he prayed it so mournfully. I really felt sure he thought praying was a disagreeable duty. This isn't poetry, but it makes me feel just the same way poetry does. 'Our Father who art in heaven hallowed be Thy name.' That is just like a line of music. Oh, I'm so glad you are making me learn this, Miss – uh, Matilda."

"Well, learn it and hold your tongue," commanded Matilda, her patience frayed.

Anne tipped the vase of apple blossoms near enough to bestow a soft kiss on a pink-cupped bud, and then studied the card diligently for some moments longer. "Matilda," she demanded presently, "do you think that I shall ever have a bosom friend in Avonlea?"

"W-what kind of friend?"

"A bosom friend – an intimate friend, you know – a really kindred spirit to whom I can confide my innermost soul. I've dreamed of meeting her all my life. I never really supposed I would, but so many of my loveliest dreams have come true all at once that perhaps this one will, too. Do you think it's possible?"

"Diana Barry lives over at Orchard Slope and she's about your age. She's a very nice little girl, and perhaps she will be a playmate for you when she comes home. She's visiting her aunt over at Carmody just now. You'll have to be careful how you behave yourself, though. Mrs. Barry is a very particular woman. She won't let Diana play with any little girl who isn't nice and good."

Anne looked at Matilda through the apple blossoms, her eyes aglow with interest. "What is Diana like? Her hair isn't red, is it? Oh, I hope not. I positively couldn't endure it on a bosom friend."

"Diana is a very pretty little girl. She has green eyes and raven-black hair and rosy cheeks. And she is good and smart, which is better than being pretty."

"She's ugly then"

"No, no, not at all. She's nearly as pretty as you. I'm sure you'll hit it off famously. In no time at all you two will be playing doctor together, poking strange objects up your pussies, and fucking neighborhood boys. That's the way of the world."

Matilda was as fond of morals as the Duchess in Wonderland, and was firmly convinced that one should be tacked on to every remark made to a child who was being brought up.

But Anne waved the moral inconsequently aside and seized only on the delightful possibilities before it.

"Oh, I'm so glad she's pretty. Next to being beautiful oneself – and that's impossible in my case – it would be best to have a beautiful bosom friend. When I lived with Mrs. Thomas she had a bookcase in her sitting room with glass doors. There weren't any books in it; Mrs. Thomas kept her best china there. One of the doors was broken. Mr. Thomas smashed it one night when he was intoxicated. But the other was whole and I used to pretend that my reflection in it was another little girl who lived in it. I called her Katie Maurice, and we were very intimate. She and I used to masturbate together when the Thomases weren't home. I used to talk to her by the hour, especially on Sunday, and tell her everything. Katie was the comfort and consolation of my life. We used to pretend that the bookcase was enchanted and that if I only knew the spell I could open the door and step right into the room where Katie Maurice lived, instead of into Mrs. Thomas' shelves of china. And then Katie Maurice would have taken me by the hand and led me out into a wonderful place, all flowers and sunshine and fairies, and we would have lived there happy forever after. When I went to live with Mrs. Hammond it just broke my heart to leave Katie Maurice. She felt it dreadfully, too, I know she did, for she was crying when she kissed me good-bye through the bookcase door. There was no bookcase at Mrs. Hammond's. But just up the river a little way from the house there was a long green little valley, and the loveliest echo lived there. It echoed back every word you said, even if you didn't talk a bit loud. So I imagined that it was a little girl called Violetta and we were great friends and I loved her almost as well as I loved Katie Maurice – not quite, but almost. The night before I went to the orphanage I said goodbye to Violetta, and oh, her goodbye came back to me in such sad, sad tones. I had become so attached to her that I hadn't the heart to imagine a bosom friend at the orphanage, even if there had been any scope for imagination there."

"I think it's just as well there wasn't," said Matilda drily. "I don't approve of such goings-on. You seem to half believe your own imaginations. It will be well for you to have a real live friend to put such nonsense out of your head. But don't let Mrs. Barry hear you talking about your Katie Maurices and your Violettas or she'll think you tell stories."

"Oh, I won't. I couldn't talk of them to everybody – their memories are too sacred for that. But I thought

I'd like to have you know about them. Oh, look, here's a big bee just tumbled out of an apple blossom. Just think what a lovely place to live – in an apple blossom! Fancy going to sleep in it when the wind was rocking it. If I wasn't a human girl I think I'd like to be a bee and live among the flowers."

"Yesterday you wanted to be a seagull," sniffed Matilda. "I think you are very fickle minded. I told you to learn that prayer and not talk. But it seems impossible for you to stop talking if you've got anybody that will listen to you. So go up to your room and learn it."

"Oh, I know it pretty nearly all now – all but just the last line."

"Well, never mind, do as I tell you. Go to your room and finish learning it, and stay there until I call you down to help me get tea."

"Can I take the apple blossoms with me for company?" pleaded Anne.

"No; you don't want your room cluttered up with flowers. You should have left them on the tree in the first place."

"I did feel a little that way, too," said Anne. "I kind of felt I shouldn't shorten their lovely lives by picking them – I wouldn't want to be picked if I were an apple blossom. But the temptation was IRRESISTIBLE. What do you do when you meet with an irresistible temptation? Like fucking Martin. I do so want to fuck your brother again. Do you think he wants to fuck me too?"

"I'm sure of it. Just wait your turn."

"I can hardly wait. Last night I dreamed he came

into my bed and put his John Thomas between my thighs and fucked me long and hard."

"That didn't happen. It was all your silly imagination. Martin was in bed fucking me."

"Oh, I wish I could have been in bed with you and your brother, fucking and sucking you both at the same time."

"Maybe later."

"Yes, but –"

"Anne, did you hear me tell you to go to your room?"

Anne sighed, retreated to the east gable, and sat down in a chair by the window. "There – I know this prayer. I learned that last sentence coming upstairs. Now I'm going to imagine things into this room so that they'll always stay imagined. The floor is covered with a white velvet carpet with pink roses all over it and there are pink silk curtains at the windows. The walls are hung with gold and silver brocade tapestry. The furniture is mahogany. I never saw any mahogany, but it does sound SO luxurious. This is a couch all heaped with gorgeous silken cushions, pink and blue and crimson and gold, and I am reclining gracefully on it, waiting for Martin to come seduce me. I can see my reflection in that splendid big mirror hanging on the wall. I am tall and regal, clad in a gown of trailing white lace. It is thin and transparent, showing my pink nipples through the fabric. A pearl cross hangs between my breasts and pearls adorn my hair. My hair is of midnight darkness and my skin is a clear ivory pallor. My name is Lady Cordelia Fitzgerald. No, it isn't – I can't make THAT seem real."

She danced up to the little looking glass and peered into it. Her solemn face and gray eyes peered back at her.

"You're only Anne of Green Gables," she said earnestly, "and I see you, just as you are looking now, whenever I try to imagine I'm the Lady Cordelia. But it's a million times nicer to be Anne of Green Gables than Anne of nowhere in particular, isn't it?"

She bent forward, kissed her reflection affectionately, and betook herself to the open window.

"Dear Snow Queen, good afternoon. And good afternoon dear birches down in the hollow. And good afternoon, dear gray house up on the hill. I wonder if Diana is to be my bosom friend and do intimate things with me. I hope she will, and I shall love her very much. But I must never quite forget Katie Maurice and Violetta. They would feel so hurt if I did and I'd hate to hurt anybody's feelings, even a little bookcase girl's or a little echo girl's. I must be careful to remember them and send them a kiss every day."

Anne blew a couple of airy kisses from her fingertips past the cherry blossoms and then, with her chin in her hands, drifted luxuriously out on a sea of daydreams.

But that evening when Martin got home, her daydreams turned serious. He stepped into her room and shut the door behind him. "I reckon my sister has told you that you're going to stay with us ...?"

"Yes, I'm so very happy."

"You know there are conditions and duties that go with it?"

"Do you mean duties of a sexual nature? I'm so

looking forward to that. You can fuck me anytime you want. I won't mind at all."

"Very well then," said Martin, unbuttoning his trousers. "We may as well get started with your first lesson in womanhood. No more fingers by those boys at the orphanage. It's time you got used to a real dick."

Anne was again amazed at the size of his member. Long and stiff with a plump purple head, it was much larger than any of the dicks on the boys at the orphanage. But they were barely teenagers and Martin Collins was a full-grown man in his early thirties.

He looked so handsome standing there, trousers about his ankles, like a Prince come to ravish the Lady Cordelia Fitzgerald with his proud lance. "My, what a big John Thomas," she said with admiration.

"All the better to fuck you with," he repeated the fairy-tale words. Well, an approximation of them.

"I can't wait." As she spoke, she shucked her dress, presenting her naked white body to him. She was wearing only stockings, their dark shade matching the sprig of hair between her legs.

"No time like the present," he said, eying his prize, the puffy lower lips swollen with desire. "All those probing fingers of the boys at the orphanage have likely stretched your maidenhead so you'll accommodate me with a snug, but comfortable fit."

"Can you call me Lady Cordelia as you fuck me? I'd like that."

"I'll call you anything you want," he said as he wedged his hips between her thighs and pushed his member inside her, forcing apart her vulva like a log-splitter's wedge.

"Mmmph," Anne said as he entered her.

"How's that," Martin inquired as he pumped energetically. "Does it feel good yet?"

"Oh yes," cried Anne, no longer thinking of the Lady Cordelia Fitzgerald. "It's such a delicious feeling. I hope you will never stop."

"I'll be stopping soon," he grunted. "I'm about to cum."

"Inside me? Won't I get pregnant?"

"If you do, we'll raise your daughter to be another fuck toy for me and Matilda. Adopting you was a bully idea."

"Oooo, I'm so glad you adopted me. But don't cum just yet. I feel like I'm going to explode with joy. Just a moment. There, there, oooooh."

And thus Anne Shirley achieved her first-ever orgasm.

Yes, she liked it.

Naked in the fields.

CHAPTER IX

Mrs. Langston Is Properly Horrified

Anne had been a fortnight at Green Gables before Mrs. Langston arrived to inspect her. Mrs. Langston, to do her justice, was not to blame for this. A severe and unseasonable attack of grippe had confined that good lady to her house ever since the occasion of her last visit to Green Gables. Mrs. Langston was not often sick and had a well-defined contempt for people who were; but grippe, she asserted, was like no other illness on earth and could only be interpreted as one of the special visitations of Providence. As soon as her doctor allowed her to put her foot out-of-doors she hurried up to Green Gables, bursting with curiosity to see Martin and Matilda's orphan, concerning whom all sorts of stories and suppositions had gone abroad in Avonlea.

Mr. Barry had said he'd seen a naked girl running through the fields like a wood sprite. Surely, he had mistaken a deer at a distance for the new girl at Green Gables. After all, he was old and his eyesight was beginning to fail.

But Anne it was. She had made good use of every waking moment of that fortnight. Already she was acquainted with every tree and shrub about the place. She had discovered that a lane opened out below the apple orchard and ran up through a belt of woodland; and she had explored it to its furthest end in all its delicious vagaries of brook and bridge, fir coppice and wild cherry arch, corners thick with fern, and branching byways of maple and mountain ash.

Martin and Matilda were a bit shocked by the girl's penchant for nudity. She rarely wore clothing when she could avoid it, preferring to "feel the caress of the sea breeze on my skin." Fortunately, the farm was large and few neighbors other than Mr. Barry had caught sight of the naked girl.

Anne had made friends with the pond down in the hollow – that wonderful deep, clear icy-cold pond that gave way to a brook lined by palm-like clumps of water fern; and there was a log bridge over the brook.

That bridge led Anne's dancing feet over to a wooded hill beyond, where perpetual twilight reigned under the straight, thick-growing firs and spruces; the only flowers there were myriads of delicate June bells, those shyest and sweetest of woodland blooms, and a few pale, aerial starflowers, like the spirits of last year's blossoms.

All these raptured exploration were made in the odd hours she was allowed to play, and Anne talked Martin and Matilda half-deaf over her discoveries. Not that Martin complained, to be sure; he listened to it all with a wordless smile on his face, anticipating the night to come in bed with Anne and his sister.

Matilda permitted Anne's chatter until she found herself becoming too interested in it, whereupon she always promptly quenched the girl by a curt command to hold her tongue. That tongue was much better put to use licking her cunt as the threesome lay entangled in bed together in the wee morning hours. Anne had not slept in her own room since those first nights.

Anne was wandering in the orchard, hidden among the lush, tremulous grasses, when Mrs. Langston came to visit. Their neighbor started off by talking about her recent illness, describing every ache and pulse beat. When all the details were exhausted, Mrs. Langston launched into the real reason of her call.

"I've been hearing some surprising things about you and Martin."

"Oh, what might that be?"

"That you allow that girl you've taken in to run around the farm like a naked savage."

"It is true I can hardly make Anne wear clothing," she admitted. "She likes to feel the sea breezes on her bare skin, she says."

"Well, it's a scandal. What if the Barston boys should spot her traipsing around in her birthday suit? They might get impious ideas."

"No doubt. Best they stay on their own farmland and not coming spying at Green Gables."

"Boys sniff out girls like dogs in heat."

"True. I'm sure our young Anne will have her share of suitors in due time."

"But surely you don't approve of her walking around bare-bottomed in front of Martin?"

"Green Gables is a small house. It would be impossible for Martin to live here with two women without seeing his share of female flesh. God knows, he's seen me naked many a time."

"I am well aware of that," huffed Mrs. Langston, reminding Matilda Collins that her spyglass provided a nightly view of her and Martin's bedroom. If not having been down with the grippe, she would have spotted

Anne's presence there also. "That's why I'm shocked you would bring a nubile young girl into your home. I thought you were getting a boy."

"I don't suppose you are any more surprised than I am myself," said Matilda. "I was expecting a boy, but Mrs. Spencer didn't honor our request. I'm getting over my surprise now."

"It was too bad there was such a mistake," said Mrs. Langston sympathetically. "Couldn't you have sent her back?"

"I suppose we could, but we decided not to. Martin took a fancy to her. And I must say I like her myself – although I admit she has her faults. The house seems a different place already. She's a real bright little thing."

Matilda said more than she had intended to say when she began, for she read disapproval in Mrs. Langston's expression.

"It's a great responsibility you've taken on yourself," said that lady gloomily, "especially when you've never had any experience with children. You don't know much about her or her real disposition, I suppose, and there's no guessing how a child like that will turn out. But I don't want to discourage you I'm sure, Matilda."

"I'm not feeling discouraged," was Matilda's dry response. "When I make up my mind to do a thing it stays made up. I suppose you'd like to see Anne. I'll call her in."

Anne came running in presently, her face sparkling with the delight of her orchard rovings; but, abashed at finding herself in the unexpected presence of a stranger, she halted confusedly inside the door. She certainly was a sight for sore eyes, standing there stark naked. Her skin was flushed from running, her cheeks nearly as rosy as the tips of her breasts. The wind had ruffled her hair into over-brilliant disorder; she had never looked more like a wild savage than at that moment.

"Well, they didn't pick you for fashion sense, that's sure and certain," was Mrs. Langston's emphatic comment. Mrs. Langston was one of those people who pride themselves on speaking their mind without fear or favor. "Come here, child, and let me have a look at you. Lawful heart, did anyone ever see so much bare skin on display? Naked as the day she was born! And her hair as tangled as a bramble bush. What an ugly visage. Come here, child, I say."

Anne "came there," but not exactly as Mrs. Langston expected. With one bound she crossed the kitchen floor and stood before Mrs. Langston, her face scarlet with anger, her lips quivering, and her whole slender form trembling from head to foot. "I hate you," she cried in a choked voice, stamping her foot on the floor. "I hate you – I hate you – I hate you – " a louder stamp with each assertion of hatred. "How dare you call me ugly? How dare you question my dress in my own home? You are a rude, impolite, unfeeling woman!"

"Anne!" exclaimed Matilda in consternation.

But Anne continued to face Mrs. Langston undauntedly, head up, eyes blazing, hands clenched, indignation exhaling from her like an atmosphere. "How dare you say such things about me?" she repeated vehemently. "How would you like to have such things said about you? How would you like to be told that you are fat and clumsy and probably hadn't a spark of imagination in you? I don't care if I do hurt your feelings by saying so! I hope I hurt them. You have hurt mine worse than they were ever hurt before even by Mrs. Thomas' intoxicated husband. And I'll NEVER forgive you for it, never, never!"

Stamp! Stamp!

"Did anybody ever see such a temper!" exclaimed the horrified Mrs. Langston.

"Anne, go to your room and stay there until I come up," said Matilda, recovering her powers of speech with difficulty.

Anne, bursting into tears, rushed to the hall door, slammed it until the tins on the porch wall outside rattled in sympathy, and fled through the hall and up the stairs like a whirlwind. A subdued slam above told that the door of the east gable had been shut with equal vehemence.

"Well, I don't envy you your job bringing THAT up, Matilda," said Mrs. Langston with unspeakable solemnity.

Matilda opened her lips to say she knew not what of apology or deprecation. What she did say was a surprise to herself then and ever afterwards. "You shouldn't have twitted her about her nudity, Rita."

"Matilda Collins, you don't mean to say that you are upholding her in such a terrible display of temper as we've just seen?" demanded Mrs. Langston indignantly.

"No," said Matilda slowly, "I'm not trying to excuse her. She's been very naughty and I'll have to give her a talking to about it. But we must make allowances for her. She's never been taught what is right. And you WERE too hard on her, Rita."

Matilda could not help tacking on that last sentence, although she was again surprised at herself for doing it. Mrs. Langston got up with an air of offended dignity.

"Well, I see that I'll have to be very careful what I say after this, Matilda, since the fine feelings of orphans, brought from goodness knows where, have to be considered before anything else. Oh, no, I'm not vexed – don't worry yourself. I'm too sorry for you to leave any room for anger in my mind. You'll have your own troubles with that child. But if you'll take my advice – which I suppose you won't do, although I've brought up ten children and buried two – you'll do that 'talking to' you mention with a fair-sized birch switch. I should think THAT would be the most effective language for that kind of a child. Her temper matches her brazen lack of social convention, running around the farm naked as a Red Injun. Well, good evening, Matilda. I hope you'll come down to see me often as usual. But you can't expect me to visit here again in a hurry, if I'm liable to be flown at and insulted in such a fashion. It's something new in MY experience."

Whereat Mrs. Langston swept out and away – if a fat woman who always waddled COULD be said to sweep away – and Matilda with a very solemn face betook herself to the east gable.

On the way upstairs she pondered uneasily as to what she ought to do. She felt no little dismay over the scene that had just been enacted. How unfortunate that

Anne should have displayed such temper before Mrs. Langston, of all people! Then Matilda suddenly became aware of an uncomfortable and rebuking consciousness that she felt more humiliation over this than sorrow over the discovery of such a serious defect in Anne's disposition. And how was she to punish her? The amiable suggestion of the birch switch – to the efficiency of which all of Mrs. Langston's own children could have borne smarting testimony – did not appeal to Matilda. She did not believe she could whip a young girl. No, some other method of punishment must be found to bring Anne to a proper realization of the enormity of her offense.

Matilda found Anne face downward on her bed, crying bitterly, quite oblivious of the woman's entrance into the room.

"Anne," she said not ungently.

No answer.

"Anne," with greater severity, "get off that bed this minute and listen to what I have to say to you."

Anne squirmed off the bed and sat rigidly on a chair beside it, her face swollen and tear-stained and her eyes fixed stubbornly on the floor.

"This is a nice way for you to behave, Anne! Aren't you ashamed of yourself?"

"She hadn't any right to call me ugly and make mean remarks about my 'fashion sense'," retorted Anne, evasive and defiant.

"You hadn't any right to fly into such a fury and talk the way you did to her, Anne. I was ashamed of you – thoroughly ashamed of you. I wanted you to behave nicely to Mrs. Langston, and instead of that you have disgraced me. I'm sure I don't know why you should lose your temper like that just because Mrs. Langston noticed you were naked. That's hard for a visitor to ignore. I've told you that you should wear clothes outside the house."

"Oh, I can't bear clothing when I'm visiting my friends, the trees and the flowers. They don't wear clothes, do they?"

"Trees and flowers are not people. Certainly no one would ever call Rita Langston a flower."

Anne sniffled. "I suppose you think I have an awful temper, but I couldn't help it. When she said those things something just rose right up in me and choked me. I HAD to fly out at her."

"Well, you made a fine exhibition of yourself I must say. Mrs. Langston will have a nice story to tell about you everywhere – and she'll tell it, too. It was a dreadful thing for you to lose your temper like that, Anne."

"Just imagine how you would feel if somebody told you to your face that you were an 'ugly visage'," pleaded Anne tearfully.

An old remembrance suddenly rose up before Matilda. She had been a very small child when she had heard one aunt say of her to another, "What a pity she is such a homely little thing." Matilda was every day of thirty before the sting had gone out of that memory.

"I don't say that I think Mrs. Langston was right in saying what she did to you, Anne," she admitted in a softer tone. "Rita is too outspoken. But that is no excuse for such behavior on your part. She was a stranger and an elderly person and my visitor – all three very good reasons why you should have been respectful to her.

You were rude and saucy and" – Matilda had a saving inspiration of punishment – "you must go to her and tell her you are very sorry for your bad temper and ask her to forgive you."

"I can never do that," said Anne determinedly. "You can punish me in any way you like, Matilda. You can shut me up in a dark, damp dungeon inhabited by snakes and toads and feed me only on bread and water and I shall not complain. But I cannot ask Mrs. Langston to forgive me."

"We're not in the habit of shutting people up in dark, damp dungeons," said Matilda drily, "especially as dungeons are rather scarce in Avonlea. But apologize to Mrs. Langston you must and shall and you'll stay here in your room until you can tell me you're willing to do it."

"I shall have to stay here forever then," said Anne mournfully, "because I can't tell Mrs. Langston I'm sorry I said those things to her. How can I? I'm NOT sorry. I'm sorry I've vexed you; but I'm GLAD I told her just what I did. It was a great satisfaction. I can't say I'm sorry when I'm not, can I? I can't even IMAGINE I'm sorry."

"Perhaps your imagination will be in better working order by the morning," said Matilda, rising to depart. "You'll have the night alone to think over your conduct and come to a better frame of mind."

"Alone?" cried Anne. "You mean I do not get to be in bed with you and Martin tonight?"

"You said you would try to be a very good girl if we kept you at Green Gables, but I must say it hasn't seemed very much like it this evening."

Leaving this Parthian shaft to rankle in Anne's stormy bosom, Matilda descended to the kitchen, grievously troubled in mind and vexed in soul. She was as angry with herself as with Anne, because, whenever she recalled Mrs. Langston's dumbfounded countenance her lips twitched with amusement and she felt a most reprehensible desire to laugh. The sight of the naked girl had completely discombobulated the old biddy. That had been worth the price of admission at a circus sideshow!

The caress of the sea breeze on my skin.

CHAPTER X

Anne's Apology

Matilda said nothing to Martin about the affair that evening; but he was curious when Anne did not join them in bed for the night. An explanation had to be made to account for her absence from their nighttime cavorting. So Matilda told Martin the whole story, taking pains to impress him with a due sense of the enormity of Anne's behavior.

"It's a good thing Rita Langston got a calling down; she's a meddlesome old gossip," was Martin's consolatory rejoinder.

"Martin Collins, I'm astonished at you. You know that Anne's behavior was dreadful, and yet you take her part! I suppose you'll be saying next thing that she oughtn't to be punished at all!"

"Well now – no – not exactly," said Martin uneasily. "I reckon she ought to be punished a little. But don't be too hard on her, Matilda. Recollect she hasn't ever had anyone to teach her right. I was surprised when she didn't join us for supper. But you're – you're going to give her something to eat for breakfast, aren't you?"

"When did you ever hear of me starving people into good behavior?" demanded Matilda indignantly. "She'll have her meals regular, and I'll carry them up to her myself. But she'll stay there in her room until she's ready to apologize to Mrs. Langston, and that's final, Martin."

For the next few days breakfast, lunch, and supper were very silent meals – for Anne still remained obdurate. After each meal Matilda carried a well-filled tray to the east gable and brought it down later on, not noticeably depleted. Martin eyed its last descent with a troubled eye. Had Anne eaten anything at all?

When Matilda went out that evening to bring the cows from the back pasture, Martin, who had been hanging about the barns and watching, slipped into the house with the air of a burglar and crept upstairs. As a general thing Martin gravitated between the kitchen and the little bedroom off the hall where he slept; once in a while he ventured uncomfortably into the parlor or sitting room when the minister came to tea. But he rarely visited the east gables bedroom. After all, Anne had been joining them in their boudoir.

He tiptoed along the hall and stood for several minutes outside the door of the east gable before he summoned courage to tap on it with his fingers and then open the door to peep in.

Naked as usual, Anne was sitting on the yellow chair by the window gazing mournfully out into the garden. Very small and unhappy she looked, and Martin's heart smote him. He softly closed the door and tiptoed over to her.

"Anne," he whispered, as if afraid of being overheard. "How are you making it, Anne?"

Anne smiled wanly.

"Pretty well. I imagine a good deal, and that helps to pass the time. Of course, it's rather lonesome. But then, I may as well get used to that." Anne smiled again, bravely facing the long years of solitary imprisonment before her.

Martin recollected that he must say what he had come to say without loss of time, lest Matilda return prematurely. "Well now, Anne, don't you think you'd better do it and have it over with?" he whispered. "It'll have to be done sooner or later, you know, for Matilda's a dreadful determined woman – dreadful determined, Anne. Do it right off, I say, and have it over."

"Do you mean apologize to Mrs. Langston?"

"Yes – apologize – that's the very word," said Martin eagerly. "Just smooth it over so to speak. That's what I was trying to get at."

"I suppose I could do it to oblige you," said Anne thoughtfully. "It would be true enough to say I am sorry, because I AM sorry now. I wasn't a bit sorry a few days ago. I was mad clear through, and I stayed mad for some time. I know I did because I woke up three times last night and I was just furious every time. But this morning it was over. I wasn't in a temper anymore – and it left a dreadful sort of goneness, too. I felt so ashamed of myself. But I just couldn't think of going and telling Mrs. Langston so. It would be so humiliating. I made up my mind I'd stay shut up here forever rather than do that. But still – I'd do anything for you – if you really want me to – "

"Well now, of course I do. It's terrible lonesome in bed at night without you. Just go and smooth things over – that's a good girl."

"Very well," said Anne resignedly. "I'll tell Matilda as soon as she comes in that I've repented."

"That's right – that's right, Anne. But don't tell Matilda I said anything about it. She might think I was putting my oar in and I promised not to do that."

"Wild horses won't drag the secret from me," promised Anne solemnly. "How would wild horses drag a secret from a person anyhow? I've never told anyone about you fucking me. Or about me licking Matilda's pretty blonde pussy. No matter what questions they put at me when I go to church on Sundays."

"Good girl," nodded Martin, then he was gone, scared at his own success. He fled hastily to the remotest corner of the horse pasture lest Matilda should suspect what he had been up to. Matilda herself, upon her return to the house, was agreeably surprised to hear a plaintive voice calling, "Matilda" over the banisters.

"Well?" she said, going into the hall.

"I'm sorry I lost my temper and said rude things, and I'm willing to go and tell Mrs. Langston so."

"Very well." Matilda's crispness gave no sign of her relief. She had been wondering what under the canopy she should do if Anne did not give in. "I'll take you down after milking."

Accordingly, after milking, behold Matilda and Anne walking down the lane, the former erect and triumphant, the latter drooping and dejected. But halfway down Anne's dejection vanished as if by enchantment. She lifted her head and stepped lightly along, her eyes fixed on the sunset sky and an air of subdued exhilaration about her. Matilda beheld the change disapprovingly. This was no meek penitent such as it behooved her to take into the presence of the offended Mrs. Langston.

"What are you thinking of, Anne?" she asked sharply.

"I'm imagining out what I must say to Mrs. Langston," answered Anne dreamily.

This was satisfactory – or should have been so. But Matilda could not rid herself of the notion that something in her scheme of punishment was going askew. Anne had no business to look so rapt and radiant.

Rapt and radiant Anne continued until they were in the very presence of Mrs. Langston, who was sitting knitting by her kitchen window. Then the radiance vanished. Mournful penitence appeared on every feature. Before a word was spoken a very well-dressed Anne suddenly went down on her knees before the astonished Mrs. Langston and held out her hands beseechingly.

"Oh, Mrs. Langston, I am so extremely sorry," she said with a quiver in her voice. "I could never express all my sorrow, no, not if I used up a whole dictionary. You must just imagine it. I behaved terribly to you – and I've disgraced the dear friends, Martin and Matilda, who have let me stay at Green Gables even though I'm not a boy. I'm a dreadfully wicked and ungrateful girl, and I deserve to be punished and cast out by respectable people forever. It was very wicked of me to fly into a temper because you told me the truth. It WAS the truth; every word you said was true. My hair was tangled and I'm freckled and skinny and ugly. I'm sure it was a shock to see me in all my naked glory. What I said to you was true, too, but I shouldn't have said it. Oh, Mrs. Langston, please, please, forgive me.

If you refuse it will be a lifelong sorrow on a poor little orphan girl. Please say you forgive me, Mrs. Langston."

Anne clasped her hands together, bowed her head, and waited for the word of judgment. There was no mistaking her sincerity – it breathed in every tone of her voice. Both Matilda and Mrs. Langston recognized its unmistakable ring. But the former understood in dismay that Anne was actually enjoying her performance of deep humiliation – was reveling in the thoroughness of her abasement. Where was the wholesome punishment upon which she, Matilda, had plumed? Anne had turned it into a species of positive pleasure.

Good Mrs. Langston, not being overburdened with perception, did not see this. She only perceived that Anne had made a very thorough apology and all resentment vanished from her kindly, if somewhat officious, heart.

"There, there, get up, child," she said heartily. "Of course I forgive you. I guess I was a little too hard on you, anyway. But I'm such an outspoken person. You just mustn't mind me, that's what. It can't be denied your hair was terrible tangled; but I knew a girl once – went to school with her, in fact – whose hair was every mite as unruly as yours when she was young, but when she grew up it easily permed into beautiful curls. I wouldn't be a mite surprised if yours did, too – not a mite."

"Oh, Mrs. Langston!" Anne drew a long breath as she rose to her feet. "You have given me a hope. I shall always feel that you are a benefactor. Oh, I could endure anything if I only thought my hair could be permed when I grew up. It would be so much easier to be good if one's hair was curly, don't you think? And now may I go out into your garden and sit on that bench under the apple trees while you and Matilda are talking? There is so much more scope for imagination out there."

"Laws, yes, run along, child. And you can pick a bouquet of them white June lilies over in the corner if you like."

As the door closed behind Anne Mrs. Langston got briskly up to light a lamp.

"She's a real odd little thing. Here, take this chair, Matilda; it's easier than the one you've got; I just keep that for the hired hand to sit on. Yes, she certainly is an odd child, but there is something kind of fetching about her after all. I don't feel so surprised at you and Martin keeping her as I did – nor so sorry for you, either. She may turn out all right. Of course, I suspect what you and Martin have in mind for that nubile young thing, if you haven't appropriated her into your fun and games already."

"Why, Rita, I shall have to start closing the curtains to my bedroom."

Mrs. Langston glanced guiltily at her spyglass, sitting there on the side table next to the window. "I only use that telescope for gazing at the moon," she fabricated a flimsy excuse. "I'm interested in astrology, you know."

"Yes, of course," smiled Matilda, her point having been made.

"Your girl Anne has a queer way of expressing herself – a little too – well, too forcible, you know; but she'll likely get over that now that she's come to live among civilized folks. And her temper's pretty quick, but children that have a quick temper just blaze up and then cool down. They ain't never likely to be sly or deceitful. Preserve me from a sly child, that's what. On the whole, Matilda, I kind of like her."

When Matilda went home Anne came out of the fragrant twilight of the orchard with a sheaf of white narcissi in her hands. "I apologized pretty well, didn't I?" she said proudly as they went down the lane. "I thought since I had to do it I might as well do it thoroughly."

"You did it thoroughly, all right – a little overly dramatic, but Mrs. but Langston bought your act."

"My act?"

"You don't fool me, young lady." Matilda had also an uneasy feeling that she ought to scold Anne for apologizing so well; but then, that was ridiculous! She compromised with her conscience by saying severely: "I hope you won't have occasion to make many more such apologies, Anne. I hope you'll try to control your temper from now on."

"That wouldn't be so hard if people wouldn't twit me about my not wearing clothes," said Anne with a sigh. "I don't get cross about other things; but that just makes me boil right over. And I'm SO tired of being twitted about my unruly hair. Do you suppose my hair will really be curly when I grow up?"

"Only if you get a permanent wave like Mrs. Langston was suggesting."

"Well, maybe you will get me a perm someday ...?"

"You shouldn't think so much about your looks,

Anne. I'm afraid you are becoming a very vain little girl. Martin shouldn't be telling you so much how pretty you are."

"I like it when Martin tells me how much he likes my boobies. They are not as round and beautiful as yours, but I'm glad he is satisfied with mine too."

"Martin thinks with his dick."

Anne sniffed at her narcissi. "Oh, aren't these flowers sweet! It was lovely of Mrs. Langston to give them to me. I have no hard feelings against Mrs. Langston now. It gives you a lovely, comfortable feeling to apologize and be forgiven, doesn't it? Aren't the stars bright tonight? If you could live in a star, which one would you pick? I'd like that lovely clear big one away over there above that dark hill."

"Anne, do hold your tongue," said Matilda, thoroughly worn out trying to follow the gyrations of Anne's thoughts.

Anne said no more until they turned into their own lane. A little gypsy wind came down it to meet them, laden with the spicy perfume of young dew-wet ferns. Far up in the shadows a cheerful light gleamed out through the trees from the kitchen at Green Gables. Anne suddenly came close to Matilda and slipped her hand into the older woman's hard palm.

"It's lovely to be going home and know it's home," she said. "I love Green Gables already, and I never loved any place before. No place ever seemed like home. Oh, Matilda, I'm so happy. I could lick your beautiful pussy all night long."

Something warm and pleasant welled up in Matilda's heart at the thought – a throb of romance she had missed, perhaps. Its very sweetness disturbed her. She hastened to restore her sensations to their normal calm by inculcating a moral.

"If you'll be a good girl you'll always be happy, Anne. And you should never feel obligated to lick my pussy unless you really want to."

"Oh, I like doing that. And fucking Martin too. I'm so happy to be wanted, even if it's for my body," said Anne excitedly.

"We care about you more than just sex," protested the blonde woman. "You're now part of the family."

"Oh, I like that thought," said the girl. "I like being part of this family. It makes me want to satisfy your and Martin's desires all the more!"

"Thank you, dear."

"Matilda, that's the first time you've called me 'dear.' Oh, do you truly mean it? I'm dizzy with happiness."

"You are a dear. I care about you more than I can say."

"Oh my, I can hardly stand the emotions. I'm just so very, very happy. I'm going to imagine that I'm the wind that is blowing up there in those treetops. When I get tired of the trees I'll imagine I'm gently waving down here in the ferns – and then I'll fly over to Mrs. Langston's garden and set the flowers dancing – and then I'll go with one great swoop over the clover field – and then I'll blow over the Lake of Shining Waters and ripple it all up into little sparkling waves. Oh, there's so much scope for imagination in a wind! So I'll not talk any more just now, Matilda."

"Thanks be to goodness for that," breathed Matilda in devout relief.

Off to Sunday School.

CHAPTER XI

Anne's Impressions of Sunday School

"**W**ell, how do you like them?" said Matilda. Anne was standing in the gable room, looking solemnly at three new dresses spread out on the bed. One was of snuffy colored gingham that Matilda had bought from a peddler the preceding summer because it looked so serviceable; that and the fact he'd serviced her nicely with a dick shaped like a curved banana. The other was of black-and-white checkered sateen which Matilda had picked up at a bargain counter this past winter; the clerk there was a sometimes tryst. And the third was a stiff print of an ugly blue shade which she had purchased a few months ago at a Carmody fabric store; a shop where the owner had a stiff member also.

She had made dresses up herself, and they were all patterned alike – plain skirts pulled tightly to plain waists, with sleeves as tight as sleeves could be.

"I'll imagine that I like them," said Anne soberly.

"I don't want you to imagine it," said Matilda, offended. "Oh, I can see you don't like any of the dresses! What is the matter with them? Aren't they neat and clean and new?"

"Yes."

"Then why don't you like them?"

"You know I don't like to wear clothes."

"Yes, but sometimes you HAVE to wear a dress – like when you go to Sunday School. It wouldn't do at all for you to show up there bare-ass naked. Why Rev.

Cleary would have a stroke."

"I know, but –"

"But what?"

"The dresses are very thoughtful of you but they're – they're not – pretty," said Anne reluctantly.

"Pretty!" Matilda sniffed. "I didn't trouble my head about getting pretty dresses for you. I don't believe in pampering vanity, Anne, I'll tell you that right off. Those dresses are good, sensible, serviceable dresses, without any frills or furbelows about them, and they're all you'll get this summer. The brown gingham and the blue print will do you for grade school when you begin to go. The sateen is perfect for Sunday School. I'll expect you to keep them neat and clean and not to tear them. I should think you'd be grateful to get most anything after those skimpy wincey things you've been wearing."

"Oh, I AM grateful," protested Anne. "But I'd be ever so much gratefuller if – if you'd made just one of them with puffed sleeves. Puffed off-the-shoulder sleeves are so fashionable now. It would give me such a thrill, Matilda, just to wear a dress with puffed sleeves."

"Well, you'll have to do without your thrill. I hadn't any material to waste on puffed sleeves. I think they are ridiculous-looking things anyhow. I prefer the plain, sensible ones."

"But I'd rather look ridiculous when everybody else does than plain and sensible all by myself," persisted Anne.

"Trust you for that! Well, hang those dresses carefully up in your closet, and then sit down and learn your Sunday School lesson. I got a quarterly from Rev.

Cleary for you and you'll go to Sunday School tomorrow," said Matilda, disappearing downstairs in a huff.

Anne clasped her hands and looked at the dresses. "I did hope there would be a flowery one with puffed sleeves," she whispered disconsolately. "I prayed for one, but I didn't much expect it on that account. I didn't suppose God would have time to bother about a little orphan girl's dress. I knew I'd just have to depend on Matilda for it. Well, fortunately I can simply imagine that one of them is of a flower-patterned muslin with lovely off-the-shoulder puffed sleeves."

The next morning warnings of a sick headache prevented Matilda from going to Sunday School with Anne. "You'll have to go down and call for Mrs. Langston, Anne," she said. "Rita will see that you get into the right class. Now, mind you behave yourself properly. Stay for preaching afterwards and ask Mrs. Langston to show you our pew. Here's a cent for collection. Don't stare at people and don't fidget. I shall expect you to tell me the text when you come home."

"Why isn't Martin going?"

"He's off to buy a cow. This morning was the only time the dairyman could see him. I doubt he'll burn in Hell for providing his family with milk rather than going to church."

"No, he's more likely to go to hell for fucking his own sister," Anne muttered under her breath.

"What did you say, young lady?"

"Nothing. Just that I was leaving now for Sunday School. See, I'm wearing that sateen dress you made for me."

"Perfect," said Matilda, applying a warm compress to her temple. She'd suffered from migraines since she was a girl about Anne's age.

≈≈≈

Anne Shirley started off irreproachable, arrayed in the stiff black-and-white sateen, which, while decent as regards length and certainly not open to the charge of skimpiness, contrived to emphasize every corner and angle of her thin figure. Her hat was a flat, glossy sunbonnet, the plainness of which had much disappointed Anne. She had permitted herself secret visions of ribbon and flowers. The latter, however, were supplied to the hat before Anne reached the main road, for halfway down the lane she stopped to pick a selection of white daisies along with a glory of purple blossoms. Anne liberally garlanded her hat with a heavy wreath of them. Whatever other people might have thought of the result didn't matter; it satisfied Anne. And she tripped gaily down the road to the steepled First Presbyterian Church, holding her head very proudly in order to display her hat with its decoration of purple and white.

In front of the church she found a crowd of little girls, all more or less gaily attired in blues and pinks, and all staring with curious eyes at this stranger in their midst, with her extraordinary head adornment. Avonlea's girls had already heard queer stories about Anne. Mrs. Langston said she had an awful temper; Harley Buote, the hired hand at Green Gables, said she talked all the time to herself or to the trees and flowers like a crazy girl. And Mr. Barry said she ran about the farm naked, but nobody believed that story. Last year he'd said he had seen water sprites down by his pond.

The girls looked at Anne and whispered to each other behind their quarterlies. Nobody made any friendly advances, then or later on when the opening exercises were over.

Anne found herself in Miss Rogerson's Sunday School class. Miss Rogerson was a middle-aged lady who had taught Sunday School for nearly twenty years. Her method of teaching was to ask the printed questions from the quarterly and look sternly over its edge at the particular little girl she thought ought to answer the question. She looked very often at Anne, and Anne, thanks to Matilda's drilling, answered promptly; but it may be questioned if she understood very much about either question or answer.

Anne did not think she liked Miss Rogerson. She felt very miserable, because every other little girl in the class had puffed sleeves and she did not. Life was really not worth living without puffed sleeves. So she tugged the dress off her shoulders, exposing the smooth skin of her shoulders. There, that was better.

"Well, how did you like Sunday School today?" Matilda wanted to know when Anne came home. Her wreath of flowers having wilted, Anne had discarded it in the lane, sparing Matilda the knowledge of that adorned hat for a time.

"I didn't like it a bit," cried Anne. "It was horrid."

"Anne Shirley!" rebuked Matilda.

"I behaved well, just as you told me. Mrs. Langston was gone, but I went right on myself. I went into the church, with a lot of other little girls, and I sat in the corner of a pew by the window while the opening exercises went on. Rev. Cleary offered an awfully long prayer. I would have been dreadfully tired before he got through if I hadn't been sitting by that window. But it looked right out on the Lake of Shining Waters, so I just gazed at that and imagined all sorts of splendid things."

"You shouldn't have done anything of the sort. You should have listened to Rev. Cleary."

"But he wasn't talking to me," protested Anne. "He was talking to God and he didn't seem to be very much interested in it, either. I think he thought God was too far off, he was shouting so. There was a long row of white birches hanging over the lake and the sunshine fell down through them, way, way down, deep into the water. Oh, Matilda, it was like a beautiful dream! It gave me a thrill and I just said, 'Thank you for it, God,' two or three times."

"Not out loud, I hope," said Matilda anxiously.

"Oh, no, just under my breath. Well, Rev. Cleary did finish his talk at last and someone told me to go into the classroom with Miss Rogerson. There were nine other girls in it. They all had puffed sleeves. I tried to imagine mine were puffed, too, but I couldn't. Why couldn't I? It was as easy as could be to imagine they were puffed when I was alone in the east gable, but it was awfully hard there among the others who had really truly puffs."

"You shouldn't have been thinking about your sleeves in Sunday School. You should have been attending to the lesson. I hope you knew it."

"Oh, yes; and I answered a lot of questions. Miss Rogerson asked ever so many. I don't think it was fair for her to do all the asking. There were lots I wanted to ask her, but I didn't like to because I didn't think she was a kindred spirit. Then all the other little girls recited a paraphrase. She asked me if I knew any. I told her I didn't, but I could recite, 'The Dog at His Master's Grave' if she liked. That's in the Third Royal Reader. It isn't a really truly religious piece of poetry, but it's so sad and melancholy that it might as well be. She said it wouldn't do and she told me to learn the nineteenth paraphrase for next Sunday. I read it over in church afterwards and it's splendid. There are two lines in particular that just thrill me.

"'Quick as the slaughtered squadrons fell
In Midian's evil day.'

"I don't know what 'squadrons' means nor 'Midian,' either, but it sounds SO tragical. I can hardly wait until next Sunday to recite it. I'll practice it all the week. After Sunday School I asked Miss Rogerson – because Mrs. Langston was too far away – to show me your pew. I sat just as still as I could and the text was Revelations, third chapter, second and third verses. It was a very long text. If I were a minister I'd pick the short, snappy ones. The sermon was awfully long, too. I suppose the minister had to match it to the text. I didn't think he was a bit interesting. The trouble with him seems to be that he hasn't enough imagination. I didn't listen to him very much. I just let my thoughts run and I thought of the most surprising things."

Matilda felt helplessly that all this should be sternly reproved, but she was hampered by the undeniable fact that some of the things Anne had said, especially about Rev. Cleary's sermons were what she herself had really thought deep down in her heart for years, but had never given expression to. It almost seemed to her that those secret, unuttered, critical thoughts had suddenly taken visible and accusing shape and form in the person of this outspoken morsel of neglected humanity.

"Enough about Sunday School," said Matilda with a wicked grin. "Let me help you get out of those clothes. May as well take mine off too."

Flower child.

CHAPTER XII

A Solemn Vow and Promise

It was not until the next Friday that Matilda heard the story of the flower-wreathed hat. She came home from Mrs. Langston's and called Anne to account.

"Anne, Mrs. Langston says you went to church last Sunday with your hat rigged out ridiculous with daisies and such. What on earth put you up to such a caper? A pretty-looking object you must have been!"

"Oh. I know white and purple aren't becoming to me," began Anne.

"Becoming fiddlesticks! It was putting flowers on your hat at all, no matter what color they were, that was ridiculous. You are the most aggravating young girl!"

"I don't see why it's any more ridiculous to wear flowers on your hat than on your dress," protested Anne. "Lots of little girls there had bouquets pinned on their dresses. What's the difference?"

Matilda was not to be drawn from the safe concrete into dubious paths of the abstract. "Don't answer me back like that, Anne. It was very silly of you to do such a thing. Never let me catch you at such a trick again. Mrs. Langston says she thought she would sink through the floor when she saw you come in all rigged out like that. She couldn't get near enough to tell you to take them off till it was too late. She says people talked about it something dreadful. Of course they would think I had no better sense than to let you go decked out like that."

"Oh, I'm so sorry," said Anne, tears welling into her eyes. "I never thought you'd mind. The flowers were so sweet and pretty I thought they'd look lovely on my hat. Lots of the little girls had artificial flowers on their hats. I'm afraid I'm going to be a dreadful trial to you. Maybe you'd better send me back to the orphanage. That would be terrible; I don't think I could endure it; most likely I would go into consumption; I'm so thin as it is, you see. But that would be better than being a trial to you."

"Nonsense," said Matilda, vexed at herself for having made Anne cry. "I don't want to send you back to the orphanage, I'm sure. All I want is that you should behave like other little girls and not embarrass us. Don't cry anymore. I've got some news for you. Diana Barry came home this afternoon. I'm going up to see if I can borrow a skirt pattern from Mrs. Barry, and if you like you can come with me and get acquainted with Diana."

Anne raised to her feet, with clasped hands, the tears still glistening on her cheeks; the dishtowel she had been hemming slipped unheeded to the floor.

"Oh, Matilda, I'm frightened – now that it has come I'm actually frightened. What if she shouldn't like me! It would be the most tragical disappointment of my life."

"Now, don't get into a fluster. I guess Diana'll like you well enough. It's her mother you've got to reckon with. If she doesn't like you it won't matter how much Diana does. If she has heard about your outburst to Mrs. Langston and your going to church with daisies round your hat it will be the icing on the cake. Her husband is already telling everybody that you run around the farm as naked as a jaybird."

"But I do."

"Normal people wear clothes."

"I don't want to be normal. What a sad goal, to strive for normalcy."

"Never mind that. You must be polite and well behaved when you meet Diana's mother. And don't make any of your startling speeches."

"O-okay."

"For pity's sake, you're actually trembling!"

Anne WAS trembling. Her face was pale and tense. "Oh, Matilda, you'd be excited, too, if you were going to meet a little girl you hoped to be your bosom friend and whose mother mightn't like you," she said as she hastened to get her hat.

"Bosom friend – next thing you know she'll be running around naked with you!"

"Oh, I hope so. I do love having sex with you and Martin, but I miss the girls my age at the orphanage putting their fingers in me. I hope Diana will become that intimate with me."

"I don't mind your playing with other girls your age, but you must keep any intimacy a secret. Just as you do your relationship with me and Martin. People would wag their tongues if they knew your doings."

"Don't worry. I will be most discrete. I'm good at keeping secrets. Why, I've never told you about Martin putting his John Thomas up my ass. He told me not to."

"He did that? I've never let him do that no matter how much he begged. Sodomy is frowned on in the Bible."

"It hurt quite a bit in the beginning, but then I relaxed and it started to feel good. But I like it better when he fucks me in my pussy because it makes me cum."

"Martin should restrict himself to the proper orifices," Matilda declared. "You're under my care and I will decide who fucks you and how."

"Yes ma'am."

"Very good. Now put your gingham dress on so you'll make an appropriate first impression on Diana and her mother."

≈≈≈

They went over to Orchard Slope by the shortcut across the brook and up through the firry hill grove. Mrs. Barry came to the kitchen door in answer to Matilda's knock. She was a tall black-eyed, black-haired woman, with a very resolute mouth. She had the reputation of being very strict with her children.

"How do you do, Matilda?" she said cordially. "Come in. And this is the little girl you have adopted, I suppose?"

"Yes, this is Anne Shirley," said Matilda.

"Spelled with an E," gasped Anne, who, tremulous and excited as she was, was determined there should be no misunderstanding on that important point.

Mrs. Barry, not hearing or not comprehending, merely shook hands and said kindly: "How are you?"

"I am well in body although considerable rumpled up in spirit, thank you ma'am," said Anne gravely. Then aside to Matilda in an audible whisper, "There wasn't anything startling in that, was there, Matilda? I didn't mention Martin fucking me in the ass."

"Hush, dear." Fortunately Mrs. Barry had her deaf ear turned toward them.

Diana was sitting on the sofa, reading a book which she dropped when the callers entered the parlor. She was a very pretty little girl, with her mother's blue eyes and a merry expression that was her inheritance from her pixelated father.

"This is my little girl Diana," said Mrs. Barry. "Diana, you might take Anne out into the garden and show her your flowers. It will be better for you than straining your eyes over that book. She reads entirely too much – " this to Matilda as the little girls went out – "and I can't prevent her, for her father aids and abets her. She's always poring over a book. I'm glad she has the prospect of a playmate – perhaps it will take her more out-of-doors. My husband says your Anne likes to commune with nature."

"Yes, she does. She takes to the farm like a new mare."

"He says she doesn't wear very much clothing, but his eyesight is failing just like his mind. He is going to be a burden on me, I can see that already."

"I'm so sorry to hear that."

"Ignore his stories about your Anne's lack of clothing. No one believes his silly tales. I do apologize," Mrs. Barry continued earnestly.

"No need to do that. I'm sure he means no harm."

"He's now convinced that the barn is infested with leprechauns, poor man."

"Well, he was born in Ireland …"

"True. I guess I never should have married an Irishman. All they do is drink and tell wild tales."

≈ ≈ ≈

Outside in the garden, which was full of mellow sunset light streaming through the dark old firs to the west of it, stood Anne and Diana, gazing bashfully at each other over a clump of gorgeous tiger lilies.

The Barry garden was a bowery wilderness of flowers, which would have delighted Anne's heart at any time less fraught with destiny. It was encircled by huge old willows and tall firs, beneath which flourished flowers that loved the shade. Prim, right-angled paths neatly bordered with clamshells intersected it like moist red ribbons. And in the beds between, old-fashioned flowers ran riot. There were rosy bleeding-hearts and great splendid crimson peonies; white, fragrant narcissi and thorny, sweet Scotch roses; pink and blue and white columbines and lilac-tinted Bouncing Bets; clumps of southernwood and ribbon grass and mint; purple Adam-and-Eve, daffodils, and masses of sweet clover white with its delicate, fragrant, feathery sprays; scarlet lightning that shot its fiery lances over prim white musk-flowers. It was a garden where sunshine lingered and bees hummed and winds purred and rustled.

"Oh, Diana," said Anne at last, clasping her hands and speaking almost in a whisper, "do you think you can like me a little – enough to be my bosom friend?"

Diana laughed. Diana always laughed before she spoke. "Why, I guess so," she said. "I'm awfully glad you've come to live at Green Gables. It will be jolly to have somebody to play house with. You can be the mommy and I'll be the daddy. There aren't any other girls who lives near enough to play with, and I've no sisters big enough."

"Will you swear to be my friend forever and ever?" demanded Anne eagerly.

Diana looked shocked. "Why it's dreadfully wicked to swear," she responded.

"Oh no, not my kind of swearing. There are two kinds, you know."

"I never heard of but one kind," said Diana doubtfully.

"There really is another. Oh, it isn't wicked at all. It just means vowing and promising solemnly."

"Well, I don't mind doing that," agreed Diana, relieved. "How do you do it?"

"We must join hands – so," said Anne gravely. "It ought to be over running water. We'll just imagine this path is running water. I'll repeat the oath first. I solemnly swear to be faithful to my bosom friend, Diana Barry, as long as the sun and moon shall endure. Now you say it and put my name in."

Diana repeated the "oath" with a laugh fore and aft. Then she said: "You're a queer girl, Anne. I heard before you came to visit that you were queer. But I believe I'm going to like you real well. I'm a bit queer myself."

"Odd like me?"

"Yes, but there are two definitions, you know. That too."

"You mean –?"

"Yes, I like girls better than boys. I'm going to enjoy playing mommy and daddy with you, Anne Shirley."

"Oh, thank you, dear Diana. Now that we've made an oath I am obliged to do anything you want me to.

I'm very good at licking pussy, if you like."

"Yes, I like that very much. But you must promise to keep it a secret. My mother does not approve of my Tomboy ways."

"I am good at secrets," Anne said. "I've promised not to tell anyone about licking Matilda's pussy as well. Or about Martin fucking me."

Diana giggled. "Oh my, Anne Shirley, I can see that we're going to get along really well."

≈≈≈

When Matilda and Anne went home Diana went with them as far as the log bridge. The two little girls walked with their arms about each other. At the brook they parted with many promises to spend the next afternoon together.

"Well, did you find Diana a kindred spirit?" asked Matilda as they went up through the garden of Green Gables.

"Oh yes," sighed Anne, blissfully unconscious of any sarcasm on Matilda's part. "Oh Matilda, I'm the happiest girl on Prince Edward Island this very moment. I assure you I'll say my prayers with a right goodwill tonight. Diana and I are going to build a playhouse in Mr. William Bell's birch grove tomorrow. Can I have those broken pieces of china that are out in the woodshed? Diana's birthday is in February and mine is in March. Don't you think that is a very strange coincidence? Diana is going to lend me a book to read. She says it's perfectly splendid and tremendously exciting. It's called the *Kama Sutra*. She says it has the most interesting pictures. And she's going to show me a place back in the woods where rice lilies grow. Don't you think Diana has got very soulful eyes? I wish I had soulful eyes. Diana is going to teach me to sing a song called 'Nelly in the Hazel Dell.' She's going to give me a picture to put up in my room; it's a perfectly beautiful picture, she says – a lovely lady in a corset with her boobies showing. A garage mechanic gave it to her. I wish I had something to give Diana in return. I'm an inch taller than Diana, but she is ever so much plumper; her boobies are bigger than mine. She says she'd like to be thin because it's so much more graceful, but I'm afraid she only said it to soothe my feelings. My boobies will get bigger as I get older, won't they? I truly hope so. Martin says they are a nice handful as they are. And you say they are a good mouthful. But I wouldn't mind them being as big as Diana's. She's so pretty, isn't she? A little boyish in manner, but those boobies are enticing. I wonder if I can get my mouth around them."

"Hush, dear. Don't talk like that. You've only just met Diana Barry."

"True, but we hit it off. We swore an oath to be bosom friends. We're going to the shore some day to gather shells. We have agreed to call the spring down by the log bridge the Dryad's Bubble. Isn't that a perfectly elegant name? I read a story once about a spring called that. A dryad is sort of a grown-up fairy, I think. She says her father sees them playing near the spring."

"Well, all I hope is you won't talk Diana to death," said Matilda. "But remember this in your planning, Anne. You're not going to spend all your time with this new playmate. You have your work around the house to do. And me and Martin to service."

"Yes, of course. You and Martin come first. You're family."

Anne's cup of happiness was full, and Martin caused it to overflow. He had just got home from a trip to the store at Carmody, and he sheepishly produced a small parcel from his pocket and handed it to Anne, with a deprecatory look at Matilda. "I heard you say you liked chocolate sweeties, so I got you some," he said.

"Humph," sniffed Matilda. "It'll ruin her teeth and stomach. There, there, Anne, don't look so dismal. You can eat those, since Martin has gone and got them. He'd better have brought you peppermints. They're wholesomer. Don't sicken yourself eating all them at once now."

"Oh, no, indeed, I won't," said Anne eagerly. "I'll just eat one tonight, Matilda. And I can give Diana half of them, can't I? The other half will taste twice as sweet to me if I give some to her. It's delightful to think I have something to give her."

"I will say it for the girl," said Matilda when Anne had gone up to her gable, "she isn't stingy. I'm glad, for of all faults I detest stinginess in a person. Dear me, it's only three weeks since she came, and it seems as if she's been here always. I can't imagine the place without her. Now, don't be acting I told-you-so, Martin. That's bad enough in a woman, but it isn't to be endured in a man. I'm perfectly willing to own up that I'm glad I consented to keep the girl and that I'm getting fond of her tongue lickings ... but don't you rub it in, Martin Collins."

Hay diddle-diddle.

CHAPTER XIII
The Delights of Anticipation

"**I**t's time Anne was in to do her sewing," said Matilda, glancing at the clock and then out into the yellow August afternoon where everything was drowsed in the heat. "She stayed playing with Diana half an hour more'n I gave her leave to; and now she's perched out there on the woodpile talking to Martin when she ought to be at her sewing work. And of course he's listening to her like a perfect ninny. I never saw such an infatuated man. The more she talks and the odder the things she says, the more he's delighted evidently. Especially when she's not wearing airy stitch of clothing!"

The blonde woman leaned out the door. "Anne Shirley, you come right in here this minute," she called. "Do you hear me?"

A series of staccato taps on the west window brought Anne flying in from the yard, eyes shining, cheeks faintly flushed with pink, unruly hair streaming behind her in a torrent of brightness. As predicted, she was stark naked, her rose-tipped breasts bobbling as she traipsed across the threshold.

"Oh, Matilda," she exclaimed breathlessly, "there's going to be a Sunday School picnic next week – in Mr. Harmon Andrews's field, right near the lake of Shining Waters. And Mrs. Superintendent Bell and Mrs. Langston are going to make ice cream – think of it, Matilda – ICE CREAM! Oh, Matilda, can I go to it?"

"Just look at the clock, if you please, Anne. What time did I tell you to come in?"

"Two o'clock – but isn't it splendid about the picnic, Matilda? Please can I go? Oh, I've never been to a picnic – I've dreamed of picnics, but I've never – "

"I told you to come in to do your sewing at two o'clock. And it's a quarter to three. I'd like to know why you didn't obey me, Anne?"

"Why, I meant to, Matilda, as much as could be. But I had to tell Martin about the picnic. Martin is such a sympathetic listener."

"Sympathetic when you're flaunting your boobies in his face."

"I can't help it if he likes to look at my boobies," she pouted. "That's not my fault."

"You bewitch him, running around naked."

"You could go naked too, Matilda. We could bewitch him together. Make his John Thomas stand at attention in the daytime, just as we do in bed at night."

"Me wearing no clothes around the farm – what would Mrs. Langston think?"

"Oh, don't mind her," giggled Anne. "I know the old witch spies on us. With her telescope she can see straight into our bedroom window. So I try to put on a good performance for her every night. Sometimes I pump up and down on Martin's John Thomas with extra enthusiasm just to entertain Mrs. Langston. I think she enjoys the show."

"No doubt she does," smiled Matilda. "I must admit that sometimes I feel like an actress in a kinescopic peep show, knowing that she's watching."

"Then I will pretend I'm an actress in a peep show

too. Tonight, let's put on a special presentation for Mrs. Langston – do something especially wicked with Martin."

"Like what?"

"I know. Let's allow him to tie us up and spank us. He can even use his riding crop. That should give Mrs. Langston a thrill."

"That would give me a thrill too," admitted the blonde woman. "I've never played sadomasochistic games before."

"The headmistress at the orphanage used to spank my bare bottom. It wasn't exactly a game, but I think she liked it. She said I had a most beautiful round butt."

"Indeed you do," agreed Matilda.

"I'm so glad you like my round butt. Would you like to spank it? We could consider it my punishment for being late."

"As starters," replied Matilda, pulling the girl over he knees, and giving her bare flesh three sharp whacks, leaving read handprints. "There," she said.

"Oww. That smarted. You could have been more gentle, Matilda."

"You got what you deserved."

"So please can I go to the picnic?"

"Before you get that privilege, you'll have to promise to mind me better. When I tell you to do your sewing at a certain time I mean that time and not half an hour later. And you needn't stop to discourse with sympathetic listeners on your way, too."

"Why do I need to learn to sew if I rarely wear clothes?"

"Because it's a skill every woman should master.

Someday you'll have a husband and he will want his socks darned."

"I don't need a husband. I have you and Martin. And I want to live with you two forever. Besides Diana and I play mommy and daddy, and that's almost like being married."

"Oh, you silly goose."

"So can I go to the picnic? I promise to do my sewing when you tell me to."

Matilda suppressed a smile. "Of course you can go to the picnic. It's not likely I'd refuse to let you go when all the other girls are going."

"Diana says that everybody must take a basket of things to eat. I can't cook, as you know, Matilda, and – and – I don't mind going to a picnic without puffed sleeves so much, but I'd feel terribly humiliated if I had to go without a basket. It's been preying on my mind ever since Diana told me."

"Well, you needn't worry. I'll bake you a basket."

"Oh, you dear good Matilda. Oh, you are so kind to me. Oh, I'm so much obliged to you."

Anne cast herself into Matilda's arms and rapturously kissed her sallow cheek. That sudden sensation of startling sweetness thrilled Matilda. She was embarrassed by Anne's impulsive caress, which is why she said brusquely: "There, there, never mind your kissing me. We'll save that for our performance for Mrs. Langston tonight."

"We could practice for it now."

"No, I have chores to do. And so do you, young lady. Remember the sewing?"

"Yes ma'am."

"Then get out your patchwork and have your square done before tea time."

"I do NOT like patchwork," complained Anne dolefully, hunting out her workbasket and sitting down before a little heap of red-and-white cotton squares with a resigned sigh. "I think some kinds of sewing might be nice; but there's no scope for imagination in patchwork. It's just one little seam after another and you never seem to be getting anywhere. But of course I'd rather be Anne of Green Gables sewing patchwork than Anne of any other place with nothing to do but play. I wish time went as quick sewing fabric patches as it does when I'm playing with Diana, though. Oh, we do have such elegant times, Matilda. I have to furnish most of the imagination, but I'm well able to do that. Diana is simply perfect in every other way. You know that little piece of land across the brook that runs up between our farm and Mr. Barry's. It belongs to Mr. William Bell, and right in the corner there is a little copse of white birches – the most romantic spot, Matilda. Diana and I have our playhouse there. We call it Idlewild. Isn't that a poetical name? I assure you it took me some time to think it out. I stayed awake nearly a whole night before I invented it. Then, just as I was dropping off to sleep, it came like an inspiration. Diana was ENRAPTURED when she heard it. We have got our house fixed up elegantly. You must come and see it, Matilda – won't you? We have great big stones, all covered with moss, for seats, and boards from tree to tree for shelves. And we have set all our dishes on them. Of course, they're all broken but it's the easiest thing in the world to imagine that they are whole.

There's a piece of a plate with a spray of red and yellow ivy on it that is especially beautiful. We keep it in the parlor and we have the fairy glass there, too. The fairy glass is as lovely as a dream. Diana found it out in the woods behind their chicken house. It's all full of rainbows – just little young rainbows that haven't grown big yet – and Diana's mother told her it was broken off a hanging lamp they once had. But it's nice to imagine the fairies lost it one night when they had a ball, so we call it the fairy glass. Martin is going to make us a table. We have great fun in our pretend bed made of moss. We got lots of ideas about sexual positions out of that book Diana lent me. It was a thrilling book, Matilda. Perhaps you and Martin could try some of these positions? Diana nibbled at my pussy until I almost fainted with ecstasy. Fainting is so romantic, don't you think?"

"I'm sure it is. But save some of your sexual desires for Martin and me."

"Oh, don't worry about that. I've got enough desire for all three of you. Maybe a few others as time goes by. I really do like sex. But as much as I enjoy it with you and Diana, I particularly like fucking with Martin. There's something about having a stiff John Thomas inside you, don't you agree? You've certainly had Martin's in you enough to appreciate its immense size. He's been fucking you since you were – what? – ten years old?"

"Thirteen. I'd just had my first period."

"Oh my. I didn't have my period until I was fourteen. Just two years ago."

"You have the body of a woman, even if your mind

is that of a ten-year-old."

"Don't tease me just because I want to go to the picnic next Wednesday and eat ice cream. I do hope it will be good weather next week. I don't feel that I could endure the disappointment if anything happened to prevent me from going to the picnic. I suppose I'd live through it, but I'm certain it would be a lifelong sorrow. It wouldn't matter if I got to a hundred picnics in later years; they wouldn't make up for missing this one. I hear they're going to have boats on the Lake of Shining Waters – and ice cream, as I told you. I have never tasted ice cream. Diana tried to explain what it was like, but I guess ice cream is one of those things that are beyond imagination."

"Anne, you have chattered on for a good ten minutes by the clock," said Matilda. "Now, just for curiosity's sake, see if you can hold your tongue for the same length of time."

"I will save it for licking your pussy tonight."

"That would be a much better use than your incessant chatter."

"Yes, ma'am."

≈≈≈

Anne held her tongue as requested. But for the rest of the week she talked picnic and thought picnic and dreamed picnic. On Saturday it rained and she worked herself up into such a frantic state lest it should keep on raining until Wednesday that Matilda made her sew an extra patchwork square to steady her nerves with the focus required by sewing.

On Sunday Anne confided to Matilda on the way home from church that she grew tingly all over when the minister announced the picnic from the pulpit. "Such a thrill went up and down my back, Matilda! I don't think I ever really believed until then that there was really going to be a picnic. I feared that I'd only imagined it – a wonderful picnic with baskets of food and homemade vanilla ice cream! But when a minister says such a thing from the pulpit you just have to believe it."

"You set your heart too much on things, Anne," Matilda said with a sigh. "I'm afraid there'll be a great many disappointments in store for you throughout life."

"Oh, Matilda, looking forward to things is half the pleasure of them," exclaimed Anne. "You mayn't get the things themselves; but nothing can prevent you from having the fun of looking forward to them. Mrs. Langston says, 'Blessed are they who expect nothing for they shall not be disappointed.' But I think it would be worse to expect nothing than to be disappointed."

Matilda wore her amethyst brooch to church that day as usual. Matilda always wore her brooch to church. She would have thought it rather sacrilegious to leave it off – as bad as forgetting her Bible or her collection dime. That amethyst brooch was Matilda's most treasured possession. A seafaring uncle had given it to her mother who in turn had bequeathed it to Matilda. It was an old-fashioned oval, containing a braid of her mother's hair, surrounded by a border of very fine amethysts. Matilda knew too little about precious stones to realize how fine the amethysts actually were; but she thought them very beautiful and was always pleasantly conscious of their violet shimmer at her throat, above her good brown satin dress, even although she could not see it.

Anne had been smitten with delighted admiration when she first saw that brooch.

"Oh, Matilda, it's a perfectly elegant brooch. I don't know how you can pay attention to the sermon or the prayers when you have it on. I couldn't, I know. I think amethysts are just sweet. They are what I used to think diamonds were like. Long ago, before I had ever seen a diamond, I read about them and I tried to imagine what they would be like. I thought they would be lovely glimmering purple stones. When I saw a real diamond in a lady's ring one day I was so disappointed I cried. Of course, it was very lovely but it wasn't my idea of a diamond. Will you let me hold the brooch for one minute, Matilda? Do you think amethysts can be the souls of good violets?"

"Oh, Anne, you're such a dreamer."

"That's true. I'm going to my room and imagine I'm wearing nothing but your amethyst broach, like a harem girl waiting for the sultan to come ravish her. If Martin is home, will you send him to my room?"

"Yes, but you have to share him with the other girl in the harem."

"Okay, if you'll let me wear your broach."

"Just this one time. I want to see it hanging there between your boobies. Then I'm going to suck them till you faint with ecstasy."

The missing broach.

CHAPTER XIV

Anne's Confession

On the Monday evening before the picnic Matilda came down from her room with a troubled face. "Anne," she said to that small personage who was shelling peas by the spotless table and singing "Nelly of the Hazel Dell" with a vigor that did credit to Diana's coaching, "did you see anything of my amethyst brooch? I thought I stuck it in my pincushion after our tryst with Martin yesterday, but I can't find it anywhere."

"I – I saw it this afternoon when you were away at the Aid Society," said Anne a little slowly. "I was passing your door when I saw it on the cushion, so I went in to look at it."

"Did you touch it?" asked Matilda.

"Y-e-e-s," admitted Anne, "I took it up and I pinned it on my breast just to enjoy its look against my blouse."

"It looked quite beautiful against your bare skin yesterday."

"Thank you."

"But you shouldn't have gone into my room today and touched a brooch that didn't belong to you. Where did you put it?"

"Oh, I put it back on the bureau. I had it on only a minute. Truly, I didn't think about its being wrong to go in and try on the brooch; but I see now that it was and I'll never do it again. That's one good thing about me. I never do the same naughty thing twice."

"That's not true. What we did with Martin yesterday was very naughty. And we plan to do it again tonight."

"You mean playing sultan with his harem?"

"Well, yes. But I'm thinking more of what the harem does with the sultan."

"You mean letting him ejaculate into our mouths? That was so much fun. I liked the taste."

"Now tell me where you put my broach after you tried it on," said Matilda. "That brooch isn't anywhere on the bureau. You've taken it out or something, Anne."

"I did put it back," said Anne quickly – pertly, Matilda thought. "I don't just remember whether I stuck it on the pincushion or laid it in the china tray. But I'm perfectly certain I put it back."

"I'll go and have another look," said Matilda, determining to be just. "If you put that brooch back it's there still. If it isn't I'll know you didn't, that's all!"

Matilda went to her room and made a thorough search, not only over the top of the bureau but in every other place she thought the brooch might possibly be. It was not to be found and she returned to the kitchen to confront the girl.

"Anne, the brooch is gone. By your own admission you were the last person to handle it. Now, what have you done with it? Tell me the truth at once. Did you take it out and lose it?"

"No, I didn't," said Anne solemnly, meeting Matilda's angry gaze squarely. "I never took the brooch out of your room and that is the truth."

"I believe you are telling me a falsehood, Anne," the woman said sharply. "I know you are. There now, don't say anything more unless you are prepared to tell the whole truth. Go to your room and stay there until you are ready to confess."

"Shall I take the peas with me?" said Anne meekly.

"No, I'll finish shelling them myself. Do as I bid you."

When Anne had gone Matilda went about her evening tasks in a very disturbed state of mind. She was worried about her valuable brooch. What if Anne had lost it? And how wicked of the child to deny having taken it, when anybody could see she must have! With such an innocent face, too!

"I don't know what I wouldn't sooner have had happen," thought Matilda, as she nervously shelled the peas. "Of course, I don't suppose she meant to steal it or anything like that. She's just taken it to play with or help along that imagination of hers. She must have taken it, that's clear, for there hasn't been a soul in that room since she was in it, by her own admission, until I went up tonight. And the brooch is gone, there's nothing surer. I suppose she is afraid to own up to losing it for fear she'll be punished. It's a dreadful thing to have a child in your house you can't trust. Slyness and untruthfulness – that's what she has displayed. I feel worse about that than about the brooch. If she'd only have told the truth about it I wouldn't mind so much."

Matilda went to her room at intervals all through the evening and searched for the brooch, without finding it. A bedtime visit to the east gable produced no satisfaction. Anne persisted in denying that she knew anything about the brooch but Matilda was only the more firmly convinced that she did.

She told Martin the story the next morning. Martin was confounded and puzzled; he could not so quickly lose faith in Anne but he had to admit that circumstances were against her.

"You're sure it hasn't fell down behind the bureau?" was the only suggestion he could offer.

"I've moved the bureau and I've taken out the drawers and I've looked in every crack and cranny" was Matilda's response. "The brooch is gone and that girl has taken it and lied about it. That's the plain, ugly truth, Martin Collins, and we might as well look it in the face."

"Well now, what are you going to do about it?" Martin asked forlornly, feeling secretly thankful that Matilda and not he had to deal with the situation. He felt no desire to put his oar in this time.

"She'll stay in her room until she confesses," Matilda said grimly, remembering the success of this method in the former case. "Then we'll see. Perhaps we'll be able to find the brooch if she'll only tell us where she took it; but in any case she'll have to be severely punished, Martin."

"Well now, you'll have to punish her," said Martin, reaching for his hat. "I've nothing to do with it, remember. You warned me off yourself."

Matilda felt deserted by everyone. She could not even go to Mrs. Langston for advice. She feared the story of their harem play might come out. So she went up to the east gable with a very serious face and left it with a face more serious still because Anne steadfastly refused to confess. She persisted in saying she had not taken the brooch.

"You'll stay in this room until you confess, Anne. You can make up your mind to that," she said firmly.

"But the picnic is tomorrow, Matilda," cried Anne. "You won't keep me from going to that, will you? You'll just let me out for the afternoon, won't you? Then I'll stay here as long as you like AFTERWARDS cheerfully. But I MUST go to the picnic."

"You'll not go to picnics nor anywhere else until you've confessed, Anne."

"Oh, Matilda," gasped Anne. "How can you be so cruel when I've shared your bed?"

But Matilda had gone out and shut the door.

Wednesday morning dawned as bright and fair as if expressly made to order for the picnic. The birches in the hollow waved joyful hands as if watching for Anne's usual morning greeting from the east gable. But Anne was not at her window. When Matilda took her breakfast up to her she found the child sitting primly on her bed, pale and resolute, with tight-shut lips and gleaming eyes.

"Matilda, I'm ready to confess."

"Ah!" Matilda laid down her tray. Once again her method had succeeded; but her success was very bitter to her. "Let me hear what you have to say then, Anne."

"I took the amethyst brooch," said Anne, as if repeating a lesson she had learned. "I took it just as you said. I didn't mean to take it when I went in. But it did look so beautiful, Matilda, when I pinned it on my breast that I was overcome by an irresistible temptation. I imagined how perfectly thrilling it would be to take it to Idlewild and play I was the Lady

Cordelia Fitzgerald. It would be so much easier to imagine I was the Lady Cordelia if I had a real amethyst brooch on. Diana and I make necklaces of roseberries but what are roseberries compared to amethysts? So I took the brooch. I thought I could put it back before you came home. I went all the way around by the road to lengthen out the time. When I was going over the bridge across the Lake of Shining Waters I took the brooch off to have another look at it. Oh, how it did shine in the sunlight! And then, when I was leaning over the bridge, it just slipped through my fingers – so – and went down – down – down, all purply-sparkling, and sank forevermore beneath the Lake of Shining Waters. And that's the best I can do at confessing, Matilda."

Matilda felt hot anger surge up into her heart again. This girl had taken and lost her treasured amethyst brooch and now sat there calmly reciting the details thereof without the least apparent repentance.

"Anne, this is terrible," she said, trying to speak calmly. "You are the very wickedest girl I ever heard of."

"Yes, I suppose I am," agreed Anne tranquilly. "And I know I'll have to be punished. It'll be your duty to punish me, Matilda. Won't you please get it over right off because I'd like to go to the picnic with nothing on my mind."

"Picnic, indeed! You'll go to no picnic today, Anne Shirley. That shall be your punishment. And it isn't half severe enough either for what you've done!"

"Not go to the picnic!" Anne sprang to her feet and clutched Matilda's hand. "But you PROMISED me I might! Oh, Matilda, I must go to the picnic. That was why I confessed. Punish me any way you like but that. Oh, Matilda, please, please, let me go to the picnic. Think of the ice cream! For anything you know I may never have a chance to taste ice cream again."

Matilda disengaged Anne's clinging hands stonily.

"You needn't plead, Anne. You are not going to the picnic and that's final. No, not a word."

Anne realized that Matilda was not to be moved. She clasped her hands together, gave a piercing shriek, and then flung herself face downward on the bed, crying and writhing in an utter abandonment of despair.

"For land's sake!" gasped Matilda, hastening from the room. "I believe the child is crazy. No one in her senses would behave as she does. Oh dear, I'm afraid Rita was right from the first. But I've put my hand to the plow and I won't look back."

That was a dismal morning. Matilda worked fiercely and scrubbed the porch floor and the dairy shelves when she could find nothing else to do. Neither the shelves nor the porch needed it – but Matilda did. Then she went out and raked the yard.

When lunch was ready she went to the stairs and called Anne. A tear-stained face appeared, looking tragically over the banisters.

"Come down to your lunch, Anne."

"I don't want any lunch, Matilda," said Anne, sobbingly. "I couldn't eat anything. My heart is broken. You'll feel remorse someday, I expect, for breaking it, Matilda, but I forgive you. Remember when the time comes that I forgive you. But please don't ask me to eat anything."

Exasperated, Matilda returned to the kitchen and poured out her tale of woe to Martin, who was a miserable man. He knew he wasn't going to get fucked by either woman tonight.

"Well now, she shouldn't have taken the brooch, Matilda, or told stories about it," he admitted, mournfully surveying his plateful of unromantic pork and greens, "but she's such a little thing – such an interesting little thing. Don't you think it's pretty rough not to let her go to the picnic when she's so set on it?"

"Martin Collins, I'm amazed at you. I think I've let her off entirely too easy. And she doesn't appear to realize how wicked she's been at all – that's what worries me most."

"Well now, there should be allowances made, Matilda. You know she's never had any bringing up."

"Well, she's having it now" retorted Matilda.

The retort silenced Martin if it did not convince him. That lunch was a very dismal meal. The only cheerful thing about it was Harley Buote, the hired hand, who came by for his pay. Matilda seemed to resent his cheerfulness as if it were a personal insult.

When her dishes were washed and her hens fed, Matilda remembered that she had noticed a small rent in her best black lace shawl when she had taken it off on Monday afternoon on returning from the Ladies' Aid. She needed to mend it.

The shawl was in a box in her trunk. As Matilda lifted it out, the sunlight falling through the window struck upon something caught in the shawl – something that glittered and sparkled in facets of violet light. Matilda snatched at it with a gasp. It was the amethyst brooch, hanging to a thread of the lace by its catch!

"Dear life and heart," said Matilda, "Here's my brooch safe and sound that I thought was at the bottom of Barry's pond. Whatever did that girl mean by saying she took it and lost it? I declare I believe Green Gables is bewitched. I remember now that when I took off my shawl Monday afternoon I laid it on the bureau for a minute. I suppose the brooch got caught in it somehow. Well!"

Matilda betook herself to the east gable, brooch in hand. Anne had cried herself out and was sitting dejectedly by the window, naked as usual. A good thing Harley Buote had left because she would be clearly visible through the window.

"Anne Shirley," said Matilda solemnly, "I've just found my brooch hanging to my black lace shawl. Now I want to know what that rigmarole you told me this morning meant."

"Why, you said you'd keep me here until I confessed," returned Anne wearily, "and so I decided to confess because I wanted to go to the picnic. I thought out a confession last night after I went to bed and made it as interesting as I could. And I said it over and over so that I wouldn't forget it. But you wouldn't let me go to the picnic after all, so all my trouble was wasted."

Matilda had to laugh in spite of herself. But her conscience pricked her. "Anne, you do beat all! But I was wrong – I see that now. I shouldn't have doubted your word. Of course, it wasn't right for you to confess to a thing you hadn't done – but I can see I drove you to it. So if you'll forgive me, Anne, I'll forgive you, and we'll start square again. And now get yourself ready for the picnic."

Anne flew up like a rocket. "Oh, Matilda, isn't it too late?"

"No, it's only two o'clock. They won't be gathered yet. It'll be another hour before they have tea. Wash your face and comb your hair and put on some clothes. You can't go naked as a jaybird."

"Yes ma'am."

"I'll fill a basket for you. There's plenty of baked goods in the house. And I'll get Martin hitch up the sorrel and drive you down to the picnic ground."

"Oh, Matilda," exclaimed Anne, flying to the washstand. "Five minutes ago I was so miserable I was wishing I'd never been born and now I wouldn't change places with an angel!"

≈≈≈

That night a thoroughly happy, completely tired-out Anne returned to Green Gables in a state of beatification impossible to describe.

"Oh, Matilda, I've had a perfectly scrumptious time. Scrumptious is a new word I learned today. I heard Mary Alice Bell use it. Isn't it very expressive? Everything was lovely. We had a splendid tea and then Mr. Harmon Andrews took us all for a row on the Lake of Shining Waters – six of us at a time. And Jane Andrews nearly fell overboard. She was leaning out to pick water lilies and if Mr. Andrews hadn't caught her by her sash just in the nick of time she'd have fallen in and prob'ly drowned. I wish it had been me. It would have been such a romantic experience to nearly drown.

It would give me such a thrilling tale to tell. And we had the ice cream. Words fail me to describe that ice cream. Matilda, I assure you it was sublime."

That evening Matilda told the whole story to Martin. "I'm willing to own up that I made a mistake," she concluded candidly, "but I've learned a lesson. I have to laugh when I think of Anne's 'confession,' although I suppose I shouldn't for it really was a falsehood. But it doesn't seem as bad as the other would have been, somehow, and anyhow I'm responsible for it. That girl is hard to understand in some respects. But I believe she'll turn out all right yet. And there's one thing certain, no house will ever be dull that she's in."

"Does that mean you gals are going to fuck me tonight?"

"Not tonight, Martin. We've had much too exciting a day."

"Oh shoot," he muttered. "I knew this wasn't going to end well for me, one way or another."

A school day.

CHAPTER XV

A Tempest in the School Teapot

"**W**hat a splendid day!" said Anne, drawing a long breath. "Isn't it good just to be alive on a day like this? I pity the people who aren't born yet for missing it. They may have good days, of course, but they can never have this one. And it's splendider still to have such a lovely way to go to school by, isn't it?"

"It's a lot nicer than going round by the road," said Diana. "That is so dusty and hot." She was peaking into her lunch pail and mentally calculating if the three raspberry tarts were divided among ten girls how many bites each girl would have.

The little girls of Avonlea School always pooled their lunches, and to eat three raspberry tarts all alone, or share them only with one's best chum, would have considered "awful mean." And yet, when the tarts were divided among ten girls you barely got enough to tantalize you.

The way Anne and Diana went to school WAS a pretty one. Anne thought those walks to school with Diana couldn't be improved upon even by imagination. Going by the main road would have been so unromantic; but to go by Lover's Lane and Violet Vale and the Birch Path was indeed romantic, if ever anything was.

Lover's Lane opened out below the orchard at Green Gables and stretched far up into the woods to the end of the Collins farm. It was the way by which the cows were taken to the back pasture. Anne had named it Lover's Lane before she had been a month at Green Gables.

"Not that lovers ever really walk there," she explained to Matilda, "but Diana and I are reading a perfectly magnificent book and there's a Lover's Lane in it. So we want to have one, too. It's a very pretty name, don't you think? So romantic!"

Anne, starting out alone in the morning, went down Lover's Lane as far as the brook. Here Diana met her, and the two girls went on up the lane under the leafy arch of maples – "Maples are such sociable trees," said Anne; "they're always rustling and whispering to you" – until they came to a rustic bridge. Then they left the lane and walked through Mr. Barry's backfield and past Violet Vale – a little green dimple in the shadow of Mr. Andrew Bell's big woods. "Of course there are no violets there now," Anne told Matilda, "but Diana says there are millions of them in spring. Oh, Matilda, can't you just imagine you see them? It actually takes away my breath. I named it Violet Vale. Diana says she never saw the beat of me for hitting on fancy names for places. It's nice to be clever at something, isn't it? But Diana named the Birch Path. She wanted to, so I let her; but I'm sure I could have found something more poetical than plain ol' Birch Path. Anybody can think of a name like that. But the Birch Path is one of the prettiest places in the world, Matilda."

It was. Other people besides Anne thought so when they stumbled on it. It was a narrow, twisting path, winding down a long hill in Rev. Cleary's woods. It was fringed all its length with slim young birches. Ferns and starflowers and wild lilies-of-the-valley and scarlet tufts of pigeon berries grew thickly along it. Now and then you might see a rabbit skipping across the road if you were quiet – which, with Anne and Diana, happened about once in a blue moon. Down in the valley the path came out on the main road and from there it was a short walk up the hill to the school.

The Avonlea School was a whitewashed building, low in the eaves and wide in the windows, furnished inside with old-fashioned desks that were carved all over their lids with the initials and hieroglyphics of three generations of school children. The schoolhouse was set back from the road and behind it was a dusky fir wood and a lake where in the morning all the children put their bottles of milk to keep them cool until lunch.

Matilda had seen Anne start off to school on the first day of September with many secret misgivings. Anne was such an odd girl. How would she get on with the other children? And how on earth would she ever manage to stay dressed during school hours?

However, things went much better than Matilda anticipated. Anne had come home that evening in high spirits.

"I think I'm going to like school," she announced. "I don't think much of the headmaster, through. He's all the time curling his mustache and making eyes at Prissy Andrews. Prissy is grown up, you know. She's eighteen and studying for the entrance examination into Queen's Academy at Charlottetown next year. Tilly Boulter says the headmaster is DEAD GONE on her. She's got a beautiful complexion and curly brown hair and she does it up so elegantly. And her titties are big as watermelons. She sits in the long seat at the back and he sits there, too, most of the time – to explain her lessons, he says. But Ruby Gillis says she saw him writing something on her slate and when Prissy read it she blushed as red as a beet and giggled; and Ruby Gillis says she doesn't believe it had anything to do with the lesson. I think he wants to fuck her!"

"Anne Shirley, don't let me hear you talking about your teacher in that way again," said Matilda sharply. "You don't go to school to criticize the headmaster. I'd guess he can teach YOU something, and it's your business to learn. And I want you to understand right off that you are not to come home telling tales about him. I hope you behaved yourself today."

"Indeed I did," said Anne comfortably. "It wasn't so hard as you might imagine, either. I sit with Diana. Our seat is right by the window and we can look down to the Lake of Shining Waters. There are a lot of nice girls in school and we had scrumptious fun playing during lunchtime. It's so nice to have a lot of girls to play with. But of course I like Diana best and always will. She's my bosom buddy and we play house together. When we do, she lets me touch her and kiss her all over."

"Careful, Anne. You cannot tell the other schoolchildren about that. Or about what you do with me and Martin."

"Of course not. It's our secret."

"How did you do with the lessons?"

"Oh, I'm dreadfully far behind the others. They're all in the fifth book and I'm only in the fourth. I feel that it's kind of a disgrace. We had reading and geography and Canadian history today. Mr. Phillips said my spelling was disgraceful and he held up my slate so that everybody could see it, all marked over. I felt so mortified, Matilda. Don't you think he could have been politer to a stranger?"

"You must study hard to catch up."

"The children in my class are so nice. Ruby Gillis gave me an apple and Charlie Sloane passed me a note that said, 'Show me your tits.' So I did show them to him at lunchtime. It seemed like the polite thing to do. I took off my blouse while we were down near the lake behind the school. Only for a moment, but he seemed satisfied with that. Particularly when I promised he could touch them tomorrow. And Jane Andrews told me that Minnie MacPherson told her that she heard Prissy Andrews tell Sara Gillis that I had very pretty boobies. Matilda, that is the first compliment I have ever had in my life from a classmate and you can't imagine what a strange feeling it gave me. Matilda, do I really have pretty boobies? I know you'll tell me the truth."

"Your bosom is quite nice. It's ample for a girl your age," said Matilda shortly. Secretly she thought Anne's titties were remarkably pretty; but she had no intention of telling her that, lest it go to her head. "But you can't go baring your breasts at school. That would be considered unseemly."

"Oh, but Matilda, Charlie Sloane liked them so much. I don't mind if he touches them tomorrow. They're not as big as Prissy Andrews's titties – not watermelons. What would compare mine to?

Kumquats?"

"Never you mind. And don't you let Charlie Sloan touch them."

"But I promised."

"This is one promise it's okay to break. You let Charlie Sloan touch them, next thing you know he'll try to fuck you."

"Oh, I wouldn't mind that. He's awfully cute."

"No, Anne, the rule is you cannot fuck your classmates. That's something you can only do at home."

"But what about Diana –?"

"That's the exception. You're allowed only one bosom buddy."

"Oh. Well, then I'm glad it's Diana."

≈≈≈

That was three weeks ago and all had gone smoothly so far. And now, this crisp September morning, Anne and Diana were tripping blithely down the Birch Path, two of the happiest little girls in Avonlea.

"I guess Gilbert Blythe will be in school today," said Diana. "He's been visiting his cousins over in New Brunswick all summer and he only came home Saturday night. He's AW'FLY handsome, Anne. And he teases the girls something terrible. He just torments our lives out, always trying to feel our boobies. He's worse than Charlie Sloan."

Diana's voice indicated that she rather liked having her life tormented by this boy.

"Gilbert Blythe?" said Anne. "Isn't that his name written on the porch wall along with Julia Bell's and a big heart drawn around them?"

"Yes," said Diana, tossing her head, "but I'm sure he doesn't like Julia Bell so very much. I've heard him say he studied the multiplication table by her freckles. He just likes her 'cause she puts out."

"Puts out? You mean she fucks her classmates?"

"Yes, Julia's the biggest whore. But truth is, I'd fuck Gilbert if he asked me."

"Diana!"

"That's how you get your name written on the porch," she explained. "It's what the most popular girls do."

Anne sighed. She wanted her name written on the porch. But there was little likelihood of it happening. Matilda had been quite clear about her not fucking any of her classmates – Charlie Sloan in particular. "My name will never make it onto the porch," she lamented.

"Nonsense," said Diana, whose black eyes and glossy tresses had played such havoc with the hearts of Avonlea schoolboys that her name figured on the porch walls in half a dozen take-notices. "Don't you be too sure your name won't ever be written up. Charlie Sloane is DEAD GONE on you. He told his mother – his MOTHER, mind you – that you were the smartest girl in school. That's better than being good looking."

"No, it isn't," said Anne, feminine to the core. "I'd rather be pretty than clever. And I hate Charlie Sloane; I can't bear a boy with goggle eyes. If anyone wrote my name up with his I'd NEVER get over it, Diana Barry. But it IS nice to be the head of your class. Mr. Phillips says I've improved the fastest of any student he's ever taught."

"Oh, he just wants to fuck you. He does all the girls who will let him."

"Have you let him?"

"Only once. Last year. He's got a very big dick. It hurt a little, but I was a virgin of course."

"But not now?"

"No, silly. Haven't you seen my name up there on the porch – four or five times at least? Besides, you're never a virgin again after the first time. Once Mr. Phillips popped my cherry I was no longer a virgin."

"Oh my, perhaps I've misled Martin and Matilda. When I came to live with them I told them I was a virgin. But Mr. Thomas, that old drunk I used to live with climbed into bed with me all the time. I thought it didn't count when it was forced on you."

"Oh Anne, you silly goose. You're far from being a virgin. You told me about having sex with BOTH Martin and his sister."

"That's a secret."

"But it's still true. You're quite the little whore yourself. Charlie Sloan will be in your panties before you know it."

"From what you say, I think I'd rather fuck Gilbert Blythe."

"No, I've got dibs on Gilbert. Besides, he'll see you as a threat."

"A threat?"

"You'll have Gilbert in your class after this," said Diana, "and he's used to being head of the class. He's very smart. You won't find it so easy to keep ahead after this, Anne."

"I'm glad for the challenge," said Anne quickly. "I

don't really feel proud of keeping ahead of little boys and girls of just nine or ten. Sometimes Josie Pye gives me some competition. Yesterday she was on top, but mind you she peeped in her book. Mr. Phillips didn't see her – he was looking at Prissy Andrews's titties – but I did. I just swept her a look of freezing scorn and she got as red as a beet and spelled it wrong after all."

"Those Pye girls are cheats all round," said Diana indignantly, as they climbed the fence of the main road. "Gertie Pye actually went and put her milk bottle in my place in the lake yesterday. Did you ever? I don't speak to her now."

When Mr. Phillips was in the back of the room hearing Prissy Andrews's Latin, Diana whispered to Anne, "That's Gilbert Blythe sitting right across the aisle from you, Anne. Just look at him and see if you don't think he's handsome."

Anne looked accordingly. She had a good chance to do so, for the said Gilbert Blythe was absorbed in stealthily patting Ruby Gillis's ass. She sat in front of him, her bottom easy to reach with his hand under his desk. Ruby didn't seem to mind. She wasn't squealing or telling him to stop as he caressed her plump little butt.

Gilbert was a tall boy, with curly brown hair, roguish hazel eyes, and a mouth twisted into a teasing smile. As he fondled Ruby, he looked over at Anne and winked with inexpressible drollery.

"Your Gilbert Blythe IS handsome," confided Anne to Diana at lunch. "But I think he's very bold. It isn't good manners to wink at a strange girl."

But it was not until the afternoon that things really

began to happen.

Mr. Phillips was back in the corner explaining a problem in algebra to Prissy Andrews and the rest of the scholars were doing pretty much as they pleased, eating green apples, whispering, and drawing naughty pictures on their slates. Gilbert Blythe was trying to make Anne Shirley look at him and failing utterly, because Anne was at that moment totally oblivious not only to the very existence of Gilbert Blythe, but of every other scholar in Avonlea School itself. With her chin propped on her hands and her eyes fixed on the Lake of Shining Waters through the west window, she was far away in a gorgeous dreamland hearing and seeing nothing save her own wonderful visions.

Gilbert Blythe wasn't used to putting himself out to make a girl look at him and meeting with failure. She SHOULD look at him, that Shirley girl with the pouty lips and the big gray-green eyes that weren't like the eyes of any other girl in Avonlea School.

Gilbert reached across the aisle and cupped his hand around Anne's left breast, giving it a squeeze. "Honk! Honk!" he said in a piercing whisper.

Then Anne looked at him with a vengeance! She did more than look. She sprang to her feet, flashing an indignant glance at Gilbert from eyes whose angry sparkle was swiftly quenched in equally angry tears.

"You mean, hateful boy!" she exclaimed passionately. "How dare you!"

And then – thwack! Anne had brought her slate down on Gilbert's head and cracked it – slate not head – clear across.

Avonlea School always enjoyed a scene. This was

an especially enjoyable one. Everybody said "Oh" in horrified delight. Diana gasped. Ruby Gillis, who was inclined to be hysterical, began to cry.

Mr. Phillips stalked down the aisle and laid his hand heavily on Anne's shoulder. "Anne Shirley, what does this mean?" he said angrily. Anne returned no answer. It was asking too much of flesh and blood to expect her to tell before the whole school that she had been molested.

Gilbert spoke up stoutly. "It was my fault, Mr. Phillips. I teased her."

Mr. Phillips paid no heed to Gilbert. "I am sorry to see a pupil of mine displaying such a temper and such a vindictive spirit," he said in a solemn tone, as if the mere fact of being a pupil of his ought to root out all evil passions from the hearts of small imperfect mortals. "Anne, go and stand on the platform in front of the blackboard for the rest of the afternoon."

Anne would have infinitely preferred a whipping to this punishment under which her sensitive spirit quivered as from a whiplash. With a white, set face she obeyed. Mr. Phillips took a chalk crayon and wrote on the blackboard above her head.

"Ann Shirley has a very bad temper. Ann Shirley must learn to control her temper," and then read it out loud so that even the primer class, who couldn't read should understand it.

Anne stood there the rest of the afternoon with that legend above her. She did not cry or hang her head. Anger was still too hot in her heart for that and it sustained her amid all her agony of humiliation. With resentful eyes and passion-red cheeks she confronted alike Diana's sympathetic gaze and Charlie Sloane's indignant nods and Josie Pye's malicious smiles. As for Gilbert Blythe, she would not even look at him. She would NEVER look at him again! She would never even speak to him!

When school was dismissed Anne marched out with her head held high. Gilbert Blythe tried to intercept her at the porch door. "I'm awfully sorry I felt your boob, Anne," he whispered contritely. "Honest I am. Don't be mad for keeps, now."

Anne swept by disdainfully, without look or sign of hearing. "Oh how could you, Anne?" breathed Diana as they went down the road half reproachfully, half admiringly. Diana felt that SHE could never have resisted Gilbert's plea.

"I shall never forgive Gilbert Blythe," said Anne firmly. "And Mr. Phillips spelled my name without an E, too. The iron has entered into my soul, Diana."

Diana hadn't the least idea what Anne meant but she understood it was something terrible.

"You mustn't mind Gilbert teasing you," she said soothingly. "Why, he makes fun of all the girls. He squeezes my titties all the time. He's called me a cow a dozen times; because my titties are so big, not as big as Prissy's but bigger than yours. And I never heard Gilbert apologize for doing anything before, either."

"There's a great deal of difference between being called a cow and being treated like one," said Anne with dignity. "Gilbert Blythe has hurt my feelings EXCRUCIATINGLY, Diana."

≈≈≈

It is possible the matter might have blown over

without more excruciation if nothing else had happened. But when things begin to happen they are apt to keep on.

On the following day Mr. Phillips was seized with one of his spasmodic fits of reform and announced before going home for lunch that he should expect to find all the students in their seats when he returned. Anyone who came in late would be punished.

Most days Avonlea scholars spent their lunch hour picking gum in Rev. Cleary's spruce grove across the big pasture field. From there they could keep an eye on Eben Wright's house, where the headmaster boarded. When they saw Mr. Phillips emerge they ran like the wind for the schoolhouse; but the distance being about three times longer than Mr. Wright's lane they were very apt to arrive there, breathless and gasping, some three minutes too late.

This time they loitered too long, only taking flight when they heard Jimmy Glover shouting from the top of a patriarchal old spruce, "Master's coming."

The girls, who were on the ground under the spruce trees, started first and managed to reach the schoolhouse just in time, without a second to spare. The boys, having to wriggle hastily down from the trees, arrived a few minutes later. And Anne, who had not been picking gum at all but was wandering happily in the far end of the grove, waist-deep among the bracken, singing softly to herself, with a wreath of rice lilies on her hair as if she were some wild divinity, was latest of all. However Anne could run like a deer, and run she did, overtaking the boys at the schoolhouse door, sweeping into the classroom just as Mr. Phillips was in the act of hanging up his hat.

Mr. Phillips's brief reforming energy was over; he didn't want the bother of punishing a dozen pupils. But it was necessary to do something to save his word, so he looked about for a scapegoat and found it in Anne, who had dropped into her seat, gasping for breath, with a forgotten lily wreath hanging askew over one ear and giving her a particularly rakish and disheveled appearance.

"Anne Shirley, since you seem to be so fond of the boys' company we shall indulge your taste for it this afternoon," he said sarcastically. "Take those flowers out of your hair and sit with Gilbert Blythe."

The other boys snickered. Diana, turning pale with pity, plucked the wreath from Anne's hair and squeezed her hand. Anne stared at the headmaster as if turned to stone.

"Did you hear what I said, Anne?" queried Mr. Phillips sternly.

"Yes, sir," said Anne slowly "but I didn't suppose you really meant it."

"I assure you I did" – still with the sarcastic inflection which all the children, and Anne especially, hated. "Obey me at once."

For a moment Anne looked as if she meant to disobey. Then, realizing that there was no help for it, she rose haughtily, stepped across the aisle, sat down beside Gilbert Blythe, and buried her face in her arms on the desk.

To Anne, this was as the end of all things. It was bad enough to be singled out for punishment from among a dozen equally guilty ones; it was worse still to be sent to sit with a boy, but that the boy should be Gilbert Blythe was heaping insult onto injury. Anne felt that she could not bear it and it would be of no use to try. Her whole being seethed with shame and anger and humiliation.

At first the other students looked and whispered and giggled and nudged. But as Anne never lifted her head and as Gilbert worked fractions as if his whole soul was absorbed in them and them only, they soon returned to their own tasks and Anne was forgotten. When Mr. Phillips called the history class out Anne should have gone, but Anne did not move, and Mr. Phillips, who had been writing some verses "To Priscilla" before he called the class, was thinking about an obstinate rhyme still and never missed her. Once, when nobody was looking, Gilbert took from his desk a little pink candy heart with a gold motto on it, "You are sweet," and slipped it under the curve of Anne's arm. Whereupon Anne arose, took the pink heart gingerly between the tips of her fingers, dropped it on the floor, ground it to powder beneath her heel, and resumed her position without deigning to bestow a glance on Gilbert.

When school went out Anne marched to her desk, ostentatiously took out everything therein, books and writing tablet, pen and ink, testament and arithmetic, and piled them neatly on her cracked slate.

"What are you taking all those things home for, Anne?" Diana wanted to know, as soon as they were out on the road. She had not dared to ask the question before.

"I am not coming back to school anymore," said

Anne.

Diana gasped and stared at Anne to see if she meant it. "Will Matilda let you stay home?" she asked.

"She'll have to," said Anne. "I'll NEVER go to school to that man again."

"Oh, Anne!" Diana looked as if she were ready to cry. "I do hope you don't mean it. What shall I do? Mr. Phillips will make me sit with that horrid Gertie Pye – I know he will because she is sitting alone. Do come back, Anne."

"I'd do almost anything in the world for you, Diana," said Anne sadly. "I'd let myself be torn limb from limb if it would do you any good. But I can't do this, so please don't ask it."

"Just think of all the fun you will miss," mourned Diana. "We'll be playing ball next week and you've never played ball, Anne. It's tremendously exciting. And we're going to learn a new song – Jane Andrews is practicing it now; and Alice Smithington is going to bring a new Pansy book next week and we're all going to read it out loud down by the lake. You know you are so fond of reading out loud, Anne."

Nothing moved Anne in the least. Her mind was made up. She would not go to school to Mr. Phillips again; she told Matilda so when she got home.

"Nonsense," said Matilda.

"It isn't nonsense at all," said Anne, gazing at Matilda with solemn, reproachful eyes. "Don't you understand, Matilda? I've been insulted."

"Insulted fiddlesticks! You'll go to school tomorrow as usual."

"Oh, no." Anne shook her head gently. "I'm not

going back, Matilda. I'll learn my lessons at home and I'll be as good as I can be and hold my tongue all the time if it's possible at all. But I will not go back to school, I assure you."

Matilda saw something remarkably like unyielding stubbornness looking out of Anne's small face. She understood that she would have trouble in overcoming it; but she resolved wisely to say nothing more just then. "I'll run down and see Rita about it this evening," she thought. "There's no use reasoning with Anne now. She's too worked up and I've an idea she can be awful stubborn if she takes the notion. Far as I can make out from her story, Mr. Phillips has been carrying matters with a rather high hand. But it would never do to say so to her. I'll just talk it over with Rita. She's sent ten children to school and she ought to know something about it. She'll have heard the whole story, too, by this time."

~ ~ ~

Matilda found Mrs. Langston knitting quilts as industriously and cheerfully as usual. "I suppose you know what I've come about," she said, a little shamefacedly.

Mrs. Langston nodded. "About Anne's fuss in school, I reckon," she said. "Tilly Boulter stopped by on her way home from school and told me about it."

"I don't know what to do with her," said Matilda. "She declares she won't go back to school. I never saw a child so worked up. I've been expecting trouble ever since she started to school. I knew things were going too smooth to last. She's so high strung. What would you advise, Rita?"

"Well, since you've asked my advice, Matilda," said Mrs. Langston amiably – Mrs. Langston dearly loved to be asked for advice – "I'd just humor her a little at first, that's what I'd do. It's my belief that Mr. Phillips was in the wrong. Of course, it doesn't do to say so to the children, you know. And of course he did right to punish her yesterday for giving way to temper. But today it was different. The others who were late should have been punished as well as Anne, that's what. And I don't believe in making the girls sit with the boys for punishment. It isn't modest. Tilly Boulter was real indignant. She took Anne's part right through and said all the students did too. Anne seems real popular among them, somehow. I never thought she'd take with them so well."

"Then you really think I'd better let her stay home," said Matilda in amazement.

"Yes. That is, I wouldn't say school to her again until she said it herself. Depend upon it, Matilda, she'll cool off in a week or so and be ready enough to go back of her own accord, that's what, while, if you were to make her go back right off, dear knows what freak or tantrum she'd take next and make more trouble than ever. The less fuss made the better, in my opinion. She won't miss much by not going to school, as far as THAT goes. Mr. Phillips isn't any good at all as a teacher. The order he keeps is scandalous, that's what, and he neglects the young fry and puts all his time on those big scholars he's getting ready for Queen's. He'd never have got the school for another year if his uncle hadn't been a trustee – THE trustee, for he just leads the other two around by the nose, that's what. I declare, I don't know what education in this Island is coming to."

Mrs. Langston shook her head, as much as to say if she were only at the head of the educational system of the Province things would be much better managed.

Matilda took Mrs. Langston's advice and not another word was said to Anne about going back to school. She learned her lessons at home, did her chores, and played with Diana in the chilly purple autumn twilights; but when she met Gilbert Blythe on the road or encountered him in Sunday School she passed him by with an icy contempt that was no whit thawed by his evident desire to appease her. Even Diana's efforts as a peacemaker were of no avail. Anne had evidently made up her mind to hate Gilbert Blythe to the end of life.

As much as she hated Gilbert, however, did she love Diana with all the love of her passionate little heart. One evening Matilda, coming in from the orchard with a basket of apples, found Anne sitting alone by the east window in the twilight, crying bitterly.

"Whatever's the matter now, Anne?" she asked.

"It's about Diana," sobbed Anne luxuriously. "I love Diana so, Matilda. I cannot ever live without her. But I know very well when we grow up that Diana will get married and go away and leave me. And oh, what shall I do? I hate her husband – I just hate him furiously. I've been imagining it all out – the wedding and everything – Diana dressed in snowy garments, with a veil, and looking as beautiful and regal as a queen; and me the bridesmaid, with a lovely dress too, and puffed sleeves, but with a breaking heart hid beneath my smiling face. And then bidding Diana goodbye-e-e–" Here Anne broke down entirely and wept with increasing bitterness.

Matilda turned quickly away to hide her twitching face; but it was no use; she collapsed on the nearest chair and burst into such a hearty and unusual peal of laughter that Martin, crossing the yard outside, halted in amazement. When had he heard Matilda laugh like that before?

"Well, Anne Shirley," said Matilda as soon as she could speak, "if you must borrow trouble, for pity's sake borrow it handier home. I should think you had an imagination, sure enough."

"Quit carrying on, you two," said Martin. "I could use a good roll in the hay. Get your clothes off and we'll play king and his court."

"Oh boy," said Anne, her spirits brightening. Martin's sexual play proved that he shared her imagination, two kindred spirits. She was so lucky to have landed at Green Gables.

"As for your little friend Diana," added Martin Collins, "invite her over some afternoon and I'll fuck her too."

"All three of us?" trilled Anne. Impressed by this magnanimous offer.

"Why not?" he grinned. "I've got the stamina of a mule."

Girls will be girls.

CHAPTER XVI
Diana Is Invited to Tea with Tragic Results

October was a beautiful month at Green Gables, when the birches in the hollow turned as golden as sunshine and the maples behind the orchard were royal crimson and the wild cherry trees along the lane put on the loveliest shades of dark red and bronzy green.

Anne reveled in the world of color about her. "Oh, Matilda," she exclaimed one Saturday morning, coming dancing in with her arms full of gorgeous boughs, "I'm so glad I live in a world where there are Octobers. It would be terrible if we just skipped from September to November, wouldn't it? Look at these maple branches. Don't they give you a thrill – several thrills? I'm going to decorate my room with them."

"Messy things," said Matilda, whose aesthetic sense was not noticeably developed. "You clutter up your room entirely too much with out-of-doors stuff, Anne. Bedrooms were made to sleep in."

"Oh, and fuck in too, Matilda. And one can fuck so much better in a room where there are pretty things. I'm going to put these boughs in this old blue jug and set them on my table."

"Mind you, don't drop leaves all over the stairs. I'm going to a meeting of the Aid Society at Carmody this afternoon, Anne, and I won't likely be home before dark. You'll have to get Martin and Harley their supper, so mind you don't forget to put the tea to draw until you sit down at the table as you did last time."

"It was dreadful of me to forget," said Anne apologetically, "but that was the afternoon I was trying to think of a name for Violet Vale and it crowded other things out. Martin was so good. He never scolded a bit. He put the tea down himself and said we could wait awhile as well as not. And I told him a lovely fairy story while we were waiting, so he didn't find the time long at all. It was a beautiful fairy story, Matilda. I forgot the end of it, so I made up an end for it myself and Martin said he couldn't tell where the join came in."

"Martin would think it all right, Anne, if you took a notion to get up and have lunch in the middle of the night as long as you fuck him regularly. But you keep your wits about you this time. And – I don't really know if I'm doing right – it may make you more addlepated than ever – but you can ask Diana to come over and spend the afternoon with you and have tea here."

"Oh, Matilda!" Anne clasped her hands. "How perfectly lovely! You ARE able to imagine things after all or else you'd never have understood how I've longed for that very thing. After all, Martin did suggest she come over and get fucked."

"Do you think she would be willing to join you and Martin for fun and games?"

"Oh yes, I'm sure of it. Diana is not a virgin. And she's said she thinks Martin is very handsome. I think she will fuck his brains out."

"Very well. But you should serve tea first."

"It will seem so nice and grown-uppish. No fear of my forgetting to put the tea to draw when I have company. Oh, Matilda, can I use the rosebud spray tea set?"

"No, indeed! The rosebud tea set! Well, what next? You know I never use that except for the minister or the Aids. You'll put down the old brown tea set. But you can open the little yellow crock of cherry preserves. It's time it was being used anyhow – I believe it's beginning to work. And you can cut some fruitcake and have some of the cookies and snaps."

"I can just imagine myself sitting down at the head of the table and pouring out the tea," said Anne, shutting her eyes ecstatically. "And asking Diana if she takes sugar! I know she doesn't but of course I'll ask her just as if I didn't know. And then pressing her to take another piece of fruitcake and another helping of preserves. Oh, Matilda, it's a wonderful sensation just to think of it. Can I take her into the spare room to lay off her hat when she comes? And then into the parlor to sit?"

"No. The sitting room will do for you and your company. But there's a bottle half full of raspberry cordial that was left over from the church social the other night. It's on the second shelf of the sitting-room closet and you and Diana can have it if you like, and a cookie to eat with it along in the afternoon, for I daresay you girls will need some energy to keep up with Martin."

Anne flew down to the hollow, past the Dryad's Bubble and up the spruce path to Orchard Slope, to ask Diana to tea. As a result just after Matilda had driven off to Carmody, Diana came over, dressed in HER second-best dress and looking exactly as it is proper to look when asked out to tea. At other times she was wont to run into the kitchen without knocking; but now she knocked primly at the front door. And when Anne, dressed in her second-best, as primly opened it, both little girls shook hands as gravely as if they had never met before. This unnatural solemnity lasted until after Diana had been taken to the east gable to lay off her hat and then had sat for ten minutes in the sitting room, toes in position.

"How is your mother?" inquired Anne politely, just as if she had not seen Mrs. Barry picking apples that morning in excellent health and spirits.

"She is very well, thank you. I suppose Mr. Collins is hauling potatoes to the Lily Sands this afternoon, is he?" said Diana, who had ridden down to Mr. Harmon Andrews's that morning in Martin's cart.

"Yes. Our potato crop is very good this year. I hope your father's crop is good too."

"It is fairly good, thank you. Have you picked many of your apples yet?"

"Oh, ever so many," said Anne forgetting to be dignified and jumping up quickly. "Let's go out to the orchard and get some of the Red Sweetings, Diana. Matilda says we can have all that are left on the tree. Matilda is a very generous woman. She said we could have fruitcake and cherry preserves for tea. But it isn't good manners to tell your company what you are going to give them to eat, so I won't tell you what she said we could have to drink. Only it begins with an R and a C and it's bright red color. I love bright red drinks, don't you? They taste twice as good as any other color."

"Raspberry cordial?" whispered Diana.

"I'm not to say."

The orchard, with its great sweeping boughs that bent to the ground with fruit, proved so delightful that the little girls spent most of the afternoon in it, sitting in a grassy corner where the frost had spared the green and the mellow autumn sunshine lingered warmly, eating apples and talking as hard as they could. Diana had much to tell Anne of what went on in school. She had to sit with Gertie Pye and she hated it; Gertie squeaked her pencil all the time and it just made Diana's blood run cold. Ruby Gillis had charmed all her warts away, true's you live, with a magic pebble that old Mrs. Garrett from the Creek gave her. You had to rub the warts with the pebble and then throw it away over your left shoulder at the time of the new moon and the warts would all go. Charlie Sloane's name was written up with Emma White's on the porch wall and Emma was AWFUL MAD about it, saying he shouldn't be bragging about bagging her because she was still a virgin. Sam Boulter had "sassed" Mr. Phillips in class and Mr. Phillips whipped him and Sam's father came down to the school and dared Mr. Phillips to lay a hand on one of his children again, else get a trashing himself. Mattie Andrews had a new red hood and a blue crossover with tassels on it and the airs she put on about it were perfectly sickening. Lizzie Wright didn't speak to Mamie Wilson because Mamie Wilson's grown-up sister had cut out Lizzie Wright's grown-up sister with her beau. And everybody missed Anne so and wished she'd come to school again. And Gilbert Blythe –

But Anne didn't want to hear about Gilbert Blythe. She jumped up hurriedly and said suppose they go in and have some raspberry cordial.

Anne looked on the second shelf of the pantry but there was no bottle of raspberry cordial there. Search revealed it way back on the top shelf. Anne put it on a tray and set it on the table with a tumbler.

"Now, please help yourself, Diana," she said politely. "I don't believe I'll have any just now. I don't feel as if I want any after all those apples."

Diana poured herself out a tumblerful, looked at its bright-red hue admiringly, and then sipped it daintily.

"That's awfully nice raspberry cordial, Anne," she said. "I didn't know raspberry cordial was so nice."

"I'm real glad you like it. Take as much as you want. I'm going to run out and stir the fire up. There are so many responsibilities on a person's mind when they're keeping house, isn't there?"

When Anne came back from the kitchen Diana was drinking her second glassful of cordial; and, being entreated thereto by Anne, she offered no particular objection to the drinking of a third. The tumbler offered a generous portion and the raspberry cordial was certainly very nice.

"The nicest I ever drank," said Diana. "It's ever so much nicer than Mrs. Langston's, although she brags of hers so much. It doesn't taste a bit like hers."

"I should think Matilda's raspberry cordial would prob'ly be much nicer than Mrs. Langston's," said Anne loyally. "Matilda is a famous cook. She is trying to teach me to cook but I assure you, Diana, it is uphill work. There's so little scope for imagination in cookery. You just have to go by rules. The last time I made a cake I forgot to put the flour in. Why, Diana, what is the matter?"

Diana had stood up very unsteadily; then she sat down again, putting her hands to her head.

"I'm – I'm awful dizzy," she said, a little thickly. "I – I – must go right home."

"Oh, you mustn't dream of going home without your tea," cried Anne in distress. "I'll get it right off – I'll go and put the tea down this very minute."

"I must go home," repeated Diana, stupidly but determinedly.

"Let me get you a lunch anyhow," implored Anne. "Let me give you a bit of fruitcake and some of the cherry preserves. Lie down on the sofa for a little while and you'll be better. Where do you feel bad?"

"I must go home," said Diana, and that was all she would say. In vain Anne pleaded.

"I never heard of company going home without tea," she mourned. "Where do you feel bad?"

"I'm awful dizzy," said Diana.

Just then Martin came in. "Hello, young ladies, have you had tea yet?"

"No, Diana's had too much raspberry cordial."

"Tipsy, huh?" said Martin, taking the girl's hand to steady her.

"Hello, Mr. Collins. I'm so embarrassed."

"Don't be, my dear. Here, let me loosen the collar of your dress so you can breathe easier."

"Yes, please."

Martin unbuttoned the top loop. Then the second and the third until he had undid Diana's gingham dress all way down the front. He tugged it off her shoulders and it fell to the floor in a rumpled heap about her feet.

"Oh my," she said, standing there in her camisole and knickers.

"It is stuffy in here," pronounced Anne. "I think I'll get more comfortable too." With no further ado, she stripped off her second-best dress and folded it over a chair the way Matilda had taught her. "Martin, why don't you get comfortable too?"

"I think I will," he agreed, stepping out of his trousers, then shucking his shirt.

"Are we going to fuck?" asked Diana, looking from one to another for confirmation.

"Yes, dear Diana. I thought you might enjoy sharing Martin with me this afternoon."

"O-okay," she muttered, stripping off the rest of her garments to reveal her fleshy young body, the skin as white as plaster.

By now Anne had removed her underwear too. Standing beside her friend it was easy to compare their bodies, Anne the more slender of the two, her breasts a cup-size smaller than Diana's.

Sporting a huge erection, Martin seemed taken with the visitor's generous titties. They were even larger than Matilda's. He took the nipples into his mouth, one at a time, teasing them with his tongue until he had the young girl moaning.

Meanwhile, Anne had engorged Martin's monstrous member with her mouth. By now she had learned how to take it deep into her throat, moving her head back and forth as she sucked. She knew he liked that, but had to be careful not to make him cum too soon. After all, she wanted that John Thomas inside her pussy before it deflated.

"Yes, let's," agreed Anne, suddenly hungry. "But we best leave Diana to sleep. I never should have served her so much cordial."

"Alright," nodded Martin. "Give me a few minutes and then I'll do you both again."

≈≈≈

Anne walked her friend Diana as far as the Barrys' yard fence. Then she ran all the way back to Green Gables, where she put the remainder of the raspberry cordial back into the pantry and got tea ready for Martin, but all the zest had gone out of the performance. Martin had fucked both girls twice, a feat of endurance that left chaffed skins and cum splatters on the couch. Matilda would be angry if it couldn't be cleaned off the porous green fabric.

"That was great fun," Anne told Martin. "Diana said she'd never had such a good time. She hopes we'll invite her back."

"We'll do that. But we must make sure Matilda is here too. She will want to sample your young friend. For a woman who had never been with a partner of the same sex until you, my sister has practically turned into a lesbian. She's certainly turned into a connoisseur of the Sapphic arts."

"I'll take that as a compliment," smiled Anne Shirley.

≈≈≈

The next day Matilda sent Anne down to Mrs. Langston's on an errand. In a very short space of time Anne came flying back up the lane with tears rolling down her cheeks. Into the kitchen she dashed and flung herself face downward on the sofa in an agony.

"Whatever has gone wrong now, Anne?" queried Matilda in dismay. "I do hope you haven't been saucy to Mrs. Langston again."

No answer from Anne save more tears and stormier sobs!

"Anne Shirley, when I ask you a question I want to be answered. Sit right up this very minute and tell me what you are crying about."

Anne sat up, tragedy personified. "Mrs. Langston was up to see Mrs. Barry today and Mrs. Barry was in an awful state," she wailed. "She says I got Diana DRUNK yesterday and sent her home in a disgraceful condition. And she says I must be a thoroughly bad, wicked little girl and she's never, never going to let Diana play with me again. Oh, Matilda, I'm just overcome with woe."

Matilda stared in blank amazement. "Got Diana drunk?" she said when she found her voice. "Anne, are you or Mrs. Barry crazy? What on earth did you give her?"

"Not a thing but raspberry cordial," sobbed Anne. "I never thought raspberry cordial would get people drunk, Matilda — not even if they drank three big tumblerfuls as Diana did. Oh, it sounds so – so – like Mrs. Thomas's husband! But I didn't mean to get her drunk."

"Drunk fiddlesticks!" said Matilda, marching to the sitting room pantry. There on the shelf was a bottle which she at once recognized as containing some of her three-year-old homemade currant wine for which she was celebrated in Avonlea. At the same moment she recollected that she'd put the bottle of raspberry cordial down in the cellar instead of in the pantry as she had told Anne.

Walking back to the kitchen with the wine bottle in her hand, Matilda's face was twitching in spite of herself. "Anne, you certainly have a genius for getting into trouble. You gave Diana currant wine instead of raspberry cordial. Didn't you taste the difference yourself?"

"I never tasted it," said Anne. "I thought it was the cordial. I meant to be so – so – hospitable. Diana got awfully sick and had to go home. But only after Martin fucked her a couple of times. Me too. Mrs. Barry told Mrs. Langston she was simply dead drunk. She just laughed silly-like when her mother asked her what was the matter and went to sleep and slept for hours. Her mother smelled her breath and knew she was drunk. Mrs. Barry is so indignant. She will never believe but what I did it on purpose."

"I should think she would better punish Diana for being so greedy as to drink three glassfuls of anything," said Matilda shortly. "Why, three of those big glasses would have made her sick even if it had only been cordial. Well, this story will be a nice handle for those folks who are so down on me for making currant wine, although I haven't made any for three years ever since I found out that the minister didn't approve. I just kept that bottle for sickness. There, there, child, don't cry. I can't see as you were to blame although I'm sorry it happened so."

"I must cry," said Anne. "My heart is broken. The stars in their courses fight against me, Matilda. Diana and I are parted forever. Oh, Matilda, I little dreamed of this when first she and I swore our vows of friendship."

"Don't be foolish, Anne. Mrs. Barry will think better of it when she finds you're not to blame. I suppose she thinks you've done it for a silly joke or something of that sort. You'd best go up this evening and tell her how it was."

"My courage fails me at the thought of facing Diana's injured mother," sighed Anne. "Besides, what if it comes out that Martin fucked her too? That would never do. I wish you'd go, Matilda. You're so much more dignified than I am. Likely she'd listen to you quicker than to me. And you're not as likely to let things slip out as I would be.""

"Well, I will go," agreed Matilda, judging that it would be the wiser course. "Don't cry anymore, Anne. Everything will be all right. You just wait and see."

≈≈≈

Matilda had revised her estimation about everything being all right by the time she got back to Green Gables. Anne was watching from the porch and flew to meet her. "Oh, Matilda, I know by your face that it's been no use," she said sorrowfully. "Mrs. Barry won't forgive me?"

"Mrs. Barry indeed!" snapped Matilda. "Of all the unreasonable women I ever saw she's the worst. I told her it was all a mistake and you weren't to blame, but she just simply didn't believe me. And she rubbed it well in about my currant wine and how I'd always said it couldn't have the least effect on anybody. I just told her plainly that currant wine wasn't meant to be drunk three tumblerfuls at a time and that if a child I had to do with was so greedy I'd sober her up with a right good spanking."

Matilda whisked into the kitchen, leaving a very distracted little soul on the porch. Anne sat there ruminating for about ten minutes, then stepped bareheaded into the autumn chill and made her way down through the clover field, over the log bridge, and up through the spruce grove, lighted by a pale little moon hanging low over the western woods. Mrs. Barry, coming to the door in answer to a timid knock, found a white-lipped eager-eyed suppliant on the doorstep.

Her face hardened at the sight of Anne. Mrs. Barry was a woman of strong prejudices and dislikes, and her anger was of the cold, sullen sort which is always hardest to overcome. To do her justice, she really believed Anne had made Diana drunk out of sheer malice prepense, and she was honestly anxious to preserve her little daughter from the contamination of further intimacy with such a child. Little did she know the sexual hijinks these girls had been up to, or her resolve would have been all the more!

"What do you want?" she said stiffly.

Anne clasped her hands nervously. "Oh, Mrs. Barry, please forgive me. I did not mean to – to – intoxicate Diana. How could I? Just imagine if you were a poor little orphan girl that kind people had adopted and you had just one bosom friend in all the world. Do you think you would intoxicate her on purpose? I thought it was only raspberry cordial. I was firmly convinced it was raspberry cordial. Oh, please don't say that you won't let Diana play with me anymore. If you do you will cover my life with a dark cloud of woe."

This speech which would have softened good Mrs. Langston's heart in a twinkling, had no effect on Mrs. Barry except to irritate her still more. She was suspicious of Anne's big words and dramatic gestures and imagined that the child was making fun of her. So she said, coldly and cruelly: "I don't think you are a fit little girl for Diana to associate with. You'd better go home and behave yourself."

Anne's lips quivered. "Won't you let me see Diana just once to say farewell?" she implored.

"Diana has gone over to Carmody with her father," said Mrs. Barry, going in and shutting the door.

Anne went back to Green Gables calm with despair.

"My last hope is gone," she told Matilda. "I went up and saw Mrs. Barry myself and she treated me very insultingly. Matilda, I do NOT think she is a well-bred woman. There is nothing more to do except to pray and I haven't much hope that that'll do much good because, Matilda, I do not believe that God Himself can do very much with such an obstinate person as Mrs. Barry."

"Anne, you shouldn't say such things," rebuked Matilda, striving to overcome that unholy tendency to laughter which she was dismayed to find growing upon her. And indeed, when she told the whole story to Martin that night, she did laugh heartily over Anne's tribulations.

But when she slipped into the east gable before going to bed and found that Anne had cried herself to sleep an unaccustomed softness crept into her face.

"Poor little soul," she murmured, lifting a loose curl of hair from the child's tear-stained face. Then she bent down and kissed the flushed cheek on the pillow. Waking up, Anne kissed her back, but with surprising passion. She had little choice but slip off her dress and crawl into bed with the naked girl. Martin was left to pleasure himself on this night.

An eternal farewell.

CHAPTER XVII

A New Interest in Life

The next afternoon Anne, bending over her patchwork at the kitchen window, happened to glance out and beheld Diana down by the Dryad's Bubble beckoning mysteriously. In a trice Anne was out of the house and flying down to the hollow, astonishment and hope struggling in her expressive eyes. But the hope faded when she saw Diana's dejected countenance.

"Your mother hasn't relented?" she gasped.

Diana shook her head mournfully. "No, and oh, Anne, she says I'm never to play with you again. I've cried and cried and I told her it wasn't your fault, but it isn't any use. I had ever such a time coaxing her to let me come down and say goodbye to you. She said I was only to stay ten minutes and she's timing me by the clock."

"Ten minutes isn't very long to say an eternal farewell in," said Anne tearfully. "Oh, Diana, will you promise faithfully never to forget me, the friend of your youth, no matter what dearer friends may caress thee?"

"Indeed I will," sobbed Diana, "and I'll never have another bosom friend – I don't want to have. I couldn't love anybody as I love you. While I may share my body with boys, I will never share it with another girl. You will remain in my heart forevermore!"

"Oh, Diana," cried Anne, clasping her hands, "do you LOVE me?"

"Why, of course I do. Didn't you know that?"

"No." Anne drew a long breath. "I thought you LIKED me of course, but I never hoped you LOVED me. Why, Diana, I didn't think anybody could love me. Nobody ever has truly loved me since I can remember. Oh, this is wonderful! It's a ray of light which will forever shine on the darkness of a path severed from thee, Diana. Oh, just say it once again."

"I love you devotedly, Anne," said Diana stanchly, "and I always will, you may be sure of that."

"And I will always love thee, Diana," said Anne, solemnly extending her hand to caress the girl's breasts, a gesture of affection. "In the years to come thy memory will shine like a star over my lonely life, as that last story we read together says. Diana, wilt thou give me a lock of thy jet-black tresses in parting to treasure forevermore?"

"Wouldn't you rather have a lock of my curly black pubic hair?"

"Even better," cried Anne, her mind picturing the hidden garden of delight.

"Have you got anything to cut it with?" queried Diana, wiping away the tears and returning to practicalities.

"Yes. I've got my patchwork scissors in my apron pocket fortunately," said Anne.

Diana leaned against a fence post and raised the hem of her dress. She wasn't wearing knickers, having dressed so hurriedly to visit her friend for the last time. "Help yourself," she said, displaying the small jungle of dark follicles.

Anne solemnly clipped a lock of Diana's curls.

"Fare thee well, my beloved friend. Henceforth we must be as strangers though living side by side. But my heart will ever be faithful to thee."

"Would you mind kissing me there," she indicated her nether regions, "as a farewell gesture?"

"With pleasure," said Anne, burrowing her face in Diana's pudendum. Her tongue found its familiar target, the pearl between her friend's lower lips. "M'mmm," she purred with delight.

"Oh yes, that's it, lick it. Make me cum one last time, dear heart."

Anne obliged.

≈≈≈

Later Anne stood and watched Diana out of sight, mournfully waving her hand to the latter whenever she turned to look back. Then she returned to the house, not a little consoled for the time being by this romantic parting.

"It is all over," she informed Matilda. "I shall never have another friend. I'm really worse off than ever before, for I haven't Katie Maurice and Violetta now. And even if I had it wouldn't be the same. Somehow, little dream girls are not satisfying after having a real friend. Diana and I had such an affecting farewell down by the spring. It will be sacred in my memory forever. Diana gave me a lock of her pubic hair and I'm going to sew it up in a little bag and wear it around my neck all my life. Please see that it is buried with me, for I don't believe I'll live very long. Perhaps when she sees me lying cold and dead before her Mrs. Barry may feel remorse for what she has done and will let Diana come to my funeral."

"I don't think there is much fear of your dying of grief as long as you can talk, Anne," said Matilda unsympathetically. "You may want to share that sprig of hair with Martin. He likes keepsakes and treasures the interlude with your friend Diana, even if she WAS drunk at the time."

≈≈≈

The following Monday Anne surprised Matilda by coming down from her room with a bundle of books under her arm, her lips formed into a line of determination. "I'm going back to school," she announced. "That is all there is left in life for me, now that my friend has been ruthlessly torn from me. In school I can look at her and muse over days departed."

"You'd better muse over your lessons," said Matilda, concealing her delight at this development. "If you're going back to school I hope we'll hear no more of breaking slates over people's heads. Behave yourself and do just what your teacher tells you."

"I'll try to be a model pupil," agreed Anne dolefully. "There won't be much fun in it, I expect. Mr. Phillips said Minnie Andrews was a model pupil and there isn't a spark of imagination in her. She is dull and poky and never seems to have a good time. But I feel so depressed that perhaps it will come easy to me now. I'm going round by the road. I couldn't bear to go by the Birch Path on my own."

≈≈≈

Anne was welcomed back to school with open arms. Her imagination had been sorely missed in games, her voice in the singing, and her dramatic ability in reading books aloud during the lunch hour.

Ruby Gillis smuggled three blue plums over to her during the math session. Ella May MacPherson gave her an enormous yellow pansy cut from the covers of a floral catalogue – a species of desk decoration much prized in Avonlea School. Carrie Sloane offered to teach her a perfectly elegant new pattern of knit lace, so nice for trimming aprons. Katie Boulter gave her a perfume bottle to keep slate water in. And Julia Bell copied carefully on a piece of pale pink paper scalloped on the edges the following effusion:

> *When twilight drops her curtain down*
> *And pins it with a star*
> *Remember that you have a friend*
> *Though she may wander far.*

And Prissy Andrews brushed past her in the cloakroom, pressing her large breasts again Anne's arm. They were as pliant as feather pillows. It caused a thrill to run through Anne's loins. If she were to ever have a new bosom friend, Prissy certainly had the bosom for it.

"It's so nice to be appreciated," sighed Anne rapturously to Matilda that night. "I'm happy to be back in school. Even Mr. Phillip was polite to me for a change."

"Perhaps losing you as a student for a while pointed out the error of his ways." That and a lecture from Rita Langston, she thought to herself.

The girls were not the only scholars who "appreciated" her. When Anne went to her seat after the lunch break – she had been told by Mr. Phillips to sit with the "perfect" Minnie Andrews – she found on her desk a luscious red apple. Anne caught it up ready to take a bite when she remembered that the only place in Avonlea where apples this size grew was in the old Blythe orchard on the other side of the Lake of Shining Waters. Anne dropped the apple as if it were a red-hot coal and ostentatiously wiped her fingers on her handkerchief. The apple lay untouched on her desk until the next morning, when little Timothy Andrews, who swept the school and kindled the fire, annexed it as one of his perquisites.

Charlie Sloane's slate pencil, gorgeously bedizened with striped red and yellow paper, costing two cents where ordinary pencils cost only one, which he sent up to her after lunch, met with a more favorable reception.

Anne was graciously pleased to accept it and rewarded the donor with a smile which exalted that infatuated youth straightway into the seventh heaven of delight and caused him to make such fearful errors in his dictation that Mr. Phillips kept him in after school to rewrite it.

But as,

>   *The Caesar's pageant shorn of Brutus' bust*
>   *Did but of Rome's best son remind her more,*

so the marked absence of any recognition from Diana Barry embittered Anne's little triumph.

"Diana might just have smiled at me once, I think," she mourned to Matilda that night. But the next morning a note most wonderfully twisted and folded, along with a small parcel, was passed across to Anne.

Dear Anne (the note read),

Mother says I'm not to play with you or talk to you even in school. It isn't my fault and don't be cross with me, because I love you as much as ever. I miss you awfully to tell all my secrets to and I don't like Gertie Pye one bit. I made you one of the new bookmarkers out of red tissue paper. They are awfully fashionable now and only three girls in school know how to make them. When you look at it remember ...

Your true friend,
Diana Barry

Anne read the note, kissed the bookmark, and dispatched a prompt reply back to the other side of the school.

My own darling Diana:
Of course I am not cross at you because you have to obey your mother. Our spirits can commune. I shall keep your lovely present forever. Minnie Andrews is a very nice little girl – although she has no imagination – but after having been Diana's bosom friend I cannot be Minnie's. Please excuse mistakes because my spelling isn't very good yet, although much improoved.

Yours until death us do part,
Anne or Cordelia Shirley
P.S. I shall sleep with your letter under my pillow tonight.

Matilda pessimistically expected more trouble

since Anne had again begun to go to school. But none developed. Perhaps Anne caught something of the "perfect" spirit from Minnie Andrews; at least she got on very well with Mr. Phillips thenceforth. She flung herself into her studies heart and soul, determined not to be outdone by Gilbert Blythe. The rivalry between them was soon apparent; it was entirely good-natured on Gilbert's side; but the same cannot be said of Anne. The girl had a tenacity for holding grudges. She was as intense in her hatreds as in her loves. She would not stoop to admit that she meant to rival Gilbert in schoolwork, because that would have been to acknowledge his existence ... which Anne persistently ignored. But the rivalry was there and honors fluctuated between them.

Now Gilbert was head of the spelling class; now Anne, with a toss of her head, spelled him down.

One morning Gilbert had all his sums done correctly and had his name written on the blackboard on the roll of honor; the next morning Anne, having wrestled wildly with decimals the evening before, would be first.

One awful day they were tied and their names were written up together. It was almost as bad as a take-notice and Anne's mortification was as evident as Gilbert's satisfaction.

When the written examinations at the end of each month were held, the suspense was terrible. The first month Gilbert came out three marks ahead. The second Anne beat him by five. But her triumph was marred by the fact that Gilbert congratulated her heartily before the whole school. It would have been ever so much sweeter to her if he had felt the sting of his defeat.

Mr. Phillips might not be a very good teacher; but a pupil so inflexibly determined on learning as Anne could hardly escape making progress under any kind of instructor.

By the end of the term Anne and Gilbert were both promoted into the next class and allowed to begin studying Latin, geometry, French, and algebra. However, in geometry Anne met her Waterloo.

"It's perfectly awful stuff, Matilda," she groaned. "I'm sure I'll never be able to make heads or tails of it. There is no scope for imagination in it at all. Mr. Phillips says I'm the worst dunce he ever saw at it. And Gil – I mean some of the others are so smart at it. It is extremely mortifying, Matilda.

"Even Diana gets along better than I do. But I don't mind being beaten by Diana. Although we meet as strangers now, I still love her with an INEXTINGUISHABLE passion. How can you ever forget someone you've been intimate with? It makes me very sad at times to think about Diana. But really, Matilda, one can't stay sad very long in such an interesting world, can one?"

"Come, dear," coaxed Matilda Collins. "Let's go up to the bedroom and be intimate with Martin. You don't want to forget either of us, do you?"

"No, never," said Anne Shirley. "Besides, I'm particularly horny tonight. I want to reach a nice long orgasm."

"Well, I'm just the woman to help you do that."

Anne is redeemed.

CHAPTER XVIII

Anne to the Rescue

All things great are wound up with all things little. At first glance it might not seem that the decision of a certain Canadian Premier to include Prince Edward Island in a political tour could have much to do with the fortunes of little Anne Shirley at Green Gables. But it had.

It was during January the Premier came, to address his loyal supporters at a mass meeting held in Charlottetown. Most of the Avonlea people were on the Premier's side of politics; hence on the night of the meeting nearly all the men and a goodly proportion of the women had gone to see him.

Mrs. Langston had gone too. She was a red-hot politician and failed to believe that the political rally could be carried through without her. So she went to town and took along her husband – Thomas would be useful in looking after the horse – inviting Matilda Collins to go along with her. Matilda thought it might be her only chance to see a real live Premier, so she promptly accompanied the old biddy, leaving Anne and Martin to keep house until her return the following day.

Hence, while Matilda and Mrs. Langston were enjoying themselves hugely at the mass meeting, Anne and Martin had the master bedroom at Green Gables all to themselves. A bright fire was glowing in the old-fashioned Waterloo stove and blue-white frost crystals were shining against the windowpanes. Martin nodded over a *Farmers' Almanac* as he lay against the pillows and Anne sat at the table studying her lessons with grim determination. She wanted to crawl into bed with Martin, but she could not bear the possibility of Gilbert Blythe triumphing over her tomorrow.

"Martin, did you ever study geometry when you went to school?"

"Well now, no, I didn't," said Martin, coming out of his doze with a start.

"I wish you had," sighed Anne, "because then you'd be able to sympathize with me. You can't sympathize properly if you've never studied it. It is casting a cloud over my whole life. I'm such a dunce at it, Martin."

"Well now, I dunno," said Martin soothingly. "You do all right at most anything. Certainly you are an A-1 cocksucker."

"What's that?"

"It mean's you're great at oral sex."

"Oh, I enjoy putting your John Thomas in my mouth. And I love the taste of your cum. Sometimes it tastes like peppermint."

"That due to the mint leaves Matilda puts in our salads. She enjoys the tangy taste of my spunk too."

"I wish geometry were as easy as – what do you call it? – sucking cock."

"You're probably better at geometry than you think. Mr. Phillips told me last week in Blair's store in Carmody that you are the smartest scholar in school and are making rapid progress. 'Rapid progress' was his very words. There's them as runs down Ted Phillips and says he ain't much of a teacher, but I guess he's all right."

Martin would have thought anyone who praised Anne was "all right."

"I'm sure I'd get on better with geometry if only he wouldn't change the letters," complained Anne. "I learn the proposition by heart and then he draws it on the blackboard and puts different letters from what are in the book and I get all mixed up. I don't think a teacher should take such a mean advantage, do you? We're studying agriculture now and I've found out at last what makes the roads red. It's a great comfort. I wonder how Matilda and Mrs. Langston are enjoying themselves. Mrs. Langston says Canada is going to the dogs the way things are being run at Ottawa and that it's an awful warning to the electors. She says if women were allowed to vote we would soon see a blessed change. What way do you vote, Martin?"

"Conservative," said Martin promptly. To vote Conservative was part of Martin's "religion."

"Then I'm Conservative too," said Anne decidedly. "I'm glad because Gil – because some of the boys in school are Grits. I guess Mr. Phillips is a Grit too because Prissy Andrews's father is one, and Ruby Gillis says that when a man is courting he always has to agree with the girl's mother in religion and her father in politics. Is that true, Martin?"

"Well now, I dunno," said Martin, turning the page in his *Farmer's Almanac*.

"Did you ever go courting, Martin?"

"Well no, I never did," said Martin. "Course I've had Matilda as a sexual partner since we was kids. Didn't need to go find a woman to fuck."

"Now you have two," she said, obviously counting herself as a grown-up woman.

"Guess I do," he allowed with a smile.

Anne reflected with her chin in her hands: "It must be rather interesting, don't you think, Martin? Ruby Gillis says when she grows up she's going to have ever so many beaus on the string, all of them crazy about her. But I'd rather have just one, so he can service me day and night. Like you do."

"Happy to oblige. But I'm not exactly a beau. After all, me and Matilda adopted you. We even have a certificate stating so."

"Yes, but you know what I mean. I'm yours to fuck until I grow up and get a real beau. Or maybe a husband."

"Got anybody in mind?" he teased.

"Not yet. But someday my prince will come. I truly believe that."

"I'm sure that will happen in due time. As it is, Matilda and I are happy to share our bed with you, Anne Shirley."

"Wish I had someone to help me study. Mr. Phillips goes up to see Prissy Andrews nearly every evening. He says it is to help her with her lessons but Sophie Sloane is studying for Queen's too, and I should think she needed help a lot more than Prissy because she's ever so much stupider, but he never goes to help her in the evenings at all. There are a great many things in this world that I can't understand very well, Martin."

"I dunno as I comprehend them all myself," acknowledged Martin. "But I don't think it's much of a mystery as to why Teddy Phillips calls on that Andrews girl. She's a fine little piece of ass. A lot of the local fellows are tapping her."

"Tapping?"

"Fucking," he clarified.

"Well, I'd almost be willing to fuck Mr. Phillips if he'd help me with geometry. I suppose I must finish up my lessons. I won't allow myself to open that new book Jane lent me until I'm through. But it's a terrible temptation, Martin. Even when I turn my back on it I can see it there just as plain. Jane said she cried herself sick over it. I love a book that makes me cry. But I think I'll carry that book into the sitting room and lock it in the jam closet and give you the key. And you must NOT give it to me, Martin, until my lessons are done, not even if I implore you on my bended knees."

"If you're on bended knees, my dick will be in your mouth, young lady."

"Oh, Martin, if I didn't have to study I'd come over there and put it in my mouth right this very minute. I like being a – what was it again? – oh yes, a cocksucker."

"Just keep studying."

"Maybe I should take a brief pause and run down to the cellar and get some russets. Wouldn't you like some russets, Martin?"

"Well now, I dunno but what I would," said Martin, who never ate russets but knew Anne's weakness for them.

Just as Anne emerged triumphantly from the cellar with her plateful of russets came the sound of footsteps on the icy walkway outside. The very next moment the kitchen door swung open and in rushed Diana Barry, white-faced and breathless, with a knit shawl wrapped snugly around her shoulders. Anne promptly let go of her candle and plate in her surprise, and plate, candle, and apples crashed together down the cellar ladder and were found at the bottom embedded in melted grease, the next day, by Matilda, who gathered them up and thanked mercy the house hadn't been set on fire.

"Whatever is the matter, Diana?" cried Anne. "Has your mother relented at last?"

"Oh, Anne, do come quick," implored Diana nervously. "Minnie May is awful sick – she's got croup. Father and Mother are at the meeting in town and there's nobody to fetch the doctor. Minnie May is awful bad – and oh, Anne, I'm so scared!"

Martin had come down the stairs to check on the commotion. Without a word, he reached for his cap and coat, slipped past Diana and disappeared into the darkness of the yard.

"He's gone to harness the sorrel mare to go to Carmody for the doctor," said Anne, who was pulling on her jacket. "I know it as well as if he'd said so. Martin and I are such kindred spirits I can read his thoughts without words at all."

"I don't believe he'll find the doctor at Carmody," sobbed Diana. "I know that Dr. Blair went to town for the big political meeting and I would guess Dr. Spencer went too. Me and the babysitter never saw anybody with croup and we don't know what to do. Oh, Anne, I'm so scared!"

"Don't cry, Diana," said Anne. "I know exactly what to do for croup. You forget that Mrs. Hammond had twins three times. When you look after three pairs of twins you naturally get a lot of experience. They all had croup regularly. Just wait till I get the ipecac bottle – you mayn't have any at your house. Come on now. Your sister will be okay."

The two girls hurried through Lover's Lane and across the crusted field beyond, for the snow was too deep to go by the shorter way through the woods. Anne, although sincerely sorry for Minnie May, was swept up with the romance of the situation and to the sweetness of once more sharing that romance with Diana.

The night was clear and frosty, shadows reflecting on the snowy slopes. Big stars were shining over the silent fields, like a Christmas tree in the sky. Here and there stood pointed firs with snow powdering their branches and the wind whistling through them. Anne thought it was truly delightful to go skimming through all this loveliness with her bosom friend who had been so long estranged.

Minnie May, aged three, was really very sick. She lay on the sofa feverish and restless, while her hoarse breathing could be heard all over the house. Margaux, a buxom, broad-faced French girl from the creek, whom Mrs. Barry had engaged to stay with the children during her absence, was bewildered, not knowing what to do.

Anne went to work with skill and promptness. "Minnie May has croup all right; she's got it pretty bad, but I've seen worse. First, we must have lots of hot water. I declare, Diana, there isn't more than a cupful in the kettle! There, I've filled it up, and, Margaux, you may put some wood in the stove. I don't want to hurt your feelings but it seems to me you might have thought of this before if you'd any imagination. Now, I'll undress Minnie May and put her to bed and you try to find some soft flannel cloths, Diana. I'm going to give her a dose of ipecac first of all."

Minnie May did not take kindly to the ipecac but Anne had not brought up three pairs of twins for nothing. Down that ipecac went, not only once, but many times during the long, anxious night when the two little girls worked patiently over the suffering Minnie May. And, Margaux, honestly anxious to do all she could, kept up a roaring fire and heated more water than would have been needed for a hospital of croupy babies.

It was three o'clock when Martin came with a doctor, for he had been obliged to go all the way to Spencervale for one. But the pressing need for assistance was past. Minnie May was much better and sleeping soundly.

"I was awfully near giving up in despair," explained Anne. "She got worse and worse until she was sicker than ever the Hammond twins were, even the last pair. I actually thought she was going to choke to death. I gave her every drop of ipecac in that bottle and when the last dose went down I said to myself – not to Diana or Margaux, because I didn't want to worry them any more than they were worried, but I had to say it to myself just to relieve my feelings – 'This is the last lingering hope and I fear, tis a vain one.' But in about three minutes she coughed up the phlegm and began to get better right away. You must just imagine my relief, doctor, because I can't express it in words. You know there are some things that cannot be expressed in words."

"Yes, I know," nodded the doctor. He looked at Anne as if he were thinking some things about her that couldn't be expressed in words. Later on, however, he expressed them to Mr. and Mrs. Barry.

"That little girl they have over at Collins's is as smart as they make 'em. I tell you she saved that baby's life, for it would have been too late by the time I got there. She seems to have a skill and presence of mind perfectly wonderful in a youngster her age. I never saw anything like it. You owe her your child's life."

Anne had gone home in the wonderful, white-frosted winter morning, heavy eyed from loss of sleep, but still talking unweariedly to Martin as they crossed the white field and walked under the glittering fairy arch of the Lover's Lane maples: "Oh, Martin, isn't it a wonderful morning? The world looks like something God had just imagined for His own pleasure, doesn't it? Those trees look as if I could blow them away with a breath – pouf! I'm so glad I live in a world where there are white frosts, aren't you? And I'm so glad Mrs. Hammond had three pairs of twins after all. If she hadn't I mightn't have known what to do for Minnie May. I'm real sorry I was ever cross with Mrs. Hammond for having twins. But, oh, Martin, I'm so sleepy. I can't go to school. I just know I couldn't keep my eyes open and I'd be so stupid. But I hate to stay home, for Gil – some of the others will get head of the class, and it's so hard to get up again – although the harder it is the more satisfaction you have when you do get up, haven't you?"

"Well now, I guess you'll manage all right," said

Martin, looking at Anne's white little face and the dark shadows under her eyes. "You just go right to bed and have a good sleep. I'll do all the chores."

Anne accordingly went to bed and slept so long and soundly that it was well on in the chilly winter afternoon when she awoke and descended to the kitchen where Matilda, who had arrived home in the meantime, was sitting knitting.

"Oh, did you see the Premier?" exclaimed Anne at once. "What did he look like, Matilda?"

"Well, he never got to be Premier on account of his looks," said Matilda. "Such a nose that man had! But he can speak. I was proud of being a Conservative. Rita Langston, of course, being a Liberal, had no use for him. Your lunch is in the oven, Anne, and you can get yourself some blue plum preserve out of the pantry. I guess you're hungry. Martin has been telling me about last night. I must say it was fortunate you knew what to do. I wouldn't have had any idea myself, for I never saw a case of croup. There now, never mind talking till you've had your food. I can tell by the look of you that you're just full up with speeches, but they'll keep."

Matilda had something to tell Anne, but she did not tell it just then for she knew if she did Anne's consequent excitement would lift her clear out of the region of such material matters as appetite or food.

Not until Anne had finished her saucer of blue plums did Matilda say: "Mrs. Barry was here this afternoon, Anne. She wanted to see you, but I wouldn't wake you up. She says you saved Minnie May's life, and she is very sorry she acted as she did in that affair of the currant wine. She says she knows now you didn't mean

232

to get Diana drunk, and she hopes you'll forgive her and be good friends with Diana again. You're to go over this evening if you like for Diana can't stir outside the door on account of a bad cold she caught last night. Now, Anne Shirley, for pity's sake don't fly up into the air."

The warning seemed not unnecessary, so uplifted and aerial was Anne's expression and attitude as she sprang to her feet, her face irradiated with the flame of her spirit.

"Oh, Matilda, can I go right now – without washing my dishes? I'll wash them when I come back, but I cannot tie myself down to anything so unromantic as dishwashing at this thrilling moment."

"Yes, yes, run along," said Matilda indulgently. "Anne Shirley – are you crazy? Come back this instant and put something on you. I might as well call to the wind. She's gone without a cap or wrap. Look at her tearing through the orchard with her hair streaming. It'll be a mercy if she doesn't catch her death of cold."

Martin smiled. "You're just lucky she's wearing any clothes at all. You know how she likes to go naked."

"Not so much in the winter – although the other day I did catch her out in the snow with nary a stitch on. She said she liked the tingle of snowflakes on her bare skin."

≈≈≈

Anne came dancing home in the purple winter twilight across the snowy landscape. Afar in the southwest sky was the pearl-like sparkle of an evening star. The sky itself was a hue of pale gold and ethereal rose over the gleaming white fields and dark glens of spruce. The tinkles of sleigh bells among the snowy hills came like elfin chimes through the frosty air. But nothing was sweeter than the song in Anne's heart.

"You see before you a perfectly happy person, Matilda," she announced. "I'm perfectly happy – yes, in spite of being raised as a poor orphan. Just moments ago Mrs. Barry kissed me and cried and said she was so sorry and she could never repay me. I felt fearfully embarrassed, Matilda, but I just said as politely as I could, 'I have no hard feelings for you, Mrs. Barry. I assure you that I did not mean to intoxicate Diana and henceforth let us cover the past with the mantle of oblivion.' That was a pretty dignified way of speaking wasn't it, Matilda?"

"I barely understand you myself," admitted Matilda.

"Diana and I had a lovely afternoon. Diana showed me a new fancy crochet stitch her aunt over at Carmody taught her. Not a soul in Avonlea knows it but us, and we pledged a solemn vow never to reveal it to anyone else. Diana gave me a beautiful card with a wreath of roses on it and a verse of poetry:

> *"If you love me as I love you*
> *Nothing but death can part us two.*

"And that is true, Matilda. We're going to ask Mr. Phillips to let us sit together in school again, and Gertie Pye can go with Minnie Andrews. We had an elegant tea. Mrs. Barry had the very best china set out, just as if I was real company. I can't tell you what a thrill it gave me. Nobody ever used their very best china on my account before. And we had fruitcake and pound cake and doughnuts and two kinds of preserves. And Mrs. Barry asked me if I took tea and said, 'Pa, why don't you pass the biscuits to Anne?' It must be lovely to be grown up, treated so nice."

"I don't know about that," said Matilda, with a brief sigh.

"Well, anyway, when I am grown up," said Anne decidedly, "I'm always going to talk to little girls as if they were grown up too, and I'll never laugh when they use big words. I know from sorrowful experience how that hurts one's feelings. After tea Diana and I made taffy. The taffy wasn't very good, I suppose because neither Diana nor I had ever made any before. Diana left me to stir it while she buttered the plates and I forgot and let it burn; and then when we set it out on the platform to cool the cat walked over one plate and that had to be thrown away. But the making of it was splendid fun. Then when I left Mrs. Barry invited me to come over as often as I could and Diana stood at the window and threw kisses to me all the way down to Lover's Lane. I assure you, Matilda, that I'm going to say a very special prayer tonight in honor of the occasion."

"That's nice."

"Oh, I'm so excited. I'm going to be extra passionate in bed tonight to show you and Martin how happy I feel."

"That's *very* nice," said the blonde woman.

Giving in to the headmaster.

CHAPTER XIX

A Concert and a Confession

"**M**atilda, can I go over to see Diana just for a minute?" asked Anne, running breathlessly down from the east gable one February evening.

"I don't see what you want to be traipsing about after dark for," said Matilda shortly. "You and Diana walked home from school together and then stood down there in the snow for half an hour more, your tongues going the whole blessed time, clickety-clack. So I don't think you're very badly off to see her again."

"But she wants to see me," pleaded Anne. "She has something very important to tell me."

"How do you know that?"

"Because she just signaled to me from her window. We have arranged a way to signal with our candles and cardboard. We set the candle on the windowsill and make flashes by passing the cardboard back and forth. So many flashes mean a certain thing. It was my idea, Matilda."

"Oh, I'm sure it was you," nodded Matilda emphatically. "And the next thing you'll be setting fire to the curtains with your signaling nonsense."

"Oh, we're very careful, Matilda. And it's so interesting. Two flashes mean, 'Are you there?' Three mean 'yes' and four 'no.' Five mean, 'Come over as soon as possible, because I have something important to reveal.' Diana has just signaled five flashes, and I'm really suffering to know what it is."

"Well, you needn't suffer any longer," said Matilda sarcastically. "You can go, but you're to be back here in just ten minutes, remember that."

Anne did remember it and was back in the stipulated time, although probably no mortal will ever know just what it cost her to confine the discussion of Diana's important communication within the limits of ten minutes. But at least she had made good use of them.

"Oh, Matilda, what do you think? You know tomorrow is Diana's birthday. Well, her mother told her she could ask me to go home with her from school and stay all night with her. And her cousins are coming over from Newbridge in a big sleigh to go to the Debating Club concert at the hall tomorrow night. And they are going to take Diana and me to the concert – if you'll let me go, that is. You will, won't you, Matilda? Oh, I feel so excited."

"You can calm down then, because you're not going. You're better at home in bed with me and Martin. And as for that concert, it's all nonsense, and little girls should not be allowed to go out to such places at all."

"I'm sure the Debating Club is a most respectable affair," pleaded Anne.

"I'm not saying it isn't. But you're not going to begin gadding about to concerts and staying out all hours of the night. Pretty doings for young girls. I'm surprised Mrs. Barry's letting Diana go."

"But it's such a very special occasion," mourned Anne, on the verge of tears. "Diana has only one birthday in a year. It isn't as if birthdays were common things, Matilda. Prissy Andrews is going to recite 'Curfew Must Not Ring Tonight.' That is such a good moral piece, Matilda, I'm sure it would do me lots of good to hear it. And the choir is going to sing four lovely songs that are pretty near as good as hymns. And oh, Matilda, the minister is going to take part; yes, indeed, he is. He's going to give an address on the virtues of a good life. That's almost the same thing as a sermon. Please, mayn't I go, Matilda?"

"You heard what I said, Anne, didn't you? Take off your clothes now and go to bed. Martin will be waiting for us up there."

"There's just one more thing, Matilda," said Anne, with the air of producing an ace from the deck. "Mrs. Barry told Diana that we might sleep in the spare bedroom. Think of the honor of your little Anne being put in the spare bedroom at the Barrys' house."

"It's an honor you'll have to get along without. Go to bed, Anne, and don't let me hear another word out of you. When I get up there, you can put your tongue to better use."

Anne, with tears rolling over her cheeks, went tearing up the steps. Great sobs echoed down the stairwell in her wake. A few minutes later Martin came downstairs, a solemn expression on his face.

"Did she send you as an emissary to plead her case," sighed his sister.

"Not exactly, Matilda. But I do think you ought to let Anne go."

"Who's bringing this child up, Martin, you or me?" retorted Matilda. He could tell she was irked.

"Well now, you," admitted Martin.

"Don't interfere then."

"Well now, it ain't interfering to have your own opinion. And my opinion is that you ought to let Anne go."

"I've no doubt you'd think I ought to let Anne go to the moon if she took the notion," came Matilda's rejoinder. "I might have let her spend the night with Diana, if that was all it was. But I don't approve of this concert plan. She'd go there and get her head filled with nonsense. It would unsettle her for a week. I understand that girl's disposition and what's good for it better than you, Martin."

"I think you ought to let Anne go," repeated Martin firmly. Argument was not his strong point, but holding fast to his opinion certainly was.

Matilda gave a gasp of helplessness and took refuge in silence.

There was no sex for anybody that night. Anne slept in her own room. Martin and his sister kept to their respective sides of the bed.

≈≈≈

The next morning, when Anne was washing the breakfast dishes in the pantry, Martin paused on his way out to the barn to say to Matilda again: "I think you ought to let Anne go, Matilda."

For a moment Matilda got angry. Then yielding to the inevitable, she replied tartly: "Very well, she can go, since nothing else will please you."

Having overheard them, Anne came flying out of the pantry with a dripping dishcloth in her hand. "Oh, Matilda, Matilda, say those blessed words again."

"I guess once is enough to say them. This is

Martin's doings and I wash my hands of it. If you catch pneumonia sleeping in a strange bed or coming out of that hot hall in the middle of the night, don't blame me, blame Martin."

"Yes, whatever you say."

Matilda stamped her foot. "Anne Shirley, you're dripping greasy water all over the floor. I never saw such a careless girl."

"Oh, I know I'm a great trial to you, Matilda," said Anne repentantly. "I make so many mistakes. But then just think of all the mistakes I don't make, although I might. And you've got to admit I perform well in bed. Martin says I'm a great little cocksucker. And you like it when I find your pearl."

"That is true," the blonde woman admitted.

"Don't worry, I'll scrub up the spots before I go to school. Oh, Matilda, my heart was just set on going to that concert. I've never been to a concert in my whole life, and when the other girls talk about them in school I feel so out of it. You didn't know just how important it is for me to go, but Martin did. Martin understands me, and it's so nice to be understood, Matilda."

"I'm glad someone in this household is understood," she sighed.

≈≈≈

Anne was much too excited to do herself justice with her lessons that morning in school. Gilbert Blythe spelled her down in class and left her clear out of sight in arithmetic. Anne's consequent humiliation was less than it might have been, however, in view of going to the concert and sleeping with Diana in the Barrys' spare bedroom. She and Diana talked so constantly about it all day that a stricter teacher than Mr. Phillips might have dished out dire punishment.

Anne felt that she could not have borne it if she had not been going to the concert, for nothing else was discussed that day in school. The Avonlea Debating Club, which met fortnightly all winter, had had several smaller free entertainments; but this was to be a big affair, admission ten cents, in aid of the library. The Avonlea young people had been practicing for weeks, and all the scholars were especially interested in it by reason of older brothers and sisters who were going to take part. Everybody in school over nine years of age expected to go, except Carrie Sloane, whose father shared Matilda's opinions about small girls going out to night concerts. Carrie Sloane cried into her grammar textbook all the afternoon, convinced that life was not worth living.

For Anne the real excitement began with the dismissal of school for the rest of the day and culminated with the positive ecstasy of attending the concert. Anne and Diana started off the afternoon with a "perfectly elegant tea" – and then came the fun of getting dressed for the concert in Diana's little room upstairs. Diana did Anne's hair in the new pompadour style and Anne tied Diana's bows with the special knack she possessed. They paused now and then to kiss, using their tongues. At last they were ready, cheeks scarlet and eyes glowing with excitement.

True, Anne could not help a little pang when she contrasted her shapeless, homemade dress with Diana's smart gown. But she remembered that she had an imagination and could use it to imagine her own finery.

Then Diana's cousins, the Murrays from Newbridge, arrived. They all crowded into the big pung sleigh, among heaps of straw and furry robes. Anne reveled in the drive to the hall, the runners slipping along the satin-smooth roads that were layered with crisp snow. Tinkles of sleigh bells and distant laughter, that seemed like the mirth of wood elves, came from every quarter.

"Oh, Diana," breathed Anne, squeezing Diana's mittened hand under the fur robe, "isn't it all like a beautiful dream? Do I really look the same as usual? I feel so different that it seems to me it must show in my looks."

"You look awfully nice," said Diana, who having just received a compliment from one of her cousins, felt that she ought to pass it on. "You've got the loveliest color."

Diana's cousin Tommy Murray was sitting on the far side of Anne. The sleigh was bouncing along the snowy road behind the horses. About halfway to the concert, Tommy snuggled closer, his hand landing on Anne's thigh. "Ooo," she said.

"What was that?" asked Diana.

"Nothing. Just a bump in the road."

"It's so thrilling, isn't it? Racing through the night behind two powerful dray horses."

"Yes, thrilling," Anne repeated as she felt Tommy's fingers slide under the hem of her dress and work its way up to her panties. They were her very best pair, made of real silk, a gift from Martin. She hoped Tommy's clumsy fingers wouldn't tear them. She might never get another pair made of silk. Nonetheless, she didn't resist as he wedged a finger under the smooth fabric to explore the nest of her pubis. She felt a tremor run through her body as he touched her holy of holies.

"Are you comfortable, Miss Anne?" he asked, code for permission to go farther.

"Yes, quite," she replied politely, flashing a smile in his direction.

She felt his index finger push past her labia, entering her. She was already wet with anticipation. "Ummm," she said as the digit slid in and out, in and out.

"What did you say?" asked Diana, distracted by the tinkling bells on the horses.

"I said, what a wonderful night." She shut her eyes and let Tommy do his ministrations. It was like when she snuggled under the covers with boys at the orphanage, letting them finger her to orgasm.

It didn't take Tommy long to do just that. "Agggh," she muffled a scream as she felt the Big O wash over her.

"Are you all right?" inquired Diana. "Do you have a tummy ache? We shouldn't have eat all that fudge this afternoon."

"Yes, the fudge," Anne said as Tommy's finger retreated.

≈≈≈

The program that night was a series of thrills for at least one listener in the audience, and, as Anne assured Diana, every succeeding thrill was thrillier than the last.

When Prissy Andrews made her appearance, she

looked as radiant as an angel sent down from Heaven. She was attired in a pink silk gown, cut so low her oversized boson was practically spilling out of the taffeta flange. A string of pearls adored her smooth white throat. Real carnations decorated her hair – it was rumored that the headmaster sent all the way to Charlottetown for them for her. Anne shivered with envy; if only she could be as beautiful as the blonde girl.

And when Mr. Phillips gave Mark Antony's oration over the dead body of Caesar in the most heart-stirring tones – looking at Prissy Andrews at the end of every sentence – Anne felt that she could rise and mutiny on the spot if but one Roman citizen led the way.

Only one number on the program failed to interest her. When Gilbert Blythe recited "Bingen on the Rhine," Anne picked up a library book and read it until he had finished, then sat rigidly stiff while Diana and the rest of the audience clapped their hands in thunderous applause.

≈≈≈

Afterwards, Diana and her cousins led Anne backstage to congratulate the performers. While they crowded around Gilbert Blythe, she wandered over to tell Mr. Phillips how much she'd enjoyed his stirring oration.

"Why thank you, Miss Shirley. I must say you've become my star pupil."

"What about Gil – uh, Gilbert Blythe?"

"He's good, but you have so much more potential."

"Me – potential?"

"Indeed. Perhaps you'd like some special tutoring?"

"I thought you were busy tutoring Prissy Andrews for Queen's Academy."

"Oh, I am. But I could make time for you, Miss Shirley."

"Can't you call me Anne when we're not in school?" she interjected.

"Of course I can, Annie."

"Anne," she corrected. "With an E."

"Anne with an E it is. Want to step over there in the storage room to discuss some lesson plans? We'd have more privacy there."

Anne glanced around, but didn't see Prissy. "Don't you have someone to take home?"

"You mean Miss Andrews? She will be tied up for the next twenty minutes with her admirers. Her recitation tonight drew much attention."

"That and her low-cut gown."

"Prissy does have magnificent tits, doesn't she?"

"I wish mine were that nice."

"Oh, but they are. Not as large as Prissy's, but more perfectly formed."

That stopped her. "How do you know that?"

"I saw you that day down by the lake when you took off your blouse and showed your titties to Charlie Sloane. I was taking the shortcut back from lunch at Eben Wright's house where I board."

"I'm so embarrassed."

"Don't be. I found the sight of your titties very exhilarating."

"Thank you."

"Shall we step into the storage room?"

"Why not?" said Anne with an E.

≈ ≈ ≈

In the cluttered storage room, Ted Phillips wasted no time, stripping her naked without asking permission. After all, he had to hurry before Prissy Andrews came looking for her escort to take her home.

Anne didn't protest. She found it exciting for the headmaster of her school to be gazing on her bared body with a countenance of lust. "Do you like what you see?" she asked.

"Indeed I do. I think you are about to get straight A's on your next report card."

"I'd like that. What can I do to earn those grades?"

"You could let me fuck you."

"I must warn you I'm not a virgin. So there would be no cherry to pop like with my friend Diana."

"So I was her first?"

"But not her last."

"Yes, I've seen her name carved there on the porch."

"So perhaps you'd like me to do something else. Suck your cock perhaps? I'm told I'm quite good at that?"

"Go ahead. Think of this as earning extra credit."

Anne unbuttoned his trousers and removed his stiff member. Wrapping her lips around it, she set to the task. She worked her frizzy head up and down with a steady rhythm, hardly able to believe she had her teacher's John Thomas in her pretty little mouth.

Klang!

Her concentration was interrupted by the sound of the storage room door banging open. Ted Phillips's rigid staff slipped from her lips as he turned to face the intruder. "Oh, there you are, Prissy," he said without a trace of embarrassment. "Anne and I were just killing time while waiting for you to tear yourself away from your adoring fans."

"Fans!" sniffed the busty blonde. "Those boys just wanted to stare down the front of my dress."

"Can't blame them," grinned Ted Phillips. "Why don't you lock the door and join us?"

"You're going to fuck Anne Shirley? She's such an egghead."

Anne spoke up in her own defense. "Just because I'm smart does not mean I'm a bad lay. As a matter of fact, I am the best cocksucker on Prince Edward Island."

"Better than me?" Prissy asked the headmaster.

"I have to admit she was doing a damn fine job when you walked in."

"Well, we'll just see about that," exclaimed Prissy, reaching back to unsnap her gown. The large breasts came tumbling out, wide pink nipples on display.

"Oh my," said Anne, transfixed by the sight. She'd never seen boobies as big as these. Watermelons indeed.

"Move aside," commanded Prissy. "I'm going to suck Teddy's brains out his dick."

Anne blinked her eyes excitedly. "Before you do that, Prissy, would you mind if I touch your breasts? I've never seen such magnificent orbs before."

Prissy thrust out her bosom, invitingly. "Sure, go ahead, you silly cunt. Practically all the boys in Avonlea School have felt me up. Why not a girl too?"

Anne reached out and weighed the fleshy mounds

in her hands, as if inspecting produce at William J. Blair's store over in Carmody. "Nice," she whispered, amazed by their weight. "But don't those heavy bazongas give you a backache."

"Sometimes. But I frequently wear a corset that offers some support. Teddy dislikes my corset though. He hates helping me lace it back up after we fuck."

"Would you mind if I let him fuck me? I've never been fucked by a teacher. I think I'd find it a most interesting experience."

"Oh, go ahead," shrugged Prissy, a gesture that made her breasts bounce in Anne's palms. "I can suck his dick any ol' time. I think I'd like to watch a goody two-shoes like you get fucked. Let's see if how far you'll go. Sometimes I let Teddy fuck me in the ass."

"I've let Martin fuck me in the ass too," declared Anne, her competitiveness getting the better of her.

"Martin? You let Martin Collins fuck you?" Prissy stepped back, just out of Anne's reach, the interlude over.

"Uh, did I say Martin? I mean to say Marvin. Marvin was a custodian at the orphan's orphanage I came from," she lied.

Prissy smiled to show she recognized prevarication when she heard it. "Martin Collins fucked me one time," she said. "I was about fifteen as I recall. He's got a very big dick. You ought to try it if you haven't. It's not like he's your real father."

"I wish he were," mused Anne, dreamily. She barely noticed when Ted Phillips entered her, his thick member forcing her labia apart as if pushing past a heavy curtain.

"How's that?" he asked, once he got the in-and-out movement going. "Does it feel good?"

"Oh yes," breathed Anne, almost as if experiencing pain. "I think I like being tutored by you."

≈≈≈

It was close to eleven o'clock when the entourage got home, sated with dissipation, but with the exceedingly sweet pleasure of talking it all over still again on the sleigh ride back to Barry's Pond. Everybody seemed asleep and the house was dark and silent. Anne and Diana tiptoed into the parlor, a long narrow room out of which the spare bedroom opened. It was pleasantly warm and dimly lighted by the embers of a fire in the grate.

"Let's undress here," said Diana. "It's so nice and warm."

"Hasn't it been a delightful time?" sighed Anne rapturously. "It must be splendid to get up and recite at the Debate Club concert. Do you suppose we will ever be asked to do it, Diana?"

"Yes, of course, someday. They're always wanting the big scholars to recite. Gilbert Blythe does often and he's only two years older than us. Oh, Anne, how could you pretend not to listen to him? When he came to the line, *'There's another, not a sister,'* he looked right down at you."

"Diana," said Anne with dignity, "you are my bosom friend, but I cannot allow even you to speak to me of that horrid person. He does not exist in my world. Are you ready for bed? Let's run a race and see who'll get to the bed first."

The suggestion appealed to Diana. The two naked

figures flew down the long room and bounded onto the bed at the same moment.

And then – something – moved beneath them. There was a muffled gasp – and somebody exclaimed: "Merciful goodness!"

Anne and Diana were never able to tell just how they got off that bed and out of the room. They only knew that after a frantic rush they found themselves tiptoeing up the stairs, shivering in the winter's chill without any clothing.

"Oh, who was it – WHAT was it?" whispered Anne, her teeth chattering with cold and fright.

"It was Aunt Josephine," said Diana, gasping with laughter. "Oh, Anne, it was Aunt Josephine. However she came to be there I have no idea. Oh, she will be furious. It's dreadful – it's really dreadful – but did you ever know anything so funny, Anne?"

"Who is Aunt Josephine?"

"She's my father's aunt and she lives in Charlottetown. She's awfully old – seventy anyhow – and I don't believe she was EVER a little girl. We were expecting her to come out for a visit, but not so soon. She's awfully prim and proper and she'll scold us dreadfully about this. Well, we'll just have to sleep with Minnie May – and you can't imagine how that child kicks."

"What are you girls doing out in the hall way without a stitch on?" came a masculine voice. They practically jumped out of their skin. It was Tommy Murray, the boy who had been so saucily familiar with Anne on the ride to the concert.

"Oh goodness, do not look upon us," shrieked

Diana, *sotto voce*. "We're forced to bunk with my baby sister because Aunt Josephine took our bed."

"You two don't have to bed down with that little brat. Come into my and Jimmy's room. You can stay with us."

"Your and Jimmy's room. I think you're referring to my bedroom that I gave up during your visit."

"Then it's your rightful place. Come along, Jimmy will be delighted to see those big titties of yours, Cousin Diana. He's always fancied you."

"Me? I'm his blood kin."

"He doesn't want to marry you – just fuck you. And I'd like to finish what I started with your pretty friend Anne."

"Started with Anne – when was that?"

"On the sleigh ride to the concert. I fingered her under the blanket. Didn't you notice? She was near to fainting when I got her going."

"I thought she had a tummy ache."

"More like a Tommy ache."

"You bad boy, do you and your brother think we're going to crawl in bed with you boys and let you pork us like we're farm breeding stock?"

"I certainly hope so, lest my dick swells to bursting while I stand here looking at your titties."

"Diana, don't tease your cousin so. I for one would like Tommy to finish the job he started in the sleigh," declared Anne.

"Oh, alright," relented her friend. "Wake Jimmy up. Truth is, I've always fancied him too. Nobody is going to get sleep tonight!"

≈≈≈

Miss Josephine Barry did not appear at breakfast the next morning. Mrs. Barry smiled kindly at the two girls.

"Did you have a good time last night? I tried to stay awake until you came home, for I wanted to tell you that Aunt Josephine had come and you would have to go upstairs after all, but I was so tired I fell asleep. I hope you didn't disturb your aunt, Diana."

Diana preserved a discreet silence, but she and Anne exchanged furtive smiles across the table. Anne hurried home after breakfast and thus remained in blissful ignorance of the hubbub within the Barry household until that afternoon when she went to Mrs. Langston's on an errand for Matilda.

"I hear you and Diana nearly frightened her poor old Aunt Josephine to death last night," said Mrs. Langston with a twinkle in her eye. "Mrs. Barry was here a few minutes ago on her way to Carmody. She's feeling real worried over it. Old Josephine was in a terrible temper when she got up this morning – and her temper is no joke, I can tell you that. She wouldn't speak to Diana at all."

"It wasn't Diana's fault," said Anne contritely. "It was mine. I suggested racing to see who would get into bed first."

"I knew it!" said Mrs. Langston, with the exultation of a correct guesser. "I knew that idea came out of your head. Well, it's made a nice lot of trouble, that's what. Diane's Aunt Josephine came out to stay for a month, but she declares she won't stay another day and is going right back to town tomorrow. They pleaded for her to stay, but she's resolute. The old woman had promised to pay for music lessons for Diana, but now she refuses to do anything at all for such a tomboy."

"This is terrible."

"Oh, I guess they had a lively time of it there this morning. The old woman is rich and they'd like to keep on the good side of her. Of course, Mrs. Barry didn't say exactly that to me, but I'm a pretty good judge of human nature, that's what."

"I feel horrible."

"To make matters worse, those two Murray boys broke Diana's bed last night while wrestling around."

"I'm such an unlucky girl," mourned Anne. "I'm always getting into scrapes myself and getting my best friends – people I'd shed my heart's blood for – into trouble too. Can you tell me why it is so, Mrs. Langston?"

"It's because you're too heedless and impulsive, that's what. You never stop to think – whatever comes into your head to say or do, you say or do it without a moment's reflection."

"Oh, but that's the best of it," protested Anne. "Something just flashes into your mind, so exciting, and you must be out with it. If you stop to think it over you spoil it. Haven't you never felt that yourself, Mrs. Langston?"

No, Mrs. Langston had not. She shook her head sagely as she said, "You must learn to think a little, Anne, that's what. The proverb you need to go by is 'Look before you leap' – especially into spare-room beds."

Mrs. Langston laughed comfortably over her mild joke, but Anne remained pensive. She saw nothing to laugh at in the situation, which to her eyes appeared very serious. When she left Mrs. Langston's she made her way across the crusted fields to Orchard Slope. Diana met her at the kitchen door.

"Your Aunt Josephine was very cross about it, wasn't she?" whispered Anne.

"Yes," answered Diana, stifling a giggle with an apprehensive glance over her shoulder at the closed sitting-room door. "She was fairly dancing with rage, Anne. Oh, how she scolded. She said I was the worst-behaved girl she ever saw and that my parents ought to be ashamed of the way they had brought me up. She says she won't stay and I'm sure I don't care. But Father and Mother do."

"Why didn't you tell them it was my fault?" demanded Anne.

"Do you think it's likely I'd do such a thing?" said Diana with just scorn. "I'm no telltale, Anne Shirley, and anyhow I was just as much to blame as you."

"Well, I'm going in to tell her myself," said Anne resolutely.

Diana stared. "Anne Shirley, you'd never! Why – she'll eat you alive!"

"Don't frighten me any more than I am," implored Anne. "I'd rather walk up to a cannon's mouth. But I've got to do it, Diana. It was my fault and I've got to confess. I've had practice in confessing, fortunately."

"Well, she's in the room," said Diana. "You can go in if you want to. I wouldn't dare. And I don't believe you'll do a bit of good."

With this faint encouragement Anne bearded the lion in its den – that is to say, walked resolutely up to the sitting-room door and knocked. A sharp "Come in" followed.

Miss Josephine Barry, thin, prim, and rigid, was knitting fiercely by the fire, her wrath quite unappeased and her eyes snapping through her gold-rimmed glasses.

She wheeled around in her chair, expecting to see Diana, and beheld a white-faced girl whose great eyes were brimmed up with a mixture of desperate courage and shrinking terror.

"Who are you?" demanded Aunt Josephine without ceremony.

"I'm Anne of Green Gables," said the small visitor tremulously, clasping her hands together as if trying to hold together her courage, "and I've come to confess, if you please."

"Confess what?"

"That it was all my fault about jumping into bed on you last night. I suggested it. Diana would never have thought of such a thing, I am sure. Diana is a very ladylike girl, Miss Barry. So you must see how unjust it is to blame her."

"Oh, I must, hey? I rather think Diana did her share of the jumping at least. Such carryings on in a respectable house!"

"But we were only having fun," persisted Anne. "I think you ought to forgive us, Miss Barry, now that we've apologized. And anyhow, please forgive Diana and let her have her music lessons. Diana's heart is set on her music lessons, Miss Barry, and I know too well what it is to set your heart on a thing and not get it. If you must be cross with anyone, be cross with me. I've been so used to having people cross at me that I can endure it much better than Diana can."

Much of the snap had gone out of the old lady's eyes by this time and was replaced by a twinkle of amused interest. But she still said severely: "I don't think it is any excuse for you that you were only having fun. Little girls never indulged in that kind of fun when I was young. You don't know what it is to be awakened out of a sound sleep, after a long and arduous journey, by two naughty girls bouncing down on you."

"I don't KNOW, but I can IMAGINE," said Anne eagerly. "I'm sure it must have been very disturbing. But then, there is our side of it too. Have you any imagination, Miss Barry? If you have, just put yourself in our place. We didn't know there was anybody in that bed and you nearly scared us to death. It was simply awful the way we felt. And then we couldn't sleep in the spare bedroom after being promised. I suppose you are used to sleeping in spare bedrooms. But just imagine what you would feel like if you were a little orphan girl who had never had such an honor."

All the snap had gone by this time. Miss Barry actually laughed – a sound that caused Diana, waiting in speechless anxiety in the kitchen outside, to give a great gasp of relief.

"I'm afraid my imagination is a little rusty – it's so long since I used it," she said. "I dare say your claim to sympathy is just as strong as mine. It all depends on the way we look at it. Sit down here and tell me about yourself."

"I am very sorry I can't," said Anne firmly. "I would like to, because you seem like an interesting lady, and you might even be a kindred spirit although you don't look very much like it. But it is my duty to go straight home to Miss Matilda Collins. Miss Matilda Collins is a very kind lady who has adopted me in order to bring me up properly. She is doing her best, but it is very discouraging work. You must not blame her because I jumped on the bed. But before I go I do wish you would tell me if you will forgive Diana and stay just as long as you meant to in the first place."

"I think perhaps I will if you will come over and talk to me occasionally," said Miss Barry.

"Yes, I would enjoy doing that."

"Very well, off with you then. I must get back to my knitting."

≈ ≈ ≈

That evening Miss Josephine Barry gave Diana a silver bangle bracelet and told the senior members of the household that she had unpacked her valise.

"I've made up my mind to stay simply for the sake of getting better acquainted with that Anne of Green Gables girl," she said frankly. "She amuses me, and at my time of life an amusing person is a rarity."

"Oh thank heavens," said Diana's mother.

"And what's more, I will not only pay for piano lesson for your daughter, but for that Anne girl too."

Matilda's only comment when she heard the story was, "I told you so." This was for Martin's benefit.

Miss Barry stayed her month out and over. She was a more agreeable guest than usual, for Anne kept her in good humor. They became firm friends.

When Miss Barry went away she said: "Remember, you Anne girl, when you come to town you're to visit me and I'll put you in my very sparest spare-room bed to sleep."

"Miss Barry was a kindred spirit, after all," Anne confided to Matilda. "You wouldn't think so to look at her, but she is. You don't find it right out at first, as in Martin's case, but after a while you come to see it. Kindred spirits are not so scarce as I used to think. It's splendid to find out there are so many of them in the world."

"So you enjoyed Miss Josephine Barry's visit?"

"Yes, I did. I enjoyed Diana's cousin Tommy's visit too. I hope he comes back."

A Spring day on Prince Edward Island.

CHAPTER XX

A Good Imagination Gone Wrong

Spring had come once more to Green Gables – the beautiful capricious, reluctant Canadian spring, lingering along through April and May in a succession of sweet, fresh days with pink sunsets and miracles of resurrection and growth. The maples in Lover's Lane were red-budded and little curly ferns pushed up around the Dryad's Bubble. Away up in the barrens, behind Mr. Silas Sloane's place, the Mayflowers blossomed out, pink and white stars of sweetness under their brown leaves. All the schoolchildren had a golden afternoon gathering them, coming home in the clear, echoing twilight with arms full of their flowery bounty.

"I'm so sorry for people who live in lands where there are no Mayflowers," said Anne. "Diana says perhaps they have something better, but there couldn't be anything better than Mayflowers, could there, Matilda? Diana says if they don't know what they are like they don't miss them. But I think that is the saddest thing of all. I think it would be TRAGIC, Matilda, not to know what Mayflowers are like and NOT to miss them. Do you know what I think Mayflowers are, Matilda? I think they must be the souls of the flowers that died last summer and this is their heaven. But we had a splendid time today. We ate our lunch down in a big mossy hollow by an old well – such a ROMANTIC spot. Charlie Sloane dared Arty Gillis to jump over it, and

Arty did because he wouldn't take a dare. It is very fashionable to dare. Mr. Phillips gave all the Mayflowers he found to Prissy Andrews and I heard him to say 'sweets to the sweet.' He got that out of a book, I know; but it shows he has some imagination. Not that Mayflowers taste sweet. He offered me some Mayflowers too, but I rejected them. I don't think just because a person fucks you once gives them the right to treat you like a girlfriend, do you? Someone else offered me a bouquet of Mayflowers too, but I refused them with scorn. I can't tell you the person's name because I have vowed never to let it cross my lips. We made wreaths of the Mayflowers and put them on our heads; and when the time came to go home we marched in procession down the road, two by two, with our bouquets and wreaths, singing 'My Home on the Hill.' Oh, it was so thrilling, Matilda. Everybody we met on the road stopped and stared after us. We made a real sensation."

"Not much wonder! Such silly doings!" was Matilda's response.

After the Mayflowers came the violets, and Violet Vale was empurpled with them. Anne walked through it on her way to school with reverent steps and worshiping eyes, as if she trod on holy ground.

"Somehow," she told Diana, "when I'm going through here I don't really care whether Gil – whether anybody gets ahead of me in class or not. But when I'm up in school it's all different and I care as much as ever. There's such a lot of different Annes in me. I sometimes think that is why I'm such a troublesome person. If I was just the one Anne it would be ever so much more comfortable, but then it wouldn't be half so interesting."

One June evening, when the orchards were pink blossomed again, when the frogs were singing silvery sweet in the marshes about the head of the Lake of Shining Waters, and the air was full of the savor of clover fields and balsamic fir woods, Anne was sitting naked by her gable window. She had been studying her lessons, but it had grown too dark to see the book, so she had fallen into wide-eyed reverie, looking out past the boughs of the trees outside her window.

In all essential respects the little gable chamber was unchanged. The walls were as white, the pincushion as hard, the chairs as stiffly and yellowly upright as ever. Yet the whole character of the room was altered. It was full of a new vital, pulsing personality that seemed to pervade it quite independent of schoolgirl books and dresses and ribbons, and even of the cracked blue jug full of apple blossoms on the table. It was as if all the dreams, sleeping and waking, of its vivid occupant had taken a visible although unmaterial form and had tapestried the bare room with splendid filmy tissues of rainbow and moonshine.

Presently Matilda came briskly in with some of Anne's freshly ironed school clothes. She hung them over a chair and sat down with a short sigh. She had had one of her headaches that afternoon, and although the pain had gone she felt "tuckered out," as she expressed it. Anne looked at her with eyes limpid with sympathy.

"I do truly wish I could have had the headache in

your place, Matilda. I would endure it joyfully for your sake."

"I guess you did your part in attending to the work and letting me rest," said Matilda. "You seem to have got on fairly well and made fewer mistakes than usual. Of course, it wasn't exactly necessary to starch Martin's handkerchiefs, but he won't mind. And most people when they put a pie in the oven to warm up for dinner take it out and eat it when it gets hot instead of leaving it to be burned to a crisp. But that doesn't seem to be your way evidently." Headaches always left Matilda somewhat sarcastic.

"Oh, I'm so sorry," said Anne penitently. "I was firmly resolved, when you left me in charge this morning, not to imagine anything, but keep my thoughts on the facts before me. I did pretty well until I put the pie in, and then an irresistible temptation came to me to imagine I was an enchanted princess shut up in a lonely tower with a handsome knight riding to my rescue on a coal-black steed. So that is how I came to forget the pie. I didn't know I starched the handkerchiefs. All the time I was ironing I was trying to think of a name for a new island Diana and I have discovered up the brook. It's the most enchanting spot, Matilda. There are two maple trees on it and the brook flows right around it. At last it struck me that it would be splendid to call it Victoria Island because we found it on the Queen's birthday. Both Diana and I are very loyal to the Crown. But I'm sorry about that pie and the handkerchiefs. I wanted to be extra good today because it's an anniversary. Do you remember what happened this day last year, Matilda?"

"No, I can't think of anything special."

"Oh, Matilda, it was the day I came to Green Gables. I shall never forget it. It was the turning point in my life. Of course, it wouldn't seem so important to you. I've been here for a year and I've been so happy. Needless to say, I've had my troubles, but one can live down troubles. Are you sorry you kept me, Matilda?"

"No, I can't say I'm sorry," said Matilda, who sometimes wondered how she could have lived before Anne came to Green Gables. "If you've finished your lessons, Anne, I want you to run over and ask Mrs. Barry if she'll lend me Diana's apron pattern."

"Oh – it's – it's too dark," cried Anne.

"Too dark? Why, it's only twilight. And goodness knows you've gone over often enough after dark."

"I'll go over early in the morning," said Anne eagerly. "I'll get up at sunrise and go over, Matilda."

"What has got into your head now, Anne Shirley? I want that pattern to cut out your new apron this evening. Go at once and be smart too."

"I'll have to go around by the road, then," said Anne, pulling on a dress reluctantly.

"Go by the road and waste half an hour! I'd like to catch you!"

"I can't go through the Haunted Wood, Matilda," cried Anne desperately.

Matilda stared. "The Haunted Wood! Are you crazy? What under the canopy is the Haunted Wood?"

"The spruce wood over the brook," said Anne in a whisper.

"Fiddlesticks! There is no such thing as a haunted wood anywhere. Who has been telling you such stuff?"

"Nobody," confessed Anne. "Diana and I just imagined the wood was haunted. All the places around here are so – so – COMMONPLACE. We just got this up for our own amusement. We began it in April. A haunted wood is so very romantic, Matilda. We chose the spruce grove because it's so gloomy. Oh, we have imagined the most harrowing things. There's a white lady who walks along the brook just about this time of the night and wrings her hands and utters wailing cries. She appears when there is to be a death in the family. And the ghost of a little murdered child haunts the corner up by Idlewild; it creeps up behind you and lays its cold fingers on your neck. Oh, Matilda, it gives me a shudder to think of it. And there's a headless man who stalks up and down the path. And skeletons glower at you between the boughs. Oh, Matilda, I wouldn't go through the Haunted Wood after dark now for anything. I'd be sure that creepy things would reach out from behind the trees and grab me."

"Did ever anyone hear the like!" exclaimed Matilda, who had listened in dumb amazement. "Anne Shirley, do you mean to tell me you believe all that wicked nonsense of your own imagination?"

"Not exactly believe," faltered Anne. "At least, I don't believe it in daylight. But after dark, Matilda, it's different. That is when ghosts walk."

"There are no such things as ghosts, Anne."

"Oh, but there are, Matilda," cried Anne eagerly. "I know people who have seen them. And they are respectable people. Charlie Sloane says that his grandmother saw his grandfather driving home the cows one night after he'd been buried for a year. You know Charlie Sloane's grandmother wouldn't tell a lie for anything. She's a very religious woman. And Mrs. Thomas's father was pursued home one night by a lamb with its head cut off hanging by a strip of skin. He said he knew it was the spirit of his brother and that it was a warning he would die within nine days. He didn't, but he died two years after, so you see it was really true. And Ruby Gillis says – "

"Anne Shirley," interrupted Matilda firmly, "I never want to hear you talking in this fashion again. I've had my doubts about that imagination of yours right along, and if this is going to be the outcome of it, I won't countenance any such doings. You'll go right over to Barry's, and you'll go through that spruce grove, just for a lesson and a warning to you. And never let me hear a word out of your head about haunted woods again."

Anne might plead and cry as she liked – and did, for her terror was very real. Her imagination had run away with her and she held the spruce grove in mortal dread after nightfall. But Matilda was inexorable. She marched the shrinking ghost-seer down to the spring and ordered her to proceed straightaway over the bridge and into the dusky retreats of wailing ladies and headless specters beyond.

"Oh, Matilda, how can you be so cruel?" sobbed Anne. "What would you feel like if a creepy thing did snatch me up and carry me off?"

"I'll risk it," said Matilda unfeelingly. "You know I always mean what I say. I'll cure you of imagining ghosts into places. March, now. I mean it!"

Anne marched. That is, she stumbled over the

bridge and went shuddering up the horrible dim path beyond. Anne never forgot that walk. Bitterly did she repent the license she had given to her imagination. The goblins of her fancy lurked in every shadow about her, reaching out their cold, fleshless hands to grasp the terrified girl who had called them into being. A white strip of birch bark blowing up from the hollow over the brown floor of the grove made her heart stand still. The long-drawn wail of two old boughs rubbing against each other brought out the perspiration in beads on her forehead. The swoop of bats in the darkness over her was as the wings of unearthly creatures. When she reached Mr. William Bell's field she fled across it as if pursued by an army of monsters, arriving at the Barry's kitchen door so out of breath that she could hardly gasp out her request for the apron pattern. Diana was away so she had no excuse to linger. The dreadful return journey had to be faced. Anne went back over it with shut eyes, preferring to take the risk of dashing her brains out among the boughs to that of seeing a creepy thing. When she finally stumbled over the log bridge she drew one long shivering breath of relief.

"Well, so nothing caught you?" said Matilda unsympathetically.

"Oh, M-Matilda," chattered Anne, "I'll b-b-be contented with c-c-commonplace places after this."

Meetings and partings.

CHAPTER XXI

A New Departure in Flavorings

"**D**ear me, there is nothing but meetings and partings in this world, as Mrs. Langston says," remarked Anne plaintively, putting her slate and books down on the kitchen table on the last day of June and wiping her red eyes with a very damp handkerchief. "Wasn't it fortunate, Matilda, that I took an extra handkerchief to school today? I had a presentiment that it would be needed."

"I never thought you were so fond of Mr. Phillips that you'd require two handkerchiefs to dry your tears just because he's going away," said Matilda.

"I don't think I was crying because I was fond of him," reflected Anne. "Although I did let him fuck me, so that counts for something."

"I told you not to fuck anyone at school," Matilda sternly pointed out. "That was the rule."

"I thought you meant only classmates. And you told me to do whatever the headmaster said – I clearly remember those instructions."

"I didn't mean you should fuck him. That's not part of the curriculum."

"I think I cried because all the others did. It was Ruby Gillis who started it. Ruby Gillis has always declared she hated Mr. Phillips, but just as soon as he got up to make his farewell speech she burst into tears. Then all the girls began to cry, one after the other. I tried to hold out, Matilda. I tried to remember the time

Mr. Phillips made me sit with Gil – with a, boy; and the time he spelled my name without an E on the blackboard; and how he said I was the worst dunce he ever saw at geometry and how he laughed at my spelling; and all the times he was so horrid and sarcastic; but somehow I couldn't, Matilda, and I just had to cry too."

"Probably most of those crying were girls he has taken sexual advantage of. That's why he's leaving, you know. Prissy Andrews's father complained to the school board after he caught them having intercourse in his barn."

"Not all of them have had sexual congress with him," insisted Anne. "Take Carrie Sloane, for instance. She swears she's a virgin – well, if you don't count that one time she played doctor with her brother. Charlie Sloane gave her a pelvic exam using a very personal instrument. Carrie has been talking for a month about how glad she'll be when Mr. Phillips goes away and she declared she'd never shed a tear. That's because he flunked her in geography. Probably because she wouldn't let him fuck her. Turns out, she carried on worse than any of us and had to borrow a handkerchief from her brother Charlie, being she hadn't brought one of her own, not expecting to need it."

"I can't believe he was that popular," said Matilda, failing to mention she'd let Teddy Phillips fuck her one time too. It was soon after he got the appointment as headmaster of Avonlea School and she's paid a welcome visit to him at Eben Wright's house where he was boarding. She barely got seated in the parlor before he had her knickers off and began laying it to her.

Fortunately, the Wrights were away, shopping in Carmody, and thereby had no clue as to the debauchery that took place on their couch.

"Oh, Matilda, it was heartrending," continued Anne. "Mr. Phillips made such a beautiful farewell speech beginning, 'The time has come for us to part.' It was very affecting. Oh, I felt dreadfully remorseful for all the times I'd talked in school and drawn pictures of him on my slate and made fun of him and Prissy. I can tell you I wished I'd been a perfect pupil like Minnie Andrews. She hadn't anything on her conscience. She's still a virgin too. The girls cried all the way home from school. Carrie Sloane kept saying every few minutes, 'The time has come for us to part,' and that would start us off again whenever we were in any danger of cheering up. I do feel dreadfully sad, Matilda. But one can't feel quite in the depths of despair with two months' vacation before them, can they, Matilda? And besides, we met the new minister and his wife coming from the station. For all I was feeling so bad about Mr. Phillips going away I couldn't help taking a little interest in a new minister, could I? His wife is very pretty. Not exactly regally lovely, of course – it wouldn't do, I suppose, for a minister to have a regally lovely wife, because it might set a bad example. Mrs. Langston says the minister's wife over at Newbridge sets a very bad example because she dresses so fashionably. Our new minister's wife was dressed in blue muslin with lovely puffed sleeves and a hat trimmed with roses. Jane Andrews said she thought puffed sleeves were too worldly for a minister's wife, but I didn't make any such uncharitable remark,

Matilda, because I know what it is to long for puffed sleeves. Besides, she's only been a minister's wife for a little while, so one should make allowances, shouldn't they? They are going to board with Mrs. Langston until the parsonage is ready."

≈ ≈ ≈

Matilda went over to Mrs. Langston's that evening on the excuse of returning the quilting frames she had borrowed. It was an excuse shared by many curious neighbors. Numerous objects that Mrs. Langston had lent, never expecting to see it again, came home that night in charge of the borrowers hoping for a glimpse of the new minister. After all, a new minister with a wife was a lawful object of curiosity in a quiet little country settlement where sensations were few and far between.

Rev. Cleary, the former minister whom Anne found so lacking in imagination, had been pastor of Avonlea for eighteen years. He was a widower when he came, and a widower he remained, despite the fact that gossip regularly married him to this, that, or the other one, from parishioner to choirgirl, every year of his sojourn. However, the preceding February he had resigned his charge and departed for Montreal amid the regrets of his people, most of whom had grown to like him despite of his shortcomings as an orator.

Since then, the congregation of the First Presbyterian Church of Avonlea had listened to many candidates who came Sunday after Sunday to preach on trial. These eager applicants stood or fell by the judgment of the church's deacons; but a certain girl who sat meekly in the corner of the Collins pew also had opinions about them and discussed the same in full with Martin, while Matilda always declined from criticizing ministers in any shape or form as a matter of principle.

"I don't think Rev. Smith was very qualified," Anne summed up the latest candidate. "Mrs. Langston says his delivery was poor, but I think his worst fault was just like Rev. Cleary's – he had no imagination. And that Rev. Terry had too much imagination for the job; he let it run away with him just as I did in the matter of the Haunted Wood. Besides, Mrs. Langston says his theology wasn't very sound. That Rev. Gresham seemed to be a good religious man, but he told too many funny stories and made the congregation laugh; that was undignified, and you must have some dignity about a minister, mustn't you, Martin? I thought Rev. Marshall was decidedly attractive; but Mrs. Langston says he isn't married, or even engaged, because she made special inquiries about him, and she says it would never do to have a young unmarried minister in Avonlea, because he might diddle women in the congregation and that would make trouble. I know I would have been willing to fuck him, a handsome man like that with blue eyes and a square chin and broad shoulders. But I suppose one should never lay down with one's own minister, should one? At least that's what Mrs. Langston says. She is a very farseeing woman, isn't she?"

"Mrs. Langston is quite the pillar of the community," Martin allowed, although he may have been referring to the woman's sturdy build rather than her civic contributions. He was wary of the old hag, knowing she spied in his bedroom window.

Anne babbled on: "I'm very glad they've selected Rev. Allan. I liked him because his sermon was interesting and he prayed as if he meant it and not just because he was in the habit of it. Mrs. Langston says he isn't perfect, but she says we couldn't expect to get a perfect minister for what we pay. She says his theology is sound because she questioned him thoroughly on all the points of doctrine. And she knows his wife's people and they are most respectable and the women are all good housekeepers. Mrs. Langston says that sound doctrine in the man and good housekeeping in the woman make an ideal combination for a minister's family."

"I'm sure they're a good choice," Martin nodded absently, more interested in the shapely legs on the new minister's wife. She wore her skirts awfully short for a woman of God. But he didn't mind.

Rev. Jonathan Allan and his wife Cynthia were a young, pleasant-faced couple, still on their honeymoon, and full of enthusiasms for their chosen life's work. Avonlea opened its heart to them from the start. Old and young liked the frank, cheerful young man with his high ideals, and the bright, gentle little lady who assumed the mistress-ship of the manse.

With Cynthia Allan our girl Anne fell promptly and wholeheartedly in love. She had discovered another kindred spirit.

"Mrs. Allan is perfectly lovely," she announced one Sunday afternoon. "She's taken over our Bible School class and she's a splendid teacher. She said right away she didn't think it was fair for the teacher to ask all the questions, and you know, Matilda, that is exactly what

I've always thought. She said we could ask her any question we liked and I asked ever so many. I'm good at asking questions, you know."

"Indeed you are," was Matilda's emphatic comment.

"Nobody else asked any except Ruby Gillis, and she asked if there was going to be a Sunday School picnic this summer. I didn't think that was a very proper question because it hadn't any connection with the lesson – the lesson was about Daniel in the lions' den – but Mrs. Allan just smiled and said she thought there would be. Mrs. Allan has a lovely smile; she has such EXQUISITE dimples in her cheeks. I wish I had dimples in my cheeks, Matilda. I'm not half so skinny as I was when I came here, but I have no dimples yet. If I had, perhaps I could influence people for good. Mrs. Allan said we ought always to try to influence other people for good. She talked so nice about everything. I never knew before that religion was such a cheerful thing. I always thought it was kind of melancholy, but Mrs. Allan's isn't, and I'd like to be a Christian if I could be one like her. I wouldn't want to be like old Rev. Cleary. He was such a sourpuss."

"It's wrong of you to speak that way about Rev. Cleary," said Matilda severely. "Rev. Cleary was a real good man. You didn't like it because he reprimanded you when he came across you running naked down near Barry's Pond."

"Oh, of course he's a good man," agreed Anne, "but he doesn't seem to get any comfort out of it. If I could be good I'd dance and sing all day because I was glad of it. I don't suppose it would be dignified for a minister's wife to dance and sing but I bet Mrs. Allan does it in private. We all do things we enjoy in private, like me sharing your and Martin's bed. I wonder what Cynthia Allan does in private. Do you think she'd be willing to share our bed with us?"

"Anne! What a thing to say about the new minister's wife. Do you think she's some kind of harlot?"

"I'm not a harlot and I share your bed. That's because I like pleasuring the two of you. Maybe that does make me a harlot on second thought. I do so like fucking. And I'd like pleasuring Cynthia Allan. I'd bet Martin would too."

"No doubt. I've seen how he looks at her legs. I think her skirts are a little short for a minister's wife, if you want to know the truth."

"She does have such shapely legs, don't you think? And her bottom is so nice and round, adding balance to her ample bosom. God was generous when handing out a curvy body to Mrs. Allan. I understand what Martin sees in her. I see it too, a woman with carnal lust lurking beneath a placid exterior. Maybe she *is* a secret harlot, like me?"

"Girl, your imagination runs wild. Harlot indeed! I can tell Mrs. Allan is glad she's a devout Christian and that she'd be one even if she could get to heaven without it."

"When she leans over my shoulder to show me a Bible verse, I can see down the front of her blouse. She leaves the top buttons undone, affording me a view of those twin mounds of flesh. I'd like to see her breasts unfettered by clothing. Do you think she might ever run through the meadows naked with me?"

"No, and I'm not going to do that either – no matter how many times you invite me."

"You're just afraid Mrs. Langston would see us. But that wouldn't really matter. She watches us through our bedroom window with her spyglass. She has already seen every mold and freckle on your otherwise flawless body."

"Do you think she knows that you share my and Martin's bed?" the blonde woman asked nervously. There was no question she knew the brother and sister enjoyed an incestuous relationship, for the old wag had dropped broad hints. That damn spyglass!

"Oh, I'm sure she does. She sometimes admonishes me that I should wear a nightgown to bed. How would she know I crawl into bed naked with you and Martin if she wasn't spying on the three of us."

"Well, I hope she continues to hold her tongue. We would be driven from the community in shame if word of our arrangement ever got out. Avonlea is not a tolerant place."

"I'll bet Rev. Allan is tolerant. Elsewise would he let his wife wear such short skirts? And leave the top of her blouse unbuttoned? I do think she's a secret harlot and I will dream of her joining us in our pleasurable nighttime activities. Wouldn't that be so lovely, you and I licking Cynthia Allan's naked body from stem to stern? I wonder what her pussy would taste like, don't you? I do so hope she joins us in bed sometime. I wonder if her public hair is red, like the hair that adorns her head?"

"I suppose we must have Rev. and Mrs. Allan up to

tea someday soon," said Matilda reflectively. "They've been most everywhere but here. Let me see. Next Wednesday would be a good time to have them. But don't say a word to Martin about it, for if he knew they were coming he'd find some excuse to be away that day. He'd got so used to Rev. Cleary he didn't mind him, but he's going to find it hard to get acquainted with a new minister, and especially a new minister's wife with such shapely legs. She will frighten him to death."

"I'll be as secret as the dead," assured Anne. "But oh, Matilda, will you let me make a cake for the occasion? I'd love to do something for Mrs. Allan, and you know I can make a pretty good cake by this time."

"Yes, you can make a layer cake," promised Matilda. "But get those ideas about Cynthia Allan sharing our bed out of your silly head. That will never happen."

≈≈≈

On Monday and Tuesday great preparations were underway at Green Gables. Having the minister and his wife to tea was a serious and important undertaking. Matilda Collins was determined not to be eclipsed by any of the other Avonlea housekeepers. Everything had to be just perfect.

Anne was wild with excitement and delight. She talked it all over with Diana Tuesday night in the twilight, as they sat naked on the big red stones by the Dryad's Bubble and made rainbows in the water with little twigs dipped in fir balsam.

"Everything is ready, Diana, except my cake which I'm to make in the morning, and the baking-powder biscuits which Matilda will make just before teatime.

Matilda calls them scones, but they are really just biscuits with raisins in them."

"That sounds delicious," said Diana. She'd put on a few pounds over the winter thanks to her insatiable appetite, but Anne thought the extra weigh merely made her bosom friend's bosom all the more "cushiony." She enjoyed burrowing her face between the large mounds and going "*Brrrrrrrr.*"

Tonight she was licking the tips of Diana's breasts with her snake-like tongue, making the nipples stand up. She thought that was so cute, her friend's nips standing at attention like little pink soldiers.

Pausing between licks, Anne said, "I assure you, Diana, that Matilda and I have had a busy two days of it. It's such a responsibility having a minister's family over to tea. I never went through such an experience before. You should just see our pantry. It's a sight to behold. We're going to have jellied chicken and cold pig's tongue. We're to have two kinds of jelly, red and yellow, and whipped cream and lemon pie, and cherry pie, and three kinds of cookies, and fruitcake, and Matilda's famous yellow plum preserves that she keeps especially for ministers, and pound cake and my layer cake, and biscuits as aforesaid; and new bread and old both, in case the minister is dyspeptic and can't eat new. Mrs. Langston says ministers are often dyspeptic, but I don't think Rev. Allan has been a minister long enough for it to have had a bad effect on him."

"You're making me hungry."

"Don't worry, Diana dear. There shall be plenty of leftovers for us to feast on for days to come. However, I grow cold with fear when I think of my layer cake. Oh,

Diana, what if it shouldn't be good! I dreamed last night that I was chased all around by a fearful goblin with a big layer cake for a head."

"It'll be good, all right," assured Diana, who was a very comfortable sort of friend. She leaned forward to push her left breasts into Anne's willing mouth. "I can assure you that layer cake you made that we had for lunch in Idlewild two weeks ago was perfectly elegant."

"Mmmph."

"Don't talk with your mouth full. It isn't polite," reprimanded her friend, gently pulling her breast away.

"I can't help but worry," said Anne when she regained her breath. "Layer cakes have such a terrible habit of turning out bad just when you especially want them to be good." Anne set a particularly well-balsamed twig afloat. "I suppose I shall just have to trust to Providence and be careful to put in the flour. I forget that sometimes when I'm baking a cake. I get distracted so easily." As if giving testament to her words, she added, "Oh, look, Diana, what a lovely rainbow! Do you suppose the dryad will come out after we go away and take it for a colorful scarf?"

"You know there is no such thing as a dryad," said Diana. Diana's mother had found out about the Haunted Wood and had been decidedly angry over it. As a result Diana had abstained from any further imitative flights of imagination and did not think it prudent to cultivate a spirit of belief even in harmless dryads.

"But it's so easy to imagine there is," said Anne. "Every night before I go to bed, I look out of my window and wonder if the dryad is really sitting here, combing her locks with the spring for a mirror. Sometimes I look for her footprints in the dew in the morning. Oh, Diana, don't give up your faith in the dryad!"

"You're the only dryad I know of," smiled Diana. "Sitting here naked by the pond, stirring a stick in the mirror-like water, you could be a painting by Maxfield Parrish."

"Oh, Diana, I like that idea. Perhaps when I grow up I could go off to Paris and become a nude model for a famous painter. I think I'd be good at it. My body is quite presentable. And goodness knows, I like being naked. Wouldn't it be grand for thousands of men to gaze upon your nude body and desire you?"

"Anne Shirley, you are indeed crazy as a loon. What would Rev. Allan think if he heard you talking that way?"

"You know who else would make a wonderful nude model? Rev. Allan's wife! Cynthia has such a magnificent body. Oh, how I wish she were sitting here enjoying the fresh air on her bare skin with us. Wouldn't that be fun? Maybe I shall invite her one day!"

≈≈≈

Wednesday morning came. Anne got up at sunrise because she was too excited to sleep. She had caught a severe cold in the head by reason of her running about naked with Diana at Dryad's Bubble on the preceding evening; but nothing short of absolute pneumonia could have quenched her interest in culinary matters that morning. After breakfast she proceeded to make her layer cake. When she finally shut the oven door upon it she drew a long breath of relief. This time she had remembered to include the flour.

"I'm sure I haven't forgotten anything, Matilda. But do you think the cake will rise? Just suppose perhaps the baking powder isn't good? I used it out of the new can. And Mrs. Langston says you can never be sure of getting good baking powder nowadays when everything is so adulterated. Mrs. Langston says the Government ought to take the matter up, but she says we'll never see the day when a Tory Government will do that. Matilda, what if that cake doesn't rise?"

"We'll have plenty without it" was Matilda's unimpassioned way of looking at the subject.

The cake did rise, however, and came out of the oven as light and feathery as golden foam. Anne, flushed with delight, clapped it together with layers of ruby jelly and, in imagination, saw Mrs. Cynthia Allan eating it and possibly asking for another piece!

"You'll be using the best tea set, of course, Matilda," she said. "Can I fix the table with ferns and wild roses?"

"I think that's all nonsense," sniffed Matilda. "In my opinion it's the eatables that matter and not flummery decorations."

"Mrs. Barry had HER table decorated," noted Anne, a girl not entirely guiltless of the wisdom of the serpent. "And the new minister paid her an elegant compliment. He said it was a feast for the eye as well as the palate."

"Well, do as you like," huffed Matilda, quite determined not to be surpassed by Mrs. Barry or anybody else. "Only mind you leave enough room for the dishes and the food."

Anne laid herself out to decorate in a manner that would outdo Mrs. Barry's table setting. Having an abundance of roses and ferns, and very artistic tastes of her own, she made that tea table into such a thing of beauty that when the minister and his wife sat down at it they exclaimed in chorus over it loveliness.

"It's Anne's doings," said Matilda. And Anne felt that Mrs. Allan's approving smile was almost too much happiness for this world.

Martin was there, having been inveigled into attending the party by Anne. He had been in such a state of shyness that Matilda had given up the idea of his participation, but Anne had her ways with him. Matilda suspected it involved the promise of an extra special blowjob, the kind referred to as a "hummer." Anne often chose patriotic songs for such occasions.

Now Martin sat at the table in his best clothes and white collar and talked to the minister not uninterestingly. He never said a word to Mrs. Allan, but that was to be expected. Now and then he snuck a glance at her exposed calves, her legs demurely crossed as she sat there in the chair next to him.

All went merry as a marriage bell until Anne's layer cake was passed. Mrs. Allan, having already been helped to a bewildering variety, declined it. But Matilda, seeing the disappointment on Anne's face, said smilingly: "Oh, you must take a piece of this, Mrs. Allan. Anne made it especially for you."

"In that case I must sample it," laughed Cynthia Allan, helping herself to a plump triangle, as did also the minister and Matilda.

Mrs. Allan took a mouthful of hers and a most

peculiar expression crossed her face; not a word did she say, however, but steadily ate away at it. Matilda saw the expression and hastened to taste the cake.

"Anne Shirley!" she exclaimed. "What on earth did you put into that cake?"

"Nothing but what the recipe said," cried Anne with a look of anguish. "Oh, isn't it all right?"

"All right! It's simply horrible. Rev. Allan, don't try to eat it. Anne, taste it yourself. What flavoring did you use?"

"Vanilla," said Anne, her face scarlet with mortification after tasting the cake. "Only vanilla. Oh, Matilda, it must have been the baking powder. I had my suspicions of that bak – "

"Baking powder fiddlesticks! Go and bring me the bottle of vanilla you used."

Anne fled to the pantry and returned with a small bottle partially filled with a brown liquid and labeled yellowly, "Best Vanilla."

Matilda took it, uncorked it, smelled it. "Mercy on us, Anne, you've flavored that cake with anodyne liniment. I broke the liniment bottle last week and poured what was left into an old empty vanilla bottle. I suppose it's partly my fault – I should have warned you – but for pity's sake why couldn't you have smelled it?"

Anne dissolved into tears under this double disgrace. "I couldn't – I had such a cold!" and with this she fairly fled to the gable chamber, where she cast herself on the bed and wept as one who refuses to be comforted.

Presently a light step sounded on the stairs and somebody entered the room.

"Oh, Matilda," sobbed Anne, without looking up, "I'm disgraced forever. I shall never be able to live this down. It will get out – things always do get out in Avonlea. Diana will ask me how my cake turned out and I shall have to tell her the truth. I shall always be pointed at as the girl who flavored a cake with anodyne liniment. Gil – the boys in school will never get over laughing at it. Oh, Matilda, if you have a spark of Christian pity don't tell me that I must go down and wash the dishes after this. I'll wash them when the minister and his wife are gone, but I cannot ever look Mrs. Allan in the face again. Perhaps she'll think I tried to poison her. Mrs. Langston says she knows an orphan girl who tried to poison her benefactor. But the liniment isn't poisonous. It's meant to be taken internally – although not in cakes. Won't you tell Mrs. Allan so, Matilda?"

"Suppose you jump up and tell her so yourself," said a merry voice.

Anne flew up, to find Cynthia Allan standing by her bed, surveying her with laughing eyes.

"My dear girl, you mustn't cry like this," she said, genuinely disturbed by Anne's tragic face. "Why, it's all just a funny mistake that anybody might make."

"Oh, no, it takes me to make such a mistake," said Anne forlornly. "And I wanted to have that cake so nice for you, Mrs. Allan."

"Yes, I know, dear. And I assure you I appreciate your kindness and thoughtfulness just as much as if it had turned out all right. Now, you mustn't cry anymore, but come down with me and show me your flower garden. Miss Collins tells me you have a little plot all your own. I want to see it, for I'm very much interested in flowers."

Anne permitted herself to be led down and comforted, reflecting that it was really providential that Mrs. Allan was a kindred spirit. Nothing more was said about the liniment cake, and when the guests went away Anne found that she had enjoyed the evening more than could have been expected, considering that terrible incident.

Nevertheless, she sighed deeply as she said, "Matilda, isn't it nice to think that tomorrow is a new day with no mistakes in it yet?"

"I'll warrant you'll make plenty in it," said Matilda. "I never saw your beat for making mistakes, Anne."

"Yes, and well I know it," admitted Anne mournfully. "But have you ever noticed one encouraging thing about me, Matilda? I never make the same mistake twice."

"I don't know as that's much benefit when you're always making new ones."

"Oh, don't you see, Matilda? There must be a limit to the mistakes one person can make, and when I get to the end of them, then I'll be through with them. That's a very comforting thought, isn't it?"

"Well, you'd better go and give that cake to the pigs," said Matilda. "It isn't fit for any human to eat, not even Harley Boute."

But Anne couldn't focus on the likes of Harley, the boy who helped out on the farm. Her thoughts were of Cynthia Allan dancing naked with her in the garden, flowers surrounding them like a painting by Maxfield Parrish. Oh, if only it were true and not just a product of her vivid imagination!

Tea time for Anne.

CHAPTER XXII

Anne is Invited Out to Tea

"**A**nd why are your eyes popping out of your head?" asked Matilda when Anne came in from a run to the post office. "Have you discovered another kindred spirit?" Excitement hung around Anne like a garment, shone in her eyes, reflected in every feature. She had come dancing up the lane, like a wind-blown sprite, through the mellow sunshine and lazy shadows of the August evening.

"No, Matilda, but oh, what do you think? I am invited to tea at the parsonage tomorrow afternoon! Mrs. Allan left the letter for me at the post office. Just look at it, Matilda. 'Miss Anne Shirley, Green Gables.' That is the first time I was ever formally called 'Miss.' Such a thrill it gave me! I shall cherish this letter forever among my choicest treasures."

"Mrs. Allan told me she meant to have all the members of her Sunday School class to tea in turn," said Matilda, regarding the wonderful event very coolly. "You needn't get in such a fever over it. Do learn to take things calmly, my dear."

For Anne to take things calmly would have been to change her nature. All "spirit and fire and dew" as she was, the pleasures and pains of life came to her with trebled intensity. Matilda troubled over this, realizing that the ups and downs of existence would be hard on this impulsive soul, but not understanding that the equally great capacity for delight might more than compensate for such hardships. Therefore Matilda considered it her duty to drill a tranquil disposition into the exuberant young girl – a task as impossible as training a sunbeam to dance.

Matilda did not make much headway, as she sorrowfully admitted to herself. The attempt often plunged Anne into "deeps of affliction." Matilda had almost begun to despair of ever fashioning this waif of the world into a model little girl of demure manners and prim deportment. Neither would she have believed that she in fact really liked Anne better as she was.

Anne went to bed that night speechless with misery because Martin had said the wind was round northeast and she feared it would be a rainy day tomorrow. The rustle of the poplar leaves about the house worried her, for it sounded like pattering raindrops. And the faraway roar of the sea, to which she listened delightedly at other times, loving its strange, sonorous, haunting rhythm, now seemed like a prophecy of storm – disaster to a girl who particularly wanted a fine day.

Anne thought that the morning would never come. But all things have an end, even nights before the day on which you are invited to take tea at the minister's manse. The morning, in spite of Martin's predictions, turned out fine, causing Anne's spirits to soar to their highest. "Oh, Matilda, there is something in me today that makes me just love everybody," she exclaimed as she washed the breakfast dishes. "You don't know how good I feel! Wouldn't it be nice if it could last? I believe I could be a model child if I were just invited out to tea every day. But oh, Matilda, it's a solemn occasion too. I feel so anxious. What if I shouldn't behave properly?

You know I never had tea at a parsonage before, and I'm not sure that I know all the rules of etiquette, although I've been studying the rules given in the Etiquette Department of the *Family Herald* ever since I came here. I'm so afraid I'll do something silly or forget to do something I should do. Would it be good manners to take a second helping of anything if you wanted to VERY much?"

"The trouble with you, Anne, is that you're thinking too much about yourself. You should just think of Mrs. Allan and what would be nicest and most agreeable to her," offered Matilda, hitting for once in her life on a very sound and pithy piece of advice.

Anne instantly realized this. "You are right, Matilda. I'll try not to think about myself at all."

≈≈≈

The tea went fine, Mrs. Allan a charming hostess. Her husband was away at a regional church conference, so the woman and the girl took their tea with tiny cucumber sandwiches, just the two of them in the back parlor overlooking the sea. The sky was as blue as an aggie marble, with a slight breeze whipping up the sea foam along the beach. It was truly a beautiful day, everything Anne had dreamed it could be.

"How long have you lived with the Collins family?" asked Cynthia Allen to make polite conversation.

"A little over a year," replied the girl. "I'm sure I've been quite a trial for them. But I try to make it up to them in other ways."

"Oh, what ways, may I ask?"

Anne almost replied, "By fucking their brains out," but caught herself in the nick of time. Matilda had warned her that too much honesty was not always a good thing. "I do extra chores around the house," she corrected herself. "Green Gables takes a lot of upkeep."

"I'm sure," smiled the minister's wife. "It's such a lovely place, snuggled there among all those verdant fields and green forests."

"I've given most of the spots thereabouts new names, secret names."

"Really now, that sounds interesting. Would you tell me one?"

"Well, Barry's Pond is now known as Lake of Shining Waters. Don't you think that sounds oh-so-much better?"

"Yes, I do." She gave the girl a dazzling smile, her teeth as white as the keys on Diana's new piano, a gift from Aunt Josephine. "Any others you can share?"

"There's one special place we call Dryad's Bubble. It's a beautiful spring down near the Log Bridge where Diana and I like to go."

"It sounds perfectly wonderful. Will you invite me to see it someday?"

"I would love to, but that may not be possible," replied Anne, after taking another sip of tea. "You see, dryad's are grown-up fairies who run naked through the woods. You can only be there at their gathering place when you're nude like them."

"Oh my. Are you saying you and Diana pull off all your clothes when you're visiting Dryad's Bubble?"

Anne smiled weakly. "Yes, that's the requirement. We don't want to offend the fairies."

"I suppose not," answered Cynthia Allan with a wisp of a smile on her lips. She wore a lipstick called

Valentine's Heart, its hue as bright as fresh blood. It complimented her flaming-red hair. "Fairies can be very finicky, as we both know."

"Yes," nodded Anne, surprised that this adult lady would confirm such a notion. "I'd like to be a dryad, wouldn't you?"

"Would I have to run through the woods naked?"

"Yes, of course ... if you were a dryad. That's what they do."

"I see your point." Cynthia Allan paused, as if considering her next words. "I would be willing to do that sometime if only you were present. Being a minister's wife I have to maintain the appearance of proper decorum. So it would have to be our secret, telling no one. Not Matilda or Martin, not Diana, not even my husband."

"I can keep a secret," Anne assured her, thinking her heart might burst from her chest. "Truly I can."

Cynthia Allen reached across the table to pat the girl's hand. "I believe you," she said.

"I'd very much like to show you Dryad's Bubble."

"Then it's a play date. Perhaps next week or the week after if it's warm."

"Yes, a date," repeated Anne, almost in a stupor of delight.

≈≈≈

Anne got through her visit without any serious breach of etiquette, other than the conversation about a proposed "play date." She came home under a great, high-sprung sky gloried over with trails of saffron and rosy cloud. Finding herself in an exhilarated state of mind, she happily told Matilda all about it while reclining on the big red-sandstone slab at the kitchen door, her tired head snuggled in Matilda's gingham lap. Of course, she left out the part about dryads.

She wondered why Cynthia Allan could believe in dryads when Matilda could not? Perhaps it was a difference in brain development, one having a more sophisticated frontal lobe devoted to imagination than the other.

A cool wind was blowing over the harvest fields from the distant rims of the firry western hills. One clear star hung over the orchard like the decoration atop a Christmas tree. And twinkling fireflies flitted along Lover's Lane, weaving in and out among the ferns and rustling boughs. Anne watched them as she told Matilda about the absolutely perfect tea with the minister's pretty redheaded wife.

"Oh, Matilda, I've had a most FASCINATING time. I feel that I have not lived in vain and I shall always feel like that even if I should never be invited to tea at a manse again. When I got there Mrs. Allan met me at the door. She was dressed in the sweetest dress of pale-pink organdy, with dozens of frills and elbow sleeves, and she looked just like a seraph. I really think I'd like to be a minister's wife when I grow up, Matilda. A minister mightn't mind my clumsy mistakes because he wouldn't be thinking of such worldly things. But then of course one would have to be naturally good and I'll never be that, so I suppose there's no use in wishing for such a union. Some people are naturally good, you know, and others are not. I'm one of the others. Mrs. Langston says I'm full of Original Sin. No matter how hard I try to be good I can never make a success of it. I expect it's a good deal like geometry, you either have the ability to understand it or you don't. But shouldn't trying hard count for something? Mrs. Allan is one of the naturally good people. I love her passionately. You know there are some people, like Martin and Mrs. Allan that you can love right off without any trouble. And there are others, like Mrs. Langston, that you have to try very hard to love. You know you OUGHT to love them because they are such active workers in the church, but you have to keep reminding yourself of it all the time or else you forget."

"I take it you liked Mrs. Allan?"

"Oh, yes. We are indeed kindred spirits. Mrs. Allan and I had a heart-to-heart talk. I told her everything – about Mrs. Thomas and the twins and Katie Maurice and Violetta and coming to Green Gables and my troubles over geometry. And would you believe it, Matilda? Mrs. Allan told me she was a dunce at geometry too. You don't know how that encouraged me. Mrs. Langston came to the manse just before I left, and what do you think, Matilda? The school board has hired a new teacher and it's a lady. Her name is Miss Muriel Stacy. Isn't that such a romantic name? Mrs. Langston says they've never had a female teacher in Avonlea before and she thinks it is a dangerous innovation. But I think it will be splendid to have a lady teacher, and I really don't see how I'm going to live through the two weeks before school begins. I'm so impatient to see her."

"Well, I hope you learned something from your association with Mr. Phillips. It is not a good idea to become too fixated on a teacher. Let's hope Miss Stacy is not some old lesbian spinster who wants to have sex with her girl students."

"I do regret fucking Teddy Phillips," avowed Anne. "Not that I didn't enjoy it. But doing so did not advance my cause."

"Your cause is –?"

"Why, to spend as much time servicing you and Martin as possible. Teachers come and go, as we have seen. But family is forever – isn't that right, Matilda?"

"Yes, I suppose so," sighed the Collins woman, realizing that adopting Anne Shirley had been a bigger commitment than she'd ever imagined. Rather than acquiring a teenage sex slave, she and her brother Martin had been enslaved for the rest of their life by this enchantress Anne Shirley.

The minister's wife and Anne.

CHAPTER XXIII

Anne Comes to Grief in an Affair of Honor

As it happened, Anne had to live through more than two weeks before Mrs. Allan visited Dryad's Bubble. Almost a month having elapsed since the liniment cake episode, she got a note from the minister's wife that said simply:

> Dearest Anne,
> I am ready to visit Dryad's Bubble. Is this afternoon suitable? If so, I will be waiting for you at the Log Bridge.
> Cordially yours,
> Cynthia

Anne's heart was beating like a hummingbird's wings. "Dearest," she had written. And signed her name "Cynthia," as if they were the best-est of friends. And she wanted to visit the hidden spring with Anne. Oh my.

Promptly at 2 p.m. Anne came racing down the path to the Log Bridge. Never mind the Haunted Wood or creepy things lurking behind trees or any of that silliness – she was on her way to Fairyland!

As promised, Cynthia Allan was waiting for her on this side of the bridge. She looked ethereal, standing there in a wide-brimmed sunbonnet and white taffeta dress. The woman's auburn hair shimmered like burnished copper in the bright sunlight.

"You came, you actually came," gushed Anne, garbed more plainly in a tan cotton pullover. But her face radiated an excitement that made her look like a storybook princess who was yet to kiss the frog.

"I said I would," nodded the minister's wife. "I'm ready to become a dryad for the afternoon."

"Oh, that's wonderful. Follow me, the spring is over this way, hidden among the foliage."

Anne guided her guest under a low-hanging copse of maple trees and down a winding trail that dead-ended at a lovely pool, its mirror-like surface the very embodiment of tranquility.

"So this beautiful spot is Dryad's Bubble?"

Anne blushed. "That's what I named it. Because I could imagine dryads gathering about to study their reflections, like those fairies recently photographed by those two little girls in Cottingley, England."

"I read about that," said Mrs. Allen, removing her sunbonnet and tossing it aside, the hat landing atop a nearby prickleberry bush. She unpinned her reddish hair and shook it free, letting the tresses tumble down her neck. "Do you believe those photographs are real?"

"Oh, I want to. Don't you?"

"Fairies live in our imaginations. So I think we can pretend they are real, whether or not it's true."

"I knew you'd understand," said Anne. "I knew we'd be kindred spirits."

"Yes, I think we are," said Mrs. Allan, beginning to unbutton the front of her taffeta dress. "You did say we had to be nude in order not to disturb the fairies, did you not?"

"Yes, that is true. But I could never imagine – try

as I might – a proper minister's wife ever taking off her clothing out here in the fields with me."

"You might be surprised," said Cynthia Allan as she shrugged off her dress and stepped out of it. She was wearing a tight white corset and flimsy knickers. Her rounded breasts perched over the corset like twin moons, an astrological phenomenon of significant proportions. "Are you not getting undressed too?" she asked the astonished girl.

"I am," confirmed Anne as she hauled her dress over her head and shook her unruly brunette hair free. Having prepared for the meeting, she wore no undergarments at all. "There, I am ready to transform into a dryad."

"And a beautiful dryad indeed," observed Cynthia Allan as she unlaced the corset and wiggled it down her hips. That left her standing by the pool in only her white panties, a dark triangle showing beneath the thin silk.

"Thank you," said Anne, thrilled by the compliment. Other than Matilda, she'd never paraded her exposed epidermis in front of a grown-up woman. "You are as lovely as a fairy princess yourself, Mrs. Allan."

"Call me Cynthia when we're alone. After all, anyone who shares my husband's intimate view of my body deserves to be on a first-name basis."

"Cynthia then. Are you going to remove your knickers? I'd so love to see your pussy."

"Fairies have nothing to hide from each other," said the redhead, slipping the silk down her tapered thighs. The dark patch hinted at by her panties proved to be nothing less than a tangled nest of auburn hair. As if this triangle were an arrow pointing downward, Anne could clearly see the puffy lips of her vulva.

"Other than Matilda's I have never seen a grown woman's pussy," the girl trilled, eyes affixed to Cynthia Allan's nether regions.

"Oh? Do you have an intimate relationship with your adopted mother?"

"Yes, but she's more like a big sister."

"And do you fuck her brother Martin too?"

Anne was shocked to hear the word "fuck" falling from the lips of a minister's wife. But it was equally amazing to be standing naked with her under this copse of trees. "Yes," nodded the girl. "But I am not supposed to tell. However, I suppose it's all right for you to know, in that we have declared ourselves to be kindred spirits."

"I hope we will be more than that, dear girl. A minister's wife gets lonely, particularly when her husband's pious ways foreswear sex. But that's okay for I have always fancied women more than men."

"But I am not quite a woman, I've just recently turned sixteen."

"Close enough. Come over here and lie down next to me. I think my tongue can find the little man in the boat."

"Little man in the boat?" She glanced at the pool, expecting to see a tiny vessel.

"Your clitoris – that is what it's sometimes called. You do know what a clit is, don't you, dear Anne?"

"You mean my pearl? Yes, here it is." She spreads her legs to display her slit, its arched top housing a fleshy bulge.

"Oh how wonderful," said Cynthia Allan, elbowing her way between the girl's thighs. "That berry looks good enough to eat."

And she did, after a fashion.

≈≈≈

With no one catching onto Anne's frequent meetings with the minister's errant wife, it was high time for her to get into fresh trouble. Little mistakes, such as absentmindedly emptying a pan of skim milk into a basket of yarn balls in the pantry instead of into the pigs' bucket, or walking clean over the edge of the log bridge into the brook while enjoying an imaginative reverie, were really not worth counting.

But Anne's unplanned aerial act qualified as what even Martin termed a "fuck up."

It happened that week Diana Barry threw her own tea party.

"Small and select," Anne assured Matilda. "Just the girls in our class."

The schoolmates had a very good time and nothing untoward happened until after tea, when they found themselves in the Barry's garden, a little tired of all their party games and ripe for any enticing form of mischief which might present itself. This presently took the form of "daring."

Daring was the fashionable amusement among the Avonlea small fry just then. It had begun among the boys, but soon spread to the girls, and all the silly things that were done in Avonlea that summer because the doers thereof were "dared" to do them would fill a book by themselves.

First of all Carrie Sloane dared Ruby Gillis to climb to a certain point in the huge old willow tree in the schoolyard; which Ruby Gillis, albeit in mortal dread of the fat green caterpillars which infested the tree and a fear that she might tear her new muslin dress, did nonetheless.

Then Josie Pye dared Jane Andrews to hop on her left leg around the garden without stopping or putting her right foot to the ground; which Jane Andrews gamely tried to do, but gave out at the third corner and had to confess herself defeated.

Josie's triumph was short-lived, for Anne Shirley dared her to walk along the top of the board fence which bounded the garden to the east. Now, walking board fences requires more skill and balance than one who has never tried it might suppose. But Josie Pye had a natural gift, duly cultivated, for walking board fences.

Thus Josie walked the Barry fence with an airy unconcern which seemed to imply that a little thing like that wasn't worth a "dare." Reluctant admiration greeted her exploit, for most of the other girls had suffered minor injuries in their own efforts to walk fences. Josie descended from her perch, flushed with victory, and darted a defiant glance at Anne.

Anne tossed her unruly hair, a sign of disdain. "I don't think it's such a wonderful thing to walk a low board fence," she sniffed. "I knew a girl in Marysville who could walk the ridgepole of a roof."

"I don't believe it," said Josie flatly. "I don't believe anybody could walk a ridgepole. YOU couldn't, anyhow."

"Couldn't I?" cried Anne rashly.

"Then I dare you to do it," said Josie defiantly. "I dare you to climb up there and walk the ridgepole of Mrs. Barry's kitchen roof."

Anne turned pale, but there was clearly only one thing to be done. She walked toward the house, where a ladder was leaning against the kitchen roof. All the fifth-class girls said, "Oh!" partly in excitement, partly in dismay.

"Don't you do it, Anne," entreated Diana. "You'll fall off and be killed. Never mind Josie Pye. It isn't fair to dare anybody to do anything so dangerous."

"I must do it. My honor is at stake," said Anne solemnly. "I shall walk that ridgepole, Diana, or perish in the attempt. If I am killed you are to have my pearl bead ring."

"Oh, go ahead then. I'd really like to have that ring."

"I hope Gil – that is, I mean the other students in our class will remember how bravely I died," declared Anne. She climbed the ladder amid breathless silence, gained the ridgepole, balanced herself uprightly on that precarious footing, and started to walk along it, dizzily conscious that she was uncomfortably high up in the world and that walking ridgepoles was not a thing in which your imagination helped much. Nevertheless, she managed to take several steps before the catastrophe came. Then she swayed, lost her balance, stumbled, staggered, and fell, sliding down over the sunbaked roof and crashing off it through the tangle of Virginia creeper beneath – all before the dismayed circle below could give a simultaneous, terrified shriek.

If Anne had tumbled off the roof on the side she

had ascended, Diana definitely would have fallen heir to the pearl bead ring. Fortunately, she fell on the other side, where the roof extended down over the porch so near to the ground that a fall therefrom was a much less serious thing. Nevertheless, when Diana and the other girls rushed frantically around the house – except Ruby Gillis, who remained as if rooted to the ground while going into hysterics – they found Anne lying all white and limp among the wreck and ruin of the Virginia creeper.

"Anne, are you killed?" shrieked Diana, throwing herself on her knees beside her friend. "Oh, Anne, dear Anne, speak just one word to me and tell me if you're killed."

To the immense relief of all the girls, and especially of Josie Pye, who, in spite of lack of imagination, had been seized with horrible visions of a future branded as the girl who was the cause of Anne Shirley's early and tragic death, Anne sat dizzily up and answered uncertainly: "No, Diana, I am not killed, but I think I am rendered unconscious."

"Where?" sobbed Carrie Sloane. "Oh, where, Anne?"

Before Anne could answer Mrs. Barry appeared on the scene. At the sight of Diana's mother, Anne attempted to scramble to her feet, but sank back again with a sharp little cry of pain.

"What's the matter? Where have you hurt yourself?" demanded Mrs. Barry.

"My ankle," gasped Anne. "Oh, Diana, please find your father and ask him to take me home. I know I can never walk there. And I'm sure I couldn't hop that far on one foot when Jane couldn't even hop around the garden."

≈≈≈

Matilda Collins was out in the orchard picking a panful of summer apples when she saw Mr. Barry coming over the log bridge and up the slope, with Mrs. Barry beside him and a whole procession of little girls trailing after them. In his arms he carried Anne, whose head lay limply against his shoulder.

At that moment Matilda had a revelation. In the sudden stab of fear that pierced her very heart she realized what Anne had come to mean to her. She would have admitted that she liked Anne – nay, that she was very fond of Anne. But now she knew as she hurried wildly down the slope that Anne was dearer to her than anything else on earth.

"Mr. Barry, what has happened to her?" she gasped, more white and shaken than the self-contained, sensible Matilda had been for many years.

Anne herself answered, lifting her head.

"Don't be very frightened, Matilda. I was walking the ridgepole and I fell off. I expect I have sprained my ankle. But let us look on the bright side of things – I could have broken my neck."

"I might have known you'd go and do something of the sort when I let you go to that party," said Matilda, sharp and shrewish in her very relief. "Bring her in here, Mr. Barry, and lay her on the sofa. Mercy me, the child has gone and fainted!"

Martin, hastily summoned from the harvest field, left straightway for the doctor, who in due time came, to discover that the injury was more serious than they had supposed. Anne's ankle was broken.

That night, when Matilda went up to the east gable, where a white-faced girl was lying, a plaintive voice greeted her from the bed. "Aren't you very sorry for me, Matilda?"

"It was your own fault," said Matilda, twitching down the blind and lighting a lamp. No need to give Mrs. Langston a bird's-eye view.

"And that is just why you should be sorry for me," said Anne, "because the thought that it is all my own fault is what makes it so hard. If I could blame it on anybody I would feel so much better. But what would you have done, Matilda, if you had been dared to walk a ridgepole?"

"I'd have stayed on good firm ground and let them dare away. Such absurdity!"

Anne sighed. "But you have such strength of mind, Matilda. I haven't. I just felt that I couldn't bear Josie Pye's scorn. She would have crowed over me all my life. And I think I have been punished so much that you needn't be very cross with me. It's not a bit nice to faint, after all. And the doctor hurt me dreadfully when he was setting my ankle. I won't be able to go around for six or seven weeks and I'll miss the new lady teacher. She won't be new anymore by the time I'm able to go to school. And Gil – everybody will get ahead of me in class. Oh, I am an afflicted mortal. But I'll try to bear it all bravely if only you won't be cross with me, Matilda."

"There, there, I'm not cross," said Matilda. "You're an unlucky child, there's no doubt about that; but as you say, you'll have the suffering of it. Here now, try to eat some supper."

"Isn't it fortunate I've got such an imagination?" said Anne. "It will help me get through this splendidly, I expect. What do people who haven't any imagination do when they break their bones, Matilda?"

"I have no idea." But she felt a pang of guilt in her answer, for she realized she fell in the no-imagination camp when compared to Anne Shirley.

Anne had good reason to bless her imagination many a time during the tedious seven weeks that followed. But she was not solely dependent on it. She had numerous visitors. Not a day passed without one or more of the schoolgirls dropping in to bring her flowers and books and tell her all the happenings in the juvenile world of Avonlea.

"Everybody has been so good and kind, Matilda," sighed Anne happily, on the day when she could first limp across the floor. "It isn't very pleasant to be laid up; but there is a bright side to it, Matilda. You find out how many friends you have. Why, even School Superintendent Bell came to see me, and he's really a very fine man. Not a kindred spirit, of course; but still I like him and I'm awfully sorry I ever criticized him. He told me all about the time he broke his ankle when he was a boy. It does seem so strange to think of Superintendent Bell ever being a boy. Even my imagination has its limits, for I can't imagine THAT. When I try to imagine him as a boy I see him with gray whiskers and spectacles, just as he looks today, only smaller. Now, it's so easy to imagine Mrs. Allan as a little girl. Mrs. Allan has been to see me fourteen times. Isn't that something to be proud of, Matilda? When a minister's wife has so many claims on her time! She is such a cheerful person to have visit you, too. She never tells you it's your own fault and she hopes you'll be a better girl on account of it. Mrs. Langston always told me that when she came to see me; and she said it in a way that indicated she hoped I'd be a better girl but didn't really believe I would accomplish that goal. Of course, she watches us fucking through our bedroom window, so she knows how debauched I really am."

"There, there, Anne. Our family life is between us – none of Mrs. Langston's beeswax."

"Even Josie Pye came to see me," Anne rattled on. "I received her as politely as I could, because I think she was sorry she dared me to walk a ridgepole. If I had been killed she would had to carry a dark burden of remorse all her life. Diana has been a faithful friend. She's been over every day to cheer my lonely pillow. Sometimes she gets naked and climbs into bed with me. She's so much fun under the covers. But oh, I shall be so glad when I can go back to school for I've heard such exciting things about the new teacher. The girls all think she is perfectly sweet. Diana says she has the loveliest curly hair and such fascinating eyes. She dresses beautifully, and her sleeve puffs are bigger than anybody else's in Avonlea. Every other Friday afternoon she has recitations and everybody has to say a piece or take part in a dialogue. Oh, it's just glorious to think of it. Josie Pye says she hates it but that is just because Josie has so little imagination. Diana and Ruby Gillis and Jane Andrews are preparing a dialogue, called 'A Morning Visit,' for next Friday. And on those other Friday afternoons Miss Stacy takes the class to the woods for a field day and they study ferns and flowers and birds. And they have an exercise period every morning. Mrs. Langston says she never heard of such goings-on and that it comes from having a lady teacher. But I think it's splendid and believe I shall find that Miss Stacy is a kindred spirit."

Matilda shook her head wearily. "There's one thing plain to be seen, Anne Shirley, and that is that your fall off the Barry roof hasn't injured your tongue at all."

Anne giggled. "Take off your dress and crawl into bed with me and I'll show you that my tongue still works just fine."

Back to school.

CHAPTER XXIV

Miss Stacy and Her Pupils Get Up a Concert

It was October again when Anne was ready to go back to school – a glorious October, all red and gold, with mellow mornings when the valleys were filled with delicate mists as if the potable spirit of autumn had been poured into them – amethyst, pearl, silver, rose, and smoke-blue. The dews were so heavy that the fields glistened like cloth of silver and there were heaps of rustling leaves in the hollows for dryads to run through. The Birch Path was a canopy of yellow and the ferns were seared brown all along it. There was a tang in the air that inspired the hearts of small maidens racing willingly to school.

Anne found it jolly to be back at the little wooden desk beside Diana, with Ruby Gillis nodding across the aisle and Carrie Sloane sending up notes and Julia Bell passing a chew of gum down the aisle. Anne drew a long breath of happiness as she sharpened her pencil and arranged her picture cards on her desk. Life was certainly very interesting.

In the new teacher she found another helpful friend. Miss Muriel Stacy was a bright young woman with a talent for winning the affections of her pupils. She was truly gifted with bringing out the best that was in them academically. Anne thrived like a flower under this teacher's influence and carried home glowing accounts of schoolwork and accomplishments.

"I love Miss Stacy with my whole heart, Matilda.

She is so ladylike and has such a sweet voice. Her hair is just as blonde as yours. Isn't that a wonderful coincidence? And when she pronounces my name I feel INSTINCTIVELY that she's spelling it with an E. We had recitations this afternoon. I just wish you could have been there to hear me recite 'Mary, Queen of Scots.' I put my whole soul into it. Ruby Gillis told me coming home that the way I said the line 'my woman's heart farewell' made her tingle."

"Well now, you might recite it for me one of these days, out in the barn," suggested Martin.

"Of course I will," said Anne meditatively, "but I won't be able to do it so well, as when I have a whole schoolroom filled with students hanging breathlessly on my every word. I know I won't be able to make you tingle."

"Oh, you might," he said with a wink that told her he had more in mind for her in the barn than simply listening to her recite "Mary, Queen of Scots."

"Our field trips are wonderful, Matilda. Miss Stacy explains everything so beautifully. We have to write compositions about our experiences in the field and I write the best ones."

"It's very vain of you to say that. You'd best let your teacher say it."

"But she DID say it, Matilda. And indeed I'm not vain about it. How can I be, when I'm such a dunce at geometry? But I think I'm beginning to see through geometry a little. Miss Stacy makes it so clear. Still, I'll never be good at it and I assure you that is a humbling experience."

"Learn from it," advised Matilda.

"Yes, I will. Of all our activities, I love writing compositions. Mostly Miss Stacy lets us choose our own subjects; but next week we are assigned to write a composition about some remarkable person. It's hard to choose among so many remarkable people who have lived. Mustn't it be splendid to be remarkable and have compositions written about you after you're dead? Oh, I would dearly love to be remarkable. I think when I grow up I'll be a trained nurse with the Red Cross and go into the field of battle as a messenger of mercy. That is, if I don't go out as a church missionary. That would be very romantic, but I think one would have to be very good to be a missionary. That might be a stumbling block for me. I'm not sure how I would take to fucking black-skinned Zulus if I were stationed in Africa and did not have you and Martin to satisfy my physical needs."

"Zulus, my lord. Can't you graduate to the next form before you start planning who you're going to have sex with as an adult?"

"You're right, Matilda. I should be thinking who I'm going to have sex with at the concert that's coming up. I wonder if Gil – I mean, some boy will ask me to go to it with him."

"Concert? Yes, I suppose it's approaching that time of year again." Matilda wasn't big on concerts. Besides, she had mixed feeling about Anne fucking boys in her class. It was so easy to get a reputation as a tart in an isolated province like Prince Edward Island.

≈≈≈

All the field trips and recitations and physical culture paled against the upcoming concert. Here the

317

scholars of Avonlea School would put on a variety show on Christmas Night for the laudable purpose of helping to pay for a schoolhouse flag. The pupils one and all took enthusiastically to this plan, beginning preparations for an interesting program. But of all the potential performers none was more excited than Anne Shirley. She threw herself into the undertaking heart and soul.

Matilda thought it all rank foolishness. "It's just filling students' heads up with nonsense and taking time away from their lessons," she grumbled. "I don't approve of children performing like trained monkeys. It makes them vain and forward and fond of gadding."

"But think of the worthy goal," argued Anne. "A flag will cultivate a spirit of patriotism for our school."

"Fudge! There's precious little patriotism in the thoughts of any of you. All you want is to have a good time."

"Well, when you can combine patriotism and fun, isn't it all right? Of course, it's fun to strut your stuff in a concert. We're going to have choreographed dancers. There will be six chorales. Diana will sing a solo. And I'm in a recitation of *The Faerie Queene*. I just tremble when I think of it, but it's a nice thrilly kind of tremble."

"Bully for you."

"Diana and Ruby and I are to be in the tableau, all decked out with wings and long flowing hair. I'm going to practice my recitations in the east garret. Don't be alarmed if you hear me groaning. I have to groan heartrendingly in one scene, and it's really hard to get up a good artistic groan. Josie Pye is acting sulky because she didn't get the part she wanted. She wanted to be the Faerie Queene, but that would have been ridiculous, for who ever heard of a fairy queen as fat as Josie? Diana was too plump also. Fairy queens must be slender. Therefore I get to be the queen and they are my maids of honor. I'm to wear a wreath of white roses on my hair and fairy wings, but I plan to be nude for the recitation. It's necessary for fairies to be naked, you know. You couldn't imagine a fairy wearing clothes, could you?"

"Anne Shirley, get that silly notion out of your head. Miss Stacy is not going to let you appear on stage naked. This is Avonlea School we're talking about, not Minksy's Burlesque!"

"But Matilda –"

"Don't try to sway me. It's one thing for you to run naked around the farm, but another for you to stand bare-butt on a stage in front of all the other students and their parents. I won't hear of it."

"Oh, okay. But a fairy wearing clothing will look plain silly."

The Faerie Queene.

CHAPTER XXV

An Unfortunate Lily Maid

"**A**nne, of course you must be Gloriana, the faerie queene," said Diana Barry. "I can't think of a more suitable leader of the fairies than you."

"Nor I," agreed Ruby Gillis. "You talk about fairies and elves and dryads all the time. You might as well be one."

"Sometimes I think I am," giggled Anne Shirley. "At least in my imagination."

"It would be romantic to be a fairy," conceded little Emma White, "but I know I couldn't run around naked. I'd be so embarrassed. And that would spoil the effect."

"I'd love to be Gloriana," said Anne. "But Prissy Andrews would make a much better faerie queene because she is so fair and has such lovely long golden hair – not piss-burnt brown tresses like mine."

"Your hair is not so bad," offered Jane. "Just unruly."

"But Prissy has bigger boobs. A faerie queene must have proud, full breasts, don't you think?"

"Prissy's boobs are TOO big," opined Ruby. "I don't see how she carries them, as heavy as they must be."

"Your boobs are just right," said little Emma White, daring to touch them. Anne didn't seem to mind.

"Here, let us make a comparison," suggested Diana, reaching over to unbutton her friend's dress with accustomed familiarity. "I think your fairy court might be a better judge of your boobs than you."

"Okay," responded Anne, shrugging the dress off her shoulders to expose her pointy breasts. Yes, they were much smaller than Prissy's exaggerated mammaries, but well rounded with perky pink tips. "What do you think of them, my fairy maidens?"

"Ooo, they're very pretty," said Emma, touching them again. "I wish my boobies were as nice as these."

"Be patient," advised Anne. "In time they will grow. You're only fourteen, younger than the rest of us."

"Not bad titties indeed," admitted Josie, her sometimes nemesis. "I'd offer to suck on them if the other girls weren't here." She was a tomboy, with perhaps a few Sapphic tendencies.

"Go ahead if you want to," said Anne. "I wouldn't mind. And I'm sure the other girls won't tell."

"Maybe some other time," Josie backed off her impulse. But you could tell she was disappointed in turning down the offer. "But I agree you'd make a better faerie queene than that cow Prissy."

"Your complexion is just as fair as Prissy's," said Diana earnestly, "and your hair is ever so much nicer than it used to be before Matilda trimmed it."

"Oh, do you really think so?" exclaimed Anne, flushing with delight. "I've sometimes thought it was nicer myself – but I never dared to ask anyone for fear I'd be told it wasn't."

"I think your hair is real pretty," said Jane, looking admiringly at the brunette tresses clustered about Anne's head, held in place by a very jaunty black velvet ribbon and bow. "I hate being a dishwater blonde."

"Your blonde hair is quite lovely," countered Anne. "Does it match the hair between your legs?"

"I don't have much hair down there yet. I only recently got my first period. My mother says I'm a late bloomer."

"I've been having my periods for three years now," said Anne, "but the hair down below is fairly sparse. Here, I'll show you."

With that, Anne Shirley stepped out of her dress and shed her knickers in one downward curtsey. "There," she said, displaying her dark pubes as she leaned back against a huge tree.

"Oh my, you are indeed a faerie queene," declared Ruby at the sight of Anne posing *au naturale*.

"Yes, you must be our queen," echoed the others, unanimously ratifying Anne's lead in the upcoming production of *The Faerie Queene*.

They were standing on the bank of the pond, just below Orchard Slope where a wooden platform extended into the waters. Diana's father kept a small flatboat moored there. It was a bit chilly this time of year, but these were Canadian girls who came from hardy stock, immune to the cold.

Turns out, Ruby and Jane were spending the afternoon with Diana, and Anne had come over to play with them. Little Emma White had happened along on her way to buy some eggs for her mother from Mrs. Langston.

That past summer Anne and Diana had spent most of their spare time on and about the pond. Idlewild was a thing of the past, for Mr. Barry had ruthlessly cut down the little circle of trees in his back pasture that defined the pretend house. Anne had sat among the stumps and wept, not without an eye to the romance of it; but she was speedily consoled, for, after all, as she and Diana said, big girls of sixteen, going on seventeen, were too old for such childish amusements as playhouses, and there were more fascinating sports to be found about the pond. It was splendid to fish for trout over the bridge and the two girls learned to row themselves about in the little flat-bottomed dory Mr. Barry kept for duck shooting. That, and pleasuring each other at Dryad's Bubble.

It was Anne's idea that they dramatize *The Faerie Queen* for Avonlea School's Christmas concert. They had studied Edmund Spenser's epic poem in school that preceding spring, Mr. Superintendent Bell having made it required reading for English courses in all Prince Edward Island schools. He was a big fan of Spenser. The students had analyzed and parsed it and torn it to pieces in general until it was a wonder there was any meaning at all left in it for them, but at least King Arthur and Acrasia and Belphoebe had become very real people to them. Anne harbored a secret regret that she had not been born in Camelot. Those days, she said, were so much more romantic than the present.

Anne's plan had been hailed with enthusiasm. Miss Stacy said she was awarding Anne extra points for coming up with such a brilliant suggestion.

With scripts in hand, the schoolgirls began memorizing their lines. Only a limited number of passages could be selected for the poem was very long and they had been allotted only a half hour of the concert.

Anne tried out her lines:

"For whatsoever from one place doth fall,
Is with the tide unto an other brought:
For there is nothing lost, that may be found, if
sought."

"Do you suppose it's really right to act out a poem like this?" interrupted Emma. "Mrs. Langston says that all play-acting is abominably wicked."

"Emma, you shouldn't be talking about Mrs. Langston," said Anne severely. "It spoils the effect because this takes place hundreds of years before Mrs. Langston was born."

Ruby rose to the occasion. "Anne is standing there reciting her lines in the buff. She so looks like a true fairy against all this foliage. We should take off our clothes and join her to establish a proper mood."

"Yes, I'm game," said Diana, stepping out of her puffy-sleeved dress.

"Me too," agreed Jane, shucking her gingham pullover.

Soon all the girls were in a natural state, save Emma White. "Don't be shy," coaxed Anne. "We're transforming ourselves into fairies and water sprites and lily maidens."

"I'm not shy. I'm just afraid everyone will tease me over my small boobies."

"They can't be much smaller than mine," replied Jane Andrews, turning to display her modest bosom, "and nobody is teasing me." One would think her sister Prissy had inherited all the bosom genes in the Andrews family.

Hesitantly, Emma White undressed, revealing

pancake-flat boobies. But no one made fun of her diminutive state of development. Since Prissy wasn't present, Diana had the largest set, Anne second.

"Anne, you lay in Mr. Barry's flatboat and we'll launch you out into the pond where you can reign over the water sprites," suggested Jane.

"Where are the water sprites," little Emma said, looking around as if she expected to see some.

"Ruby and I will pretend to be sprites," explained Jane. "We will swim out to Anne – uh, I mean the Fairy Queen. We're both very good swimmers. We learned last year at 4H Canada camp."

"I'm not sure I know how to swim," admitted Anne.

"What do you mean you don't know if you know how," laughed Jane. "You either know how or you don't."

"Well, what I mean to say is that I've never tried to swim."

"Don't worry, you'll be in the boat," Diana assured her friend. "My father said that dory's nigh impossible to sink."

"If you say so, dear Diana." Stepping onto the boat, Anne looked quite regal, chin held high, boobs thrust forward, tummy sucked flat, her boyish hips cocked jauntily to one side.

"Lay down as if this is your funeral barge," directed Jane, enjoying this diversion from the script. She hated memorizing lines from a dusty old poem by a long-dead bard.

Anne obediently stretched out in bottom of the wooden boat and placed her hands over her breasts as she imagined a dead queen would be positioned.

"Ready, my water sprites," she intoned.

The flatboat was accordingly pushed off, scraping roughly over an old embedded stake in the process. Diana and Jane and Ruby only waited long enough to see it caught in the current before scampering through the woods, heading to the lower headland where, as water sprites and lily maids, they were to be in readiness to receive the faerie queene.

For a few minutes Anne drifted slowly down, enjoying the romance of her situation to the fullest. Then something happened not at all romantic. The boat began to leak. In a very few moments it was necessary for Anne to scramble to her feet, and gaze in horror at a big crack in the bottom of her barge through which the water was literally pouring. That sharp stake at the landing had torn off the strip of batting nailed on he bottom of the flatboat. So much for Mr. Barry's boat being unsinkable!

It did not take Anne long to realize that she was in a dangerous plight. At this rate the shallow boat would fill with water long before it reached the lower headland. She had to get to shore, but where were the oars? Drat! – Left behind at the landing.

Anne gave a scream which nobody heard; the other girls were already on the far side of the pond. She was white to the lips, but did not lose her self-possession. There was one chance – just one.

"I was horribly frightened," she told Mrs. Allan the next day, "and it seemed like years while the boat was drifting down to the bridge and the water rising in it every moment. I prayed most earnestly, for I knew the only way I could be saved was if the boat floated close enough to one of the bridge pilings for me to climb up on it. You know the pilings are just old tree trunks and there are lots of knots and old branch stubs on them. I just said, 'Dear God, please take the boat close to a piling and I'll do the rest.' As it happened, my prayer was answered, for the flatboat bumped right into a piling and I scrambled onto a big stub. And there I was, Mrs. Allan, clinging to that slippery old piling with no way of getting up or down. It was a very unromantic position, but I didn't think about that at the time. You don't think much about romance when you have just escaped from a watery grave. I endeavored to hold on tight, for I knew I would have to depend on human aid to get back to dry land."

The flatboat drifted under the bridge and then promptly sank in midstream. Ruby, Jane, and Diana were awaiting it on the lower headland. When they saw it disappear before their very eyes, there was not a doubt but that Anne had gone down with it. For a moment they stood still, white as sheets, frozen with horror at the tragedy; then, shrieking at the tops of their voices, they started on a frantic run up through the woods, pulling on their dresses, never pausing to look back at the bridge.

Meanwhile, Anne clung desperately to her precarious foothold while watching their flying forms and hearing their shrieks. Help would soon come, she was sure, but for the moment her position was a very precarious one. Not to mention her state of nudity, which might prove embarrassing if Mr. Barry came to her rescue.

The minutes passed by, each seeming an hour to

the unfortunate faerie queen. Why didn't somebody come? Where had the girls gone? Suppose they had fainted, one and all! Suppose nobody ever came! Suppose she grew so tired and cramped that she could hold on no longer! Anne looked at the wicked green depths below her, shimmering with long, oily shadows. Her imagination began to suggest all manner of gruesome possibilities to her. Perhaps a sea monster lurked below, waiting to gobble her up the moment she fell into the icy cold waters.

Then, just as she thought she could not endure the ache in her arms and wrists a moment longer, Gilbert Blythe came rowing under the bridge in Thomas Langston's dory!

Gilbert glanced up and, much to his amazement, beheld a little white face looking down on him with big, frightened but also scornful gray-green eyes.

"Anne Shirley! How on earth did you get up there?" he exclaimed. "And where are your clothes?"

Without waiting for an answer he pulled close to the piling and extended his hand. There was no help for it; Anne, clinging to Gilbert Blythe's hand, scrambled down into the dory, where she sat, drabbled and furious, in the stern with her arms crossed to hide her breasts. No need to give him a free show. Oh my, it was certainly difficult to be dignified under such circumstances!

"What has happened, Anne?" asked Gilbert, taking up his oars.

"We were rehearsing *The Faerie Queene* for the Christmas concert," explained Anne frigidly, without even looking at her rescuer, "and I was drifting down to Camelot in the barge – I mean Mr. Barry's flatboat. The boat began to leak and I climbed out on the piling while the girls went for help."

"And they left you there totally naked?"

"Yes, to your good fortune. I hope you enjoyed the view. Now will you be kind enough to row me to the landing?"

Gilbert obligingly rowed to the landing and Anne, disdaining assistance, sprang nimbly on shore. The clearing was empty. Emma White had abandoned her post, no doubt running home in a panic.

"Take your time climbing out of the boat," he told her. "You don't want to fall overboard." But he was clearly delaying her egress in order to enjoy her nudity.

"I'm very much obliged to you," she said haughtily as she turned away.

But Gilbert had also sprung from the boat to lay a detaining hand on her arm. "Anne," he said hurriedly, "look here. Can't we be friends? I'm awfully sorry I made fun of you that time. I didn't mean to vex you. It was only meant as a joke. Besides, it was so long ago. I think you are awfully pretty – honest I do. Especially without any clothes on. Can't we be friends?"

For a moment Anne hesitated. She had an odd, newly awakened consciousness under all her outraged dignity that the half-shy, half-eager expression in Gilbert's hazel eyes was something very good to see. Her heart gave a quick, queer little beat. But the bitterness of her old grievance served to maintain her determination. She hated Gilbert Blythe! She would never forgive him!

"No," she said coldly, "I shall never be friends with

you, Gilbert Blythe; and quit staring at my breasts."

"All right!" Gilbert sprang into his skiff with an angry color in his cheeks. "I'll never ask you to be friends again, Anne Shirley. And I don't care, even if you do have great tits!"

He pulled away with swift defiant strokes, and Anne strode up the steep path, her head held very high, as if her nudity was an everyday occurrence. Let Gilbert Blythe look if he wanted. All he'd see was her retreating backside. Nonetheless, she was conscious of an odd feeling of regret. She almost wished she had answered Gilbert differently. Of course, he had insulted her terribly, but still –!

Halfway up the path she met Jane and Diana rushing back to the pond in a state narrowly removed from positive frenzy. They had found nobody at Orchard Slope, both Mr. and Mrs. Barry being away. Here Ruby Gillis had succumbed to hysterics, and was left to recover as best she might, while Jane and Diana flew through the Haunted Wood and across the brook to Green Gables. There they had found nobody either, for Matilda had gone to Carmody and Martin was making hay in the backfield.

"Oh, Anne," gasped Diana, fairly falling on the former's neck and weeping with relief and delight. "Oh, Anne – we thought – you were – drowned – and we felt like murderers – because we had made – you be – Gloriana. And Ruby is in hysterics. Oh, Anne, how did you escape?"

"I climbed up on one of the bridge's pilings," explained Anne wearily, "and Gilbert Blythe came along in Mr. Langston's dory and brought me to land."

"Oh, Anne, how splendid of him! Why, it's so romantic!" said Diana, finding breath enough for utterance at last. "Of course you'll speak to him after this."

"Of course I won't," flashed Anne, with a momentary return of her old spirit. "And I don't want ever to hear the word 'romantic' again, Diana Barry. I'm only sorry he got to see me naked, a privilege I reserve for only my dearest friends."

"Like us?" asked Jane.

"Yes, like you, my wonderful fairy court." She began to tug on her dress, just in case Mr. Barry returned home and, alerted by Ruby, came to her rescue.

"What an adventure," sighed Diana.

"I'm awfully sorry you were so frightened, Diana. It is all my fault. I feel sure I was born under an unlucky star. Everything I do gets me or my dearest friends into a scrape. We've gone and lost your father's flatboat, and I have a premonition that we'll not be allowed to row on the pond anymore."

≈≈≈

Anne's premonition proved to be accurate. Great was the consternation in the Barry and Collins households when the events of the afternoon became known.

"Will you ever have any sense, Anne?" groaned Matilda.

"Oh, yes, I think I will, Matilda," returned Anne optimistically. A good cry, indulged in the grateful solitude of the east gable, had soothed her nerves and restored her to her wonted cheerfulness. "I think my prospects of becoming sensible are brighter now than ever."

"I don't see how," said Matilda.

"Well," explained Anne, "I've learned a new and valuable lesson today. Ever since I came to Green Gables I've been making mistakes, and each mistake has helped to cure me of some great shortcoming. The affair of the amethyst brooch cured me of meddling with things that didn't belong to me. The Haunted Wood mistake cured me of letting my imagination run away with me. The liniment cake mistake cured me of carelessness in cooking. And today's mistake is going to cure me of being too romantic. I have come to the conclusion that it is no use trying to be romantic in Avonlea. It was probably easy enough hundreds of years ago in Camelot, but romance is not appreciated now. I feel quite sure that you will soon see a great improvement in me in this respect, Matilda."

"I'm sure I hope so," said Matilda skeptically.

But Martin, who had been sitting mutely in his corner, laid a hand on Anne's shoulder when Matilda had gone out. "Don't give up all your romance, Anne," he whispered shyly. "A little of it is a good thing – not too much, of course – but keep a little of it, Anne. Romance improves your performance in the bedroom."

Martin picks a wife.

CHAPTER XXVI

Martin Insists on Puffed Sleeves

Martin had come into the kitchen in the twilight of a cold, gray December evening, and perched on the corner of the woodbox to take off his heavy boots, unaware that Anne and a bevy of her schoolmates were having a practice of *The Faerie Queene* in the sitting room. Presently they came trooping through the hall and out into the kitchen, laughing and chattering gaily. They did not see Martin, who shrank bashfully back into the shadows beyond the woodbox with a boot in one hand and a bootjack in the other.

All the girls were naked, save for garlands about their hair. He could hardly believe his eyes. He watched them as they chattered about the upcoming concert and boys in their class and tomorrow's homework assignment.

Yes, there was Diana Barry and Ruby Gillis and Emma White, all exposed for him to examine from perky boobs to bushy pubes. Josie Pye and Julia Bell were starkers too. And Prissy Andrews was a sight to rival all the Seven Wonders of the World, her huge breasts defying the laws of gravity. He thought he might faint from shortness of breath.

Anne stood out among them, bright eyed and animated. Her perfect boobies bobbling like twin bowls of gelatin. As Martin watched his adopted ward, he suddenly became conscious that there was something about her different from her schoolmates. Anne had a brighter face, starrier eyes, and more delicate features than the others; even unobservant Martin took note of these things; but the difference that disturbed him did not consist in any of these respects.

Then what was this difference?

"What a delicious idea Anne had, us doing *The Faerie Queene* in the nude," remarked Diana.

"That's how fairies dress," agreed Ruby.

"Miss Stacy's sure going to be surprised," said little Emma.

"Not as surprised as the boys in our class," giggled Josie, taken with the naughtiness of the production.

"Do we dare do it?" asked Julia.

"I say give them a thrill," voted Prissy. "We will all be assured of dates after displaying our wares for all to see."

"Yes, let's do it," echoed Josie. "I want to get fucked by Charlie Sloane."

"Oh, Josie, you want to get fucked by anybody," retorted Anne.

"And you don't?"

"No, I am quite selective in whom I let fuck me."

"You did Mr. Phillips," accused Prissy who had witnessed the copulation.

"So has everyone in this room," Anne replied, not knowing of Martin's presence.

"I didn't," protested little Emma White. "I'm still a virgin."

"You're the only one in the entire school," laughed Josie.

"I'd do Martin Collins," offered Ruby. "I think he's so handsome."

"No," said Anne, "he's mine."

Martin almost revealed himself with a gasp of delight, but the girls took it to be the sound of the wind outside the kitchen window and continued on with their rehearsal.

≈≈≈

What made Anne stand out so clearly from the other girls? Martin was haunted by this question long after the girls had gone, now dressed, arm in arm, skipping down the long, hard-frozen lane, and Anne had betaken herself to her books in her room. He could not refer it to Matilda, who, he felt, would be quite sure to sniff scornfully and remark that the only difference she saw between Anne and the other girls was that they sometimes kept their tongues quiet while Anne never did. This observation, Martin felt, would be no great help.

He lit his pipe that evening to help him study it out, much to Matilda's disgust. After two hours of smoking and hard reflection Martin arrived at a solution of his problem. Anne was different from the other girls because he was in love with her!

The more Martin thought about the matter the more he was convinced that Anne might just love him too. He was surprised by this conclusion. She was just a poor little orphan girl who had come to live with him and his sister through mistaken circumstance. Keeping her as a legal sex slave had been the plan, but somewhere along the way he had started to truly care for Anne. Sure, he had affection for Matilda – after all, she was his sister. But that emotion was more of familiarity and convenience, not an outpouring of genuine romantic love as he realized he felt for Anne Shirley.

Now this complicated things. Should he confess his feelings and find out if she returned them? He was much too shy for that. Should he cease having a conjugal relationship with his sister, pledging fidelity to the girl he loved? Should he propose marriage, perhaps to the shock of the entire island? Should he and Anne move out, relocating elsewhere, perhaps someplace where their adoptive relationship was unknown, and allow Matilda to get on with her own life.

As he considered the matter, it became clear he had robbed his sister of many chances for happiness. Living with him did not allow a proper atmosphere for suitors or for her to find a man of her own. With her sexual needs satisfied, her financial security assured, she'd had less use for a husband than most women.

How old was Anne? Almost seventeen, that was a marriageable age. What if she selected a husband of her own, while he dithered around, unable to declare his true feelings? That would be – to use Anne's phrase – "tragical."

Why not declare himself and marry Anne? Matilda could live with them here at Green Gables for as long as she liked. Heck, maybe Anne would be agreeable they keep the threesome going. The girl seemed to enjoy sex with a woman as well as with a man.

Maybe he should propose. But that required a ring. He and Matilda kept their sainted mother's wedding ring in a music box on their dresser. However, Matilda wanted to preserve that ring as a family heirloom, so he'd need a new one for his marriage to Anne.

After much thought, Martin decided that he would give her one for Christmas. That wondrous holiday was only a fortnight away. A nice new ring would be the very thing for a present. And letting her find it in a gift box was the perfect way to propose, elegant yet not requiring him to prostate himself in front of her. Even being a kindred spirit, he was more of a listener than a talker.

That decided, Martin felt better. With a sigh of satisfaction, he put away his pipe and went to bed, while Matilda opened all the doors and aired the house.

≈ ≈ ≈

The very next day Martin hitched up the sorrel mare and drove to Carmody to buy the ring, determined to get the worst over and have done with it. It would be, he felt assured, no trifling ordeal. There were some things Martin could buy and in doing so prove himself no mean bargainer; but he knew he would be at the mercy of shopkeepers when it came to buying a wedding ring.

After much cogitation Martin resolved to go to Samuel Lawson's store instead of William Blair's. To be sure, the Collins siblings had always gone to William Blair's; it was almost as much a matter of conscience with them as attending the First Presbyterian Church or voting Conservative. But William Blair's two daughters frequently waited on customers and Martin held them in absolute dread. He had fucked one of them after a Farmers' Association dance two years ago and she resented that he'd never called on her again. No apology needed, he thought. She had been as cold as stone, laying there like a statue while he pounded away, the two of them in the back room of her father's store.

At the store he could contrive to deal with the angry sister when he knew exactly what he wanted and could point it out; but in a matter such as this, requiring explanation and consultation, Martin felt that he must be sure of dealing with a stranger. So he would go to Lawson's, where Samuel or his son would wait on him. They barely knew him, being he always shopped at William Blair's.

Alas! Martin did not know that Samuel, in the recent expansion of his business, had added a lady clerk; she was his niece, a very dashing young woman indeed, with huge breasts, big brown eyes, and a most bedazzling smile. She was dressed with exceeding smartness and wore several bangle bracelets that glittered and rattled and tinkled with every movement of her hands. Martin was filled with confusion at finding her there at all; and those noisy bangles completely wrecked his wits at one fell swoop.

"What can I do for you this evening, Mr. Collins?" Miss Lucilla Harris inquired, briskly and ingratiatingly, tapping the counter with both hands. She recognized him from church.

"Have you any – any – any – well now, any garden rakes?" stammered Martin.

Miss Harris looked confused, as well she might be, to hear a customer inquiring for garden rakes in the middle of December. "Rakes?"

"Uh, yes, rakes."

"I believe we might have one or two left over," she

said, "but they're upstairs in the lumber room. I'll go and see." During her absence Martin collected his scattered senses for another effort.

When Miss Harris returned with the rake and cheerfully inquired: "Anything else today, Mr. Collins?" Martin took his courage in both hands and replied: "Well now, since you suggest it, I might as well – take – that is – look at – buy some – some hayseed."

Miss Harris had heard Martin Collins called odd. She now concluded that he was entirely crazy. "We only keep hayseed in the spring," she explained loftily. "We've none on hand just now."

"Oh, certainly – certainly – just as you say," stammered unhappy Martin, seizing the rake and making for the door. At the threshold he recollected that he had not paid for it and he turned miserably back. While Miss Harris was counting out his change he rallied his powers for a final desperate attempt.

"Well now – if it isn't too much trouble – I might as well – that is – I'd like to look at – at – some sugar."

"White or brown?" queried Miss Harris patiently.

"Oh – well now – brown," said Martin feebly.

"There's a barrel of it over there," said Miss Harris, shaking her bangles at it. "It's the only kind we have."

"I'll – I'll take twenty pounds of it," said Martin, with beads of perspiration standing out on his forehead.

"I'll have the stock boy get it for you."

Martin had driven halfway home before he was his own man again. It had been a gruesome experience, but it served him right, he thought, for committing the heresy of going to a strange store. When he reached home he hid the rake in the tool house, but the sugar he carried in to Matilda.

"Brown sugar!" exclaimed his sister. "Whatever possessed you to get so much? You know I never use it except for the hired man's porridge or black fruitcake. It's not good sugar, either – it's coarse and dark – William Blair doesn't usually keep sugar like that."

"I – I thought it might come in handy sometime," said Martin, making good his escape.

When Martin came to think the matter over he decided that a woman was required to cope with the situation. Matilda was out of the question. Martin felt sure she would throw cold water on his project at once. Marrying Anne Shirley would be an anathema, upsetting the balance of the household, with Anne's position reversing itself, changing from orphaned ward to mistress of Green Gables.

Martin decided that only Mrs. Langston could help him, for there was no other woman in all of Avonlea he had the courage to ask advice. Turned out, Mrs. Langston was quite receptive, and she promptly took the matter out of the harassed man's hands.

"Pick out a ring for you to give Anne? To be sure I will. I'm going to Carmody tomorrow and I'll attend to it. Have you something particular in mind? Gold? Silver? No? Well, I'll just go by my own judgment then. I believe a nice gold band would best suit our Anne. And I've noticed William Blair has some rings in his jewelry section that are real pretty. Perhaps you'd like me to plan the wedding, too, seeing that if Matilda was to do the planning Anne would probably get wind of it before the proper time, spoiling the surprise? Well, you don't have to ask me twice, I'll do it. No, it isn't a mite of trouble. I like weddings."

"Well now, I'm much obliged," sputtered Martin, "and – and – I dunno – but I'd like – I hope Anne will accept my proposal when she opens the ring box on Christmas morn."

"Accept your proposal? Of course, she will. You needn't worry a speck more about it, Martin. The girl adores you. And you're a landholder, a successful farmer, a pillar of the community – quite the catch," said Rita Langston.

To her husband she added when Martin had gone: "It'll be a real satisfaction to see Martin do decent by that poor child. Sleeping with his own sister is bad enough, but taking advantage of a helpless orphan is another. The things I've seen through that bedroom window with my spyglass would shock a bawdyhouse madam. The way Martin and Matilda debase that girl – both of them having at her together – is positively scandalous, that's what, and I've ached to tell them so plainly a dozen times. I've held my tongue though, for I can see Martin and Matilda don't want anyone revealing their family secrets. But that's always the way. Folks like to keep their sex life private, particularly when it would not meet public approval. For example, Roscoe Andrews screws his daughter Prissy. Bruce Matthews is a closet homosexual. Old John Barry gets drunk and has his way with Margaux, the pretty French girl who babysits his daughter. And Ruby Gillis's father has sex with his sheep. Avonlea was a hotbed of scandal when you came right down to it. Even her husband Thomas preferred masturbation to connubial sex. She herself hadn't been porked since Rev. Cleary moved away.

Mrs. Langston felt sorry for Matilda Collins, about to be the odd one out. It would be hard for her to be replaced by a girl she'd treated as a daughter. "But sexual dynamics is never as easy as a Rule of Three – where you just set your three terms down, and the sum'll work out correct. But flesh and blood don't come under the heading of arithmetic and that's where Matilda Collins made her mistake," she told her husband after Martin had left. "I suppose she's trying to cultivate a spirit of humility in Anne by debasing her as she does; but it's more likely to cultivate envy and discontent. I'm sure the girl must feel a difference between her and Matilda in the bedroom pecking order. Of course, Anne Shirley will accept Martin's marriage proposal – why would she pass up the chance to be on top? It will be difficult for Matilda when the roles are reversed. I can hardly fathom it! To think of Martin replacing his sister in his bed is almost as shocking as knowing she was there in the first place!"

≈≈≈

Matilda knew all the following fortnight that Martin had something on his mind, but what it was she could not guess, until Christmas Eve, when Mrs. Langston brought up the wedding plans she'd been making in Martin's behalf. Matilda behaved pretty well on the whole, although it is very likely she distrusted Mrs. Langston's diplomatic explanation that she had made the wedding plans because Martin was afraid Anne would find out about it too soon if Matilda made them.

"So this is what Martin has been looking so mysterious over and grinning about to himself for two weeks, is it?" she said a little stiffly but tolerantly. "I knew he was up to some foolishness. Well, I must say I don't think Anne needs to marry him to secure her place in this household. I've made her feel perfectly at home, and anything more is unnecessary. But if Martin has decided to marry her, there will be no stopping him."

"Perhaps he felt it necessary to make an honest woman out of her," Mrs. Langston delicately allowed. "After all, your sleeping arrangements would not meet the church's standards."

"Martin doesn't give a whit about church standards. He's just smitten with her young pussy. She does things with him in the bedroom I deign to do. She lets him fuck her in the ass. She sucks his cum out of my pussy and swallows it. She lets him put his fist all way inside her. She doesn't mind when he ties her up and whips her with the buggy whip. She's quite the little whore."

"Shocking," muttered the neighbor lady, although she had witnessed most of these licentious acts through her trusty spyglass. Quite a show!

"Martin marrying Anne will just pamper her vanity. She's as vain as a peacock now – wanting to wear dresses with puffy sleeves, attending fancy concerts, fucking her old schoolteacher when he had a perfectly fine girlfriend in Prissy Andrews. Well, I hope she'll be satisfied at last, for I know she's been hankering after Martin ever since he brought her home, although she's never said a word to me about loving him. I fear he will get his rusty old heart broken."

"Like you say, there's no stopping him," nodded Mrs. Langston with false sympathy. "But don't you worry. I've planned them a fine wedding."

≈≈≈

Christmas morning broke on a beautiful white world. It had been a very mild December and people were looking forward to a green Christmas; but just enough snow fell in the night to transfigure Avonlea into a Winter Wonderland. Anne peeped out from her frosted gable window with delighted eyes. The firs in the Haunted Wood were all feathery and wonderful; the birches and wild cherry trees were outlined in pearl; the plowed fields were stretches of snowy dimples; and there was a crisp tang in the air that was glorious.

Anne ran downstairs singing, her voice echoing throughout Green Gables. "Merry Christmas, Matilda! Merry Christmas, Martin! Isn't it a lovely Christmas? I'm so glad it's white. Any other kind of Christmas doesn't seem real, does it? I don't like green Christmases. They're not green – they're just nasty faded browns and grays. What makes people call them green?"

As usual, Anne was as naked as a newborn child, her breasts bouncing as she hopped around in a state of excitement. Martin was bare-chested himself, having pulled on his Levis for the opening of the presents. Even Matilda was but half-dressed, her breasts exposed through her open robe.

Martin gave Anne a hug, cupping one of her boobs, as if trying to stop its jiggling. "Calm down," he said. I have a special present for you."

"A Christmas morn fuck? I was hoping Old St. Nick might deliver such a gift during the night."

"The fuck comes later. I hope you'll accept this small gift for now."

"Why – why – Martin, is that for me? Oh, Martin!"

Martin had sheepishly produced a gaily-wrapped box, resplendent in its colorful paper swathings, and held it out with a deprecatory glance at Matilda, who feigned to be filling the teapot, but nevertheless watched the scene out of the corner of her eye with a rather interested air.

Anne took the gift and looked at it in reverent silence. There was a curly red bow on top. Oh, how pretty the package was – she almost hated to tear the pretty paper to open it.

"Yes, that's a special Christmas present for just you, Anne," said Martin shyly. "Why – why – don't you open it? Well now – well now."

The girl's fingers fumbled with the wrapping, but presently revealed the ring box. She pried the clamshell box open to reveal a 14k gold band with an intricate filigree design circling it.

"D-do you like it," stuttered Martin

Anne's eyes had suddenly filled with tears. "Like it! Oh, Martin!" Anne set the ring box on the kitchen table and clasped her hands. "Martin, it's perfectly exquisite. Does this mean what I think it does? That you wish to marry me?"

He nodded dumbly. "I'd say we've already had the wedding night – many times over. Now we may as well have the wedding."

"Oh, I can never thank you enough. Look at that beautiful golden ring! It seems to me this must be a happy dream."

"Well, well, let us have breakfast," interrupted Matilda. "I must say, Anne, I don't think you have any need to marry Martin; but since my brother has got his heart set on it, see that you take good care of him. Here's a letter Mrs. Langston left for you. It's an outline of the wedding plans she has made for you two. Come now, sit down and eat your breakfast."

"I don't think I can eat anything," said Anne rapturously. "Breakfast seems so commonplace at such an exciting moment. I'd rather feast my eyes on that golden ring. I'm so glad Martin wants to marry me. I don't think I'd ever get over leaving your bed if I married someone else. I do so love fucking the two of you, I doubt anyone else could truly satisfy me."

"Well, I expect I'll be moving into your old room. Married folks shouldn't have to share their bed with anyone."

"Oh no, Matilda. Marrying Martin will be like marrying you too. I can't imagine not having you in bed with us."

"We'll see."

Anne picked up the envelope and surveyed its contents. "It was lovely of Mrs. Langston to plan the wedding. She's already reserved the church, but didn't tell Rev. Allan who it was for. Oh, I'll bet his wife Cynthia will be so surprised. But marrying Martin shouldn't keep me from being a dryad with her, it's so much fun."

"Being a dryad with the minister's wife?" asked

Matilda, confused by the statement.

"Oh yes, she's a kindred spirit. We get naked together down at Dryad's Bubble. She has the most lovely reddish hair covering her pussy. It matches her head, as if dyed by a professional beautician."

"You've been carrying on with Rev. Allan's wife –!" croaked Martin, shocked by the revelation.

Anne frowned. "'Carrying on' is such a pejorative term, don't you think. That's certainly not the way to describe the communion she and I share down at Dryad's Bubble. Oh, it's magnificent, Cynthia stretched out there on the mossy bank, as nude as a real fairy, me exploring that forest of red hair that tops her pubis. It's magical!"

"My lord," muttered Matilda. Across the table Martin was looking stricken, his face almost as pale as the white tablecloth.

"Why are you reacting this way? Martin just asked me to marry him. We should all be happy."

"Happy that you're diddling the minister's wife?" Martin croaked. "Why, if that comes out we'll be the disgrace of Avonlea. We'll have to leave Prince Edward Island in shame. Even I know better than fuck the wife of the local minister. That's violating the sanctity of the church. I'm not sure I can marry someone who'd do such a sacrilegious act." This was a greater speech than Martin Collins had made in years, a sign of how upsetting this news about Anne and Mrs. Allan had been.

Anne looked contrite, realizing her engagement was hanging in the balance. "It's at times like this I'm sorry I'm not a model little girl; and I resolve that I will be in future. But somehow it's hard to carry out your resolutions when irresistible temptations come. Like Mrs. Allan. Still, I really will make an extra effort after this to be good."

"I must cogitate on this," mumbled Martin, pulling on his hat and coat as he stumbled out the door to face the snowy weather.

≈≈≈

When the commonplace breakfast was over, Diana Barry appeared, crossing the white log bridge in the hollow, a gay little figure in her crimson ulster. Anne flew down the slope to meet her.

"Merry Christmas, Diana! And oh, it's a wonderful Christmas. I've something splendid to show you. Martin has given me the loveliest ring, and asked me to marry him. I couldn't even imagine any nicer Christmas present."

"I've got something more for you," said Diana breathlessly. "Here – this box. Aunt Josephine sent us out a big box with ever so many things in it – and this is for you. I'd have brought it over last night, but it didn't come until after dark, and I never feel very comfortable coming through the Haunted Wood in the dark now."

Anne opened the box and peeped in. First a card with "For Anne of Green Gables, Merry Christmas," written on it; and then, a pair of the daintiest little kid slippers, bright red with beaded toes and satin bows and glistening buckles.

"Oh," said Anne, "Diana, this is too much. I must be dreaming. These are just like Dorothy's slippers in *The Wizard of Oz.*"

"I call it providential," said Diana. "You won't have to borrow Ruby Gillis's slippers now for your wedding, and that's a blessing, for hers are two sizes too big for you."

"Perhaps I can wear them for our presentation of *The Faerie Queene* at the concert tonight," mused Anne, studying the beautiful shoes.

"Don't be silly. Fairies don't shuffle along in shoes. They flit about in the nude. You said so yourself. That's why we've all agreed to go on stage naked tonight. Oh, I can't wait to see all the boys' faces!"

"Yes, that's true," acquiesced Anne. But she was wondering how Martin might take her appearing on stage in the nude. Another scandal might tip him over the edge, causing him to break off their new engagement.

"Is it true that you're going to marry Martin. Oh, that would make you the first girl in our class to wed. I thought Prissy Andrews would beat us all to the altar by marrying Teddy Phillips, but word is their romance is on the rocks. He's found a new girlfriend in Charlottetown. One of his students there,"

"Teddy Phillips would fuck a snake," Anne said contemptuously.

"Hey, don't say that. He fucked both you and me."

"That meant nothing. No more than me licking Cynthia Allan's pussy – a mere moment of joy with no long-term commitment."

"You licked the minister's wife's pussy!" Even Diana was shocked by the news.

"What of it? I lick yours too. After all, you and I are bosom friends."

"But the minister's wife. That's almost like having sex with God."

"I'd suck God's dick if he ever asked. Why not? That might be even better that praying. I'm not very good at praying, but Martin says I'm a great cocksucker."

"Anne Shirley, if Gilbert Blythe ever heard you talk this way he's send you no more Valentine's cards. And he's bought you a muffler as a Christmas present, but don't let him know I told you."

"Gil – Gilbert Blythe is nothing to me. I don't even acknowledge he exists other than as a student for me to best in geometry. Not that I seem to be having muck luck at that."

"Gilbert Blythe adores you. He's going to take badly to this news of your engagement to Martin Collins. He will be heartbroken, I can assure you."

"Gilbert only cares that I'm the only girl in Avonlea School he hasn't yet fucked. He finally got to you on that field trip last month. Did you think Ruby and Josie and me didn't notice that the two of you disappeared into the bushes for a half hour? Miss Stacy was certain you'd got lost."

"Like you said about Teddy Phillips, it meant nothing. Gilbert only has eyes for you."

"His John Thomas does not seem to be so discriminating."

"He's a man. You know how men are."

"He's a boy. Martin is a man. And that's why I'm going to marry him. That will make me the mistress of Green Gables. Matilda has already agreed to step aside for Martin's new wife. So why should I give a piffle about Gilbert Blythe and his wandering eye?"

"You fancy him, I know you do. You pretend to hate him, but I know better. That's why I let him fuck me, to make you jealous. I thought that might wake you up to your true affection for him." Diana paused, and then added, "By the way, Gilbert is a great fuck. His dick is as big as a mule's. And he certainly knows how to use it, more'n I can say about most of the boys in our class."

"Thank you for that testimonial. But you'd best get on home. I have a wedding to plan."

"Oh, don't be that way. No doubt that old busybody Mrs. Langston already has your wedding planned down to the last grain of rice. I'll see you this afternoon for the rehearsal"

"In all this excitement, I almost forgot – we have the dress rehearsal for tonight's performance of *The Faerie Queene*."

"Don't you mean 'undress rehearsal'?" Diana teased as she crossed the log bridge, heading home.

≈≈≈

All the Avonlea scholars were in a fever of excitement that day, for the hall had to be decorated and a last grand rehearsal held, the centerpiece of the evening being a performance of Edmund Spenser's The *Faerie Queene*.

When the girls revealed to Miss Stacy that they planned to give the performance in the nude, their teacher put her foot down. "No way I'm allowing that," she told them. "It would be a major scandal. You'd get me fired."

"But fairies don't wear clothes," protested Ruby Gibbs. "We want this to be authentic."

"Whose idea was this? Anne Shirley's no doubt."

She whirled to face the girl. "I've heard the stories of you running through the fields at Green Gables without a single stitch on you. But your nudist proclivities cannot be thrust on these innocent girls. Their families would be up in arms if they marched naked onto that stage tonight. Don't you see that?"

"But we took a vote," said Anne. "It was unanimous that we perform in the nude – well, everyone but Emma. But she came around."

"Are all of you insane?" shrieked Miss Stacy, proving she was not the permissive free spirit that most parents in Avonlea accused her of being, with her field trips and exercise classes and dance recitals.

"Wait," interjected Mrs. Cynthia Allan. The minister's wife had volunteered to help Miss Stacy with tonight's concert. "Perhaps we should consider the girls' proposal. Ruby is correct that fairies do not wear cloth, at least not much."

"What? A woman of the church advocating nudity?" responded the teacher, confused by this unexpected viewpoint.

"Keep in mind, Adam and Eve were nude in the Garden of Eden."

"Until they realized the shame of it," countered Miss Stacy, more of the prude than anyone would have thought.

"That was because of Satan's intervention in the form of a serpent. God's original plan was for them to glory in their nudity."

"Oh, well, you have a point. But nude students – that would be quite a scandal. Whatever should we do?"

"Perhaps there's a compromise," said Mrs. Allan, smiling directly at Anne.

≈≈≈

When the curtain raised on Avonlea School's production of *The Faerie Queene*, there was an audible gasp from the audience. For twelve young female students were posed on a stepped backdrop, costumed only in head garlands, fake fairy wings, and the filmiest of gauze togas. Onlookers weren't quite sure whether the girls were naked beneath the gauze or if their eyes were deceiving them.

"Look I can see Prissy's titties," whispered Charlie Sloane.

"Hard to miss those big balloons," nodded Ron White, Emma's brother.

"Ain't your sister naked too?"

Ron squinted. "Hard to tell," he allowed.

Just then, Anne Shirley stepped forward to recite her lines. The way she stood caught stage lights behind her, silhouetting her body. When she turned to the side – Stage Left, the play's script called it – you could see the pointy tips of her nipples.

Martin Collins sunk down in his seat as if trying to hide. Matilda sniffed, and said to Mrs. Langston seated beside her, "Looks like Anne's done it again."

Rita Langston, used to seeing Anne flit about the fields without even the benefit of gauze, was less dismayed. "Those togas may be thin, but they do add a degree of modesty," she noted. "Very creative."

Mrs. Langston's husband Thomas was straining his eyes to see if he could make out the shadow of public hair under Diana Barry's thin covering. He figured she was old enough to be sporting it. He'd always lusted after this neighborhood girl, as plump as he was thin. His wife was testament that he preferred females with "a little meat on their bones."

"Are they wearing anything under those robes?" Rev. Allan leaned aside to ask his wife. He knew she'd been an advisor on the production.

"The girls are covered," she responded. "Quite tastefully, I'd say."

"Yes, I suppose so. Nothing is really showing. These classical productions have different standards, I suppose."

"Edmund Spenser's *The Faerie Queene* is a work of religious allegory. Its theme is Virtue, you know."

Rev. Allan nodded happily. "Yes, yes, excellent choice for the concert."

Miss Stacy breathed a sigh of relief when the curtain rung down and Mr. Superintendent Bell turned to her to say, "A job well done. Those costumes were amazing. It almost looked like the girls were naked underneath. Quite a *trompe l'oeil*."

"Yes, the minister's wife helped with the costume design," she replied, giving credit where credit was due. If Mr. Superintendent Bell had second thoughts, he could take them up with Cynthia Allan.

"Spenser's *The Faerie Queene* was an inspired selection," the superintendent continued excitedly. "You know he created the Spenserian stanza especially for this play. There are nine iambic lines – the first eight of them five footed and the ninth a hexameter. A brilliant poetic invention. And young Anne Shirley captured the rhythm perfectly, I must say."

"Thank you, Mr. Superintendent Bell. I coached her on the rhyme pattern relentlessly – ABABBCBCC."

"Excellent work, Miss Stacy. You are sure to make your mark here at Avonlea School."

The concert was pronounced a success. All the performers did excellently well, but Anne was the bright star of the occasion; even Josie Pye could not deny that.

Gilbert Blythe confronted Anne backstage. He was wearing the same Sunday-go-to-meeting suit that he'd worn while reciting Tennyson's "Tears, Idle Tears." Anne was still clad in the gauze toga. Up close, its transparency was quite evident. "That was an outstanding performance," he congratulated her. "But I can't believe you did it while practically naked, all the boys in school staring at your titties."

"Oh, do you like them?" she inquired, matter-of-factly, stepping back to give him a better view.

He couldn't believe Anne Shirley was standing here letting him look her over, like a prize milk cow at a 4H Canada fair. She didn't seem to mind him staring at her breasts, glancing down at her sparse bush, admiring her long slender legs.

"Miss Stacy and Mrs. Allan encouraged us to give an authentic performance, like you might see on Broadway. The costumes were well researched as to what Elizabethan actresses might wear."

"But weren't all the actors back then men – they played the women's roles too."

"That's true. But isn't this version so much better, with girls playing the fairies?"

He stared at her all-but-exposed breasts. The pink

areolae of her nipples showed through the gauze. "I'll say."

"Since *The Faerie Queene* consists of over two thousand stanza, we could only do a small portion of it tonight. Next year we may choose another selection from it. I'm thinking about "The Rape of Lucretia." Perhaps you'd like to audition for the part of the Etruscan king's son. He's the cad who rapes Lucretia. We want the production to be as authentic as possible. I may agree to have sex on stage. How does one portray a rape without actual fucking, don't you agree?"

"You wouldn't dare."

"You didn't think I'd get up on stage in front of half of Avonlea like this either, did you?" As emphasis, she twitched her shoulders just enough to make her breasts jiggle.

"No, I admit I didn't." He eyed her up and down, impressed by the body she'd been hiding under those drab dresses she wore to school. If he'd liked her before, he was now totally, irrevocably, unquestionably smitten. This confirmed the exposed view he'd had that day at Barry's Pond.

"So, are you in or out?" she asked. The sexual innuendo was obvious.

"Uh, in."

Anne could see a growing bulge in his trousers. Hadn't Diana said he was hung like a mule? That, she couldn't wait to see. "Good, we can start rehearsal soon, I think." She stared down at the bulge, a lengthy cylindrical outline against the tweed fabric. "Yes, you'll be perfect for the role."

≈≈≈

"Oh, hasn't it been a brilliant evening?" sighed Anne when it was all over and she and Diana were walking home together under a dark, starry sky. Snuggled up in heavy coats against the winter's chill, they felt quite toasty compared to their half hour on stage.

"Everything came off very well," said Diana practically. "I guess we must have made as much as ten dollars toward buying a flag. Mind you, Mr. Superintendent Bell is going to send an account of it to the Charlottetown papers. He promised to give us a glowing review."

"Oh, Diana, will we really see our names in print? It makes me thrill to think of it. Your solo was perfectly elegant. I felt so proud you. I said to myself, 'It is my dear bosom friend who is being applauded.'"

"That's kind of you to say, but my performance was naught compared to yours, dear Anne. Your recitations brought down the house. That sad one was simply splendid. And you looked so beautiful out there, your body silhouetted in light."

"Oh, I was so nervous, Diana. When Rev. Allan called out my name I wasn't sure I could get up on that platform. I felt as if a million eyes were looking at me, and for one dreadful moment I doubted I could begin at all. Although I run around the farm like a naked wood sprite, I wasn't sure I had the courage to stand before audience with my body practically exposed in that gauze tunic. Then I started in, and my voice seemed to be coming from ever so far away. I just felt like a parrot. It's providential that I practiced those recitations so often up in the garret, or I'd never have been able to get through. Did I groan all right?"

"Yes, indeed, you groaned lovely," assured Diana.

"I saw old Mrs. Sloane wiping away tears when I sat down. It was splendid to think I had touched somebody's heart. It's so romantic to take part in a concert, isn't it? Oh, it's been a very memorable occasion indeed."

"Wasn't the boys' dialogue fine?" said Diana. "Gilbert Blythe was just splendid. Anne, I do think it's awful mean the way you treat Gil. Wait till I tell you. When you ran off the platform after the fairy dialogue one of your roses fell out of your hair. I saw Gil pick it up and put it in his breast pocket. There now. You're so romantic that I'm sure you ought to be pleased at that."

"It's nothing to me what Gilbert Blythe does," said Anne loftily. "I refuse to waste a single thought on him, Diana."

"Don't be so hard-hearted."

"There's a faint hope for Gilbert's redemption. I've extended an olive branch in the form of asking him to co-star with me next year. But it requires him fucking me from now on, not you."

"Oh Anne, I told you my tryst with him was a one-time thing to make you jealous. I can see it has worked. I'm much more interested in Moody MacPherson?"

"That weasel?"

"Hey, I've given you your precious Gil. Leave Moody for me."

≈≈≈

That night Matilda and Martin, having been out to a concert for the first time in twenty years, sat for a while by the kitchen fire after Anne had gone up to bed.

Exhausted, she was sleeping in her own room tonight.

"Well now, I guess our Anne did as well as any of them," Martin said sullenly. He was having misgiving about his proposal to the flighty young girl.

"Yes, she recited her part beautifully," nodded Matilda. "She's a bright girl, Martin. And she looked real nice too, even if she was half-naked. I was proud of our Anne tonight, although I'm not going to tell her so."

"Well now, I did tell her so 'fore she went upstairs," said Martin. "But you and I must talk about this marriage business. Have I gone off half-cocked?"

"Well, your cock has certainly played a role in it," she replied archly.

"Rather than marry her maybe I should send her off to college in Charlottetown. She'd make a fine teacher."

Matilda nodded, obviously relieved by her brother's change of heart. "I figured she'd need something more than Avonlea School by and by," his sister agreed. "Maybe we should send her to Queen's after a spell. But nothing need be said about that till next year."

"Well now, it'll do no harm to be thinking it over," nodded Martin.

"Things like that are all the better for lots of thinking over. Like marriage proposals."

"Guess you're right about that."

Matilda patted him on the shoulder. "You can back out of it quietly, if you can get Mrs. Langston to keep her big trap shut. Nobody else but Anne – and maybe her friend Diana – knows about it yet."

"Diana Barry – she was a good fuck that time me

and Anne got her drunk. Maybe I should keep my eye on her. She might be better wife material than our Anne. At least she wouldn't go cavorting with the minister's wife. It's not that I care if Anne fucks around, but having sex with the minister's wife is kind of sacrilegious, don't you think?"

Anne celebrates a birthday.

CHAPTER XXVII

Vanity and Vexation of Spirit

Avonlea School found it hard to settle down to humdrum existence again. To Anne in particular things seemed fearfully flat, stale, and unprofitable after the goblet of excitement she had been sipping for weeks. Could she go back to the former quiet pleasures of those faraway days before the concert?

At first, as she told Diana, she did not really think she could. "I'm positively certain, Diana, that life can never be quite the same again as it was in those olden days," she said mournfully, as if referring to a period of at least fifty years back. "Perhaps after a while I'll get used to it, but I'm afraid concerts spoil people for everyday life. I suppose that is why Matilda disapproves of them. Matilda is such a sensible woman. It must be a great deal better to be sensible; but still, I don't believe I'd really want to be a sensible person, because they are so unromantic. Mrs. Langston says there is no danger of my ever being one, but you can never tell. I feel just now that I may grow up to be sensible yet. But perhaps that is only because I'm tired. I simply couldn't sleep last night for ever so long. I just lay awake and imagined the concert over and over again. That's one splendid thing about such affairs — it's so lovely to look back to them."

"The event was so very sophisticated. It's something I will never ever forget," vowed Diana Barry, all a-swoon.

365

"Yes," said Anne, "we will keep it in our memories – and in our hearts."

≈ ≈ ≈

Eventually, however, the students slipped back into their old groove and took up their old interests. To be sure, the concert left traces. Ruby Gillis and Emma White, who had quarreled over a point of precedence in their platform seats, no longer sat at the same desk, and a promising friendship of three years was broken up. Josie Pye and Julia Bell did not speak for three months, because Josie Pye had told everybody that boys in the front row laughed at Julia's tiny titties when she got up to recite. Finally, Charlie Sloane got into a fight with Moody MacPherson, because Moody said that Anne Shirley put on airs about her recitations. Consequently Moody's sister, Ella May, would not speak to Anne all the rest of the winter. And Moody refused to acknowledge Diana because she was Anne's best friend.

With the exception of these trifling frictions, work in Miss Stacy's little kingdom went on with regularity and smoothness.

Martin Collins had taken back the ring he'd given Anne on Christmas morning – and with it his proposal of marriage. Her feelings were hurt and she refused to sleep with him and his sister for practically a month. Not that she minded the wedding being off; more that she hated to give up that beautiful 14k gold ring. "Indian giver," she said, that being the worst name she could come up with.

The winter weeks slipped by. It was an unusually mild January, with so little snow that Anne and Diana could go to school nearly every day by way of the Birch Path. On Anne's birthday they were tripping lightly down it, keeping eyes and ears alert amid all their chatter, for Miss Stacy had assigned them to write a composition on "A Winter's Walk in the Woods," and it behooved them to be observant.

"Just think, Diana, I'm seventeen years old today," remarked Anne in an awed voice. "I can scarcely believe I'm that old. It's a great comfort to think that I'll be able to use big words now without being laughed at."

"Don't count on that," said Diana, well aware that people made fun of Anne's airs behind her back. Moody wasn't the only one.

"When I awoke this morning it seemed to me that everything must be different. You've been seventeen for months, so I suppose it doesn't seem such a novelty to you as it does to me. It makes life seem so much more interesting. Just think, in another year I'll be able to vote."

"Ruby Gillis says she means to be married by the time she's eighteen," said Diana. "She says we're on our way to becoming old maids."

"Ruby Gillis thinks of nothing but getting married," said Anne disdainfully. "She's actually delighted when anyone writes her name up in a take-notice for all to see, even though she pretends to be mad."

"Those boys who delight in writing her name on the porch care nothing of marrying her," sniffed Diana. "They just want an easy lay."

"I'm afraid we're being uncharitable toward poor

Ruby. Mrs. Allan says we should never make uncharitable remarks; but they often slip out before you can stop them, don't they? I simply can't talk about Josie Pye without making an uncharitable speech, so I never mention her at all. You may have noticed that. I'm trying to be as much like Mrs. Allan as I possibly can, for I think she's perfect. Rev. Allan thinks so too. Mrs. Langston says he just worships the ground she walks on, but the old busybody doesn't really think it right for a minister to set his affections so much on a mortal being."

"Mrs. Allan is so beautiful, how could anyone not worship her?"

"That is true, Diana. But even ministers' wives are human and have their besetting sins just like everybody else. Some people might call the time Mrs. Allan and I spend together sinful. But I don't care what other people think. I had an interesting talk with Cynthia about besetting sins last Sunday afternoon. There are just a few things it's proper to talk about on Sundays and that is one of them, I think. My besetting sin is imagining too much and forgetting my duties. I'm striving very hard to overcome these shortcomings and now that I've turned seventeen I'm quite sure I'll get better."

"You were with Mrs. Allan on Sunday afternoon? Are you still carrying on with her? I thought you promised Martin you wouldn't do that any more."

"That was before he took his ring back. That kind of action cancels all promises, don't you think?"

"Is it true Cynthia Allan's pussy hair is red like the hair on her head?" Diana wished she could see for herself, but Anne had made it clear that her "affair" with the minister's wife was private.

"That is true and I can prove it," announced Anne. "She gave me a lock as a keepsake."

"A lock of her pussy hair!" exclaimed Diana, hardly able to believe such a claim. "Will you show it to me?"

"Maybe sometime. I keep those precious auburn curls pressed between the pages of a book in my room."

"Which book? You have so many."

"Why, John Milton's *Paradise Lost*, of course. Being a married woman, I can never really claim her as my own."

"Do you have any other keepsakes?" asked the eager girl.

"A few," Anne giggled. "Yours for instance."

"My public hair —how did you get it without my knowledge?"

"Remember, you allowed me to clip a sprig as a keepsake when we thought we were being parted forever."

"That's right. And what book are my cunt hairs in?"

"*The Secret Garden* by Frances Hodgson Burnett. Appropriate, don't you think?"

"Indeed I do. Any others?"

Anne hesitated. "Well, I did clip some follicles from Martin's pubes while he slept."

"And where do you keep those?"

"They're safely ensconced in Herman Melville's *Moby Dick*," she whispered, indicating it was a secret to be kept close.

Diana paused. "Even though I was drunk when Martin fucked me last year, I remember he had a goodly sized dick. I wonder why he never did it with me again?"

Anne patted her friend's hand. "Oh, I think he will. Only last week he suggested I invite you over for fun and games."

"Really? Why didn't you tell me sooner?"

"I'm telling you now, silly. But tonight Martin promised to spend the night with just me, a special fuck on my birthday. He's going to show me a sexual move known as the Ultimate Houdini. I can't wait to see what it is."

"That sounds exciting. Please, oh, please, you will tell me all about it, won't you?"

"Of course, you're my bosom friend. Then next week we will have you over for your very own fuck session."

"Why does Martin have renewed interest in me now, after all this time?"

"I'm not sure," Anne said. "But I suspect after calling off his engagement to me he's shopping for a new matrimonial prospect."

"Oh, that would be nice. I could become the mistress of Green Gables. But don't worry, dear Anne, we would always have a place for you."

Anne laughed at her friend's silly dreams. "Don't count your chickens before you've bought the henhouse," she warned. "As you've seen with me, Martin's heart can be fickle. I think that's because it truly belongs to Matilda."

Surprise! Surprise!

CHAPTER XXVIII

The Ultimate Houdini

That night Matilda went over to Mrs. Langston's to help plan an upcoming church social. Cynthia would be there, of course. And Diana's mum and Mrs. Nell and Mrs. Andrews and Mrs. White. All the good ladies of First Presbyterian Church.

That was fine with Anne, for tonight was her birthday surprise from Martin. She could wait to see what new sexual treat he had in mind for her. Despite the broken engagement, he still savored his moment in bed with the pubescent teenager.

The Ultimate Houdini – that wasn't a sexual position listed in the Kama Sutra, the instruction book Diana had shared with her. It included such gymnastic techniques as the Crisscross, the Sideways Samba, the Indian Handstand, and the Lotus Blossom. But no Houdini.

Perhaps it referred to that magician she read about in the newspapers, Harry Houdini. He was a famous escape artist, breaking free from handcuffs, busting out of locked safes, freeing himself from all manner of restrains. In 1904 Houdini had escaped a special pair of handcuffs commissioned by the London Daily Mirror. It had taken him an hour and ten minutes.

Therefore, she suspected Martin's surprise might involve handcuffs. Her locked to the bedpost while he had his way with her.

She was partially right. Handcuffs were involved.

Shortly after Matilda had departed for her church meeting, he asked Anne to disrobe there in the living room of Green Gables. When she was completely naked, he cuffed her hands to the radiator in front of the window, a position that forced her to lean forward. She glanced back over her shoulder as he undressed himself, taking in his lean, muscled body, the result of physical farm work. My, but he was handsome. Maybe she would still marry him one day. Too bad about Diana or Matilda. He was worth claiming for herself. A prosperous landholder with a big dick – what more could she want in a man?

"Don't look back," he cautioned. "Stare out the window. Eventually you will see a surprising sight."

"Yes, Martin. Anything you say."

He entered her from behind, doggy style. Was this the Ultimate Houdini? He had fucked her doggy style many times before, one of his favorite positions. But who was to complain? As always, it felt good, his long rod sliding in and out with a steady rhythm. Ummmm.

She felt a slight breeze, as if a door had been opened, but she was too distracted to pay it much mind. Then Martin missed a stroke, his John Thomas sliding out of her slot, then resuming its position with even greater vigor. Oooo, that felt good.

The pounding continued until she was in a frenzy, on the verge of orgasm. She had closed her eyes to savor the moment – the Big O – but opened them when a tap came on the windowpane inches from her face.

Anne couldn't believe here eyes. There was Martin Collins on the other side of the glass, waving at her. But that couldn't be. He was still fucking her. She could feel his enormous pile driver ramming er from behind.

But if Martin was out there …?

She turned her head to see their farmhand Harley Buote grinning at her. Like a magician, Martin had done a disappearing act, replacing himself with this big stud from the Creek with her none the wiser.

At that moment she couldn't hold off any longer. With a shriek, she achieved an orgasm to top all orgasms, electricity running through her body from clitoris to brain. She thought she might have passed out, because when she regained her senses, she was laying on the couch, with Martin bending over her sporting a wide smile. There was no sign of Harley.

Had she dreamed it? Or had she just been fucked by their handyman?

≈≈≈

The next day the wind was mild and the sun was as bright as a 100-watt electric bulb. Anne saw Harley Buote leading the cows down to the far pasture. He didn't look up or acknowledge that he saw her, but she was sure he did. Had he partook of her body last night, and now was ignoring her as if it had never happened.

Martin wasn't talking either. When she asked him about the Ultimate Houdini, he merely characterized it as "a magic trick."

"Fooled you, didn't it?" he chuckled. "Me being in two places at the same time."

"But how –?"

"Now, now. A magician never reveals his secrets."

She wondered if the image of Martin in the window had been some kind of projection, like those kinescopes she had read about in the newspaper. There was said to be a kinescopic theater in Charlottetown.

Or had he just shared her with that over-muscled dimwit Harley Buote?

Nothing to complain about either way. It had been a mighty good fuck. Maybe the best she'd ever had.

She wondered what it would be like to fuck Gil — that is, one of her classmates. All the other girls did. What could it hurt? Obviously, Martin wouldn't mind.

For that matter, what if she fucked Harley Buote again. That is, for real — in case last night had been a figment of her vivid imagining. He saw her running around Green Gables naked all the time. Strange that he'd never tried to stick his John Thomas in her before last night. Maybe he had just been waiting for an invitation.

If Matilda was in on the Ultimate Houdini magic trick, she didn't let on to it. The day's choirs went on as usual for a Saturday. Anne helped with the housework and washed the dishes and made her bed nice and tight, the way Matilda liked it.

Martin came in for lunch. Harley took his outside as usual. Matilda had prepared plates of cold chicken with a side of cole slaw. There was corn bread left over from night before last. A big pitcher of milk sat in the center of the table.

"I must quit fucking so many people," Anne announced as they cleaned the table.

"Why is that?" asked Matilda. "You enjoy sex more than any human being I've ever met."

"Because if I became pregnant I would know whom the father is. That could be problematic. I'm sure you and Martin wouldn't want to take in any children not of your own lineage. I've been more than enough of that burden. And I wouldn't want to send a child of mine to an orphanage. That's a fate I wouldn't wish on my worst enemy. I know how that feels."

"The solution is simple," said Matilda. "Have more sex with your girlfriends. Females don't get each other pregnant."

"Now, hold on there," argued Martin. "Anne should be able to fuck who she wants to. If there's a mishap, we will take the baby in."

"Martin, you are being very generous!" rejoined his sister.

"Odds are high it would be mine anyway," he shrugged.

"Matilda, if your advice is to have sex with more females, does that mean it's alright for me to continue playing dryad with the minister's wife."

"That dalliance has already cost you marriage to my brother. I suppose you have little to lose."

"Sacrilegious," muttered Martin.

"You would like her," said Anne. "Really you would. You should come with me to Dryad's Bubble some day and fuck her for yourself. I bet she would be willing. Her husband does not believe in consummating their marriage, so she's welcoming to intimate attention."

"Hmm, I bet she would be a great piece of ass. Those long legs and perky tits topped off by that thatch of red hair – it gives me a hard-on thinking about them. I can understand why you do it, Anne. But a woman like that might be too much for me. Why don't you invite your friend Diana over next week. I may have some tricks I could show her."

Acting out Anne's story.

CHAPTER XXIX

The Story Club Is Formed

"**O**h, Diana, look, there's a rabbit," Anne said during one of their walks to school. "That's something to remember for our composition. I really think the woods are just as lovely in spring as in summer. They're so green with newborn leaves, as if they were just waking up from dreaming pretty dreams."

"I won't mind writing that composition when its time comes," sighed Diana. "I can manage to write about the woods, but the one we're to hand in Monday is challenge. The idea of Miss Stacy telling us to write a story out of our own heads!"

"Why, it's as easy as a wink," said Anne.

"It's easy for you because you have a vivid imagination," retorted Diana, "but what would you do if you had been born without one? I suppose you have your composition all done?"

Anne nodded, trying hard not to look virtuously complacent and failing miserably. "I wrote it last Monday evening. It's called 'The Jealous Rival; or In Death Not Divided.' I read it to Matilda and she said it was stuff and nonsense. Then I read it to Martin and he said it was fine. That is the kind of critic I like. It's a sad, sweet story. I just cried like a child while I was writing it. It's about two beautiful maidens called Cordelia Montmorency and Geraldine Seymour who lived in the same village and were devotedly attached to each other.

Cordelia was a regal brunette with a coronet of midnight hair and flashing gray-green eyes. And Geraldine was a queenly blonde with hair like spun gold and eyes as blue as the sea."

"That sounds like you and me," said Diana dubiously.

"All great fiction is based on the author's experiences," Anne explained. "This is no less."

"Well, what became of Cordelia and Geraldine?" asked Diana, who was beginning to feel rather interested in their fate.

"They grew in beauty side by side until they were seventeen. Then a handsome young man named Bertram DeVere came to their village and fell in love with the fair Geraldine. He saved her life when her horse ran away with her in a carriage, and she fainted in his arms and he carried her home three miles; because, you understand, the carriage was all smashed up. Right away, he asked her uncle for her hand in marriage. I found it rather hard to imagine the proposal because Martin never gave me a proper one. I asked Ruby Gillis if she knew anything about how men proposed because I thought she'd likely be an authority on the subject, having such blatant matrimonial ambitions. Ruby told me she was hiding in the hall pantry when Malcolm Andres proposed to her sister Susan. She said Malcolm told Susan that his dad had given him the farm in his own name and then said, 'What do you say, darling pet, if we get hitched this fall?' And Susan said, 'Yes – no – I don't know – let me see' – and there they were, engaged as quick as that. But I didn't think that sort of a proposal was a very romantic one, so in the end I had to imagine it out as well as I could. I made it very flowery and poetical and Bertram got down on his knees, although Ruby Gillis says it isn't done nowadays. Geraldine accepted him in a speech a page long. I can tell you I took a lot of trouble with that speech. I rewrote it five times and I look upon it as my masterpiece. Bertram gave her a diamond ring and a ruby necklace and told her they would go to Europe for a wedding tour, for he was immensely wealthy. But then, alas, shadows began to darken over their path. Cordelia was secretly in love with Bertram herself and when Geraldine told her about the engagement she was simply furious, especially when she saw the necklace and the diamond ring. All Cordelia's affection for Geraldine turned to bitter hate and she vowed that she should never marry Bertram. But she pretended to be Geraldine's friend the same as ever. One evening they were standing on the bridge over a rushing turbulent stream and Cordelia, thinking they were alone, pushed Geraldine over the brink with a wild, mocking, 'Ha, ha, ha.' But Bertram saw it all and he at once plunged into the current, exclaiming, 'I will save thee, my peerless Geraldine.' But alas, he had forgotten he couldn't swim, and they were both drowned, clasped in each other's arms. Their bodies were washed ashore soon afterwards. They were buried in the one grave and their funeral was most imposing, Diana. It's so much more romantic to end a story up with a funeral than a wedding. As for Cordelia, she went insane with remorse and was shut up in a lunatic orphanage. I thought that was a poetical retribution for her crime."

"Are you sure you're not writing about Gilbert Blythe? I suspected that you were angry when he invited me out on a date."

"You didn't have to go, us being bosom friends."

"Why should you care? You've said he means nothing to you time and again."

"Well, the situation has slightly changed. At the Christmas concert I promised he could fuck me."

"My darling friend, you should have told me. Now I fear you are a day late and a dollar short. Gil fucked me like a two-dollar whore on our date. Didn't you see the notice on the porch?"

Anne had seen it. It nearly broke her heart, although she'd told herself it didn't matter because Diana was her best-est friend and they shared everything. "It's of no consequence. My story is purely fiction, you see?"

Diana sighed. "I don't see how you can make up such things out of your head, Anne. I wish my imagination was as good as yours."

"It would be if you'd only cultivate it," Anne encouraged. "I have a bully idea, Diana. Let's you and me start a story club all our own and write stories for practice. I'll help you along until you can do them by yourself. You ought to cultivate your imagination, you know. Miss Stacy says so. Only we must go about it the right way."

"Okay, I'm game. I could use a tad more imagination."

≈≈≈

That was how the Story Club came into existence. It was limited to Diana and Anne at first, but soon it was extended to include Jane Andrews and Ruby Gillis and one or two others who felt that their imaginations needed cultivating. No boys were allowed in it – although Ruby Gillis argued that their admission would make it more exciting – and each member had to produce one story a week.

"It's extremely interesting," Anne told Matilda. "Each girl has to read her story out loud and then we act it out. We each write under a *nom-de-plume*. Mine is Rosamond Montmorency. All the girls do pretty well. Ruby Gillis is rather sentimental. She puts too much lovemaking into her stories and you know too much is worse than too little. Jane never puts in any romance because she says it makes her feel so silly when she has to read it out loud. Like Jane, her stories are extremely sensible. Josie Pye's stories are often mean-spirited, just like her. And Diana puts too many murders into hers. She says most of the time she doesn't know what to do with the people so she kills them off to get rid of them. I mostly always have to tell them what to write about, but that isn't hard for I've millions of ideas."

"I think this story-writing business is the foolishest thing you've come up with yet," scoffed Matilda. "You girls will get a pack of nonsense into your heads and waste time that should be put on your lessons. Reading stories is bad enough but writing them is worse."

"But we're so careful to put a moral into them all, Matilda," explained Anne. "I insist upon that. All the good people are rewarded and all the bad ones are suitably punished. I'm sure that must have a wholesome effect. The moral is the great thing. Rev. Allan says so. I read one of my stories to him and Mrs.

Allan and they both agreed that the moral was excellent. Only they laughed in the wrong places. I like it better when people cry. Jane and Ruby almost always cry when I come to the pathetic parts. Diana wrote her Aunt Josephine about our Story Club and her aunt wrote back that we were to send her some of our stories. So we copied out four of our very best and sent them to her. Miss Barry wrote back that she had never read anything so amusing in her life. That kind of puzzled us because the stories were all very pathetic and tragic and almost everybody died. But I'm glad Miss Barry liked them. It shows our club is doing some good in the world. Mrs. Allan says that ought to be our object in everything. I do really try to make it my object but I forget so often when I'm having fun. I hope I shall be a little like Mrs. Allan when I grow up. Do you think there is any prospect of it, Matilda?"

"I think you're already like her. I know you still sneak away for secret trysts with Mrs. Allan. It's difficult to say how Rev. Allan would react if he knew you was diddling his wife."

"You make it sound as though I'm corrupting her. Being older than me by a dozen years, isn't SHE the one corrupting a minor?"

"Oh, I'd say you know what you're doing. And it doesn't take any encouragement. You're a little whore at heart. It's a good thing you've come back into my and Martin's bed or no telling what mischief you'd find yourself in."

≈≈≈

At the next meeting of the Story Club it was Anne's time to read. Her new composition was titled "Virtue

Lost," and it was about a young girl who has a brief affair with an older man. It was very sexually explicit.

"Wow," said Diana, "that left NOTHING to the imagination."

"Hey," protested little Emma White, "I though the point of the Story Club was to teach us to HAVE imagination."

"Never mind that," said Jane Andrews. "Read it again. My panties are wet."

"No more reading," Josie Pye spoke up. "Now she has to act it out. Them are the rules."

There was silence throughout the church as everyone considered the implication of Josie's demand. They met at First Presbyterian on every Thursday afternoon, a dozen or so girls at a time. Most of the stories so far had been rather tame, acted out by performers drawn from their group.

"Maybe we better skip this story," Anne allowed. "It might be a little too racy for acting out in a Presbyterian church."

But Josie Pye wouldn't let it go. "You made the rules, Anne Shirley. I dare you to live up to them."

"Well, uh, all right –" Anne wasn't about to back down from a dare by her chief antagonist.

"How are we going to act THAT out?" asked Mamie Wright. "We don't have an older man to play the part."

"You can use my brother," volunteer Carrie Sloane. "Charlie would be glad to play the part. He already has a thing for Anne." Everyone already assumed that Anne would take the lead role, that of the young girl who falls under an older man's spell.

"Charlie's our age," protested Diana. "He can't

portray an older man."

"How about Tilly's older brother? Reggie is nearly twenty. And VERY handsome."

Tilly Boulter shook her head. "He's off the island at the moment. Visiting a friend in Montreal."

"Who then?" said Ruby, about to cry. "We can't act out Anne's story without an older man."

Josie Pye spoke up: "How about Rev. Allan? He's probably in the parsonage next door."

"A minister can't play Anne's paramour," Emma White objected. "That would be sacrilegious."

"Oh, you're such a goody two-shoes," Josie dismissed the younger girl's concern. "This is only acting. Didn't Rev. Allan mention in a recent sermon that he'd done some stage work before he entered the ministry?"

"Yes, I remember that," said Tilly. "He told us he starred in a production of *The Gentleman Caller*."

"See?" retorted Josie. "It's practically the same kind of role."

Jane said, *"The Gentleman Caller* is a comedy. Anne's story is ... well, a torrid romance."

Josie turned to Anne. "Are you going to go ask Rev. Allan or not? He's a grown man; he can say 'no' if he so chooses. Besides, aren't you supposed to be buddy-buddy with his wife? I'll bet he'd do it as a favor to you."

"Cynthia Allan and I are friends," Anne admitted. But she wasn't so sure about her relationship with Jonathan Allan.

"Cynthia?" jeered Josie Pye. "Aren't you the hoity-toity one – on a first name basis with the minister's pretty redheaded wife?"

"Just give me a minute to go next door," Anne replied defiantly.

To Anne Shirley's surprise, Rev. Allan agreed to help the girls out with their acting assignment. He came in through the sanctuary, Anne in tow. "Well, girls, I hear you need my acting ability for a play that one of you wrote. As it happens, I did some off-Broadway work before I got the calling. I'm agreeable to sight read a few lines with one of you."

"It's Anne's story," offered Diana. "So she gets to star in it with you."

"Do we have a script?"

"Just the story itself," apologized Anne. "You take the papers. I know it by heart."

"You may not want to do this story," warned little Emma. "It's kind of naughty."

"Tsk, tsk. A professional actor can do any part he's given," winked Rev. Allan. "You can't scare me away that easily."

"No, seriously –" Emma persisted.

"An actor is merely playing a role, dear girl. He can be a villain or hero, it doesn't matter which. On stage it's all pretend." He glanced down at the sheaf of papers and began skimming through Anne's story. "Oh dear Lord," he muttered by the second page. "Emma's right. We'd better rethink my doing this."

"But Rev. Allan," chided Josie Pye, "I thought you said a professional actor could play any part, hero or villain? How is this any different?"

"Well, this material may be a bit too adult for young girls like you," he began.

"But Anne wrote it. She's the same age as us. All

except for Emma White, that is. We can ask Emma to leave if you think it appropriate."

Rev. Allan had turned to the third page, his face as red as a beet. "Perhaps we can do an abridged version," he said, trying to think of a way out of this pickle. If only he'd kept his mouth shut about being a big-deal actor, able to take on any part. Written by a seventeen-year-old or not, this story about an older man seducing a young girl bordered on pornography.

"We don't have to do the whole thing," Anne offered. "Just a scene or two."

"I guess we can handle that," the minister said uneasily. "Which part do you suggest?"

"The seduction scene," Josie interjected. "We want to see you emote with Anne as if you were doing an off-Broadway audition."

"I don't know," he again tried to wiggle out of the awkward situation. "I haven't had a chance to study the lines. Perhaps we'd best postpone this performance."

"Don't worry about the lines," goaded Josie. "Just do improvisation. We learned about that in school from Miss Stacy."

He wondered if Miss Stacy had a hand in this, setting him up to assure his support of her next concert. Come to think of it, he wouldn't mind playing this part opposite Muriel Stacy. The teacher was a slender blonde with shapely legs. Better her than a student. Anne Shirley was a sexy little tart but he couldn't afford taking a risk. He'd been kicked out of his last church for diddling one of the choirgirls. He knew his wife told people they were celibate, but that wasn't true. He and Cynthia had an active sex life, fucking like bunnies night in and night out.

"You don't have to do this if you don't want to," said Anne. It wasn't that she wouldn't enjoy doing a make-out scene with Jonathan Allan, but being friends – well, more than friends – with his wife put this on a different plane.

"No, I said I would," he screwed up his courage. "But because of the sensitive nature of this scene, I must ask all you girls to swear an oath of silence. You can't tell anyone about this little exercise in thespian artistry, especially my wife."

"We promise," came the chorus.

"Anne, are you sure you're okay with this. It does get a little personal."

"I wrote it, didn't I?"

"Okay, here goes."

Clearing his throat, he began: "'Oh, Miss Wintworth, do not spurn my affections. I know I'm old enough to be your father, but you have won my heart. I must have you, no matter what you say.'

Anne was standing close. "'Mr. Cunningham, my loins throb for you. I cannot wait to feel your warm member inside me.'"

Her uninhibited lines almost threw him. What the hell was he doing? Spouting licentious dialogue with a teenager was surely a shortcut to Satan's Unholy Realm.

However, Anne brought him out of his paralysis when she pressed her torso against him and her hand grasped his cock through his woolen trousers. "'Take me, Mr. Cunningham, my body is yours," she adlibbed. "'I may be no more than a child in age, but I'm a woman in my emotions. Ravish me if thou wilt.'"

Jonathan Allan wasn't sure what to do. This was happening so fast. He could feel the heat of her body against him; her hand on his cock. He couldn't remember his next line. "Uh ... uh ..." he stuttered.

Removing her hand from his crotch, she began to unbutton his shirt. "'Oh, Mr. Cunningham, I can't say no to your advances. I burn with desire.'"

"Wait," he said. "Perhaps we'd better stop here."

But Anne stayed in character. "No, Mr. Cunningham, don't stop. I am all yours."

"But –"

"Here, she said, guiding his hands to her breasts. "Feel my heart. It throbs with unbridled passion."

He could feel the hardness of her nipples beneath the palms of his hands. She brushed her lips against his cheek. He seemed mesmerized by her attention, his lines lost by the wayside. "Uh, uh, uh –" he tried to remember what came next in the story.

Anne exhibited no hesitation in following the graphic storyline. Fumbling with the catch on her skirt, she let the garment slide down her legs and bunch on the vestry floor. As it turned out, she'd worn her scarlet underwear today. It made her classmates gasp; oddly enough, they seemed more shocked by the color of her panties than by her lascivious make-out session with Rev. Allan. Go figure!

Rev. Allan needed a little help. "Now's the time to rip open my blouse and burrow your face between my breasts," she stage-whispered. He seemed a little confused, so she returned her hand to his now-engorged member. It felt like a cucumber through his trousers. She gave it a little squeeze, and that provided the spark to motorize him into action.

With a sudden motion, he ripped open her white blouse to reveal a camisole top that matched her panties. That drew another gasp from the audience, but it wasn't clear whether they were startled by his action or the red undergarment.

"'Mr. Cunningham, I am but putty in your hands,'" the would-be actress intoned. "'Take me if you want me. Here, let me free your John Thomas so it can do its work.'" Unbuttoning his fly, she drew out what Emma White would later describe as a "large Kielbasa sausage." That certainly drew a gasp from the crowd.

Blindly into his role, Jonathan Allan jerked downward on her camisole, snapping the thin straps, and exposing her breasts. The pink nipples were standing up like corks. He brushed his lips over them, his tongue tasting the skin.

With his hands now clutching her ass, she had trouble working the silk panties past them without tearing the shiny red fabric. She managed to get them far enough down her hips to bare the thin patch of pubic hair. The sight of his fleshy shaft rubbing against her vulva drew yet another gasp.

"He actually going to fuck her," exclaimed Ruby Gillis, both frightened and fascinated by that possibility.

"I've never seen anybody get fucked before," said Tilly Boulter.

"What? You don't have a mirror in your bedroom for when Charlie Sloane comes over?" sniped Josie.

"Hey!" said Charlie's sister Carrie.

"Don't tell me Charlie hasn't fucked you too," Josie rejoined with a look of amusement on her face. She knew that the brother and sister had shared a single bed in the crowded Sloane household until just last year.

Meanwhile, Anne Shirley had reared up to lock her slender legs around her partner's hips, fully supported by his splayed hands on her bottom. The position allowed his cock to slide into her moist pussy, burying its way till their pubic ridges met, her curls flattened against the wool of his trousers. "Ooooo," she moaned. By now, she had forgotten her lines too.

"Jesus our Savior," cried Ruby Gillis at the sight of her classmate impaled on the Presbyterian minister's shaft. She began to cry, her usual response to confusing situations.

"Look at that," muttered Jane Andrews, eyes wide as hen's eggs.

"Jiminy!" gulped little Emma White. "They're really doing it."

The words snapped Jonathan Allan out of his fugue state, causing him to drop Anne onto the church's hard oak floorboard. She would have a bruise on her butt for weeks to come. "Merciful Heavens," he yelped, "what am I doing?"

"You were fucking me," said Anne helpfully. But by then Rev. Allan had made a hasty exit through the side door, heading straight for the parsonage.

"Well, that was rude," Anne sniffed as she straightened her disheveled clothing.

≈≈≈

Anne had achieved a new status among her

classmates at Avonlea School. She was the girl who had fucked the minister, besting Josie Pye in a dare. None had the courage to talk about what they'd seen, for the consequences would be dire even if no one believed them. As close as anyone came to spilling the beans was when Josie posted a notice on the porch that said "Anne Shirley and ???" – but even she didn't have the courage to fill in the blank.

Gilbert Blythe's curiosity was aroused by the posting. A girl's name appearing on the porch usually meant she had been fucked by the boy who name appear adjacent hers. But in this case there was no second name.

He cornered Anne after school that day. "Hold on," he said, catching her by the arm, nearly causing her to drop her books.

"Unhand me, Gilbert Blythe!" she said with an air of the dramatic. "I won't be accosted by the likes of you."

Quickly, he removed his restraining hand. "Sorry, Anne, I just wanted to speak with you. I hope you don't mind."

"Speak with me about what? I will not allow you to copy my geometry homework, if that's what you have in mind."

He smirked. "I'd never ask to copy your geometry. That's your worst subject."

"Yes, I know it. But I'm making gains." On today's test she has scored a 97. But to her consternation, Gilbert had attained a perfect 100. She suspected Miss Stacy favored him, being he was tall and handsome with dark wavy hair.

"I want to ask if you were serious about rehearsing for next year's Christmas concert?" he asked shyly. He couldn't bring himself to look her in the eyes.

"Why? Is this merely a ruse to see me in the nude again?"

"Well, I wouldn't mind that. I enjoyed that first viewing when I rescued you at Barry's Pond. And you looked quite fetching at the Christmas concert, your accouterments peeking through that flimsy gauze."

"Thank you, I'm sure. That may be the first compliment you ever gave me."

"Not so," he protested. "I told you I liked what I saw when we stood backstage after the concert. That was a compliment."

"You were just trying to get me to touch that bulge you had in your pants."

"Oh? Would you have done it if I asked?"

"Are you asking now?"

"Maybe."

"I thought you were interested in rehearsing, not having me stroke your John Thomas."

"Perhaps the two are the same thing. You spoke of actually fucking on the stage in front of an audience. Isn't that what you wanted to rehearse?"

"Yes, but now that I think of it, I'm not sure you're the proper candidate. Charlie Sloane may be more suitable. He has a flair for the theatrical."

Gilbert was an intelligent boy. He didn't think for a moment that Anne's proposed performance would ever happen. Miss Stacy would never go along with such a crazy idea. But he'd play along in hopes of getting laid. The posting on the porch indicated she was putting out to someone. "You should at least give me a tryout," he urged. "That's only fair. I promise to try so hard to please you. I'm told I take direction well."

"Trying HARD is the operative word," she said, glancing at his crotch.

"C'mon, give me a chance. I know we've had our differences, but we're talking about doing something for the sake of art, right?"

Anne sniffed as if discounting his words. "Very well then. Tomorrow is Saturday. Why don't you meet me at Mrs. Langston's dairy barn? That might be an acceptable place to rehearse. If we wait until after milking, the barn should be deserted. Mr. and Mrs. Langston always goes into Carmody on Saturdays around noon."

"Noon it is," he said, offering a dazzling smile that almost made her look forward to the rendezvous.

≈≈≈

Gilbert Blythe showed up at the Langston's dairy barn promptly at twelve o'clock. As a tactic to demonstrate her lack of eagerness – although in truth she could hardly wait – Anne arrived fifteen minutes late.

"Oh, there you are," she hailed Gilbert. "I hope I haven't kept you waiting. I was trying to decide whether to come or not. As I think about it, I may be wasting your time. I've all but decided that Charlie Sloane is a better candidate."

"Charlie! He couldn't act his way out of a paper bag."

"And you can?"

"Try me," he challenged.

"Alright. Since we're both here I suppose there's nothing to lose. My concept is to realistically portray "The Rape of Lucretia" from Spenser's *The Faerie Queene*. That should be quite attention-getting, don't you think?"

"Just how realistic do you have in mind," he endeavored to clarify the plan. Not that it mattered. He would do whatever she asked. He'd been quite taken with Anne Shirley for some time now.

"Well, I'd think we'd have to be nude – totally, not covered in gauze. And we'd actually fuck. I would scream and resist, but you would force yourself upon me. You could cum in me if you want to."

"I'd like that."

"Shall we rehearse part of the scene then?" she suggested, stepping into the privacy of the barn. Milk cows were lined up in their stalls. A large pile of dried hay lay just beyond the milking stalls. "Over there would be a good place," she pointed toward the hay.

"Sure. Which part of the scene do you have in mind?"

"Since we don't have a script with us today, we'd best forgo the speaking parts and concentrate on the rape scene."

"Makes sense," Gilbert nodded. Even as he said this, he knew that Mr. Superintendent Bell would never allow such debauchery to take place on any stage on Prince Edward Island. This was another of Anne's flibbertigibbet ideas. She was perhaps the smartest girl in school, but her out-of-control imagination was always getting her into trouble.

Anne arched an eyebrow. "Well, aren't you going

finding a steady rhythm. "You're equally as large as Rev. Allan, I'd say."

"Rev. Allan? How would you know HIS size?"

Snared by her own words, Ann had no choice but admit her breech of sanctimony. "Josie Pye dared me to fuck him. It was only the one time – a very brief encounter, I didn't even get a chance to cum."

Gilbert Blythe was shocked by this declaration. Being a religious boy, he passed the collection plate every Sunday morning at First Presbyterian. He knew the minister well, or at least had thought he did. "Good gravy!" exclaimed Gilbert, rolling away from Anne, breaking their sexual contact. "I can't believe you'd do something like that, you wicked girl. You will surely roast in the fires of Hell." It wasn't clear whether he was more upset over this affront to the Presbyterian Church or jealousy. At any rate, the moment of intimacy between them was broken.

Anne leaped to her feet, sexually frustrated by this unexpected act of *coitus interruptus*. "Gilbert Blythe, you're the hypocrite – attacking my morals while fucking me yourself."

"Go get Charlie Sloane to co-star in your production of 'The Rape of Lucretia," Gil shouted as he gathered up his scattered clothing. "I'd rather fuck my own fist than you, Anne Shirley. I used to imagine that one day you might be my girlfriend. But no more. Do not endeavor to speak to me again outside of school!"

"Have it your own way, Gilbert Blythe. You're a lousy fuck anyway," she shouted as she stomped angrily out of the Langston's dairy barn, not even bothering to get dressed.

Anne was halfway home before she realized she'd left her clothing back at the barn. Thomas Langston would certainly get a shock when he came across her dress that afternoon when he came in to feed the cows. She giggled at the thought. She wondered if the old coot ever shared his wife's spyglass. She vowed to herself to put on an extra special show with Martin and Matilda that night ... just in case.

≈≈≈

As reprisal to being spurned by Gilbert Blythe, Anne set out to renew her relationship – if that's what it was – with Rev. Jonathan Allan.

She encountered him in the church vestry, where he was preparing next Sunday's sermon. When he looked up from his papers, he seemed nervous to see her. The man had studiously avoided her since that episode of Story Club play-acting that had gone astray.

"Oh, Anne Shirley – what can I assist you with?" he greeted her cautiously.

"Rev. Allan, I am feeling great guilt over our brief *tête-à-tête* in front of my classmates. Or should I call it a *pénis-à-vagin*?"

He ignored her attempt at French humor. "That was a most unfortunate lapse of judgment on my part," he shook his head sadly. "There is nothing for you to feel guilty about. The fault was entirely mine. After all, I am a grown man and you are but a mere child."

"Not too much of a child ... as you discovered. I must admit I enjoyed it very much and I've been dreaming of doing it with you again."

"Ah, that is not to be. Not only am I a man of the cloth, but I am also married."

399

"That I know. Your wife is a dear friend. But my interest is only recreational. There's no intent to come between you and your lovely wife."

"That's quite an offer from a girl of sixteen."

"Seventeen," she corrected. "And long since a virgin."

"Sex out of wedlock is a sin. We must pray for your immortal soul, my dear."

"Can't you just give me a dispensation? I've read that priests can do that."

"I am a Presbyterian minister, not a Roman Catholic priest – as you well know. After all, you sit in the front pew with your adopted family week after week."

"You've noticed me?" She found that flattering.

"I notice all my parishioners," he countered. "Take it for no more than that."

Anne decided that her quest required bold action. "I am not the little girl you think me to be," she said. "Here, let me show you." With that she slipped the straps of her dress off her shoulders, letting the garment fall to the vestry floor. "As you can see, I am quite grown up."

Jonathan Allan stared fixedly at this vision before him. It was as if an angel had descended from Heaven to reward his sacrifices to the Church. Anne Shirley stood totally nude before him as if awaiting some sort of Eucharist communion. Her breasts were full and round, with pointy pink tips. Her flat belly gave way to a sparse patch of pubic hair, brunette to match the tresses surrounding her beautiful face. He couldn't withstand the temptation.

"My God forgive me, but I must have you."

"And you may," she assured him. "Think of me as a gift from God."

Thus it became a weekly tryst, Anne meeting Rev. Allan on Saturday afternoon in the vestry for energetic bouts of sex. She enjoyed it very much. He was very well endowed. But she found it quite a challenge to be fucking the husband while at the same time secretly fucking his wife.

≈≈≈

Matilda, walking home one late April evening from a Church Aid meeting, realized that the winter was over and gone. Breathing in the clover-scented air, she felt delight that spring was abroad in the land.

As the blonde woman picked her steps along the damp lane, enjoying the satisfaction that she was going home to a briskly snapping wood fire and a table nicely spread for tea, she hummed a little tune, a snatch of "Oh Canada!" she could see the rooftop of Green Gables up ahead. It comforted her to know Anne would be there to greet her. Yes, her and Martin's life had changed considerably since Anne had come to Green Gables.

Consequently, when Matilda entered her kitchen and found the fire out in the cast-iron stove, she was irritated. Hadn't she told Anne to be sure and have tea ready at five o'clock? Now she would have to pull an apron over her second-best dress and hurriedly prepare the evening meal before Martin returned from plowing. He always liked to find a hot meal on the table at the end of the day. He was very set in his ways.

"I'll settle Miss Anne Shirley when she comes

home," said Matilda grimly, carving off slices of roast beef with more vigor than was strictly necessary.

Martin came in and sat patiently at the table, waiting for his tea. "Where's the girl?" he asked, surprised by her absence. Anne usually prepared his supper.

"She's likely gadding off somewhere with Diana Barry or writing stories or practicing dialogues or some such tomfoolery," answered his sister. "I don't abide her ignoring her chores. She's got to be pulled up short on this sort of thing. I don't care if Rev. Allan does say she's the brightest and sweetest child he's ever known. She may be bright and sweet enough, but her head is full of nonsense. But heavens! – Here I am saying the very thing I got so riled with Rita Langston for saying today at the Church Aid Society. At the time, I was glad that Rev. Allan spoke up in Anne's behalf, for if he hadn't done so I would've likely said something sharp to Rita myself. Anne's got plenty of faults, goodness knows, but I'll not have Rita Langston enumerating them. That old biddy would pick faults with the Angel Gabriel if he lived anywhere near Avonlea."

"It's odd how Rev. Allan has taken to the girl, like he's become her self-appointed protector. You'd think she's holding something over his head – like a photograph of him having sexual congress with one of John Barry's sheep."

"Don't talk that way, Martin. You'll be paving a road straight to Hell with comments like that!"

"Now, Matilda. I'm just saying."

"Just the same, Anne has no business to leave the house like this when I told her to stay home this afternoon and look after things," grumbled Matilda. "For all her faults, I never found her disobedient or untrustworthy before and I'm real sorry to find her so now."

"Well now, I dunno," said Martin, who, being patient and wise and, above all, hungry, knew it was best to let Matilda talk her wrath out unhindered. He'd, learned by hard experience that his sister fixed supper much quicker if not delayed by untimely argument. "Perhaps you're judging her too hasty, Matilda. Don't call her untrustworthy until you're sure she has disobeyed you. Maybe it can all be explained – Anne's a great hand at explaining."

"She's not here when I told her to stay," retorted Matilda. "I reckon she'll find it hard to explain THAT to my satisfaction. Of course I knew you'd take her part, Martin. You're still feeling guilty over jilting her. But don't. Next time you're fucking her, just remind yourself you don't have to own the cow to enjoy the milk."

≈≈≈

Anne returned a half-hour later. Before Matilda could lay into her, Martin asked, "Where have you been? We were a mite worried."

"Oh, Martin, Matilda, it was the most harrowing thing. Mr. Harmon Andrews wrecked his new motor car. He ran off the road near Diana Barry's house. She sent me a signal to come quick. Mr. Andrews was badly injured. Prissy and her sisters were shook up. His wife escaped with nary a scratch. The automobile is a loss, I'm afraid. The fenders are all dented and one wheel came off."

"Mercy me," said Matilda. "What happened?"

"I was able to stop Mr. Andrews' bleeding. He had a terrible gash in his leg. I'd learned how to apply pressure to a wound when working for Mrs. Thomas. The twins were always falling down and getting cut. The doctor said Mr. Andrews might have bled to death if I hadn't been there."

"Lucky you were," said Matilda, her anger dissipated. Tell me, what would you like for supper?"

"Hm," said Martin, "our Anne might grow up to become a nurse."

A never-to-be-forgotten day.

CHAPTER XXX

An Epoch in Anne's Life

Anne was bringing the cows home from the back pasture by way of Lover's Lane. It was a September evening and all the gaps and clearings in the woods were brimmed up with ruby sunset light. Here and there the lane was splashed with it, but for the most part it was already quite shadowy beneath the maples, and the spaces under the firs were filled with a clear violet dusk like airy wine. The winds were out in their tops, and there is no sweeter music on earth than that which the wind makes in the fir trees at evening.

The cows swung placidly down the lane, and Anne followed them dreamily, repeating aloud the battle canto from *Marmion* – which had also been part of their English course the preceding winter and which Miss Stacy had made them learn by heart – and exulting in its rushing lines and the clash of spears in its imagery. When she came to the lines:

> *The stubborn spearsmen still made good*
> *Their dark impenetrable wood,*

she stopped in ecstasy to shut her eyes that she might the better fancy herself one of that heroic ring. When she opened them again it was to behold Diana coming through the gate and looking so important that Anne instantly divined there was news to be told. But betray too eager curiosity she would not.

"Anne, hello," the neighbor girl greeted her.

"Isn't this evening just like a purple dream, Diana? It makes me so glad to be alive. In the mornings I always think the mornings are best; but when evening comes I think it's lovelier still."

"It's a very fine evening," said Diana, "but oh, I have such news, Anne. Guess. You can have three guesses."

"Charlotte Gillis is going to be married in the church after all and Mrs. Allan wants us to decorate it," cried Anne.

"No. Charlotte's beau won't agree to being married in the church because he thinks it would seem too much like a funeral. That's too bad, because a church wedding would be such fun. Guess again."

"Jane's mother is going to let her have a birthday party?"

Diana shook her head, her black eyes dancing with merriment. "No, I think not."

"Then I can't think what it can be," said Anne in despair, "unless it's that Moody MacPherson saw you home from prayer meeting last night. Did he fuck you?"

"I should say not," exclaimed Diana indignantly. "And I wouldn't boast of it if he did, the horrid creature! I knew you couldn't guess it. So I'll tell you: Mother had a letter from Aunt Josephine today, and she wants you and me to visit her come next Tuesday to go the Fair!"

"Oh, Diana," whispered Anne, finding it necessary to lean up against a maple tree for support, "do you really mean it? I'm dying to go to the Fair. But I'm afraid Matilda won't let me go. She will say that she can't encourage gadding about. That was what she said last week when Jane invited me to go with them in their double-seated buggy to the American concert at the White Sands Hotel. I wanted to go, but Matilda said I'd be better at home learning my lessons and so would Jane. I was bitterly disappointed, Diana. I felt so heartbroken that I wouldn't say my prayers when I went to bed. But I repented of that and got up in the middle of the night and said them anyway."

"I'll tell you," said Diana, "we'll get my mother to ask Matilda. She'll be more likely to let you go then; and if she does we'll have the time of our lives. I've never been to a fair, and it's so aggravating to hear the other girls talking about their trips. Jane and Ruby have been twice, and they're going again this year."

The Prince Edward Island Fair was an annual event, with tents selling ice cream and hot dogs, prizes for the fattest pig and best milk cow, a pie eating competition, sideshow attractions with all manner of strange freaks, and a labyrinth of mechanical rides.

"I refuse to think about it at all until I know whether I can go or not," vowed Anne. "If I get disappointed, it would be more than I could bear. But in case I do go I'm very glad my new coat will be ready by that time. Matilda didn't think I needed a new coat. She said my old one would do very well for another winter and that I ought to be satisfied with having a new dress. The dress is very pretty, Diana – navy blue and made so fashionably. Matilda always makes my dresses fashionably now, because she says she doesn't intend to have Martin going to Mrs. Langston to make them. I'm so glad. It is ever so much easier to be good if your clothes are fashionable. At least, it is easier for me. I suppose it doesn't make such a difference to naturally good people like you. But Martin said I must have a new coat, so Matilda bought a lovely piece of blue broadcloth, and it's being made by a real tailor over at Carmody. It's supposed to be done by Saturday night, and I'm trying not to imagine myself walking up the church aisle on Sunday in my new suit and cap, because I'll be so disappointed if it doesn't get finished in time. Do you suppose it's wrong for us to think so much about our clothes? Matilda says it is very sinful. But it is such an interesting subject, don't you think?"

≈≈≈

At Mrs. Barry's insistence, Matilda agreed to let Anne go to the Fair. It was arranged that Mr. Barry should drive the girls there the following Tuesday. As Charlottetown was thirty miles away and Mr. Barry wished to return the same day, it was necessary to make an early start.

Not surprisingly, Anne was up before sunrise that morning. Her heart all-aflutter, she'd barely been able to sleep. A glance from her window assured her that the day would be fine, for the eastern sky was all silvery and cloudless. Through a gap in the fir trees she could see a light shining in the western gable of Orchard Slope, a sign that Diana was also up.

Anne had breakfast ready by the time Matilda came down, but was much too excited on her own part to eat. After breakfast Anne donned her jaunty new cap and warm jacket, then hastened over the brook and up through the firs to Orchard Slope. Mr. Barry and Diana were waiting for her, buggy already hitched, and soon they were on the road.

Thirty miles was a long drive, but Anne and Diana enjoyed every minute of it. They found it delightful to rattle along over the moist roads as the early red sunlight crept across the shorn harvest fields. The air was fresh and crisp, with smoke-blue mists curling through the valleys and floating off the hills. Sometimes the road went through woods where maples were beginning to hang out scarlet banners; sometimes it crossed rivers on shaky bridges that made Anne's flesh cringe with the old, half-delightful fear; sometimes it wound along the shoreline, passing by a cluster of weather-gray fishing huts; but wherever it went there was much of interest to discuss.

It was almost noon when they reached Charlottetown. The girls waved goodbye to Diana's father and found their way to Beechwood, the impressive mansion where Aunt Josephine resided. It was quite a fine old house, set back from the street in a seclusion of green elms and branching beeches. Not hard to guess where its name came from. Miss Barry met them at the door with a twinkle in her sharp black eyes.

"So you've come to see me at last, Anne of Green Gables," the old woman said. "Mercy, child, how you have grown! You're taller than I am, I declare. And you're ever so much better looking than you used to be, too. But I dare say you know that without being told."

"Indeed I didn't," said Anne radiantly. "I know I'm not so freckled as I used to be, so there's much to be thankful for. But I really hadn't dared to hope there was any other improvement. I'm so glad you think there is, Miss Barry."

Josephine Barry's house was furnished with "great magnificence," as Anne told Matilda afterward. The two little country girls were rather abashed by the splendor of the parlor where Miss Barry left them while she went to see about lunch.

"Isn't it just like a palace?" whispered Diana. "I've never been in Aunt Josephine's house before, and I had no idea it was so grand. I just wish Julia Bell could see this – she puts on such airs about her mother's parlor."

"Julia Bell sucks goat dicks," said Anne, just to be mean. She didn't like the girl, always acting high and mighty, as if she were a princess or some form of royalty.

"Look in this room," Diana led the way through the house. "Isn't it grand?"

"Velvet carpet," sighed Anne luxuriously, "and silk curtains! I've dreamed of such things, Diana. But do you know I don't believe I feel very comfortable with them after all. There are so many things in this room and all so splendid that there is no scope for imagination. That is one consolation when you are poor – there are so many things you can imagine being nicer. But if everything already exceeds your imagination, there's nowhere to go with it."

"Well, if Aunt Josephine leaves this mansion to me when she dies, I'm not going to complain about it."

"Wouldn't that be something, if she did? You and I could live here and play house. If would be ever so much nicer than we ever imagined Idlewald to be."

"Yes, you and I could lounge naked together in the master bedroom and eat bon-bons."

"Wonderful," trilled Anne, with eyes as large as

saucers. "I've never had a bob-bon before."

≈ ≈ ≈

On Wednesday Miss Barry took them to the fair grounds and kept them there all day. "It was splendid," Anne related to Matilda later on. "I never imagined anything so interesting. I don't really know which section was the most interesting. I think I liked the trained horses and the pie-eating contest and the jugglers best. Josie Pye took first prize for knitted lace. I was real glad she did. And I was glad that I felt glad, for it shows I'm improving, don't you think, Matilda, when I can rejoice in Josie's success? After all, I don't like Josie very much. She acts more like a boy than a girl. I'm surprised she's so skilled at knitting."

"Who else was there?" asked Matilda as if she were compiling a list of saints and sinners. "Anyone from Avonlea?"

"Oh yes, plenty. Mrs. Harmon Andrews took second prize for her Gravenstein apples and Mr. Richard Gillis took first prize for a pig. Clara Louise MacPherson took a prize for painting, and Mrs. Langston got first prize for her homemade butter and cheese. So Avonlea was pretty well represented, wasn't it? There were thousands of people there, Matilda. It made me feel dreadfully insignificant. And Miss Barry took us up to the grandstand to see the horse races. Mrs. Langston wouldn't go; she said horse racing was an abomination and, she being a church member, thought it her duty to set a good example by staying away. But there were so many there I don't believe Mrs. Langston's absence would ever be noticed. I shouldn't go to horseraces very often, because they offer an awful temptation to gamble. Diana got so excited that she bet me ten cents that the red horse would win. I didn't believe he would, but I refused to bet, because I wanted to tell Mrs. Allan all about everything, and I felt sure it wouldn't do to tell her that. It's always wrong to do anything you can't tell the minister's wife."

Matilda shook her head at the girl's double standard. Anne didn't mind doing things with the minister's wife she couldn't tell her friends.

Anne rattled on: "I was very glad I didn't bet Diana, because it turns out the red horse DID win, and I would have lost ten cents. So you see that virtue was its own reward. We saw a man go up in a balloon. I'd love to go up in a balloon, Matilda; it would be simply thrilling; and we saw a man selling fortunes. You paid him ten cents and a little bird picked out your fortune for you. Miss Barry gave Diana and me ten cents each to have our fortunes told. Mine said I would marry a dark-complexioned man who was very wealthy, and I would go across water to live. After that I looked carefully at all the dark men I came across, but I didn't care much for any of them. But I suppose it's too early to be looking out for him yet. I'm in no hurry now that Martin has broken my heart by calling off our nuptials."

"You have no business marrying Martin. He's like a father to you."

"I don't think I would fuck my father, Matilda. That just isn't done. Although I think Josie Pye's father fucks her. But she doesn't talk about it. But then again, maybe I would fuck my father, because you Martin is like my father, and I fuck him."

"I'm glad you had a good time," the blonde woman

said, paying little attention to the girl's words. She has socks to darn and that took concentration. Besides, Anne would repeat all these stories a dozen times, so it wasn't like she'd be missing any part of the girl's trip to the Fair."

"Oh, it was a never-to-be-forgotten day, Matilda. I was so tired I couldn't sleep at night. Miss Barry put us in the spare room, according to promise. It was an elegant room, Matilda, but somehow sleeping in a spare room isn't what I used to think it was. That's the worst of growing up, and I'm beginning to realize it. The things you wanted so much when you were a child don't seem half so wonderful to you when you get them. Like fucking a clown."

"Fucking a clown?" Matilda looked up from her handiwork. "You fucked a clown?"

"Well, he wasn't really a clown. He was a midget with one glass eye. He worked in the sideshow. But he was very funny when he juggled milk bottles. He didn't drop a single bottle, although he was always pretending he might, but he would catch it at the last moment."

"You fucked him?"

"Only once. He asked me so nicely. We stepped into a tent and I laid down on a bed of straw where he slept at night. I had to lie down, for he was too short for his John Thomas to reach my pussy while standing up. Isn't that strange, Matilda. He was barely four feet tall, but his John Thomas felt normal size."

"Anne!"

"Oh, don't worry," the girl said. "I won't marry that one-eyed midget. He was neither dark-complexioned nor wealthy."

≈ ≈ ≈

On Thursday the girls enjoyed a buggy ride in the park, and in the evening Miss Barry took them to a concert at the Academy of Music, where a noted prima donna was scheduled to sing. To Anne the evening was a glittering vision of delight.

"Oh, Matilda, it was beyond description. I was so excited I couldn't even talk, so you may know what it was like. I just sat in enraptured silence. Madame Selitsky was perfectly beautiful, and wore white satin and diamonds. But when she began to sing I never thought about anything else. Oh, I can't tell you how I felt. But it seemed to me that it could never be hard to be good anymore. I felt like I do when I look up to the stars. Tears came into my eyes, but, oh, they were such happy tears. I was so sorry when it was over, and I told Miss Barry I didn't see how I was ever to return to common life again. She said she thought if we went over to the restaurant across the street and had an ice cream it might help me. That sounded so prosaic; but to my surprise I found it true. The ice cream was delicious, Matilda, and it was so lovely and dissipated to be sitting there eating it at eleven o'clock at night. Diana said she believed she was born for city life. Miss Barry asked me what my opinion was, but I said I would have to think it over very seriously before I could tell her what I really thought. So I thought it over after I went to bed. That is the best time to think things out. And I came to the conclusion, Matilda, that I wasn't born for city life and that I was glad of it. It's nice to be eating ice cream at brilliant restaurants at eleven o'clock at night once in a while; but as a regular thing

I'd rather be in the east gable at eleven, sound asleep, but kind of knowing even in my sleep that the stars were shining outside and that the wind was blowing in the firs across the brook. I told Miss Barry so at breakfast the next morning and she laughed. Miss Barry generally laughs at anything I say, even when I say the most solemn things. I don't think I liked it, Matilda, because I wasn't trying to be funny. But she is a most hospitable lady and treated us royally."

≈≈≈

Friday brought going-home time, and Mr. Barry drove into Charlottetown to fetch the girls.

"Well, I hope you've enjoyed yourselves," said Josephine Barry, as she bade them goodbye.

"Indeed we have," said Diana.

"And you, Anne of Green Gables?"

"I've enjoyed every minute of the visit," said Anne, throwing her arms impulsively about the old woman's neck and kissing her wrinkled cheek. Diana would never have dared to do such a thing and felt rather aghast at Anne's familiarity. But Miss Barry seemed pleased. She stood on her veranda and watched the buggy out of sight, then went back into her big house with a sigh. It seemed very lonely without those fresh young lives.

Miss Barry was a rather selfish old lady, if the truth must be told, and had never cared much for anybody but herself. She valued people only as they were of service to her or amused her. Anne had amused her, and consequently stood high in the old lady's good graces. But she found herself thinking less about Anne's quaint speeches than of her fresh enthusiasms, her transparent emotions, her little winning ways, and the sweetness of her nature.

"I thought Matilda Collins was being foolish when I heard she'd adopted a girl out of an orphanage," she said to herself, "but I guess she didn't make much of a mistake after all. If I had a child like Anne in the house all the time I'd be a much happier woman."

≈≈≈

Anne and Diana found the drive home as pleasant as the drive in – pleasanter, indeed, since there was the delightful consciousness of families waiting at the end of it. The sun was setting by the time they passed through White Sands and turned onto the shore road. Before them, the moon was rising out of the sea, radiant in its reflected yellow light. Every little cove along the curving road offered a panorama of dancing ripples. The waves broke with a soft swish on the rocks below them, and the tang of the sea was strong in the air.

Beyond them, the girls could see the Avonlea hills silhouetted darkly against the saffron sky. "Oh, but it's good to be alive and to be going home," breathed Anne. When she crossed the log bridge over the brook the kitchen light of Green Gables winked her a friendly welcome back. Anne ran blithely up the hill and into the kitchen, where a hot supper was waiting on the table.

"So you've got back?" said Matilda, folding up her knitting.

"Yes, and oh, it's so good to be back," said Anne joyously. "I could kiss everything, especially you, Matilda. What's that on the table, a roasted chicken?

You don't mean to say you cooked that for me!"

"Yes, I did," she replied. "I thought you'd be hungry after such a drive and need something real appetizing. Hurry and take off your things, and we'll have supper as soon as Martin comes in. I'm glad you've got back, I must say. It's been fearful lonesome here without you, and I never put in four longer days."

After supper Anne sat before the fire, wedged between Martin and Matilda, and gave them a full account of her visit.

"I've had a splendid time," she concluded happily, "and I feel that it marks an epoch in my life. But the best of it all was the coming home."

"Good," said Martin. "Let's all go to bed and fuck."

Becoming a teacher.

CHAPTER XXXI

The Queens Class Is Organized

Matilda laid her knitting on her lap and leaned back in her chair. Her eyes were tired, and she thought vaguely that she must see about having her reading glasses changed the next time she went to town, for her eyes had grown tired very often of late.

It was nearly dark, for the full November twilight had fallen around Green Gables, and the only light in the kitchen came from the dancing flames in the Waterloo stove.

Anne was curled up Turk-fashion on the hearthrug, naked in her usual fashion, gazing into that joyous glow where the sunshine of a hundred summers was being distilled from the burning maple cordwood. She had been reading, but her book had slipped to the floor, and now she was dreaming, with a smile on her parted lips. Glittering castles in Spain were shaping themselves out of the mists of her lively fancy; enthralling adventures were happening to her in cloudland – adventures that always turned out triumphantly and never involved her in scrapes like those of actual life.

Matilda looked at the girl with a tenderness that she would never have been revealed in clearer light than that of fireshine and shadow. But she had learned to love this slim, gray-eyed girl with an affection all the deeper and stronger from its very undemonstrativeness. She had an uneasy feeling that it was rather sinful to set one's heart so intensely on any human creature as she had set hers on Anne. Perhaps she was performing a sort of unconscious penance for this by being more critical than if the girl had been less dear to her.

Certainly Anne herself had no idea how much Matilda loved her. She sometimes thought wistfully that Matilda was very hard to please and distinctly lacking in imagination. But she always checked the thought reproachfully, remembering what she owed to Matilda.

"Anne," said Matilda abruptly, "Miss Stacy was here this afternoon when you were out with Diana."

Anne came back from her other world with a start and a sigh.

"Was she? Oh, I'm so sorry I wasn't in. Why didn't you call me, Matilda? Diana and I were only over in the Haunted Wood. It's lovely in the woods now. All the little wood things – the ferns and the satin leaves and the crackerberries – have gone to sleep, just as if somebody had tucked them away until spring under a blanket of leaves. I think it was a little gray fairy with a rainbow scarf that came tiptoeing along the last moonlight night and did it. Diana wouldn't say much about that, though. Diana has never forgotten the scolding her mother gave her about imagining ghosts into the Haunted Wood. It had a very bad effect on Diana's imagination. It blighted it. Mrs. Langston says Myrtle Bell is a blighted being. I asked Ruby Gillis why Myrtle was blighted, and Ruby said she guessed it was because her young man had gone back on her. Just like Martin went back on me. But I'm not blighted, am I?"

"No, dear. You have a stronger constitution."

"Diana and I are thinking seriously of promising each other that we will never marry but be nice old maids and live together forever. Diana hasn't quite made up her mind though, because she thinks perhaps it would be nobler to marry some wild, dashing, wicked young man and reform him. Diana and I talk a great deal about serious subjects now, you know. We feel that we are so much older than we used to be that it isn't becoming to talk of childish matters. It's such a solemn thing to be almost eighteen, Matilda. Miss Stacy took all us girls who are in our teens down to the brook last Wednesday, and talked to us about it. She said we couldn't be too careful what habits we formed and what ideals we acquired in our teens, because by the time we were twenty our characters would be developed and the foundation laid for our whole future life. And she said if the foundation was shaky we could never build anything really worthwhile on it. Diana and I talked the matter over coming home from school. We felt extremely solemn, Matilda. And we decided that we would try to be very careful indeed and form respectable habits and learn all we could and be as sensible as possible, so that by the time we were twenty our characters would be properly developed. It's perfectly appalling to think of being twenty, Matilda. It sounds so fearfully old and grown up. But why was Miss Stacy here this afternoon?"

"That is what I want to tell you, Anne, if you'll ever give me a chance to get a word in edgewise. She was talking about you."

"About me?" Anne looked rather scared. Then she flushed and exclaimed: "Oh, I know what she was saying. I meant to tell you, Matilda, honestly I did, but I forgot. Miss Stacy caught me reading *Ben Hur* in school yesterday afternoon when I should have been studying my Canadian history. Jane Andrews lent it to me. I was reading it during lunch, and I had just got to the chariot race when school went in. I was simply wild to know how it turned out – although I felt sure Ben Hur must win, because it wouldn't be poetical justice if he didn't – so I spread the history open on my desk lid and then tucked *Ben Hur* between the desk and my knee. I just looked as if I were studying Canadian history, you know, while all the while I was reveling in *Ben Hur*. I was so interested in it that I never noticed Miss Stacy coming down the aisle until all at once I just looked up and there she was looking down at me, so reproachful-like. I can't tell you how ashamed I felt, Matilda, especially when I heard Josie Pye giggling. Miss Stacy took *Ben Hur* away, but she never said a word then. She kept me in at recess and talked to me. She said I had done very wrong in two respects. First, I was wasting the time I *ought* to have put on my studies; and secondly, I was deceiving my teacher in trying to make it appear I was reading a history when it was a storybook instead. I had never realized until that moment, Matilda, that what I was doing was deceitful. I was shocked. I cried bitterly, and asked Miss Stacy to forgive me and I'd never do such a thing again; and I offered to do penance by never so much as looking at *Ben Hur* for a whole week, not even to see how the chariot race turned out. But Miss Stacy said she wouldn't require that, and she forgave me freely. So I think it wasn't very kind of her to come up here to you about it after all."

"Miss Stacy never mentioned such a thing to me, Anne. It's only your guilty conscience that's bringing you to confess. You have no business to be reading storybooks during class. You read too many novels anyhow."

"Oh, how can you call *Ben Hur* a novel when it's really such a religious book?" protested Anne. "Of course it's a little too exciting to be proper reading for Sunday, and so I only read it on weekdays."

"You have a lot of books in your room, I notice."

"Yes, they are gifts from Mrs. Allan. Mostly classics like *Paradise Lost* and *The Secret Garden* and *Moby Dick*. They are each dedicated to people I love or have been intimate with. For instance, "

"Oh? Do you have a book for me?"

"Yes, I do. Given your efforts in trying to raise me, I've chosen a play by William Shakespeare – *The Taming of the Shrew*. Remember when I asked you for a sprig of your public hair as a souvenir? Well, that's where I keep it, pressed between the pages."

"So that's why you did with it. I wondered. I thought your request was most bizarre, but it seemed harmless enough. I knew I wouldn't miss it, for I regularly trim my bush."

"I've noticed how neat you keep it. After all, I often have a close-up view of your lady garden." Anne smiled.

Matilda smiled slyly. "Do you have a book for your own locks?"

"Perhaps. I'm thinking Daniel Dafoe's *The Fortunes and Misfortunes of the Famous Moll Flanders*. That, or Hawthorne's *The Scarlet Letter*.

What do you think?"

"I'd suggest Dickens's *Great Expectations*. That's you to a T, Anne Shirley."

"Do you really think so? If so, I must procure a copy. Perhaps Mrs. Allan has one she can contribute to my collection."

"What other books do you have in this collection?"

"Not many. Hawthorne's *Tanglewood Tales for Boys and Girls*. Jane Austen's *Emma*. *Jane Eyre*, too! John Barrington's *Ruby Red*. Harriet Beecher Stow's *The Minister's Wooing*. Victor Hugo's *The Hunchback of Notre Dame* – that's the misshapen midget from the Fair."

"Some of those I can guess," sighed Matilda. "But what of *The Minister's Wooing* –?"

"Since I've revealed my book code, I'm sure you can figure it out."

"Surely not Rev. Allan?" The blonde woman was aghast. They were speaking of the minister of the First Presbyterian Church!

"That book is incomplete," admitted Anne shyly.

"Thank God," Matilda breathed a sigh of relief. "Then you haven't slept with Jonathan Allan after all."

"Oh, he stuck his big John Thomas inside me. All the girls were witnesses, although they've taken blood oaths never to reveal what they saw. It's so sensitive fucking a married man, isn't it? – moreover a minister. Even Cynthia doesn't know. I do hate keeping a secret from her, but that seems best under the circumstances, don't you think?"

"I thought you said the book wasn't complete."

"It's not. Rev. Allan had his cock in me, all right.

But I never collected a lock of his hair for the book. Now he refuses to give me one. Don't you think that is rude? If a girl lets you fuck her, I'd think giving her a souvenir is the least you can do to show your appreciation?"

"Dear God," gasped Matilda Collins, feeling a restrictive shortness of breath. Maybe I'm having a heart attack, she thought to herself. Dying would be preferable to hearing more of this blasphemy.

"Matilda, I almost forgot. You were about to tell me why Miss Stacy came by."

"Well, Miss Stacy wants to organize a class among her advanced students who mean to study for the entrance examination into Queen's Academy. She intends to give them extra lessons for an hour after school. And she came to ask Martin and me if we would like to have you join it. What do you think about it yourself, Anne? Would you like to go to Queen's and become a teacher?"

"Oh, Matilda!" Anne straightened to her knees and clasped her hands. "It's been the dream of my life – that is, for the last six months, ever since Ruby and Jane began to talk of studying for the Entrance. But I didn't say anything about it, because I supposed it would be perfectly useless. I'd love to be a teacher. But won't it be dreadfully expensive? Mr. Andrews says it's costing him more'n one hundred and fifty dollars to put Prissy through, and Prissy wasn't a dunce in geometry like me."

"I guess you needn't worry about that part of it, dear. When Martin and I agreed to bring you up we resolved that we would do the best we could for you and give you a good education. I believe in a girl being qualified to earn her own living whether she ever has to or not. You'll always have a home at Green Gables as long as Martin and I are here, but nobody knows what is going to happen in this uncertain world, and it's just as well to be prepared. So you can join the Queen's class if you like, Anne."

"Oh, Matilda, thank you." Anne flung her arms about Matilda's waist and looked up earnestly into her face. "I'm extremely grateful to you and Martin. And the two of you can have your way with me for the rest of my life. But I'd so like to attend Queen's Academy and be trained to become a teacher. I promise I'll study as hard and do my very best to be a credit to you. I warn you not to expect much in geometry, but I think I can hold my own in anything else."

"I dare say you'll get along well enough. Miss Stacy says you are bright and diligent." Not for worlds would Matilda have told Anne just what Miss Stacy had said about her; that would have been to pamper vanity. "You needn't rush to any extreme of killing yourself over your books. There is no hurry. You won't be ready to try the Entrance for a year yet. But it's well to begin in time and be thoroughly grounded, Miss Stacy says."

"I shall take more interest than ever in my studies now," said Anne blissfully, "because I have a purpose in life. Rev. Allan says everybody should have a purpose in life and pursue it faithfully. Only he says we must first make sure that it is a worthy purpose. I would call it a worthy purpose to want to be a teacher like Miss Stacy, wouldn't you, Matilda? I think it's a very noble profession."

"Rev. Allan should have a purpose of his own other

than putting his dick into young girls. What would his wife say, if she knew?"

"I doubt Cynthia would be very upset, for they lead separate lives when it comes to matters of the heart. She prefers the same sex – like me. And he prefers young girls – like me. I'm the winner no matter which way I turn."

≈≈≈

The Queen's class was organized in due time. Gilbert Blythe, Anne Shirley, Ruby Gillis, Jane Andrews, Josie Pye, Charlie Sloane, and Moody MacPherson joined it. Diana Barry did not, as her parents did not intend to send her to Queen's. This seemed nothing short of a calamity to Anne. Never, since the night on which Minnie May had had the croup, had she and Diana been separated in anything. On the evening when the Queen's class first remained in school for the extra lessons and Anne saw Diana go slowly out with the others, to walk home alone through the Birch Path and Violet Vale, it was all Anne could do to keep her seat and refrain from rushing impulsively after her chum. A lump came into her throat, and she hastily uplifted her Latin grammar book to hide the tears. Not for the world would Anne have had Gilbert Blythe or Josie Pye see those tears.

"But, oh, Matilda, I really felt that I had tasted the bitterness of death, as Rev. Allan said in his sermon last Sunday, when I saw Diana go out alone," she said mournfully that night. "I thought how splendid it would have been if Diana had only been going to study for the Entrance, too. But we can't have things perfect in this imperfect world, as Mrs. Langston says. Mrs.

Langston isn't exactly a comforting person sometimes, but there's no doubt she says a great many very true things. And I think the Queen's class is going to be extremely interesting. Jane and Ruby are just going to study to be teachers. That is the height of their ambition. Ruby says she will only teach for two years after she gets through, and then she intends to be married. Jane says she will devote her whole life to teaching, and never, never marry, because you are paid a salary for teaching, but a husband won't pay you anything, and growls if you ask for a share in the egg and butter money. I expect Jane speaks from mournful experience, for Mrs. Langston says that her father is a perfect old crank, and meaner than second skimmings. Josie Pye says she is just going to college for education's sake, because she won't have to earn her own living; her family is quite wealthy, you know. Moody MacPherson says he's going to become a minister. I hope it isn't bad of me to say this, but the thought of Moody being a minister makes me laugh. He's so wicked. Charlie Sloane says he's going to go into politics and be a member of Parliament, but Mrs. Langston says he'll never succeed at that, because the Sloanes are all honest people, and it's only rascals that get on in politics nowadays."

"What is Gilbert Blythe going to be?" queried Matilda, seeing that Anne was opening her Caesar.

"I don't happen to know what Gilbert Blythe's ambition in life is – if he has any," said Anne scornfully.

There was open rivalry between Gilbert and Anne now. Previously the rivalry had been rather one-sided, but there was no longer any doubt that Gilbert was as determined to be first in class as Anne was. He was a foe worthy of her steel. The other members of the class tacitly acknowledged the pair's superiority, and never dreamed of trying to compete with them.

Since that day by the pond when she had refused to listen to his plea for forgiveness, Gilbert had evinced no recognition whatever of the existence of Anne Shirley – other than that night at the Christmas concert. He talked and jested with the other girls, exchanged books and puzzles with them, discussed lessons and plans, sometimes walked home with one or the other of them from prayer meeting or Debating Club.

Anne found that she did not like being ignored. She tried to conjure up that old satisfying anger but the effort was in vain. She tried to recall the humiliation she'd felt that day at the pond, standing there in the nude, while he laughed at her. But as she tried to dredge up those old emotions, Anne realized that she had forgiven Gilbert Blythe without even knowing it. But it was too late.

≈≈≈

The winter semester passed away in a round of pleasant duties and studies. For Anne, there were lessons to be learned and honors to be won; delightful books to read; new pieces to be practiced for the Sunday School choir; pleasant Saturday afternoons lounging in the bedroom at the manse with Mrs. Allan. And then, almost before Anne realized it, spring had come again to Green Gables and all the world was abloom once more.

Teacher and student alike were glad when the term ended and vacation days stretched rosily before them.

"You've done good work this past year," Miss Stacy told them on that last day of school, "and you deserve a good, jolly vacation. Have the best time you can in the out-of-door world and lay in a good stock of health and vitality and ambition to carry you through next year. It will be the tug of war, you know – the last year before the Entrance."

"Are you going to be back next year, Miss Stacy?" asked Josie Pye.

Josie Pye never hesitated to ask questions; in this instance the rest of the class felt grateful to her for none of them would have dared to ask it. But all had wanted to, for alarming rumors were running through the school that Miss Stacy was not coming back the next year – that she had been offered a position in the grade school of her own home district and meant to accept. The Queen's class listened in breathless suspense for her answer.

"Yes, I think I will," said Miss Stacy. "I thought of taking another school, but I have decided to come back to Avonlea. To tell the truth, I've grown so interested in my pupils here that I found I couldn't leave them. So I'll stay and see you through."

"Hurrah!" said Moody. The boy had never been so carried away by his feelings before, and he blushed uncomfortably every time he thought about it for a week.

"Oh, I'm so glad," said Anne, with shining eyes. "Dear Miss Stacy, it would be perfectly dreadful if you didn't come back. I don't believe I'd have the heart to go on with my studies if another teacher took your place."

When Anne got home that night she stacked all her textbooks away in an old trunk in the attic, locked it, and threw the key into the blanket box.

"I'm not even going to look at a schoolbook during vacation," she told Matilda. "I've studied as hard all the term as I possibly could and I've pored over that geometry until I know every proposition in the first book by heart, even when the letters ARE changed. I'm tired of being sensible and I'm going to let my imagination run riot for the entire summer. Oh, you needn't be alarmed, Matilda. I'll only let it run riot within reasonable limits. But I want to have a jolly good time this summer, for maybe it's the last summer I'll be a little girl. Mrs. Langston says that if I keep stretching out next year as I've done this I'll have to put on longer skirts. She says I'm all running to legs and eyes. And when I put on longer skirts I shall feel that I have to live up to them and be very dignified. It won't even do to believe in fairies then, I'm afraid; so I'm going to believe in them with all my whole heart this summer. I think we're going to have a very gay vacation. Ruby Gillis is going to have a birthday party soon and there's the Sunday School picnic and the missionary concert next month. And Mr. Barry promises that one evening he'll take Diana and me over to the White Sands Hotel and have dinner there. They have dinner there in the evening, you know. Jane Andrews was over once last summer and she says it was a dazzling sight to see the electric lights and the flowers and all the lady guests in such beautiful dresses. Jane says it was her first glimpse into high life and she'll never forget it to her dying day."

≈≈≈

Mrs. Langston came up the next afternoon to find out why Matilda had not been at the Church Aid meeting on Thursday. Whenever Matilda missed an Aid meeting, you could be sure there was something wrong at Green Gables.

"Martin had a bad spell with his heart Thursday," Matilda explained, "and I didn't feel comfortable leaving him. Oh, yes, he's all right again now, but he takes them spells oftener than he used to and I'm anxious about him. The doctor says he must be careful to avoid excitement. That's easy enough, for Martin doesn't go about looking for excitement by any means and never did, but he's not to do any very heavy work either and you might as well tell Martin not to breathe as not to work. Come and lay off your things, Rita. You'll stay to tea?"

"Well, seeing you're pressing the invitation, perhaps I might stay," said Mrs. Langston, who had not the slightest intention of doing anything but.

Mrs. Langston and Matilda sat comfortably in the parlor while Anne poured the tea and served hot biscuits that were light and white enough to defy even Mrs. Langston's criticism. "I must say Anne has turned out a real smart girl," admitted Mrs. Langston, as Matilda accompanied her to the end of the lane at sunset. "She must be a great help to you."

"She is," said Matilda. "I used to be afraid she'd never get over her featherbrained ways, but I wouldn't be afraid to trust her in anything now."

"I never would have thought she'd have turned out so well that first day I was here three years ago," said

Mrs. Langston. "Lawful heart, shall I ever forget that tantrum of hers! When I went home that night I says to Thomas, says I, 'Mark my words, Thomas, Matilda Collins will live to rue the step she's took.' But I was mistaken and I'm real glad of it. I ain't one of those kind of people, Matilda, as can never be brought to own up that they've made a mistake. No, that never was my way, thank goodness. I did make a mistake in judging Anne, but it weren't no wonder, for an odder, unexpecteder witch of a child there never was in this world, that's what. There was no ciphering her out by the rules that worked with other children. It's nothing short of wonderful how she's improved these three years, but especially in looks. She's turned out to be a real pretty girl, though I can't say I'm overly partial to that pale, big-eyed style myself. I like more snap and color, like Diana Barry has or Ruby Gillis. Ruby Gillis's looks are real showy. But somehow – I don't know how it is but when Anne and the other girls are together, she makes them look kind of common and overdone – something like them white June lilies alongside of those beautiful red peonies, that's what."

A good summer.

CHAPTER XXXII

Where the Brook and River Meet

Anne had her "good" summer and enjoyed it wholeheartedly. She and Diana fairly lived outdoors, running around naked, reveling in all the delights that Lover's Lane and the Dryad's Bubble and Willowmere and Victoria Island afforded. Matilda offered no objections to Anne's gypsyings. That's because the Spencervale doctor who had come the night Minnie May had the croup had met Anne at the house of a patient one afternoon early in vacation, looked her over sharply, screwed up his mouth, shook his head, and gave Anne a note to deliver to Matilda Collins.

It read: "Keep that girl of yours in the open air all summer until she gets more spring into her step."

This message frightened Matilda. She read it as a warrant of Anne's death by consumption unless the doctor's advice was scrupulously obeyed. As a result, Anne had the golden summer of her life as far as freedom and frolic went. She walked, rowed, berried, and dreamed to her heart's content; and when September came she was bright-eyed and alert, with a step that would have satisfied the Spencervale doctor and a heart full of ambition and zest once more.

His real message had simply said: "Anne looks healthy. Give her some Cod Liver Oil from time to time and she will be as healthy as a young filly."

Anne did not like taking Cod Liver Oil, so she had

substituted a different message, one that guaranteed her a satyric summer fill with wonderful sexual adventures. In addition to Martin and Matilda, Jonathan and Cynthia, and her bosom friend Diana, she added Miss Muriel Stacy to her conquests. As for the book in which to place a clip of the teacher's pubic hair, she naturally chose *She Stoops to Conquer*.

≈≈≈

Early in the summer Anne had bumped into Miss Stacy at William J. Blair's store over at Carmody. The teacher seemed glad to see her.

"I've wondered how your vacation is going?" smiled Miss Stacy. She was buying gingham to make a new dress. Everybody said she was an excellent seamstress, creating her own stylish wardrobe, beautiful calf-length dresses with large puffy sleeves.

"Just perfect so far. I've been released from household duties, so I have loads of extra time."

"Perhaps then you'd enjoy going to the beach with me some day."

"Yes, I would. But I don't own a bathing suit. Matilda Collins, my benefactor, things them immodest."

Muriel Stacy offered a sly smile. "Well, you wouldn't need a bathing suit with me. I go to a hidden cover where one can go skinny-dipping."

"You mean, swimming in the buff."

"Exactly. You're not timid about that are you? After all, you're the brazen girl who recited *The Faerie Queene* in the nude."

"No, you made us wear gauze tunics, although I admit the audience could see straight through them."

"Indeed. I was quite taken with your youthful body. Slender, but with a slight curve to your hips and full bosom. Quite fetching, I must say. I hear the boys were quite taken with your performance."

"Not Gilbert Blythe. He's not speaking to me."

"Forget Gilbert. You need more feminine companionship."

"I have the girls of the Story Club."

"I'm suggesting a more grown-up influence. Like me, for instance."

"You want to befriend me?"

"Why not? You're smart. You're pretty. And you're adventuresome. I heard about you and Rev. Allan."

"Who talked?" hissed Anne, suddenly wary.

"Don't worry, your secret is safe with me. And I'm sure Josie Pye will tell no others after the talking-to I gave that little snit."

Anne felt a wave of relief, as if she had discovered a new protector. "Thank you, Miss Stacy. It was a moment of indiscretion. I won't be doing that again."

"Not with a man perhaps. But what would you say to an intimate relationship with an older woman?"

Was Miss Stacy suggested what she thought? "You're not so old," replied Anne. "Only a few more years than me. This was your first term out of Queen's Academy. Likely you're only twenty. And I will be eighteen before you know it."

"I'm glad you see it that way," smiled the blonde teacher. "I'd like us to be more than friends."

"Bosom friends perhaps? Where we do nice things with each other using our fingers and tongues?"

"Yes, bosom friends," nodded Miss Stacy. "Shall we

go to my hidden cove tomorrow. I'd like to see your bosom without any gauze covering."

"That you shalt," replied Anne. "I look forward to our ... skinny-dipping."

≈≈≈

That next day Anne accompanied Miss Stacy to a small cove formed by two imposing cliffs, a few miles to the east of Horace Sloane's farmstead. The water was shallow enough for wading, but to swim you'd have to go out beyond the boulders that blocked the entrance to the cove.

"It's beautiful here," observed Anne, admiring the rocky precipices surrounding the spot.

"And it's quite private," said Miss Stacy as she set aside her sunbonnet and pulled her dress over her hear. "Go ahead and get undressed," she urged, shaking out her blonde hair.

"Just give me a moment," replied the girl, hurriedly unbuttoning her skirt.

Shortly, both of them were splashing about in the shallow water like two uninhibited water sprites, white skin flashing in the sun.

Miss Stacy was statuesque to the eye, her breasts much larger than they appeared behind the loose white blouses. While her long blonde tresses spilled down her shoulders when unpinned, her pubes were a darker shade -- evidence that she applied peroxide to the follicles on her head.

"I've never skinny-dipped with a grownup before," commented Anne. "Especially one of my teachers."

"Were not in school today, so you don't have to think of me as a teacher. Today we're just two free spirits, enjoying the bracing waters of the North Atlantic."

"The water, the sun, and the salt air," gushed Anne, "it couldn't be more perfect."

"I come out here on the weekends," Muriel Stacy told her. "You're welcome to join me anytime you like."

"I'm tied up most weekends. I have, uh, Bible studies with Rev. Allan on Saturday afternoon, and outing with his wife on Sundays. But perhaps I cold meet you here on Saturday mornings."

"That would be nice. I don't have a boyfriend. But it would be nice to have a girlfriend to do things with."

They came trotting out of the water, bare skin covered with goosebumps.

"You'd like me to be your girlfriend?" asked Anne as they spread a blanket on the sand and stretched out to warm in the sun."

"Why not? We are kindred spirits in some ways. We share a love of books and both have wondrous imaginations. And there are not too many years between our ages."

"And we'd go skinny-dipping together? And sunbathing?"

"Yes," smiled the blonde. "And perhaps sometimes we would pleasure each other." At which point she leaned over and kissed Anne on the lips.

"M'mm," murmured the girl. "I like that."

"Let me kiss you in a more intimate way," said Miss Stacy, tracing her lips down Anne's body to the *mons veneris* below.

And thus began another weekly tryst. It was explained away to others as special tutoring in geometry.

≈≈≈

441

"Matilda," said Anne in a burst of confidence, "I want to tell you something and ask what you think about it. It has worried me terribly – something Mrs. Langston said."

"What, dear?"

"When I'm in bed with you or Mrs. Allan or Miss Stacy I try so hard to do whatever pleases you. But when I talk about that with Mrs. Langston she makes me feel like I've been desperately wicked. Her words compel me all the more to go out and do the very things she tells me I oughtn't do. Like licking your pussy and sucking Mrs. Allen's titties and playing tickle-and-grab with Miss Stacy. Now, what do you think makes me feel like defying Mrs. Langston? Is it because I'm really bad and unregenerate?"

Matilda looked dubious for a moment. Then she laughed. "If you're wicked I guess I am too," she said. "Rita often has that very effect on me. I sometimes think she'd have more influence for good, if she didn't keep nagging people to do right. But I shouldn't talk about her. Rita is a good Christian woman and she means well. There isn't a kinder soul in Avonlea and she never shirks her share of work."

"You know she still watches us through her spyglass."

"Yes, she's done that for years. Even before you joined Martin and me in our nightly adventures. Rita Langston is what psychoanalysts call a 'voyeur.' She enjoys watching."

"Ha! I don't mind putting on a show for her. I like having an audience."

"That's because you're what psychoanalysts call an

'exhibitionist.' You enjoy being watched."

"Well then, we're a perfect match."

"I must admit that I too enjoy shocking that nosy old busybody. That's why I leave the lights on night-after-night as we go through our grunt-and-groan rituals. I want her to have a good view."

"Mrs. Langston is such a good church lady, I imagine what we do must be an abomination to her."

"No doubt we're sinners in her eyes. I'm sure she prays for us."

"Hard to believe that, after all these years, she's never ratted us out," mused Anne.

"And lose her free show? No, we're her entertainment. She's told me as much."

"So what should we do?"

Matilda shrugged to show her indifference. "We keep fucking. It's up to her whether she trains her spyglass in the direction of our bedroom window or not."

"I'm so glad you feel that way," said Anne decidedly. "I shan't worry so much about her spying after this. Let her watch all she wants. But I dare say there'll be other things to worry me. They keep coming up new all the time – things to perplex you, you know. You settle one question and there's another right after. There are so many things to be thought over and decided when you're beginning to grow up. It keeps me busy all the time thinking them over and deciding what is right. It's a serious thing to grow up, isn't it, Matilda? But when I have such good friends as you and Martin and Rev. Allan and his wife Cynthia I ought to grow up successfully, and I'm sure it will be my own fault if I don't."

"I fear we've done more to train you to be a whore than a teacher," sighed the blonde woman.

"I suppose I like being a whore. I do like to fuck. Could I make a career of being a whore, do you think?"

"Some do. There are girls who service the guests at the White Sands Hotel. They make a pretty penny, I'm told."

"Oh, Matilda, maybe I should do that rather than go to Queen's Academy. I do so like to fuck. And you and Martin and Jonathan and Cynthia have given me such great practice. I do think I have an aptitude for it."

"I can assure you that you do. But being a teacher offers more decorum. Teachers are not shunned by the community as are whores."

"Why can't I be both? I'd so hate to give up fucking."

"I suppose you can. But nice girls fuck for sport; whores do it for money."

"No one has ever paid me to fuck them. Is that a sign that I'm not desirable enough to be a whore?"

"You are quite desirable, trust me on that. There's not a boy – or girl – on Prince Edward Island who wouldn't fuck you given the opportunity."

"Not Gilbert Blythe. He hates me. Oh, Matilda, I handled him so wrongly. I pushed him away when I should have been pulling him close. If I could only do over that part of my life."

"Dear girl, there are no redos in life. You must go forward. I'm sorry if you've lost that chance at love. Fucking is one thing; love is another."

"But you've done without love. You've never

married."

"No, Anne, I haven't done without love. I love Martin dearly. But we cannot marry, being brother and sister."

"But at one time he wanted to marry me –"

"He thought so. But in the end, he came back to me. Our lives are intertwined. They have been so even before birth. We're twins you know."

"Twins? I had no idea. You look nothing alike."

"We're what's called fraternal twins. Born of the same womb, but different all the same."

"Is that why you've stayed together, a bond of birth?"

"Perhaps. Or perhaps it's true love. We tried to fight it, but the pull was too strong. I even went off to Queen's Academy as a youth but came back home to Martin after graduation."

"You were a teacher, Matilda? You never told me."

"I was trained to be one, but I never taught."

"That's why you know so much. About psychoanalysis and geometry and classic books. That's why you were so good at helping me with my homework."

"Yes, but I rejected all that for a simple life with Martin. He loves being a farmer, living here at Green Gables, fucking me – and now you. He's aims have never been any higher than that."

"And yours?"

"I made my choice."

"I suppose I have to make choices too."

"We all do."

"I feel it's a great responsibility because I have only

the one chance. If I don't grow up right I can't go back and begin over again. I've grown two inches around the bosom this summer, Matilda. Mr. Gillis measured me at Ruby's party. I must say he was very clumsy about it, putting his hands all over my boobies in the process. I'm so glad you made my new dresses looser in the bust. That dark-green one was so tight you could see the imprint of my nipples. Not that the boys at school minded. I wish Gil had paid more attention to them. I certainly flaunted them in his face. But he was busy making moony-eyes at Jane Andrews. I do hope they don't start dating. That would break my heart, him fucking her instead of me."

"You really like Gilbert Blythe, do you?"

"He's got such a nice cock. I felt it at last year's Christmas concert. It was standing up so nicely after my performance in *The Faerie Queene*. I think performing in the nude – well, near-nude – was a stroke of genius. The boys so loved it."

"I can't imagine what you've got in mind for this year's Christmas concert."

"Oh, Matilda, I have such a naughty idea in mind. It will cause a big sensation no doubt. And it might be my one chance to win Gilbert Blythe back. You wait and see, I will wind up fucking him yet."

≈≈≈

School started back up in the fall. "I feel just like studying with might and main," Anne declared as she brought her textbooks down from the attic. "Oh, you good old friends," she greeted them. "I'm glad to see your honest faces once more – yes, even you, geometry. I've had a perfectly beautiful summer, Matilda, and now I'm rejoicing as a strong man to run a race, as Rev. Allan said last Sunday. Doesn't Rev. Allan preach magnificent sermons? Mrs. Langston says he is improving every day and the first thing we know some city church will gobble him up and then we'll have to break in another green preacher. But I don't see the use of meeting trouble halfway, do you, Matilda? I think it would be better just to enjoy Rev. Allan while we have him."

Anne was living up to her words. Rev. Allan and his wife Cynthia had joined forces, bringing the girl into their bed as a threesome. She usually spent Saturday afternoons in the parsonage, exploring every position in the *Kama Sutra* with her new partners. Limbs akimbo, bodies twisted into odd angles, they experimented with such sexual positions as the Congress of the Crow, the Black Bee, and the Splitting of a Bamboo.

During the week Anne returned to her nighttime activities at Green Gables. With his heart condition, Martin wasn't as active as he used to be, but Matilda made up for it as she came out of her shell, more comfortable with her body and less inhibited in the things she and Anne did in bed.

Miss Stacy came back to Avonlea School and found all her pupils eager for work once more. Especially did the Queen's class gird up their loins for the fray, for at the end of the coming year, dimly shadowing their pathway already, loomed up that fateful thing known as "the Entrance," at the thought of which one and all felt their hearts sink into their very shoes. Suppose they did not pass! That thought was doomed to haunt Anne through the waking hours of that winter, Sunday afternoons inclusive, to the almost entire exclusion of moral and theological problems. When Anne had bad dreams she found herself staring miserably at pass lists of the Entrance exams, where Gilbert Blythe's name was blazoned at the top and in which hers did not appear at all.

But it was a jolly, busy, happy swift-flying winter. Schoolwork was as interesting, class rivalry as absorbing, as of yore. New worlds of thought, feeling, and ambition, fresh, fascinating fields of unexplored knowledge seemed to be opening out before Anne's eager eyes.

"Hills peeped o'er hill and Alps on Alps arose."

Much of all this was due to Miss Stacy's tactful, careful, broadminded guidance. She led her class to think and explore and discover for themselves and encouraged straying from the old beaten paths to a degree that quite shocked Mrs. Langston and the school trustees, who viewed all innovations on established methods rather dubiously.

Apart from her studies Anne expanded socially, for Matilda, mindful of the Spencervale doctor's dictum, no longer vetoed occasional outings. The Debating Club flourished and gave several concerts; there were one or two parties almost verging on grown-up affairs; there were sleigh drives and skating frolics galore.

Between times Anne grew, shooting up so rapidly that Matilda was astonished one day, when they were standing side by side, to find the girl was taller than herself.

"Why, Anne, how you've grown!" she said, almost unbelievingly. A sigh followed on the words. Matilda felt a queer regret over Anne's inches. The child she had learned to love had vanished somehow and here was this tall, serious-eyed girl of fifteen, with the thoughtful brows and the proudly poised little head, in her place. Matilda loved the girl as much as she had loved the child, but she was conscious of a queer sorrowful sense of loss. And that night, when Anne had gone to prayer meeting with Diana, Matilda sat alone in the wintry twilight and indulged in the weakness of a cry. Martin, coming in with a lantern, caught her at it and gazed at her in such consternation that Matilda had to laugh through her tears.

"I was thinking about Anne," she explained. "She's got to be such a big girl – and she'll probably be away from us next winter. I'll miss her terrible."

"She'll be able to come home often," comforted Martin, to whom Anne was as yet and always would be the little, eager girl he had brought home from Bright River on that June evening some four years before. "The branch railroad will be built to Carmody by that time."

"It won't be the same thing as having her here all the time," sighed Matilda gloomily, determined to enjoy her luxury of grief uncomforted. "But there – men can't understand these things!"

There were other changes in Anne no less real than the physical change. For one thing, she became much quieter. Perhaps she thought all the more and dreamed as much as ever, but she certainly talked less. Matilda noticed and commented on this also.

"You don't chatter half as much as you used to, Anne, nor use half as many big words. What has come over you?"

Anne colored and laughed a little, as she dropped her book and looked dreamily out of the window, where big fat red buds were bursting out on the creeper in response to the lure of the spring sunshine.

"I don't know – I don't want to talk as much," she said, denting her chin thoughtfully with her forefinger. "It's nicer to think dear, pretty thoughts and keep them in one's heart, like treasures. I don't like to have them laughed at or wondered over. And somehow I don't want to use big words any more. It's almost a pity, isn't it, now that I'm really growing big enough to say them if I did want to. It's fun to be almost grown up in some ways, but it's not the kind of fun I expected, Matilda. There's so much to learn and do and think that there isn't time for big words. Besides, Miss Stacy says the short ones are much stronger and better. She makes us write all our essays as simply as possible. It was hard at first. I was so used to crowding in all the fine big words I could think of – and I thought of any number of them. But I've got used to it now and I see it's so much better."

"What has become of your story club? I haven't heard you speak of it for a long time."

"The story club isn't in existence any longer. We hadn't time for it – and anyhow I think we had got tired of it. It was silly to be writing about love and murder and elopements and mysteries. Miss Stacy sometimes has us write a story for training in composition, but she won't let us write anything but what might happen in Avonlea in our own lives, and she criticizes it very sharply and makes us criticize our own too. I never thought my compositions had so many faults until I began to look for them myself. I felt so ashamed I wanted to give up altogether, but Miss Stacy said I could learn to write well if I only trained myself to be my own severest critic. And so I am trying to."

"You've only two more months before the Entrance," said Matilda. "Do you think you'll be able to get through?"

Anne shivered.

"I don't know. Sometimes I think I'll be all right – and then I get horribly afraid. We've studied hard and Miss Stacy has drilled us thoroughly, but we mayn't get through for all that. We've each got a stumbling block. Mine is geometry of course, and Jane's is Latin, and Ruby and Charlie's is algebra, and Josie's is arithmetic. Moody says he feels it in his bones that he is going to fail in English history. Miss Stacy is going to give us examinations in June just as hard as we'll have at the Entrance and mark us just as strictly, so we'll have some idea. I wish it was all over, Matilda. It haunts me. Sometimes I wake up in the night and wonder what I'll do if I don't pass."

"Why, go to school next year and try again," said Matilda unconcernedly.

"Oh, I don't believe I'd have the heart for it. It would be such a disgrace to fail, especially if Gil – if the others passed. And I get so nervous in an examination that I'm likely to make a mess of it. I wish I had nerves like Jane Andrews. Nothing rattles her."

Anne sighed and, dragging her eyes from the witcheries of the spring world, the beckoning day of breeze and blue, and the green things upspringing in the garden, buried herself resolutely in her book. There would be other springs, but if she did not succeed in passing the Entrance, Anne felt convinced that she would never recover sufficiently to enjoy them.

Late-night studies.

CHAPTER XXXIII

The Pass List Is Out

With the end of June came the close of the term and the close of Miss Stacy's rule in Avonlea School. Anne and Diana walked home that evening feeling very sober indeed. Red eyes and damp handkerchiefs bore convincing testimony to the fact that Miss Stacy's farewell words must have been quite as touching as Mr. Phillips's had been under similar circumstances two years before. Diana looked back at the schoolhouse and sighed deeply.

"It does seem as if it's the end of everything, doesn't it?" she said dismally.

"You oughtn't feel half as badly as I do," said Anne, hunting vainly for a dry spot on her handkerchief. "You'll be back again next winter, but I will have left the dear old school forever – off to Queen's Academy."

"It won't be the same. Miss Stacy won't be here, nor you nor Jane nor Ruby probably. I shall have to sit all alone, for I couldn't bear to have another desk mate after you. Oh, we have had jolly times, haven't we, Anne? In school and out. I'll always remember our moments together at Dryad's Bubble. Your body intertwined with mine. Skin against skin. Kissing each other. Oh, what glorious times. It's dreadful to think they're all over."

Two big tears rolled down by Diana's nose.

"If you'd stop crying I could too," implored Anne dismally. "Just as soon as I put away my hanky I see you brimming up and that starts me off again. As Mrs. Langston says, 'If you can't be cheerful, be as cheerful as you can.' After all, I may be back next year. I'm not sure that I'm going to pass."

"Don't be daft. You came out splendidly in the exams Miss Stacy gave."

"Yes, but those college entrance exams make me nervous."

"You will be fine. I do wish I were going with you," said Diana. "Wouldn't we have a perfectly elegant time? But I suppose you'd have to cram for the exams in the evenings."

"No. Miss Stacy made us promise not to open a book at all. She says it would only confuse us and we are not to think about the exams at all. It's good advice, but I expect it will be hard to follow. Prissy Andrews told me that she sat up half the night every night of her Entrance week and crammed for dear life. And I had determined to sit up as long as she did, but then Miss Stacy advised me to get a good night's sleep instead. She says being mentally alert is more important than memorizing stray facts.

"I'd follow Miss Stacy's advice over Prissy's. I think big tits suck away brain power."

"It was so kind of your Aunt Josephine to ask me to stay at Beechwood while I'm in Charlottetown."

"You'll write to me, won't you?"

"I'll write Tuesday night and tell you how the first day goes," promised Anne.

"I'll be haunting the post office Wednesday," vowed Diana.

Anne went to Charlottetown that following

Monday and on Wednesday Diana haunted the Post Office, as agreed, and got her letter.

"Dearest Diana" [wrote Anne],

"Here it is Tuesday night and I'm writing this in the library at Beechwood. Last night I was horribly lonesome all alone in my room and wished so much you were with me. I couldn't cram because I'd promised Miss Stacy not to, but it was hard to keep from opening my history book and a story.

"This morning Miss Stacy came for me and we went to Queen's Academy, calling for Jane and Ruby and Josie on our way. Ruby asked me to feel her hands and they were as cold as ice. Josie said I looked as if I hadn't slept a wink and she didn't believe I was strong enough to stand the grind of the teacher's course even if I did get through. There are times even yet when I don't feel that I've made any great headway in learning to like Josie Pye!

"When we reached the Academy there were scores of students there from all over the Island. The first person we saw was Moody sitting on the steps and muttering to himself. Jane asked him what on earth he was doing and he said he was repeating the multiplication table to steady his nerves and for pity's sake not to interrupt him, because if he stopped for a moment he forgot everything, but saying the multiplication table kept all his facts firmly in their proper place!

"When we were assigned to our rooms Miss Stacy had to leave us there. Jane and I sat together and Jane was so composed that I envied her. No need of the multiplication table for steady, sensible Jane! Then a man came in and began distributing the English examination sheets. My hands grew cold and my head fairly whirled around as I picked it up. I wondered if they could hear my heart thumping clear across the room. Just one awful moment – Diana, I felt exactly as I did four years ago when I asked Matilda if I might stay at Green Gables – and then everything cleared up in my mind and my heart began beating again – I forgot to say that it had stopped altogether! – for I knew I could do something with THAT paper anyhow.

"At noon we went home for dinner and then back again for history in the afternoon. The history was a pretty hard paper and I got dreadfully mixed up in the dates. Still, I think I did well today. But oh, Diana, tomorrow the geometry exam comes off and when I think of it, it takes every bit of determination I possess to keep from opening my Euclid. If I thought the multiplication table would help me any I would recite it from now till tomorrow morning.

"I went down to see the other girls this evening. On my way I met Moody wandering distractedly around. He said he knew he had failed in history and he was born to be a disappointment to his parents and he was going home on the morning train; and it would be easier to be a carpenter than a minister, anyhow. I cheered him up and persuaded him to stay to the end because it would be unfair to Miss Stacy if he didn't.

"Ruby was in hysterics when I reached their boardinghouse; she had just discovered a fearful mistake she had made in her English paper. When she recovered we went uptown and had an ice cream. How we wished you had been with us.

"Oh, Diana, if only the geometry examination were over! But there, as Mrs. Langston would say, the sun will go on rising and setting whether I fail in geometry or not. That is true but not especially comforting. I think I'd rather it didn't go on if I failed!

"Yours devotedly,

"Anne"

The geometry examination and all the others were over in due time and Anne arrived home on Friday evening, rather tired but with an air of chastened triumph about her. Diana was over at Green Gables when she arrived and they met as if they had been parted for years.

"You old darling, it's perfectly splendid to see you back again. It seems ages since you went to town and oh, Anne, how did you get along?"

"Pretty well, I think, in everything but the geometry. I don't know whether I passed in it or not and I have a creepy, crawly feeling that I didn't. Oh, how good it is to be back! Green Gables is the dearest, loveliest spot in the world."

"How did the others do?"

"The girls say they know they didn't pass, but I think they did pretty well. Josie says the geometry was so easy a child of ten could do it! Moody still thinks he failed in history and Charlie says he failed in algebra. But we don't really know anything about it and won't until the pass list is out. That won't be for a fortnight. Fancy living a fortnight in such suspense! I wish I could go to sleep and never wake up until it is over."

Diana knew it would be useless to ask how Gilbert

Blythe had fared, so she merely said: "Oh, you'll pass all right. Don't worry."

"I'd rather not pass at all than not come out pretty well up on the list," flashed Anne, by which she meant – and Diana knew she meant – that success would be incomplete and bitter if she did not come out ahead of Gilbert Blythe.

With this in mind Anne had strained every brain cell during the examinations. So had Gilbert. He had passed her a dozen times in the hallway without giving any sign of recognition. And every time, Anne had held her head a little higher and wished a little more earnestly that she had made friends with Gilbert when he asked her, or that she hadn't offended him when he'd tried to fuck her in the Langston's dairy barn.

Nonetheless, she vowed to surpass Gilbert in the examination. She knew that all junior Avonlea was wondering which of them would come out first; Jimmy Glover and Ned Wright even had a bet on it. Josie Pye had said there was no doubt that Gilbert would be first. Anne felt that her humiliation would be unbearable if she failed.

But she had another and nobler motive for wanting to do well. She wanted to "pass high" for the sake of Martin and Matilda – especially Martin. Martin was convinced she "would beat the whole Island." That, Anne felt, was something foolish to expect. But she did hope to be among the first ten at least, so that she might see Martin's kindly brown eyes gleam with pride in her achievement. That, she felt, would be a sweet reward for all her hard work in grubbing among unimaginative equations and conjugations.

Near the end of the fortnight Anne took to haunting the post office along with Jane, Ruby, and Josie, opening the Charlottetown dailies with shaking hands and sinkaway feelings as bad as any experienced during Exam week. Charlie and Gilbert joined them in doing this too, but Moody stayed resolutely away.

"I haven't the grit to look at a paper in cold blood," he told Anne. "I'm just going to wait until somebody comes and tells me whether I've passed or not."

When three weeks had gone by without the pass list appearing, Anne began to feel she couldn't endure the strain any longer. Her appetite failed and her interest in Avonlea doings languished. Mrs. Langston wanted to know what else you could expect with a Tory superintendent of education at the head of affairs, and Martin, noting Anne's paleness and lagging steps coming home each day from the post office, began seriously to wonder if he shouldn't vote Grit at the next election.

But one evening the news came. Anne was sitting at her open window, for the time forgetful of the woes of examinations and the cares of the world, as she drank in the beauty of the summer dusk. The eastern sky was flushed faintly pink and the air sweet-scented from the flowers in the garden below. Anne was suddenly startled from her reverie by the sight of Diana as she came flying down through the firs, over the log bridge, and up the slope, with a fluttering newspaper in her hand.

Anne sprang to her feet, knowing at once what that paper contained. The pass list was out!

Diana burst into her east gable room without even

knocking, so great was her excitement. "Anne, you've passed," she cried. "You passed as VERY FIRST – you and Gilbert both – you're ties – but your name is listed first. Oh, I'm so proud!"

Diana flung the paper on the table and herself on Anne's bed, utterly breathless and incapable of further speech. Anne snatched up the paper. Yes, she had passed – there was her name at the very top of a list of two hundred!

"You did just splendidly, Anne," puffed Diana, recovering sufficiently to sit up and speak. "Father brought the paper home from Bright River not ten minutes ago – it came on the afternoon train, you know, and won't be here till tomorrow by mail – and when I saw the pass list I just rushed over like a wild thing. You've all passed, every one of you, Moody and all, although he's conditioned in history. Jane and Ruby did pretty well – they're halfway up – and so did Charlie. Even Josie scraped through with three marks to spare. Won't Miss Stacy be delighted? Oh, Anne, what does it feel like to see your name at the head of a pass list like that? If it were me I know I'd be crazy with joy. I am pretty near crazy as it is, but you're as calm and cool as a spring evening."

Anne, starry eyed and rapt, had not uttered a word. "I'm just dazzled inside," she said, finally finding a voice. "I never dreamed of this – that I should come out first. Excuse me a minute, Diana, for I must run right out to the field to tell Martin. Then we'll go up the road and tell the good news to the others."

They hurried to the hayfield below the barn where Martin was coiling hay, and, as luck would have it, Mrs.

Langston was talking to Matilda at the lane fence.

"Oh, Martin," exclaimed Anne, "I've passed and I'm first – or one of the first! Can you believe it?"

"Well now, I always said it," grinned Martin, gazing at the pass list delightedly. "I knew you could beat them all easy."

"You've done pretty well, I must say, Anne," said Matilda, trying to hide her extreme pride in Anne from Mrs. Langston's critical eye.

But that good soul said heartily: "You're a credit to your friends, Anne, that's what, and we're all proud of you."

That night Anne had wound up the delightful evening by visiting Mrs. Allan at the manse, swapping kisses and quite a few tears of joy. Rev. Allan came in from his duties at the church and joined the two, eventually sweeping them into bed and fucking Anne's brains out as a reward for her success.

Later, she returned home to Green Gables and crawled into bed with Martin and Matilda where said performance was repeated with the upmost vigor.

The only thing that could have made her day any better would have been to celebrate it in bed with Gilbert Blythe. But that was not to be.

A recitation at the White Sands Hotel.

CHAPTER XXXIV

The Hotel Concert

"**P**ut on your white organdy, by all means, Anne," advised Diana decidedly.

They were together in the east gable chamber; outside it was only twilight – a lovely yellowish-green twilight with a clear-blue cloudless sky. A big round moon, the color of burnished silver, hung over the Haunted Wood. The air was full of sweet summer sounds – sleepy birds twittering, freakish breezes, faraway voices and laughter. But in Anne's room the blinds were unaccustomedly drawn, for important preparations were being made.

The east gable was a very different place from what it had been on that night three years ago, when Anne had felt its inhospitable chill penetrate to the marrow of her spirit. However, changes had crept in, as Matilda helped her fix it up, until it was as sweet and dainty a nest as a young girl could desire.

The velvet carpet and pink silk curtains of Anne's early visions had certainly never materialized; but her dreams had kept pace with her. The floor was covered with a pretty matting, and the curtains that softened the high window and fluttered in the breezes were of pale-green art muslin. The walls, hung not with gold and silver brocade tapestry, but with a dainty apple-blossom paper, were adorned with a few good pictures given to Anne by Mrs. Allan. Miss Stacy's photograph occupied the place of honor, and Anne made a sentimental point of keeping fresh flowers on the bracket under it. The room also contained a cushioned wicker rocker, a toilet table befrilled with white muslin, a quaint, gilt-framed mirror with chubby pink Cupids and purple grapes painted over its arched top, and a low white bed. Also there was a white-painted bookcase filled with books, each a repository for clippings of pubic hair from each of her "conquests" – save that empty tome titled *Loves Labor Lost*, reserved for Gilbert Blythe's.

Anne was dressing for a concert at the White Sands Hotel. The guests had got it up in aid of the Charlottetown hospital, and had included all the available amateur talent from the surrounding districts to help it along. Bertha Sampson and Pearl Clay of the White Sands Baptist choir had been asked to sing a duet; Milton Clark of Newbridge was to give a violin solo; Winnie Adela Blair of Carmody was to sing a Scotch ballad; and Laura Spencer of Spencervale and Anne Shirley of Avonlea were to recite.

As Anne said, it was "an epoch in her life," and she was deliciously athrill with the excitement of it. Martin was in the seventh heaven over the honor conferred on his Anne, and Matilda was not far behind, although she would have died rather than admit it. She said she didn't think it was very proper for a lot of young folks to be gadding over to the hotel without any responsible person to chaperone them.

Anne and Diana were to drive over with Jane Andrews and her brother Billy in their double-seated buggy; and several other Avonlea girls and boys were going too. A large party of people from Avonlea was expected to attend, and after the concert a supper was to be given to the performers.

"Do you really think I should wear the organdy dress?" queried Anne anxiously. "It's not as pretty as my blue-flowered muslin – and it certainly isn't so fashionable."

"But it suits you ever so much better," said Diana. "It's so soft and frilly and clinging. The muslin is stiff, and makes you look too dressed up. But the organdy seems as if it grew on you."

Anne looked into the mirror. The organdy did cling to her body, emphasizing all the hills and valleys. You could see the imprint of her nips against the thin material. Her breasts gently swayed as she moved, causing the pointy tips to trace a pattern that was sure to garner attention from all the men. It would be a scandal, no doubt.

Anne sighed and yielded. Diana was beginning to have a reputation for notable taste in dressing, and her advice on such subjects was much sought after. She was looking very pretty herself on this particular night in a dress of wild-rose pink; but she was not performing in the concert, so her appearance was of minor importance. All her pains were bestowed upon Anne, who, she vowed, must stand out from all the other girls taking the stage. In the right light you could see through the translucent cotton, leaving little to the imagination.

"Pull out that frill a little more," instructed Diana. "Here, let me tie your sash. Now, where are your slippers? I'm going to fluff your hair, give it some body. No, don't pull that curl over your forehead. Mrs. Allan says you look like a Madonna when you part it so. I shall fasten this little white rose just behind your ear. There was just one left in my garden, and I saved it for you."

"Shall I put my pearl beads on?" asked Anne. "Martin brought me a string from town last week, and I know he'd like to see them on me."

Diana pursed up her lips, tilted her head to one side to critically appraise the young mannequin, and finally pronounced in favor of the beads, which were thereupon tied around Anne's slim milk-white throat.

"There's something so stylish about you, Anne," said Diana, with unenvious admiration. "You hold your head with such an air. I suppose it's your figure. I am just a dumpling. I've always been afraid of it, and now I know it is so. Well, I suppose I shall just have to resign myself to it."

"But you have such pretty dimples," said Anne, smiling affectionately into the pretty, vivacious face so near her own. "Lovely dimples, like little dents in cream. I have given up all hope of dimples. My dimple-dream will never come true; but so many of my dreams have that I mustn't complain. Am I all ready now?"

"One more thing," said Diana. "Remove your panties."

"But won't my bush show against this light material?"

"Exactly," grinned Diana. "You said you wanted to be a sensation."

Anne wiggled her knickers down her hips and stepped out of them. "How's this?"

"In the right light you might as well be nude."

"Oh, I do hope Gilbert Blythe will get a chance to see me. I want to remind him what he missed out on."

"You really should have let him fuck you there in the Langston's dairy barn," opined her friend.

"I was willing, but he became offended when I mentioned Rev. Allan."

"Nobody want to compete with fucking a minister – particularly a married one," Diana pointed out.

"Well, if I had to choose between them, Jonathan Allan has the bigger dick."

Diana sighed. "Oh, I so envy you, getting to fuck the minister – and his pretty redheaded wife too!"

"I am a lucky girl, am I not?"

Matilda appeared in the doorway checking on their progress. "Come right in and look at our elocutionist, Matilda," invited Diana. "Doesn't she look lovely?"

Matilda emitted a sound between a sniff and a grunt. "She looks neat and proper. I like that way of fixing her hair. But I expect she'll ruin that dress, fucking some boy in the back of his buggy."

"And what if she does? It is worth the sacrifice."

"That dress looks too thin for any semblance of modesty. But I suppose that's what you girls have in mind. Organdy's the most unserviceable stuff in the world anyhow, and I told Martin so when he bought it for her. But there is no use in saying anything to him nowadays. Time was when he would take my advice, but now he just buys things for Anne regardless, and the clerks at Carmody know they can palm anything off on him. Just let them pull out something that reveals her body, and Martin plunks his money down for it. Particularly if it is low-cut enough to show off her titties. Mind you, he'd have her go to the concert nude tonight. And she's not far from it."

"I want to make certain all the attention is on me tonight as I do my recitation," Anne spoke up in her own behalf. "Next year I will go off on a teaching assignment, but I want to make sure all the boys in Avonlea remember me fondly."

Matilda Collins shook her head, giving up on any argument. But as a parting shot, she said, "Anne, you should put some panties on. Do you want everybody to see your pussy?"

"Yes."

With that, Matilda stalked downstairs. But secretly she was thinking how sexy Anne looked, with that

> *"One moonbeam from the forehead to the crown"*

and regretting that she not going to the concert herself to hear her girl recite.

"I wonder Matilda's right, that this dress is TOO revealing," said Anne anxiously.

"Not one bit," said Diana, pulling up the window blind. "You want to show off that perfect body. Especially to Gilbert Blythe. Let him eat his heat out that he walked away from the most prime pussy on al of Prince Edward Island."

Anne liked the sound of that. She looked out her window toward the Langston house. Rita Langston was no doubt having a fit that they had pulled down the shade while Diana dressed her. "I'm so glad my window looks east into the sunrise," reflected Anne. "It's so splendid to see the morning coming up over those long hills and glowing through those sharp fir tops. Oh,

Diana, I love this little room so dearly. I don't know how I'll get along without it when I go off to a teaching assignment."

"Don't speak of your going away tonight," begged Diana. "I don't want to think of it, it makes me so miserable, and I do want to have a good time this evening. What are you going to recite, Anne? And are you nervous?"

"Not a bit. I've recited so often in public I don't mind it at all now. I've decided to give 'The Maiden's Vow.' It's so pathetic. Laura Spencer is going to give a comic recitation, but I'd rather make people cry than laugh."

"What will you recite if they encore you?"

"They won't dream of encoring me," scoffed Anne, who was not without her own secret hopes that they would, and already envisioned herself telling Martin all about it at the next morning's breakfast table. "There comes Billy and Jane now," she pointed out the window. "Come along. It's time for Cinderella and her handmaiden to go to the Ball."

≈≈≈

Billy Andrews insisted that Anne should ride on the front seat with him, so she unwillingly climbed up. She would have much preferred to sit back with the girls, where she could have laughed and chattered to her heart's content. There was not much chatter in Billy. He was a fat, stolid youth of twenty, with an expressionless face and a painful lack of conversational skill. But he was puffed up over the prospect of driving to White Sands with that slim, upright figure beside him, all the boys thinking she was his date.

Anne, by dint of talking over her shoulder to the girls and occasionally passing a sop of civility to Billy – who grinned and chuckled and never could think of any reply until it was too late – contrived to enjoy the drive in spite of all. It was a night for enjoyment. The road was full of buggies, all bound for the hotel, and laughter and excited conversations echoed along the journey. When they reached the hotel it was ablaze with light from top to bottom. They were met by the ladies of the concert committee, one of whom took Anne off to the performers' dressing room which was filled with the members of a Charlottetown Symphony Club and other local celebrities. Among them, Anne felt suddenly shy and frightened and countrified. Her dress, which, in the east gable, had seemed so sexy and tempting, now seemed gaudy and whorish among all the silks and laces that glistened and rustled around her. What were her pearl beads compared to the diamonds of the big, handsome lady near her? And how poor her single white rose must look beside all those hothouse flowers the others wore! Anne laid her hat and jacket away, and shrank miserably into a corner, wishing herself back in the upstairs room at Green Gables.

It was still worse for Anne when she was ushered onto the stage of the big concert hall of the hotel. The electric lights dazzled her eyes; the hum of the audience bewildered her. She wished she were sitting in the back of the room with Diana and Jane, who seemed to be having a splendid time as they surveyed the proceedings.

Anne found herself wedged between a stout lady in pink silk and a tall, scornful-looking girl in a white-lace dress. The stout lady occasionally turned her head to study Anne through her thick eyeglasses until the girl felt like shrinking into the floorboards. To make matters worse, the white-lace girl kept talking audibly to her next neighbor about all the "country bumpkins" and "rustic belles" in the audience, languidly anticipating "such fun" watching the amateurish displays of local talent on the program. Anne believed that she would hate that white-lace girl to the end of life.

Unfortunately for Anne, a professional elocutionist named Eloise Cathers was staying at the hotel and had consented to recite. She was a pretty, dark-eyed woman wearing a gray gown that reminded Anne of shimmering moonbeams. The woman had a marvelously flexible voice and such power of expression that grown men were known to cry when she recited.

When it came Mrs. Cathers time to perform, the audience went wild. Anne listened with rapt and shining eyes; but when the recitation ended she suddenly put her hands over her face. She could never get up and recite after that – never. How had she ever thought she could do 'The Maiden's Vow" in front of a sophisticated audience such as this? Oh, if she were only back at Green Gables!

At this unpropitious moment her name was called. Somehow Anne – who did not notice the rather guilty little start of surprise the white-lace girl gave, and would not have understood the subtle compliment implied therein if she had – got on her feet and moved dizzily out to the front of the stage. She was so pale that

Diana and Jane, sitting in the back row, clasped each other's hands in nervous sympathy.

Anne was the victim of an overwhelming attack of stage fright. As often as she had recited in public, she'd never before faced such an audience as this, and the sight of it paralyzed her completely. Everything was so strange, so brilliant, so bewildering – the rows of ladies in evening dress, the critical faces, the whole atmosphere of wealth and culture about her. Very different from the plain folk filling the benches at the Debating Club back in Avonlea.

These people, she thought, would be merciless critics. Perhaps, like the white-lace girl, they anticipated amusement from her "rustic" efforts. She felt hopelessly, helplessly ashamed and miserable. Her knees trembled, her heart fluttered, a horrible faintness came over her; not a word could she utter, and the next moment she would have fled from the platform despite the humiliation that would ever after follow if she did so.

But suddenly, as her dilated, frightened eyes gazed out over the audience, she saw Gilbert Blythe away at the back of the room, bending forward with a smile on his face – a smile which seemed to Anne at once triumphant and taunting. In reality it was nothing of the kind. Gilbert was merely smiling with appreciation of the whole grand affair. Josie Pye, whom he had driven over, sat beside him, and her face certainly was both triumphant and taunting. But Anne did not see Josie, and would not have cared if she had. She drew a long breath and flung her head up proudly, courage and determination tingling over her like an electric shock. She WOULD NOT fail before Gilbert Blythe – he should never be able to laugh at her, never, never! Her fright and nervousness vanished; and she began her recitation, her clear, sweet voice reaching to the farthest corner of the room without a tremor or a break. Self-possession was fully restored to her, and in the reaction from that horrible moment of powerlessness she recited as she had never done before. 'The Maiden's Vow" had never before come alive so vividly to an audience.

When Anne finished there were bursts of honest applause. Taking a bow, Anne stepped back to her seat, blushing with shyness and delight.

She found her hand vigorously clasped and shaken by the stout lady in pink silk. "My dear, you did splendidly," she puffed. "I've been crying like a baby, actually I have. There, they're encoring you – they're bound to have you back!"

"Oh, I can't go," said Anne confusedly. "But yet – I must, or Martin will be disappointed. He said they would encore me."

"Then don't disappoint Martin," said the pink lady, laughing.

Smiling, blushing, limpid eyed, Anne tripped back onto the stage. In a moment of questionable inspiration, she undid the clasp at the back of her organdy dress and let it fall about her to the floor, leaving her standing before the audience as unadorned as the day she was born. There was an audible gasp as they survey her proud, pink-tipped breasts and hint of a bush which she had trimmed into the perfect shape of a heart. But they calmed quickly as she began to recite Lady Macbeth's sleepwalking soliloquy with an earnest passion that made her nudity seem all the more natural. Within a few lines, the audience was mesmerized, following her as if they had never heard the words of Shakespeare before. At the end the audience gave her a standing applause. It was quite a triumph for her.

When the concert was over, Mrs. Eloise Cathers – who, it turned out, was the wife of an American millionaire – took Anne under her wing and introduced her to everybody; and everybody was very nice to her. Even the white-lace girl paid her a languid little compliment.

Having redressed in the organdy gown, she no longer felt plain and ordinary, nor that her dress was gaudy and whorish. The sponsors of the concert invited her to supper in the big, beautifully decorated dining room. Diana and Jane accompanied her, but Billy was nowhere to be found, having decamped in mortal fear of some such invitation. However, he was in waiting for them with the buggy when it was all over, as the three girls came merrily out into the calm, white moonshine looking as radiant as belles of the ball.

Anne breathed deeply, and looked into the clear sky beyond the dark boughs of the firs, hearing the murmur of the sea in the distance. Oh, how great and wonderful everything was. "Hasn't it been a perfectly splendid night?" sighed Anne as they drove away. "I just wish I were a rich American and could spend my summer at a hotel and wear jewels and low-necked dresses and have ice cream and chicken salad every blessed day. I'm sure it would be ever so much more fun than teaching school."

"Anne, your recitation was simply great," complimented Jane. "Although I thought at first you were never going to begin. But, my God, did you rally. Your recitation of "The Maiden's Virtue' brought down the house. I think you were so much better than Mrs. Cather."

"Oh, no, don't say things like that, Jane," said Anne quickly. "My presentation couldn't possibly be better than Mrs. Cather's, you know, for she is a professional, and I'm only a schoolgirl with a little knack of reciting. I'm quite satisfied if the people just liked mine pretty well."

Diana interjected, "I'd say they liked your Lady Macbeth soliloquy more than 'pretty well.' They gave you a standing ovation. I can't believe you stood up there in the nude in front of 300 people and recited Shakespeare. Oh, Prince Edward Island will be talking about this for years to come!"

"I don't know what came over me. Maybe it was spotting Gilbert Blythe sitting there in the audience with a smirk on his face."

"Oh, forget about Gil," said Jane. "Let Josie have him."

"Josie?"

"They came together, you know. She was his date tonight."

"That little bitch. I thought she preferred girls."

"Look who's talking," laughed Diana. "You're carrying on with Matilda, Cynthia Allan, Muriel Stacy – and even me!"

"But I like dick too. I'm sleeping with Martin and Jonathan Allan too."

"I wish I had that many sexual partners," bemoaned Jane. "I have to make do with Charlie Sloane and an occasional bang from Mr. Hathcock, the old man who keeps the books for Samuel Lawson's store in Carmody."

"I've another compliment for you, Anne," said Diana. "At least I think it must be a compliment because of the tone he said it in. Part of it was anyhow. There was an American sitting next to Jane and me – such a romantic-looking man, with coal-black hair and electric-green eyes. Josie Pye says he is a distinguished artist, and that her mother's cousin in Boston is married to a man that used to go to school with him. Well, we heard him say – didn't we, Jane? – 'Who is that girl on the stage with the splendid merkin? She has a body I should like to paint.' There now, Anne. How about that?"

"But what's a 'merkin'?" puzzled Jane.

"It's an artificial covering of hair for the pubic area," laughed Anne. "He was wrong about that. What he saw was my real hair."

"Oh, Anne, I cannot believe you trimmed it into the shape of a heart. How clever of you."

"I think of it as my own private topiary garden," explained Anne. "Why don't we get together one afternoon and have a hair-trimming party? Dianna, we could shape yours like a star. And, Jane, I think yours would look great as an exclamation point, as if it was saying 'Hey, look at me'!"

"Oh no, my mother would never allow it. She would skin me alive if I did something like that. I may as well go get a tattoo as trim my pubes."

"Have it your way," Anne shrugged.

"Would you do it, Anne?" interjected her pudgy friend Diana. "Would you pose nude for a famous painter?"

"Why not? It would be for the sake of art. Besides, he saw everything I have to show tonight."

"The whole world did," teased Jane.

"I just hope Gilbert Blythe got a good look. He's going to feel awfully short changed when je compares Josie Pye's boobs to mine."

"Is he in for a big disappointment," laughed Diana. She'd never really like Josie either.

"Did you see all the diamonds those ladies wore?" sighed Jane. "They were simply dazzling. Wouldn't you just love to be rich, girls?"

"We ARE rich," said Anne staunchly. "Why, we have seventeen years to our credit, and we're happy as queens, and we've all got imaginations, more or less. Look at that sea, girls – all silver and shadow and vision of things not seen. We couldn't enjoy its loveliness any more if we had millions of dollars and ropes of diamonds. You wouldn't change into any of those women if you could. Would you want to be that white-lace girl and wear a sour look all your life, as if you'd been born turning up your nose at the world? Or the pink lady, kind and nice as she is, so stout and short that you'd really no figure at all? Or even Mrs. Cather, with that sad, sad look in her eyes? She must have been dreadfully unhappy sometime to have such a look. You KNOW you wouldn't, Jane Andrews!"

"I DON'T know – exactly," said Jane unconvinced. "I think diamonds would comfort a person a good deal."

For the sake of art.

CHAPTER XXXV

A Queen's Girl

The next three weeks were busy ones at Green Gables, for Anne was getting ready to go off to Queen's Academy for her final semester, and there was much sewing to be done, and many things to be talked over and arranged. Anne's outfits were ample and pretty, for Martin saw to that, and Matilda for once made no objections whatever to anything he purchased or suggested. More – one evening she went up to the east gable with her arms full of a delicate pale green material.

"Anne, here's something for a nice light dress for you. I don't suppose you really need it; you've plenty of pretty waists; but I thought maybe you'd like something real dressy to wear if you were asked out anywhere of an evening in town, to a party or anything like that. I hear that Jane and Ruby and Josie have got 'evening dresses,' as they call them, and I don't mean for you to be behind them in pretty apparel. I got Mrs. Allan to help me pick it in town last week, and we'll get Emily Gillis to make it for you. Emily has got an excellent sense of fashion, and her fittings aren't to be equaled."

"Oh, Matilda, it's just lovely," said Anne. "Thank you so much. You should quit being so kind to me – it's making it harder every day for me to go away."

The green dress was made up with as many tucks and frills and shirring's as Emily's taste permitted.

Anne put it on one evening for Martin and Matilda's benefit, and recited "The Maiden's Vow" for them in the kitchen. As Matilda watched the bright, animated face and graceful motions her thoughts went back to the evening Anne had arrived at Green Gables, and memory recalled a vivid picture of the odd, frightened child in her preposterous yellowish-brown wincey dress, the heartbreak looking out of her tearful eyes. Something in the memory brought tears to Matilda's own eyes.

"I declare, my recitation has made you cry, Matilda," said Anne gaily stooping over Matilda's chair to drop a butterfly kiss on that lady's cheek. "Now, I call that a positive triumph."

"No, I wasn't crying over your piece," said Matilda, who would never display such weakness over poetry. "I just couldn't help thinking of the little girl you used to be, Anne. And I was wishing you could have stayed a little girl, even with all your queer ways. You've grown up now and you're going away; and you look so tall and stylish and so – so – different altogether in that dress – as if you don't belong in Avonlea any more – and I just got lonesome thinking about it."

"Matilda!" Anne sat down on the woman's gingham lap and looked tenderly into her blue eyes. "I'm not a bit changed – not really. I'm only just pruned down and branched out. The real ME – back here – is just the same. It won't make a bit of difference where I go or how much I change outwardly; at heart I shall always be your little Anne, who will always love you and Martin and dear Green Gables more than anything in the world."

Anne laid her fresh young cheek against Matilda's, and reached out a hand to pat Martin's shoulder. Matilda would have given much just then to have possessed Anne's power of putting her feelings into words; but nature and habit had willed it otherwise, and she could only put her arms close about her girl and hold her tenderly to her heart, wishing that she need never let her go.

Martin, with suspicious moisture in his eyes, got up and went out-of-doors. Under the stars of the blue summer night he walked agitatedly across the yard to the gate under the poplars. "Well now, I guess she ain't been much spoiled," he muttered proudly. "I guess my putting in my oar occasional never did much harm after all. She's smart and pretty, and loving, too, which is better than all the rest. She's been a blessing to us, and there never was a luckier mistake than what Mrs. Spencer made – if it WAS luck. I don't believe it was any such thing. It was Providence, because the Almighty saw we needed her, I reckon."

"So I turned out to be smart and pretty, did I?" said a voice behind him. Anne had followed him outside.

"Smart and pretty – and a good fuck," he chuckled.

"Come back inside with me and I'll remind you and Matilda how good a fuck I am."

≈≈≈

The day finally came for Anne to go off again to Charlottetown. She and Martin drove in one fine September morning, following a tearful parting with Diana and an untearful practical one – on Matilda's side at least – with Matilda.

For Anne and the rest of the Avonlea scholars the

first day of this new semester passed pleasantly enough in a whirl of excitement, meeting new students, learning to know the professors by sight and being assigned classes. Anne elected to take up Senior Year work, being advised to do so by Miss Stacy; and Gilbert Blythe choose to do the same. This meant getting a First Class teacher's license in one year instead of two, if they were successful; but it also meant much harder work. Jane, Ruby, Josie, Charlie, and Moody, not being troubled with the stirrings of ambition, were content to take up the normal schedule.

Anne was conscious of a pang of loneliness when she found herself in a classroom with fifty other students, not one of whom she knew, except for the tall, brown-haired boy across the room, But knowing Gilbert in the fashion she did, did not help her spirits much. Nonetheless she was glad they were in the same class, for the old rivalry could still be carried on. Anne would hardly have known what to do if the competitive situation had been lacking.

"I wouldn't feel comfortable without it," she thought. "Gilbert looks awfully determined. I suppose he's making up his mind, here and now, to win the Queen's Gold Medal. What a splendid chin he has! I never noticed it before. I do wish Jane and Ruby had gone in for Senior Year work, too. I suppose I won't feel so much like a cat in a strange garret when I get acquainted, though. I wonder which of the girls here are going to be my friends. It's really an interesting speculation. Of course I promised Diana that no Queen's girl, no matter how much I liked her, should ever be as dear to me as she is; but I've lots of second-best affections to bestow. I like the look of that girl with the brown eyes and the crimson hair. Her coloring is somewhat reminiscent of Mrs. Allen's. And there's that pale, fair girl gazing out of the window. She has a lovely bosom, large and outstanding, a bit like Prissy Andrews's. I'd like to know them both – know them well – well enough to walk with my arm about their waists, and call them nicknames. Maybe get naked with them and wiggle about under the covers. But just now I don't know them and they don't know me, and probably don't want to know me particularly. Oh, it's hard being lonesome!"

It was lonesomer still when Anne found herself alone in her tiny bedroom that night at twilight. She was not to board with the other Avonlea girls, for they had relatives in town to take pity on them. Miss Josephine Barry would have been happy to have her, but Beechwood was so far from the Academy that it was out of the question; so Miss Barry hunted up a closer boardinghouse, assuring Martin and Matilda that it was the very place for Anne.

"The lady who keeps it is a reduced gentlewoman," explained Miss Barry. "Her husband was a British officer, and she is very careful what sort of boarders she takes in. Anne will not meet with any objectionable persons under her roof. The table is good, and the house is near the Academy, in a quiet neighborhood."

All this proved to be quite true, but it did not help Anne deal with the homesickness that seized her. She looked dismally about her narrow little room, with its pictureless walls, its small iron bedstead, and empty bookcase; and a horrible choke came into her throat as she thought of her own white room at Green Gables, where she would have the pleasant consciousness of a great green still outdoors, of sweet peas growing in the garden, and moonlight falling on the orchard.

Here there was nothing of this; Anne knew that outside of her window was a hard street, with a network of telephone wires shutting out the sky, the tramp of alien feet, and a thousand lights gleaming on strangers' faces. She knew that she was going to cry, and fought against it.

"I WON'T cry. It's silly – and weak – there's the third tear splashing down by my nose. There are more coming! I must think of something funny to stop them. But there's nothing funny except what is connected with Avonlea, and that only makes things worse – four – five – I'm going home next Friday, but that seems a hundred years away. Oh, Martin is nearly home by now – and Matilda is at the gate, looking down the lane for him – six – seven – eight – oh, there's no use in counting them! They're coming in a flood presently. I can't cheer up – I don't WANT to cheer up. It's nicer to be miserable!"

The flood of tears would have come, no doubt, had not Josie Pye appeared at that moment. In the joy of seeing a familiar face Anne forgot that there had never been much love lost between her and Josie. However, as a reminder of Avonlea life even a Pye was welcome.

"I'm so glad you came up," Anne said sincerely.

"You've been crying," remarked Josie, with aggravating pity. "I suppose you're homesick – some people have so little self-control in that respect. I've no intention of being homesick, I can tell you.

486

Charlottetown's too jolly after that poky old Avonlea. I wonder how I ever existed there so long. You shouldn't cry, Anne; it isn't becoming, for your nose and eyes get red, and your skin gets blotchy. I'd a perfectly scrumptious time in the Academy today. Our French professor is simply a duck. His moustache would give you kerwollowps of the heart. Have you anything eatable around, Anne? I'm literally starving. Ah, I guessed likely Matilda would load you up with cake. That's why I called round. Otherwise I'd have gone with Frank Stockley to the park to hear the band play. He boards same place as I do, and he's a sport. He noticed you in class today, and asked me who the cute girl was. I told him you were an orphan that the Collinses had adopted, and nobody knew very much about what you'd been before that."

Anne was about to conclude that solitude and tears were preferable to Josie Pye, when Jane and Ruby appeared, each with an inch of Queen's color ribbon – purple and scarlet – pinned proudly to her coat. As Josie was not "speaking" to Jane just then she had to subside into comparative harmlessness.

"Well," said Jane with a sigh, "I feel as if I'd lived many moons since the morning. I ought to be home studying my Virgil – that horrid old professor gave us twenty lines to start in on tomorrow. But I simply couldn't settle down to study tonight. Anne, methinks I see the traces of tears. If you've been crying DO own up. It will restore my self-respect, for I was shedding tears freely before Ruby came along. I don't mind being a goose so much if somebody else is goosey, too. Cake? You'll give me a teeny piece, won't you? Thank you. It has the real Avonlea flavor."

Ruby, perceiving the Queen's calendar lying on the table, wanted to know if Anne meant to try for the Gold Medal.

Anne blushed and admitted she was thinking of it.

"Oh, that reminds me," said Josie, "Queen's Academy is to get one of the Avery Scholarships after all. The word came today. Frank Stockley told me – his uncle is one of the board of governors, you know. It will be announced tomorrow."

An Avery Scholarship! Anne felt her heart beat more quickly, and the horizons of her ambition shifted and broadened as if by magic. Before Josie had told the news Anne's highest aspiration had been a teacher's provincial license, First Class, at the end of the year, and perhaps the Queen's Medal! But now in one shifting moment Anne saw herself winning the Avery Scholarship, taking an Arts course at Redmond College, and graduating in a gown and mortar board, before the echo of Josie's words had died away. For the Avery Scholarship was in English, and Anne felt that here her foot was on native heath.

A wealthy manufacturer of New Brunswick had died and left part of his fortune to endow a large number of scholarships to be distributed among the various high schools and academies of the Maritime Provinces, according to their respective standings. There had been much doubt whether one would be allotted to Queen's, but the matter was settled at last, and at the end of the year the graduate who made the highest mark in English and English Literature would win the scholarship – two hundred and fifty dollars a year for four years at Redmond College. No wonder that Anne went to bed that night with tingling cheeks!

"I'll win that scholarship if hard work can do it," she resolved. "Wouldn't Martin be proud if I got to be a B.A.? Oh, it's delightful to have ambitions. I'm so glad I have such a lot. And there never seems to be any end to them – that's the best of it. Just as soon as you attain to one ambition you see another one glittering higher up still. It does make life so interesting."

Josie interrupted her thoughts, "Oh, I forgot to tell you. That artist who was at the concert – you know, the one who went to school was the man married to my mother's cousin – well, he wants to paint you."

"Paint me?" said Anne, caught off guard.

"That's right – in the nude. Can you imagine? You take off your clothes in front of 300 people, like a common performer in a Minksy's Burlesque Show, and next thing you know you're in a painting hanging in a gallery. Ain't life strange!"

"I don't know about posing in the nude."

"Like you have any modesty," said Josie. "You've spent the past three years running around naked in the fields around Green Gables. Everybody's seen your tits and half the boys in Avonlea have fucked you – so what's the big deal."

"Oh Anne, being in a painting hanging in a gallery would be such an honor. You'd be famous," declared Ruby.

"You're certainly pretty enough," added Jane. "I'd like being friends with a famous model."

"Aw, she won't do it," said Josie. "I told my mother to pass the word back through her cousin's husband that Anne Shirley is just a simple little country girl who could not sit still long enough to pose for a painting. I offered to do it myself, but the artist – a guy named Peter Wimple – said I was too fat. Can you imagine?"

"You ARE too fat, Josie," snapped Jane, deciding to speak to the girl after all. "That's comes from eating all Anne's cake. You didn't leave a crumb for me or Ruby."

"Sorry. I was hungry. I told Anne that."

"What makes you think I wouldn't pose for the painting?" asked Anne, frowning at the Pye girl.

"You're not sophisticated enough to appreciate fine art. Only cultured people appreciate paintings of nudes – you know, like by Michelangelo or Degas or Rubens." She turned to Jane Andrews and stuck her tongue out. "And for your information, Miss Know-Nothing, that French painter Rubens liked to paint fat women."

"Well, you better drop out of school and start posing for Mr. Rubens because you certainly qualify."

"How do I get in touch with this Peter Wimple?" Anne interrupted their bickering.

"Why do you ask?" Josie Pye wanted to know.

"Because I'm going to pose for his painting. I think I can sit still long enough."

≈≈≈

Peter Wimble, it turned out, had a studio in Charlottetown. That made it simple for Anne to go over after class and sit for him. Sitting wasn't the problem; lying on her back was. Wimble liked to fuck his models as well as paint them. It didn't take but two sittings for Anne to succumb to his charms.

"You've got green paint on your nose," the artist

teased her as they lay naked on his daybed, recovering from a strenuous bout of sex.

"That's because you've got green paint on your cock. If you could put in in my mouth more smoothly, I wouldn't have paint on my nose."

"You like my putting my cock in your mouth," he countered.

"I do not. It tastes like turpentine."

"Then I shall put it in your twat, once it returns to vigor."

"You've already got paint in my public hair. I may have to cut it all off."

"That would be jolly, you hairless as a prepubescent girl. I like young girls, you may have noticed."

"I'm seventeen years old; that's not so young. I've had hair on my pussy for nearly three years now."

"And a very nice pussy it is," he confirmed, wiggling around to bury his face in her crotch. His tongue was magical, about to bring her to orgasm faster than a good dick.

"Ooo, stop that," she giggled. "You need to get back to painting, else this canvas will never get finished."

"What's the hurry? I have you here in Charlottetown for the whole school year. Besides, I'd rather fuck than paint."

"That is obvious." The big 4' x 5' canvas was only half finished, great white spaces surrounding the nude image of Anne Shirley. He'd captured her face quite well, the joyous smile, the twinkling eyes, but he'd taken a few liberties on the body by making her breasts slightly larger than the model's. Anne was a little uncomfortable that he'd had her pose with her legs parted, revealing her pussy, the labia as clearly delineated as an upright clamshell.

"Must you show everything?" she had protested at the beginning of their first session. "I'm not sure I'd want my friends and neighbors to see quite this much of me."

"Get used to it. After we finish this one I'm going to paint your having coitus."

Anne had frowned. "You mean me getting fucked?"

"Exactly, my dear. But don't worry; I'll help you rehearse the pose."

"You're planning to fuck me?"

"Of course," he smiled tolerantly, as if conversing with a slightly retarded child. "I fuck all my models."

And by the next session, he proved his statement to be true.

Studying at Queen's Academy with a noted artist.

CHAPTER XXXVI

The Winter at Queen's

Anne's homesickness wore off, greatly helped by her weekend visits home. As long as the open weather lasted the Avonlea students went out to Carmody on the new branch railway every Friday night. Diana and several other friends were generally on hand to meet them and they all walked over to Avonlea in a merry party. Anne thought those Friday evening gypsyings over the autumnal hills in the crisp golden air, with the homelights of Avonlea twinkling beyond, were the best and dearest hours in the whole week.

Gilbert Blythe nearly always walked with Ruby Gillis and carried her satchel for her. Ruby was a very handsome young lady, now thinking herself quite as grown up as she really was; she wore her skirts as short as her mother would let her and did her hair up in a stylish pompadour. She had bright-blue eyes, a creamy complexion, and a plump showy figure. She laughed a great deal, was cheerful and good-tempered, and enjoyed the pleasant things of life frankly.

"But I shouldn't think she was the sort of girl Gilbert would like," whispered Jane to Anne. Anne did not think so either, but she didn't dare say so. Instead, she imagined it would be very pleasant for Gilbert to like her. She would enjoy jesting and chattering with him, exchanging ideas about books and studies and ambitions, making out with him under the moonlight. Gilbert had ambitions, she knew, and Ruby Gillis did not seem the sort of person with whom such things could be profitably discussed. Ruby's only ambition was to get married.

There was no silly sentiment in Anne's ideas concerning Gilbert. Boys were to her, when she thought about it, merely good fucks. If she and Gilbert had been friends she would not have cared how many other friends he had nor with whom he slept. She had a genius for friendship; girl friends she had in plenty; but she had only a vague consciousness that masculine friendship might also be a good thing to round out one's companionship – happy to make do with Martin and Rev. Allan. Not that Anne's feelings on the matter had such clear definition. But she suspected that if Gilbert had ever walked home with her from the train, over the crisp fields and along the ferny byways, they might have had many and merry and interesting conversations about the new world that was opening around them and their hopes and ambitions therein. And maybe a few good rolls in the hay.

Gilbert was a clever young fellow, with his own thoughts and a determination to get the best out of life. Ruby Gillis had told Jane Andrews that she didn't understand half the things Gilbert said. "He talks just like Anne Shirley when she's having a thoughtful fit, Ruby said. And she didn't find it any fun to be talking about books and that sort of thing when you didn't have to. Frank Stockley offered lots more dash and go, but he wasn't half as good-looking as Gilbert – so Ruby really couldn't decide which one she liked best!

At Queen's Academy Anne gradually drew a small circle of friends about her, thoughtful, imaginative, ambitious students like herself. With the "rose-red" girl, Stella Maynard, and the "dream girl," Priscilla Grant, she soon became intimate, finding the redhead to be full of mischief and pranks and fun, while the darkly exotic Stella harbored a myriad of wistful dreams, as aerial and rainbow-like as Anne's own.

After the Christmas holidays the Avonlea students gave up going home on Fridays and settled down to hard work. As a result, Anne Shirley did not get to perform her version of "The Rape of Lucretia" at Avonlea's annual concert. Just as well, because she'd never settled on a replacement for Gilbert Blythe as her partner in that little *pas de deux*. Charlie Sloane just didn't appeal to her, as he was always picking his nose. Ugh!

By this time all the Queen's scholars had gravitated into their own positions within the academic hierarchy. Certain facts had become generally accepted – for instance, that the Queen's Gold Medal contestants had been narrowed down to Gilbert Blythe, Anne Shirley, and Lewis Wilson. However, the recipient of the Avery Scholarship was more doubtful, any one of a certain six being a possible winner. The Bronze Medal for mathematics was considered as good as won by Horace Snicklebaum, a fat, funny little up-country boy with a pimply forehead and a patched coat.

Anne Shirley was the smartest girl at Queen's and perhaps the prettiest, although Stella Maynard was a close runner up in the looks department. There was something downright sensual about the young redhead, and that was why Anne had snapped her up right away as an intimate friend. Over the years Ruby

Gillis had developed as a beauty in her own right; still a tad pudgy, but great tits. No wonder Gilbert Blythe was hound-dogging her. There were other accolades to be handed out: Ethel Marr was judged to have the most stylish modes of hairdressing. And plain, plodding, conscientious Jane Andrews carried off the honors in the domestic science course. Even Josie Pye attained a certain preeminence as the sharpest-tongued young shrew currently in attendance at Queen's. As for the boys, Gilbert rivaled Anne in brains. Charlie Sloane was doing well in math. And if not for history even Moody MacPherson would have been an honor student. Yes, it may be fairly stated that Miss Stacy's old pupils were holding their own in the academic arena at Queen's Academy.

Anne worked hard and steadily. Her rivalry with Gilbert was as intense as it had ever been in Avonlea School, although it was not known in the class at large, but somehow the bitterness had gone out of it. Anne no longer wished to win for the sake of defeating Gilbert; rather, for the proud consciousness of a well-won victory against a worthy opponent. She wanted to win, but no longer thought life would be insupportable if she did not.

In spite of all the homework, the students found opportunities for pleasant times. Anne spent many of her spare hours at Beechwood and generally ate her Sunday dinners there with Miss Barry. The old woman was, admittedly, growing old, but her beady eyes had vigor in them and the fire of her tongue was not in the least abated. But Anne continued to be a prime favorite with the critical old lady.

"That Anne of Green Gables improves all the time," she said to Mrs. Langston, who was visiting her one afternoon. "I get tired of other girls – there is such an eternal sameness about them. Anne has as many shades as a rainbow and every shade is the prettiest while it lasts. I don't know that she is as amusing as she was as a child, but she makes me love her and I like people who make me love them. It saves me so much trouble in making myself love them."

≈≈≈

Anne was surprised to get the invitation to a special showing of Peter Wimble's paintings at the Left Bank Gallery. Uh-oh. Would it include the nude she had recently posed for?

The art students from Queen's Academy would surely attend. Some of the professors too. Peter Wimble's work was considered a *cause célèbre* among the Queen's students. Mainly because their school banned it due to his paintings' "overt sexuality." Queen's was a very conservative institution.

Only then did it occur to Anne that she could get expelled for posing for such an explicit painting. Bad enough that she was nude, but her legs were parted, displaying all the secrets of her budding womanhood.

She attended the exhibit with great trepidation. There was Peter Wimble surrounded by all his acolytes, champagne flutes hoisted in toast to his success. Ambling around the gallery, she found her painting in a far corner. There was quite a crowd around it, many of them fellow Queen's Academy students. Oh my goodness.

No question it was Anne in the painting. Wimble

was a skilled portraitist, and the face in the picture was her to a tee. There she was, pussy exposed for all to see.

"Young lady, you're a Queen's student, are you not?" a professor braced her. "That's clearly you in that painting. I intend to report you first thing tomorrow. You may as well pack your bags."

"But –"

"Posing in such a salacious fashion is unbecoming of a future teacher. Putting your breasts and private parts on public display is scandalous."

"Now, now, don't jump to conclusion, Jonathan," interrupted Peter Wimble. The artist had come up behind them, unseen by the professor. "That is young Anne's face to be sure. She posed for a portrait. I later painted this piece from my imagination, as a tribute to a beautiful young lady. She has done nothing wrong, other than fall victim to my admiration of her loveliness."

"Oh, Peter. Thank you for clarifying that. But you cannot prey on our students with your artistic whims. You could've caused great harm to this young woman's reputation."

"My, I suppose you're right. But worry not. This particular painting has already been sold to a private collector. It will disappear from public exhibition at the end of this show."

"Thank goodness for that. But you are still banned from the Queen's campus. A corrupt individual like you has no place among our innocent young students."

"So be it," Peter Wimble laughed, turning back to his followers and fans.

That night Anne joined him in bed to thank him for

the lie. It had saved her career as a teacher. She fucked him thoroughly to show her gratitude.

≈≈≈

Then, almost before anybody realized it, spring had come. In Avonlea the Mayflowers were peeping pinkly out on the sere barrens where snow-wreaths lingered; and a mist of green lay on the woods and across the valleys. But in Charlottetown students at Queen's thought only of the upcoming examinations.

"It doesn't seem possible that the term is nearly over," said Anne. "Why, last fall it seemed to take so long to reach its end – a whole winter of studies and classes. And here we are now, with the exams upon us next week. Girls, I used to feel those exams meant everything, but when I look out at the big buds swelling on the chestnut trees and the misty blue air hovering at the end of the streets, they don't seem half so important."

Jane and Ruby and Josie did not take this view of it. To them the coming examinations were very important indeed – far more important than chestnut buds or Maytime hazes. It was all very well for Anne, who was sure of passing, to have her moments of fancy, but when your whole future depended on the results of those exams – as the girls truly thought– you could not afford to regard them philosophically.

"I've lost seven pounds in the last two weeks," sighed Jane. "It's no use to say don't worry. I WILL worry. Worrying helps you some – it seems as if you're doing something when you're worrying. It would be dreadful if I failed to get my license after going to Queen's all winter and spending so much money."

"*I* don't care," said Josie Pye. "If I don't pass this year I'm coming back next. My father can afford to send me. By the way, Anne, Professor Tremaine predicts Gilbert Blythe is sure to get the Queen's Gold Medal and that Emily Clay will likely win the Avery Scholarship."

"That may make me feel badly tomorrow, Josie," laughed Anne, "but just now I honestly feel that as long as I know the violets are coming out all purple down in the hollow below Green Gables and that little ferns are poking their heads up in Lovers' Lane, it's not a great deal of difference whether I win the Avery or not. I've done my best and I begin to understand what is meant by the 'joy of the strife.' Next to trying and winning, the best thing is trying and failing. Girls, don't talk about exams! Picture what the fields of violets must look like back in Avonlea."

"What are you going to wear for commencement?" asked Ruby.

Jane and Josie both answered at once and the chatter drifted into a side eddy of fashions. But Anne, with her elbows on the window sill, her soft cheek against her clasped hands, and her imagination filled with visions of purple field, looked out unheedingly across city roofs and spires, toward that glorious dome of sunset sky. Her dreams were supported by the golden tissue of youth's own optimism. As it turned out, she was thinking about Gilbert Blythe and wondering what he saw in Ruby Gillis other than a nice pair of tits.

Back home in Avonlea.

CHAPTER XXXVII

The Glory and the Dream

On the morning when the final results of all the examinations were to be posted on the bulletin board at Queen's Academy, Anne and Jane walked down the street together. Jane was smiling and happy; examinations were over and she was comfortably sure she had at least made a pass. Further considerations did not trouble Jane for she had no soaring ambitions and consequently was not affected with the worries about higher achievement. On the other hand, Anne was pale and quiet for in the next ten minutes she would know who had won the Gold Medal and who the Avery. Beyond those ticking minutes there was no such thing as Time.

"Of course, you'll win one of them," encouraged Jane, who couldn't understand how fate could possibly order it otherwise.

"I have not hope of the Avery," said Anne. "Everybody says Emily Clay will win it. And I'm not going to march up to that bulletin board and look at it before everybody. I haven't the moral courage. I'm going straight to the girls' dressing room. You must read the announcements and then come and tell me, Jane. And I implore you in the name of our old friendship to do it as quickly as possible. If I have failed just say so, without trying to break it gently; and whatever you do DON'T sympathize with me. Promise me this, Jane."

Jane promised solemnly; but, as it happened, there was no necessity for such a promise. When they went up the entrance steps of Queen's they found the hall full of boys who were carrying Gilbert Blythe around on their shoulders and yelling at the tops of their voices, "Hurrah for Blythe, our Gold Medalist!"

For a moment Anne felt one sickening pang of defeat and disappointment. So she had failed and Gilbert had won! Well, Martin would be disappointed – he had been so sure she would win.

And then!

Somebody called out: "Three cheers for Miss Shirley, winner of the Avery!"

"Oh, Anne," gasped Jane, as they fled to the girls' dressing room amid hearty cheers. "Oh, Anne I'm so proud of you! Isn't it splendid?"

And then the girls crowded around them and Anne was the center of a laughing, congratulating group. Her shoulders were thumped and her hands shaken vigorously. She was pushed and pulled and hugged and among it all she managed to whisper to Jane: "Oh, won't Martin and Matilda be pleased! I must send the news home right away."

≈≈≈

Commencement was the next important happening. The exercises were held in the big assembly hall of the Academy. Addresses were given, essays read, songs sung, and diplomas, prizes, and medals awarded.

Martin and Matilda were there, with eyes and ears for only one student on the platform – a tall girl in pale green, with faintly flushed cheeks and starry eyes, who read the best essay and was pointed out and whispered about as the Avery winner.

"Reckon you're glad we kept her, Matilda?" whispered Martin, speaking for the first time since he had entered the hall, when Anne had finished her essay.

"It's not the first time I've been glad," retorted Matilda. "You do like to rub things in, Martin Collins."

Miss Josephine Barry, who was sitting behind them, leaned forward to poke Matilda with her parasol. "Aren't you proud of that Anne of Green Gables?" she said. "I know I am."

Anne went home to Avonlea with Martin and Matilda that evening. She had not been home since April and felt that she could not wait another day. The apple blossoms were out and the world was fresh with new buds. Diana was waiting at Green Gables to meet her.

In her own white room, Anne looked about her and drew a long breath of happiness. "Oh, Diana, it's so good to be back again. It's so good to see those pointed firs silhouetted against the pink sky. Isn't the breath of the mint delicious? And it's GOOD to see you again, Diana!"

"I thought you liked that Stella Maynard better than me," said Diana reproachfully. "Josie Pye told me you did. Josie said you were INFATUATED with her."

Anne laughed and pelted Diana with the faded June lilies of her bouquet. "Stella Maynard is the dearest girl in the world except one – and you are that one, Diana," she said. "I love you more than ever and I have so many things to tell you. But just now I feel as if it were joy enough to sit here and look at you. I'm tired of being studious and ambitious. I mean to spend at least two hours tomorrow lying naked in the orchard grass, thinking of absolutely nothing."

"You've done splendidly, Anne. I suppose you won't be teaching now that you've won the Avery Scholarship?"

"No. I'll be going to Redmond in September. Doesn't it seem wonderful? I'll have a brand new stock of ambition laid in by that time. Jane and Ruby are going to teach. Isn't it splendid to think we all got through, even Moody and Josie Pye?"

"The Newbridge trustees have offered Jane their school already," said Diana. "Gilbert Blythe is going to teach, too. He has to. His father can't afford to send him to college next year, so he means to earn his own way through. I expect he'll get the school here if Miss Ames decides to leave."

Anne felt a queer little sensation of dismayed surprise. She had not known this; she had expected that Gilbert would be going to Redmond also. What would she do without their inspiring rivalry?

The next morning at breakfast it suddenly struck Anne that Martin was not looking well. Surely he was much grayer than he had been a year before.

"Matilda," she said hesitatingly when he had gone out, "is Martin well?"

"No, he isn't," said Matilda in a troubled tone. "He's had some real bad spells with his heart this spring and he won't spare himself a mite. I've been quite worried about him, but we've got a good hired man to help out around here, so I'm hoping he'll get some rest. Maybe he'll take it easier now that you're home. You always cheer him up with your antics in bed. What bizarre new sexual tricks have you picked from your friends at school."

"We'll worry about that later. I did bring you a device called ben-wa balls." Then Anne leaned across the table, her face close to Matilda's. "You are not looking do well yourself, Matilda. Your eyes look tired. I'm afraid you've been working too hard also. You must take a rest, now that I'm home. I'm just going to take this one day off to visit all the dear old spots and hunt up my old dreams, and then it will be your turn to be lazy while I do the work."

Matilda smiled affectionately at the girl. "It's not the work – it's my head. I often get a pain behind my eyes. Doctor Spencer's been fussing with glasses, but they don't seem to do me any good. There is a distinguished oculist coming to the Island the last of June and the doctor says I must see him. I guess I'll have to. I can't read or sew with any comfort now."

"Oh, Matilda –"

The blonde woman changed the subject. "Well, Anne, you've done real well at Queen's I must say. To take First Class License in one year and win the Avery Scholarship – that's pretty impressive. Mrs. Langston is always saying she doesn't believe in the higher education of women, but I don't believe a word of that hogwash. I'm right proud of you. I know I've never told you that enough. I didn't want you to get a Big Head. But you've earned the compliment."

"Why thank you, Matilda."

"Speaking of Rita Langston reminds me – have you heard anything about the Abbey Bank lately?"

"I heard it was shaky," answered Anne. "Why?"

"That's what Rita said. She was up here one day last week and said there was some talk about it. Martin seemed real worried. We have all our savings in that bank – every penny. I wanted Martin to put it in the First Savings Bank, but old Mr. Abbey was a great friend of father's and we've always banked with him. Martin said any bank with Karl Abbey at its helm was good enough for us."

"I think for many years Mr. Abbey has been its head in name only," said Anne. "He is a very old man; his nephews are actually running the institution."

"Well, when Rita told us the bank was shaky, I wanted Martin to draw our money out, but he hasn't done so yet. I'm worried about it."

"I'll ask around about the bank," Anne promised. "Don't worry."

≈≈≈

Anne had her day of communing with nature. Despite the chill, she shucked her clothing and ran naked through the pastures and fields as she used to do. At noon she met Diana at Dryad's Bubble and they happily spent the afternoon entwined in a 69 position.

She never forgot that day; it was so bright and golden and fair, so free from shadow and so lavish of blossom.

At twilight, she visited the parsonage and had a satisfying romp in bed with both Jonathan and Cynthia Allan; someone they all three realized this was farewell sex, the end of their longtime tryst. A bittersweet mood hung over them, but they each knew the end had come.

Finally in the evening Anne went with Martin for

the cows, taking a shortcut through Lovers' Lane to the back pasture. Martin walked slowly with bent head; Anne, tall and erect, matched her springing step to his.

"You've been working too hard today, Martin," she said reproachfully. "Why won't you take things easier?"

"Well now, I can't seem to," said Martin, as he opened the yard gate to let the cows through. "I've always worked pretty hard and I'd rather drop in harness. It's my heart, you know. Doc Spencer says it has a weak valve or some such."

"If I had been the boy you sent for," said Anne wistfully, "I'd be able to help you so much now and spare you in a hundred ways. I could find it in my heart to wish I had been, just for that."

"Well now, I'd rather have you than a dozen boys, Anne," said Martin patting her hand. "You can't fuck a boy. Or least I can't bring myself to try that."

Anne laughed at his jest. "I'm taking about farm work, not bedtime antics."

"Don't change my thinking. Just mind you that — I'd rather have you than a dozen boys."

"Why so?"

"Well now, I guess it wasn't a boy that took the Avery Scholarship, was it? It was a girl – my girl – my girl that I'm proud of."

He smiled his shy smile at her as they put away the cattle for the night and went into the yard toward the light of Green Gables. Anne took the memory of it with her when she went to her room that night and sat for a long while at her open window, thinking of the past and dreaming of the future. Outside the Snow Queen was mistily white in the moonshine; the frogs were singing in the marsh beyond Orchard Slope. Anne always remembered the silvery, peaceful beauty and fragrant calm of that night. It was the last night before sorrow touched her life; and no life is ever quite the same again when once that cold, sanctifying touch has been laid upon it.

A vigil with sorrow.

CHAPTER XXXVIII

The Reaper Whose Name Is Death

"**M**artin – Martin – what is the matter? Martin, are you sick?"

It was Matilda who spoke, alarm in every jerky word. Anne came through the hall, her hands full of white narcissus, – it was long before Anne could love the sight or odor of white narcissus again, – in time to hear her and to see Martin standing in the porch doorway, a folded paper in his hand, and his face strangely drawn and gray. As usual, Anne had been wandering about in the nude, or today wearing only cutoff jeans so her butt wouldn't get dirty as she stooped to pick flowers in the garden. Upon seeing Martin's ashen face, Anne dropped her flowers and sprang toward him at the same moment as Matilda. They were both too late; before they could reach him Martin had fallen across the threshold.

"He's fainted," gasped Matilda. "Anne, run for Harley – quick, quick! He's at the barn."

Harley, the hired man, started at once for the doctor, calling at Orchard Slope on his way to send Mr. and Mrs. Barry over. Mrs. Langston, who was there on an errand, came too. They found Anne and Matilda distractedly trying to restore Martin to consciousness.

Mrs. Langston pushed them gently aside, tried his pulse, and then laid her ear over his heart. She looked at their anxious faces sorrowfully and the tears came into her eyes.

"Oh, Matilda," she said gravely. "I don't think we can do anything for him."

"Mrs. Langston, you don't think – you can't think Martin is – is – " Anne could not say the dreadful word; she turned sick and pallid.

"Child, yes, I'm afraid of it. Look at his face. When you've seen that look as often as I have you'll know what it means. Martin's gone."

Anne looked at the still face and there beheld the seal of the Great Presence.

"Best get on some clothes, dear," said Mrs. Barry. "Don't want you to be too distracting when the doctor and others show up."

When the doctor came he said that death had been instantaneous and probably painless, caused in all likelihood by some sudden shock. The secret of the shock was discovered to be in the paper Martin had held and which Martin had brought from the office that morning. It contained an account of the failure of the Abbey Bank.

The news spread quickly through Avonlea, and all day friends and neighbors thronged to Green Gables. For the first time, shy Martin Collins was a person of central importance; the majesty of death had set him apart as one crowned.

When the calm night came softly down over Green Gables the old house was hushed and tranquil. In the parlor lay Martin Collins in his coffin, his blonde hair framing his placid face on which there was a little kindly smile as if he but slept, dreaming pleasant dreams. There were flowers about him – sweet old-fashioned flowers which his mother had planted in the homestead garden in her bridal days and for which Martin had always had a secret, wordless love. Anne had gathered them and brought them to him, her anguished, tearless eyes burning in her white face. It was the last thing she could do for him.

The Barrys and Mrs. Langston stayed with them that night. Diana, going up to the east gable, where Anne was standing at her window, said gently: "Anne dear, would you like to have me sleep with you tonight?"

"Thank you, Diana." Anne looked earnestly into her friend's face. "I think you won't misunderstand me when I say I want to be alone. I'm not afraid. I haven't been alone one minute since it happened – and I want to be. I want to be silent and try to realize it. I can't realize it. Half the time it seems to me that Martin can't be dead; and the other half it seems as if he must have been dead for a long time and I've had this horrible dull ache ever since."

Diana did not quite understand. It was easier to comprehend Matilda's impassioned grief, breaking all the bounds of natural reserve and lifelong habit in its stormy rush, than Anne's tearless agony. But Diana went away quietly, leaving Anne alone to keep her first vigil with sorrow.

Anne hoped that the tears would come in solitude. It seemed to her a terrible thing that she could not shed a tear for Martin, whom she had loved so much and who had been so kind to her, Martin who had walked with her last evening at sunset and was now lying in the dim room below with that awful peace on his brow. But no tears would come, even when she knelt by her window in the darkness and prayed, looking up to the stars beyond the hills – no tears, only the same horrible dull ache of misery that kept on aching until she fell asleep, worn out with the day's pain and excitement.

In the night she awakened, with the stillness and the darkness about her, and the recollection of the day came over her like a wave of sorrow. She could see Martin's face smiling at her as he had smiled when they parted at the gate that last evening. She could hear his voice saying, "My girl – my girl that I'm proud of." Then the tears came and Anne wept her heart out. Matilda heard her and crept in to comfort her.

"There – there – don't cry so, dear. It can't bring him back. It – it – isn't right to cry so. I knew that today, but I couldn't help it then. He'd always been such a good, kind helpmate to me – but God knows best."

"Oh, just let me cry, Matilda," sobbed Anne. "The tears don't hurt me like that ache did. Stay here for a little while with me and keep your arm around me – so. I couldn't have Diana stay, she's good and kind and sweet – but it's not her sorrow – she's outside of it and she couldn't come close enough to my heart to help me. It's our sorrow – yours and mine. Oh, Matilda, what will we do without him?"

"We've got each other, Anne. I don't know what I'd do if you weren't here – if you'd never come. Oh, Anne, I know I've been kind of strict with you over the years – but you mustn't think I didn't love you as well as Martin did, for all that. I want to tell you now when I can. It's never been easy for me to say things out of my heart, but at times like this it's easier. I love you as if you were my own flesh and blood and you've been my joy and comfort ever since you came to Green Gables."

Two days afterwards they carried Martin Collins over his homestead threshold and away from the fields he had tilled and the orchards he had loved and the trees he had planted; and took him to the cemetery behind the First Presbyterian Church. Rev. Allan said the prayers and his wife Cynthia played an organ recital afterwards. Anne and Matilda, both clad in black, sat side-by-side, treated by one and all as if they were two widows rather than ward and sister. Despite the secrecy, most of Avonlea had long suspected the relationships but chose to look the other way.

Then Avonlea settled back to its usual placidity and even at Green Gables affairs slipped into their old groove and work was done and duties fulfilled with regularity as before, although always with the aching sense of "loss in all familiar things." Anne, new to grief, thought it almost sad that it could be so – that they COULD go on in the old way without Martin. She felt something like shame and remorse when she discovered that the sunrises behind the firs and the pale pink buds opening in the garden gave her the old inrush of gladness when she saw them – that Diana's visits were pleasant to her and that Diana's merry words and ways moved her to laughter and smiles – that, in brief, the beautiful world of blossom and love and friendship had lost none of its power to please her fancy and thrill her heart, that life still called to her with many insistent voices.

"It seems like disloyalty to Martin, somehow, to find pleasure in these things now that he has gone," she said wistfully to Mrs. Allan one evening when they were together in the manse garden. "I miss him so much – all the time – and yet, the world and life still seem very beautiful and interesting to me. Today Diana said something funny and I found myself laughing. I'd thought when it happened I could never laugh again. And it somehow seems as if I oughtn't to."

"When Martin was here he liked to hear you laugh and he liked to know that you found pleasure in the wondrous things around you," said Cynthia Allan gently. "He is just away now; and he likes to know it just the same. I am sure we should not shut our hearts against the healing influences that nature offers us. But I can understand your feeling. I think we all experience the same thing. We resent the thought that anything can please us when someone we love is no longer here to share the pleasure with us, and we almost feel as if we were unfaithful to our sorrow when we find our interest in life returning to us. But that's the way it works."

"I was down to the graveyard to plant a rosebush on Martin's grave this afternoon," said Anne dreamily. "I took a slip of the little white Scotch rosebush his mother brought out from Scotland long ago; Martin always liked those roses the best – they are so small and sweet on their thorny stems. It made me feel glad that I could plant it by his grave – as if I were doing something that must please him in taking it there to be near him. I hope he has roses like them in heaven. Perhaps the souls of all those little white roses that he has loved so many summers were all there to meet him. I must go home now. Matilda is all alone and she gets lonely at twilight."

"She will be lonelier still, I fear, when you go away again to college," said Mrs. Allan.

Anne did not reply; she said good night and went slowly back to Green Gables. Matilda was sitting on the front doorstep and Anne sat down beside her. The kitchen door was open behind them, held back by a big pink conch shell with hints of sea sunsets in its smooth inner convolutions.

Anne gathered some sprays of pale-yellow honeysuckle and put them in her hair. She liked the delicious hint of fragrance, as some aerial benediction, above her every time she moved.

"Doctor Spencer was here while you were away," Matilda said. "He says that the specialist will be in town tomorrow and he insists that I must go in and have my eyes examined. I suppose I'd better go and have it over. I'll be more than thankful if the man can give me the right kind of glasses to suit my eyes. You won't mind staying here alone while I'm away, will you? Harley will have to drive me in and there's ironing and baking to do."

"I shall be all right. Diana will come over and be company for me. I shall attend to the ironing and baking – you needn't fear that I'll starch the handkerchiefs or flavor the cake with liniment."

Matilda smiled. "What a girl you were for making mistakes in them days, Anne. You were always getting into scrapes. I use to think you were possessed. Always running around naked. Your hair as wild as a Medusa."

"I laugh now when I think what a worry my unruly hair used to be to me," smiled Anne, touching the heavy braid of hair that was wound about her shapely head. "Thank goodness I learned how to style it. Ethel Marr showed me some simple ways of managing it. She was one of my classmates at the Academy. Now people tell me my hair is pretty – all except Josie Pye. She informed me yesterday that she really thought it was more tangled than ever, and suggested I should consider cutting it all off. Matilda, I've almost decided to give up trying to like Josie Pye. I've made what I would once have called a heroic effort to like her, but Josie Pye won't BE liked."

"Josie is a Pye," said Matilda sharply, "so she can't help being disagreeable. I suppose people of that kind serve some useful purpose in society, but I must say I don't know what it is any more than I know the use of thistles. Is Josie going to teach?"

"No, she is going back to Queen's next year. So are Moody and Charlie Sloane. Jane and Ruby are going to teach and they have both got schools – Jane at Newbridge and Ruby at some place up west."

"Gilbert Blythe is going to teach too, isn't he?"

"Yes" – briefly.

"What a nice-looking fellow he is," said Matilda absently. "I saw him in church last Sunday and he seemed so tall and manly. He looks a lot like his father did at the same age. John Blythe was a nice boy. We used to be real good friends, he and I. People called him my beau."

Anne looked up with swift interest. "Oh, Matilda – and what happened? – why didn't you –?"

"We had a quarrel. I wouldn't forgive him when he asked me to. I meant to, after awhile – but I was sulky and angry and I wanted to punish him first. He never came back – the Blythes were all mighty independent. But I always felt – rather sorry. I've always kind of wished I'd forgiven him when I had the chance."

"So you've had a bit of romance in your life, too," said Anne softly. "Aside from Martin, I mean."

"Yes, I suppose you might call it that. You wouldn't think so to look at me, would you? But you never can tell about people from their outsides. Everybody has forgot about me and John. I'd forgotten myself. But it all came back to me when I saw Gilbert last Sunday."

A happy ending.

CHAPTER XXXIX

The Bend in the Road

Matilda went to town the next day and returned in the evening. Anne had gone over to Orchard Slope with Diana and came back to find Matilda in the kitchen, sitting by the table with her head leaning on her hand. Something in her dejected attitude struck a chill to Anne's heart. She had never seen Matilda sit limply like that.

"Are you very tired, Matilda?"

"Yes – no – I don't know," said Matilda wearily, looking up. "I suppose I am tired but I haven't thought about it. It's not that."

"Did you see the oculist? What did he say?" asked Anne anxiously.

"Yes, I saw him. He examined my eyes. He says that if I give up all reading and sewing entirely and any kind of work that strains the eyes, and if I'm careful not to cry, and if I wear the glasses he's given me he thinks my eyes may not get any worse and my headaches will be cured. But if I don't, he says I'll certainly be stone-blind in six months. Blind! Anne, just think of it!"

For a minute Anne, after her first quick exclamation of dismay, was silent. It seemed to her that she could NOT speak. Then she said bravely, but with a catch in her voice: "Matilda, DON'T think of it. You know he has given you hope. If you are careful you won't lose your sight altogether; and if his glasses cure your headaches it will be a great thing."

"I don't call it much hope," said Matilda bitterly. "What am I to live for if I can't read or sew or do anything like that? I might as well be blind – or dead. And as for crying, I can't help that when I get lonesome. But there, it's no good talking about it. If you'll get me a cup of tea I'll be thankful. I'm about done out. Don't say anything about this to anyone, at least not yet. I can't bear that folks should come here to question and sympathize and talk about it."

When Matilda had eaten her lunch Anne persuaded her to go to bed. Then Anne went herself to the east gable and sat down by her window in the darkness, alone with her tears and her heaviness of heart. How sadly things had changed since she had sat there the night after coming home! Then she had been full of hope and joy and the future had looked rosy with promise. She had won the coveted Avery Scholarship. All things were possible!

Anne felt as if she had lived years since then, but before she went to bed there was a smile on her lips and peace in her heart. She had looked her duty courageously in the face and found it a friend – as duty can be when we meet it frankly.

One afternoon a few days later Matilda came slowly in from the front yard where she had been talking to a caller – a man whom Anne knew by sight as George Sadler from Carmody. Anne wondered what he could have been saying to bring that look to Matilda's face.

"What did Mr. Sadler want, Matilda?"

Matilda sat down by the window and looked at Anne. There were tears in her eyes in defiance of the oculist's prohibition and her voice broke as she said: "He heard that I was going to sell Green Gables and he wants to buy it."

"Buy it! Buy Green Gables?" Anne wondered if she had heard aright. "Oh, Matilda, you don't mean to sell Green Gables!"

"Anne, I don't know what else is to be done. I've thought it all over. If my eyes were strong I could stay here and make out to look after things and manage, with a good hired man. But as it is I can't. I may lose my sight altogether; and anyway I'll not be fit to run things. Oh, I never thought I'd live to see the day when I'd have to sell my home. But things would only go behind worse and worse all the time, till nobody would want to buy it. Every cent of our money went in that bank; and there's some notes we're obligated to pay. Mrs. Langston advises me to sell the farm and board somewhere – with her I suppose. It won't bring much – it's small and the buildings are old. But it'll be enough for me to live on I reckon. I'm thankful you're provided for with that scholarship, Anne. I'm sorry you won't have a home to come to in your vacations, that's all, but I suppose you'll manage."

Matilda broke down and wept bitterly.

"You mustn't sell Green Gables," said Anne resolutely.

"Oh, Anne, I wish I didn't have to. But you can see for yourself. I can't stay here alone. I'd go crazy with trouble and loneliness. And my sight would go – I know it would."

"You won't have to stay here alone, Matilda. I'll be with you. I'm not going to Redmond."

"Not going to Redmond!" Matilda lifted her tearstained face from her hands and stared at Anne. "Why, what do you mean?"

"Just what I say. I'm not going to take the scholarship. I decided so the night after you came home from town. You surely don't think I could leave you alone in your trouble, Matilda, after all you've done for me. I've been thinking and planning. Let me tell you my plans. Mr. Barry wants to rent the farm for next year. So you won't have any bother over that. And I'm going to teach. I've applied for the school here – but I don't expect to get it for I understand the trustees have promised it to Gilbert Blythe. But I can have the Carmody School – Mr. Blair told me so last night at the store. Of course that won't be quite as convenient as the Avonlea School, but I can board home and drive myself over to Carmody and back, in the warm weather at least. And even in winter I can come home Fridays. We'll keep a horse for that. Oh, I have it all planned out, Matilda. And I'll read to you and keep you cheered up. You won't be lonesome. And we'll be real cozy and happy here together, you and I."

Matilda had listened like a woman in a dream. "Oh, Anne, I could get along quite well if you were here, I know. But I can't let you sacrifice yourself for me. It would be terrible."

"Nonsense!" Anne laughed merrily. "There is no sacrifice. Nothing could be worse than giving up Green Gables – nothing could hurt me more. We must keep the dear old place. My mind is quite made up, Matilda. I'm NOT going to Redmond; and I AM going to stay here and teach. Don't you worry about me a bit."

"But your ambitions – and – "

"I'm just as ambitious as ever. Only, I've changed the object of my ambitions. I'm going to be a good teacher – and I'm going to save your eyesight. Besides, I mean to study at home here and take a little college course all by myself. Oh, I've dozens of plans, Matilda. I've been thinking them out for a week. I shall give life here my best, and I believe it will give its best to me in return. When I left Queen's Academy my future seemed to stretch out before me like a straight road. I thought I could see along it for many a mile. Now there is a bend in it. I don't know what lies around the bend, but I'm going to believe that the best does. It has a fascination of its own, that bend. I wonder how the road beyond it goes – what new landscapes – what new beauties – what curves and hills and valleys lie further on."

"I don't feel as if I ought to let you give it up," said Matilda, referring to the scholarship.

"But you can't prevent me. I'm nearly eighteen, and 'obstinate as a mule,' as Mrs. Langston likes to tell me," laughed Anne. "Oh, Matilda, don't you go pitying me. I don't like to be pitied, and there is no need for it. I'm ecstatic at the very thought of staying at dear Green Gables. Nobody could love it as you and I do – so we must keep it."

"You blessed girl!" said Matilda, yielding. "I feel as if you'd given me new life. I guess I ought to hold fast and make you go to college – but I know I can't, so I'm not going to try. I'll make it up to you though, Anne. I'll do anything in bed you want me to, I promise."

"You always have," Anne smiled cheekily.

529

≈≈≈

When it became known in Avonlea that Anne Shirley had given up the idea of going to college and intended to stay home and teach there was a good deal of discussion over it. Most of the good folks, not knowing about Matilda's eyes, thought she was foolish. Mrs. Allan did not. She told Anne so in approving words that brought tears of pleasure to the girl's eyes. Neither did good Mrs. Langston. She came up one evening and found Anne and Matilda sitting at the front door in the warm, scented summer dusk. They liked to sit there when the twilight came down and the white moths flew about in the garden and the odor of mint filled the dewy air.

Mrs. Langston deposited her substantial person upon the stone bench by the door with a long breath of mingled weariness and relief. "I declare I'm glad to sit down," she said. "I've been on my feet all day, and two hundred pounds is a good bit for two feet to carry round. It's a great blessing not to be fat, Matilda. I hope you appreciate it. You still have your slender figure, even in your mid thirties. How do I know? My trusty spyglass still works. And you and Anne still fail to close your bedroom window."

"We leave it open for you," replied Matilda is the sweetest voice. "We wouldn't want to deprive you of your nightly enjoyment."

"Well, you've got me there. I've enjoyed the spectacle of you and Martin going at it like dogs in heat. And then when you took in this little tart here, things got even more interesting. But I've kept your secret, you have to give me that. You've all been good neighbors – except missy here in the very beginning – and I've repaid that with my silence."

"And we thank you, Rita."

"I've got to say, you folks did some things in bed together that defied both the laws of nature and the laws of gravity. Anne is quite the limber young thing, if I do say so."

"I have an acrobatic nature," the girl said.

"Well, be as that may, Anne, I hear you've given up your notion of going to college. I was real glad to hear it. You've got as much education now as a woman can be comfortable with. I don't believe in girls going to college with the men and cramming their heads full of Latin and Greek and all that nonsense."

"But I'm going to study Latin and Greek just the same, Mrs. Langston," said Anne laughing. "I'm going to take my Arts course right here at Green Gables, and study everything that I would at college."

Mrs. Langston lifted her hands in holy horror. "Anne Shirley, you'll kill yourself. The brain can only hold so much knowledge. Then it explodes!'"

"Not at all. As far as education, I shall thrive on it. Oh, I'm not going to overdo things. I'll have lots of spare time for studying in the long winter evenings, and I've no vocation for fancy work. I'm going to teach over at Carmody, you know."

"I don't know it. I guess you're going to teach right here in Avonlea. The trustees have decided to give you the school."

"Mrs. Langston!" cried Anne, springing to her feet in her surprise. "Why, I thought they had promised it to Gilbert Blythe!"

"So they did. But as soon as Gilbert heard that you had applied for it he went to them – they had a business meeting at the school last night, you know – and he told them that he was withdrawing his application, and urged that they accept yours. He said he was going to teach at White Sands. Of course, he knew how much you wanted to stay with Matilda, and I must say I think it was real kind and thoughtful in him, that's what. Real self-sacrificing, too, for he'll have his board to pay at White Sands, and everybody knows he's got to earn his own way through college. So the trustees decided to take you. I was tickled to death when Thomas came home and told me."

"I don't feel that I ought to take it," murmured Anne. "I mean – I don't think I ought to let Gilbert make such a sacrifice for – for me."

"I guess you can't prevent him. He's already signed papers with the White Sands trustees. So it wouldn't do him any good now even if you did refuse. Of course you'll take the school. You'll get along all right, now that there are no Pyes going. Josie was the last of them, and a good thing she was, that's what. There's been some Pye or other going to Avonlea School for the last twenty years, and I guess their mission in life was to keep school teachers reminded that earth isn't their home." The old woman looked up, squinting her eyes at something in the distance. "Bless my heart! What does all that winking and blinking at the Barry gable mean?"

"Diana is signaling for me to go over," laughed Anne. "You know we keep up the old custom. Our secret code. Excuse me while I run over and see what she wants."

With a polite wave, Anne was across the yard and racing down the clover-covered slope like a whitetail deer, quickly disappearing into the firry shadows of the Haunted Wood.

Mrs. Langston looked after her indulgently. "There's a good deal of the child about her yet in some ways."

"There's a good deal more of the woman about her in others ways," retorted Matilda, with a momentary return of her old crispness. "You've seen her fucking me and Martin like a grown-up trollop. She didn't look so childish then, did she?"

"Lordy no. That girl's certainly got a talent for it, I'll give you that."

"Well, watch all you want. We don't mind."

"Not that we're having this frank discussion, I have a confession of my own. I'm not the one what watches. That spyglass belongs to my husband Thomas. He sits there and watches you while pleasuring himself. I don't mind at all. With you and Anne satisfying his carnal needs I don't have to perform my wifely duties. Never did care for that obligation. It was so messy, all that gooey jism and such."

"Well, then, does your Thomas have any special requests? We'll put on a show just for him."

"Matter of fact, he did suggest that you and Anne ought to invite your hired hand into your bed to replace Martin."

"Harley? I'm not sure Anne would go along with that. As she's growing up, she's getting more selective about who she fucks. I would be surprised if she don't settle down to one boy sooner than later."

"What about you and Harley then?" Mrs. Langston suggested helpfully.

"I might just consider that," grinned Matilda. "I've been noticing his nice muscles lately. And I am getting lonely for a man. Tell Thomas to keep watching. He may get his wish."

"Truth is," confessed Mrs. Langston, "That's my wish, not Thomas's. He's quite content with you two females going at it. But I wouldn't mind seeing that strapping farmhand strip down and show me what he got under them overalls."

"Mrs. Langston!"

"Oh, don't take on so. You're the one gets to fuck him."

≈≈≈

Anne went to the little Avonlea graveyard the next evening to put fresh flowers on Martin's grave and water the Scotch rosebush. She lingered there until dusk, liking the peace and calm of the little place, with its poplars whose rustle was like low, friendly speech, and its whispering grasses growing at will among the graves. When she finally left it and walked down the long hill that sloped to the Lake of Shining Waters it was past sunset and all Avonlea lay before her in a dreamlike afterlight – "a haunt of ancient peace." There was a freshness in the air as of a wind that had blown over honey-sweet fields of clover. Home lights twinkled out here, barely visible through the trees. To the left lay the sea, misty and purple, with its haunting, unceasing murmur. And to the west was a glory of sunset hues, the pond reflecting them like an underwater bonfire. The beauty of it all thrilled Anne's heart, and she gratefully opened the gates of her soul to it.

"Dear old world," she murmured, "you are very lovely, and I am glad to be alive in you."

Halfway down the hill a tall lad came whistling out of a gate before the Blythe homestead. It was Gilbert, and the whistle died on his lips as he recognized Anne. He lifted his cap courteously, but he would have passed on in silence, if Anne had not stopped and held out her hand.

"Gilbert," she said, with scarlet cheeks, "I want to thank you for giving up the school for me. It was very good of you – and I want you to know that I appreciate it."

Gilbert took the offered hand eagerly. "It wasn't particularly good of me at all, Anne. I was pleased to be able to do you some small service. Are we going to be friends after this? Have you really forgiven me my old faults? I do so wish I'd finished the job that day in the Langston's dairy barn. I can't blame you for being angry that I left you high and dry."

Anne laughed and tried unsuccessfully to withdraw her hand. "I forgave you long ago, although I didn't know it. What a stubborn little goose I was. I've been – I may as well make a complete confession – I've been sorry ever since. Although, like you, I wish we'd been sensible enough to finish what we started. I think I was more sexually frustrated than angry."

"Too bad I'll never have the chance to make it up to you, do it right."

"Oh, you can – if you want to. I'd like that."

"Wouldn't Rev. Allan mind?"

"Let's not plow that old field again. But I've broken off with Jonathan. Cynthia too."

"What about Stella Maynard?" He'd heard the rumors at the Academy.

"Not more tickle-and-grab with Stella Maynard. Nor with Pricilla Grant. Even Diana Barry sand I have agreed to just be friends – although we will always treasure our memories of being bosom friends."

"Really?"

"There's no one to be jealous of. Martin is dead."

"But what about Matilda? People talk you know."

Anne smiled. "Don't worry about Matilda. She has a boyfriend. Harley, her farmhand. He's plowed new fields at Green Gables it would seem. I sleep in my own room now."

"We are going to be the best of friends," said Gilbert, jubilantly. "We were born to be good friends, Anne. You've thwarted destiny enough. I know we can help each other in many ways. You are going to keep up your studies, aren't you? So am I. Come, I'm going to walk home with you."

"I want to ne more than friends," said Anne.

"Of course we will be more than friends, Anne Shirley. I'm going to marry you."

"I'd like that," she said. "Maybe then I'll finally get to fuck you."

≈≈≈

Matilda looked curiously at Anne when the latter entered the kitchen.

"Who was that came up the lane with you, Anne?"

"Gilbert Blythe," answered Anne, vexed to find

herself blushing. "I met him on Barry's hill."

"I didn't think you and Gilbert Blythe were such good friends that you'd stand for half an hour at the gate talking to him," said Matilda with a dry smile.

"We haven't been – we've been good enemies. But we have decided that it will be much more sensible to be good friends in the future. Were we really there half an hour? It seemed just a few minutes. But, you see, we have nearly three years' lost conversations to catch up with, Matilda. And lots of fucking to do"

"Oh?"

"I'm not going to make the same mistake you made with his father. Gilbert has just asked me to marry him."

"Oh, Anne, I'm so happy for you. And with Harley here as the man of the house, you are free to go live with Gilbert. Or take up your scholarship. Or whatever you choose."

"I choose to not be far from you. And I'm going to become the best teacher that Avonlea School has ever had."

≈≈≈

Anne sat long at her window that night companioned by happy thoughts. The wind purred softly among the cherry boughs, and the breath of mints came wafting up to her. The stars twinkled over the pointed firs in the hollow and Diana's light gleamed reassuringly through the old gap.

Anne's horizons had closed in since the night she had sat there after coming home from Queen's Academy, with her fresh triumph in winning the Avery Scholarship; how the world had seemed different then.

But if the path before her feet turned out to be narrow she knew that nevertheless flowers of quiet happiness would bloom alongside it. The joy of sincere work and worthy aspiration and conjugal bliss were to be hers. Nothing could rob her of her birthright of fancy or her world of dreams. But reality wasn't bad either.

She looked forward to facing that bend in the road!

"'God's in his heaven, all's right with the world,'" whispered Anne softly.

The Erotic Anne of Green Gables

A new imaging of the Anne of Green Gables *story.*

Publisher's Footnote

This retelling of the popular children's book, *Anne of Green Gables*, is strictly for the entertainment of adults, those who look back with fondness on L.M. Montgomery's tales of an orphan girl on Prince Edward Island in Nova Scotia. But these readers imagine a more salacious story about a young girl who comes to live with a couple on a small farm known as Green Gables.

Obviously, Lucy Maud Montgomery had nothing to do with this version of her classic story. But being in the public domain, that randy purveyor of eroticism Frank Holtzer has revised Anne of Green Gables, giving you a titillating adventure in much the same way those Tijuana Bible's offered alternative vision of popular comic book characters and movie stars.

So enjoy this volume for what it is, a sexual dalliance with your libido.

Meet the Authors

Lucy Maud Montgomery (1874 - 1942) was born in the village of Clifton (now New London) on Prince Edward Island, a province of Canada. Young Maud went to live with her maternal grandparents, a stern Presbyterian couple who maintained the Post Office on Prince Edward Island's north shore. Their rambling farm was the inspiration for "Green Gables," now part of a Provincial Park established in 1937. Although trained as a teacher, she became known for a series of young adult novels beginning with *Anne of Green Gables,* first published in 1908. Her stories about the lovable orphan girl Anne Shirley made Prince Edward Island an international tourist destination She was made an Officer of the Order of the British Empire in 1935.

Frank Holtzer has been called "an international adventurer" and "a lothorio of some note." Well, at least *he* makes those engrandized claims. As an experienced journalist, he's covered poverty in Port-au-Prince, Oktoberfest beer bashes in Munich, the swinging Carnaby Street scene in London, independence in the Bahamas, and the drug trade in Mexico. He's hiked across glaciers in Switzerland, whitewater rafted in Deliverance country, whalewatched in Hawaii, hunted submarines with the US Navy in the Gulf, cave explored in Appalachia, and treasure hunted in the Caymans.

Secret Kiss Erotic Literature

AbsolutelyAmazingeBooks.com
or AA-eBooks.com